Vampire Mistress

"Keep a fan and a glass of ice water handy; this one will raise your temperature."
—*Romantic Times*

"The Vampire Queen novels are more than a reader ever needs to indulge
in a world where connection with the characters is amazingly intense and
all-consuming, leaving you very, very satisfied."
—*Fresh Fiction*

Beloved Vampire

"Lock the door, turn off the television and hide the phone before starting
this book, because it's impossible to put down! . . . The story is full of action, intrigue, danger, history and sexual tension . . . This is definitely a
keeper!"
—*Romantic Times*

"This has to be the best vampire novel I've read in a very long time! Joey
... Hill has outdone herself . . . [I] couldn't put it down and didn't want it
—*ParaNormal Romance*

...pire's Claim

"*A Vampire's Claim* had ... its thrall. Joey W. Hill pulled me in and
didn't let me go. I Joyfully Recommend that everyone should sink their
teeth into [this book]."
—*Joyfully Reviewed*

"*A Vampire's Claim* is so ardent with action and sex you won't remember
to breathe . . . another stunning installment in her vampire series."
—*TwoLips Reviews*

"Hill does not disappoint with the third book in her well-written vampire
series. Sure to enthrall and delight not only existing Hill fans, but also
those new to her writing."
—*Romantic Times*

continued . . .

The Mark of the Vampire Queen

"Superb . . . This is erotica at its best with lots of sizzle and a love that is truly sacrificial. Joey W. Hill continues to grow as a stunning storyteller."
—*A Romance Review*

"Packs a powerful punch . . . As the twists and turns unfold, you will be as surprised as I was at the ending of this creative story."   —*TwoLips Reviews*

"Joey W. Hill never ceases to amaze us . . . She keeps you riveted to your seat and leaves you longing for more with each sentence."
—*Night Owl Romance*

"Dark and richly romantic. There are scenes that will make you laugh and cry, and those that will be a feast for your libido and your most lascivious fantasies. The ending will surprise and leave you clamoring for more."
—*Romantic Times*

"Fans of erotic romantic fantasy will relish *The Mark of the Vampire Queen*."
—*The Best Reviews*

The Vampire Queen's Servant

"This book should come with a warning: intensely sexy, sensual story that will hold you hostage until the final word is read. The story line is fresh and unique, complete with a twist."   —*Romantic Times*

"Hot, kinky, sweating, hard-pounding, oh-my-god-is-it-hot-in-here-or-is-it-just-me sex . . . so compelling it just grabs you deep inside. If you can keep an open mind you will be treated to a love story that will tug at your heartstrings."
—*TwoLips Reviews*

Vampire Instinct

Joey W. Hill

HEAT
New York

THE BERKLEY PUBLISHING GROUP
Published by the Penguin Group
Penguin Group (USA) Inc.
375 Hudson Street, New York, New York 10014, USA
Penguin Group (Canada), 90 Eglinton Avenue East, Suite 700, Toronto, Ontario M4P 2Y3, Canada
(a division of Pearson Penguin Canada Inc.)
Penguin Books Ltd., 80 Strand, London WC2R 0RL, England
Penguin Group Ireland, 25 St. Stephen's Green, Dublin 2, Ireland (a division of Penguin Books Ltd.)
Penguin Group (Australia), 250 Camberwell Road, Camberwell, Victoria 3124, Australia
(a division of Pearson Australia Group Pty. Ltd.)
Penguin Books India Pvt. Ltd., 11 Community Centre, Panchsheel Park, New Delhi—110 017, India
Penguin Group (NZ), 67 Apollo Drive, Rosedale, Auckland 0632, New Zealand
(a division of Pearson New Zealand Ltd.)
Penguin Books (South Africa) (Pty.) Ltd., 24 Sturdee Avenue, Rosebank, Johannesburg 2196,
South Africa

Penguin Books Ltd., Registered Offices: 80 Strand, London WC2R 0RL, England

This book is an original publication of The Berkley Publishing Group.

This is a work of fiction. Names, characters, places, and incidents either are the product of the author's imagination or are used fictitiously, and any resemblance to actual persons, living or dead, business establishments, events, or locales is entirely coincidental. The publisher does not have any control over and does not assume any responsibility for author or third-party websites or their content.

PRINTING HISTORY
Heat trade paperback edition / July 2011

Library of Congress Cataloging-in-Publication Data

Hill, Joey W.
    Vampire instinct / Joey W. Hill. — Heat trade pbk. ed.
        p. cm.
    ISBN 978-0-425-24126-4 (trade pbk.)
    1. Vampires—Fiction.   I. Title.
    PS3608.I4343V347 2011
    813'.6—dc22
                        2010036503

PRINTED IN THE UNITED STATES OF AMERICA

10   9   8   7   6   5   4   3   2   1

Acknowledgments

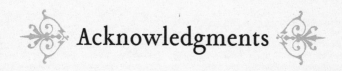

Every one of my books is the result of more than one person's efforts, and for the support of all those often unnamed individuals, I'm exceedingly grateful. However, I want to particularly note the generous offerings and kindness of several people.

Thank you to Jo, whose great insights and skills in the child development field helped me believably reflect the overlap of vampire and human nature in young fledglings. Her compassion and intelligence made me very glad people like her are out there looking out for our children.

Thank you to Helen and Mary, two wonderful Australian ladies on the Joey W. Hill fan forum who also offered their valuable time to review the manuscript. They not only made sure my references were accurate, but kept me from going overboard with delightful Aussie expressions. Or at least they tried their best! As always, any mistakes that remain are mine.

Finally, a great thanks to the Big Cat Rescue organization in Tampa, Florida. The information resources they provide both at their facility and on their website helped bring Mal's sanctuary to life. Above and beyond that, I am grateful an organization such as theirs exists, bringing dignity and ease to creatures who have suffered at the hands of human ignorance and cruelty. Like all of us, wild animals have the right to be what Nature intended them to be. Thank you, Big Cat Rescue, for being here to remind us of that.

1954, Eastern U.S. coastline

S INCE Elisa was gazing out the west-facing window of the private plane, she had first glimpse of the string of islands. Outlined in white foam, they were like flecks of green and brown jewels amid a vast expanse of deep blue sea. The islands were shaped like a question mark, a symbol that became even more pronounced as the plane dropped out of the filmy white cloud cover. The sudden flash of sunset made her squint and start back, despite its rose and gold beauty. She steeled herself against the heave of anxiety that flopped on an empty stomach. Well, not empty. A cold, tight knot she couldn't loosen had become her belly's permanent companion these days, like a dour, stillborn fetus, its potential terminated before it was realized.

Stop it. Pushing that away, she focused on the islands. This was a new place. A new start. She tried to make herself feel that, drawing a deep breath, letting it out. She'd started over countless times, hadn't she? Ever since she was a child, born to an Irish prostitute in Perth. She'd been thrown on the streets to beg, steal and fend for herself practically before she could walk. Pulled in by a copper with a kinder heart than most, he'd found her work in a household as a cook's helper, where she'd earned herself up from that to a housemaid. When she got pretty, she rucked up her skirts for the man of the house if her job was on the line. Getting rooted was nowhere near as bad as hunger or facing the dangers of the streets.

Things changed again, though, when an unusual dinner guest, a woman with sad but oddly still eyes, had paid a considerable sum to take her into her employ on her Western Australia sheep station. Elisa hadn't known Lady Constance was a vampire. Not then. She'd sent Elisa to school, taught her how to dress and take care of her hair and nails properly. Even how to speak like a proper lady, eradicating the colorful common vernacular that might have kept her relegated to a lower rank in a household. By the time she learned the nature of her current Mistress, Elisa was so grateful for her kindnesses it didn't really matter. Vampires were just another part of an unpredictable life.

The purpose of all those preparations had become clear the day Lady Constance brought Elisa to her room and explained her circumstances. "My daughter will come soon. When she does, you will repay my kindness by giving her your absolute loyalty." The next morning, the sad-eyed woman had walked into the sun, disintegrating into ash while her consort, Lord Ian, slept on undisturbed. After he heard the news, Elisa remembered he'd drummed his fingers once on the table in irritation, then asked his human servant to season his breakfast blood with the cranberry-flavored sherry. He'd moved that servant into Lady Constance's room before the wind had carried away the lingering remains of her ashes.

The arrival of her daughter, Lady Daniela, had put an end to all that. Elisa tightened her chin, vicarious satisfaction in the recollection. The female vampire had decapitated Ian at the dining table—that was a mess to clean up, for sure—and within a month had taken over as Region Master of the northwest territory with the help of her bushman servant, the quiet, handsome and altogether likable Devlin. Lady Danny made Elisa her second-marked servant right away, teaching her things about herself and her own sensuality that those previous ham-handed, clumsy employers never had, making Elisa feel strangely empowered. Until that fateful night.

Closing her eyes, she tried to shake away the horrific images before her mind could fill with them. She guessed she'd always been a simple soul, with a sturdy cheerfulness to prepare her for the life God had seen fit to give her. No matter her lot, there were always things to be thankful for. Particularly since Lady Danny had taken over. For a while, she'd been able to laugh with the other staff over nonsense, enjoy the cook's dry humor, take secret glimpses at a new stockman who had a handsome smile and arse. Stretch out in her soft bed after a hard day's work, knowing that in Lady Danny's house, no one would be creeping in to bother her.

She'd pulled herself out of the muck that others had thrown upon her often enough, but she'd never experienced the bog of her own mind. Blood and screams were pushing in at the corners of such memories even now. In desperation, she groped for one of her best, though she'd never shared it with anyone, not even Willis.

He might not have called her a fool for it, but others would, and she didn't want the memory sullied by the truth. It had been in her second employer's home. He was far wealthier than Mr. Collins, her first employer. One of her tasks was laying out the dining room for grand dinners. Usually, she was all alone in the room, and that one day, the silence of it had caught her. After she'd finished the job, she'd gone to the door, turned to survey her handiwork. Dust motes had moved lazily in the sunbeams pouring through the tall windows, drenching her corner of the room. The mahogany sheen of the table, the beautiful gold-edged dishes, the sparkle of the wineglasses, the polish of the silver—it was all like that because of her, because she'd cleaned and arranged it.

When they sat down to eat that night, they might or might not notice how lovely and perfect it all was, but she did, and knowing she'd helped make it so gave her a swelling contentment. Hard work didn't bother her none, and truth, this was really what she most liked doing. Making small corners of the world lovely to give pleasure to others, take care of them. Lately, she'd decided that Heaven would be having the mind wiped of everything but such simple memories.

Of course, with Danny, maybe she'd gotten too used to life being soft, which made it easier for something terrible to knock her off her feet. Like having the man she loved torn to pieces ten feet away and then being raped by the vampire who did it. Victor had been soaked in Willis's blood, had it dripping from his fangs before he'd stabbed them into her flesh, punctured her with sharp talons, rutted upon her . . .

She shuddered, pressing her fingers hard into the chair arms.

"It's all right," Thomas murmured next to her. "Just a little turbulence is all."

Opening her eyes, she glanced at him with despair. The somber brown eyes behind the wire spectacles reflected he wasn't talking about the plane. He'd stated it that way just to save embarrassing her. He didn't touch her, despite her obvious distress, and for that she was grateful and unhappy at once. She'd been skittish about a man's touch, not because she feared Thomas, Dev or any of the others, but because it brought back Victor's brutal, bruising grip. She craved contact to save her from the void of her own grief, her guilt, only not just any contact. A touch like Willis's, gentle and loving, the merest graze of his fingertips communicating that he knew her, saw her . . . loved her. Would Willis have been so eager to help her with the vampire children if he hadn't felt that way?

She'd thought her affection for the lean stockman was one-sided. But when Danny had taken in the seven children that the previous Region Master had unnaturally turned into vampires, Willis had volunteered to serve with Elisa as a blood source to them. She'd known it wasn't one-sided then. Not the way he met her gaze, sending heat prickling over her skin, a flush rising to her cheeks.

He'd been such a good man, too. Spoke little, but there was nothing on the place he couldn't do. When Dev traveled, Willis served as station manager. She could watch him all day long and never tire of it. Working with the sheep, mending fencing, riding a horse. Willis put her on one of the brumbies, sat her in front of him to teach her how to ride. He wouldn't let her get scared. That was where he'd kissed her the very first time. Making her lean her head back on his shoulder, he'd placed his lips over hers, giving her the taste of sun and tobacco, sweat and man, the press of his thighs on the outsides of hers. A man who was integrated into the world around him, the earth, air, wind and blazing heat of it.

She expected him to coax her to raise her skirts that very night, maybe in a corner of the stables. She might have done it, for the earlier ones had simply taken what they felt she owed them. Coated with courtesy or not, their demands had been implacable. Willis was the first who could make her heart pound up in her throat, who obsessed her with the way his brown, callused hands moved over a horse's reins or handled everything from a fence post to a bucket. She'd been quite mad over him, like a girl with her first crush, and maybe it had been. The first time in her life she'd had that luxury.

Lady Daniela had marked her, so of course Danny could read her thoughts at will. When her feelings came to light, Danny surprised Elisa with her protectiveness. Dev was sent to give Willis a thorough talking-to, reinforcing that her maid was not a simple tumble. But Elisa knew it wasn't that not-so-veiled warning that made Willis deal honorably with her.

He didn't find a stable for her after that first kiss, or even the second. The third time he kissed her, though, it was with more urgency, but he broke away first, his hands flexing on her shoulders. She would have done for him then, but he'd given her a little shake, a fierce look.

"Value yourself more than that, girl. I want you bad, I do, but I want you to take me as the man you love, not the man you expect no better from. When you think that's the case, then I'll make you mine. For keeps."

An incredible thought. For keeps. Man and wife.

But that dream was gone, lost in blood and savage animal grunts, the echo of her painful screams.

Thomas was there, with a handkerchief for the overflowing tears. With the right timing, when the need to flinch was overwhelmed by the need to cling, he eased his arm around her. Turning into his chest, she buried her sobs there as he held her close.

She felt safer with Thomas than most, because he was a monk. A monk who also happened to be a third-marked servant. He belonged to Lady Lyssa, a powerful friend of Lady Danny's. It wasn't Elisa's place to pry about it, but she certainly wondered about him. A resolute celibate, he emanated the care and compassion a true man of God could offer. She took it now, seeking no answers where there were none, giving in to another bout of the endless grief.

$$\sim$$

He really was the biggest idiot in the world, Mal reflected. Just because he owed Danny a favor didn't mean he owed her a bloody pound of flesh. The trouble with women was they had a serpent's ability to coax and persuade a man to do unlikely nonsense. Like taking in six fledgling vampires who should have been exterminated as mistakes of nature. He guessed it could have been worse. It had been eight.

One of them had died before Danny could ever get the creature back to her place. Apparently unable to handle the transition from predictable brutality to unprecedented kindness, the fledgling had so lost herself in a bloodlust attack she ran up against a wooden pin used to hold a saddle and staked herself. The other one had been executed by Danny herself.

She should have done them all at the same time.

Malachi eyed the lights of the plane coming in for a nighttime landing on his airstrip. Every vampire in the world knew you didn't turn children. But when Lord Charles Ruskin had done so to cultivate his unique and diabolical pack of "hunting hounds," Danny hadn't had the heart to dispatch them the way she'd dispatched their sire.

Of course, the Vampire Council didn't want to be involved, because they had the typically European attitude that Australia was the ass-end of the world, the least of their concerns. While Mal wasn't any fonder of the Vampire Council than Danny was, their heavy-handed attitude might have taken care of this problem before it ever got to his door.

She'd been trying to civilize them, for fuck's sake. Take the savagery out of them that Charles had exacerbated with torture and starvation. Malachi had cursed when she explained she'd used two of her household staff to help feed and manage them. She hadn't needed to tell him the inevitable tragedy, one dead and the other violated and almost killed. At least she'd been smart enough to kill the fledgling that had perpetrated the crime.

The same female who'd been injured had insisted they keep trying, and, incomprehensibly, Danny had agreed. The Lady Daniela that Mal remembered looked like a fairy-tale character with her guileless blue eyes and golden blond hair, but she didn't have a sentimental bone in her body. She'd put her foot up someone's ass in a heartbeat and kick their internal organs out their throat. Instead, in this case, she'd called Mal for help.

So in addition to seeing what could be done about this impossible situation, he had to manage this woman, this *Elisa*. He had to put up with her for only three days, though. Danny had said to give her that much time to provide background on the "children"—and to say good-bye. Then he was free to bundle her back on the plane with Thomas, if he thought that was best.

It would have been *best* if Danny's human hadn't come at all. *Children.* He snorted. That was part of the problem. Calling them that altered the true perception of them. Essentially unnatural, savage creatures with no sense of impulse control, or right or wrong. In any other environment except sentiment, they would be called monsters. Sociopaths, with fangs and superhuman strength.

~

By the time the plane began its approach, Elisa was composed again, her face washed. The children had traveled in a separate compartment, but she'd checked on them several times, assuring them and herself all was well. She hated the steel cages in which they were confined, but at least they were roomy enough for traveling. Each child had a bed and some stretching room. Malachi was supposed to have a secure facility for them that included a communal area.

At her latest check-in, Jeremiah had given her the closest thing to a grateful look. Leonidas spat at her. She hated the spurt of fear that had her hurrying by his cage, not meeting his eyes. The other responses fell somewhere in between. The two girls and four boys ranged in visual age from six to fifteen. Lady Danny had guessed they might be anywhere from a few months to ten years older than their apparent age. It wasn't likely any child could have survived longer than that under what Lord Ruskin had inflicted upon them, even as turned vampires. From his bookkeeping, they knew he'd gone through at least fifty or sixty before this lot, the average life expectancy a horrifying two years.

Danny had said little about the vampire who would now be overseeing their well-being, except that he was a friend she had known some years, and that he was young for all he'd accomplished. Over a hundred and twenty years old, he'd operated this private sanctuary for predatory cats for the last several decades, and owned the island where it was located.

"He's the quiet sort, Elisa," Danny had explained. Giving her maid a straightforward look, her Mistress had added, "I expect you to obey him as you would obey me, particularly where these children are concerned. Remember what we discussed. Continuing this goes against my better judgment, but this is their last chance. If we don't see improvement, if Mal determines it's time to end this, we follow his direction. I've told Mal he may send you back with Thomas at the end of three days if he chooses, and then their future is up to him."

"But—"

"You are getting three days. Consider it fortunate I'm allowing you to go at all."

Elisa had wanted to argue, but a warning flicker in Dev's expression made her bite her tongue. Danny didn't pull the "I'm an all-powerful vampire" mantle of authority too often, but when she did, disobedience or argument wasn't tolerated. Plus, this wasn't easy for Danny. She'd initially decided to spare the children, when they'd found them at Ruskin's estate. Now Willis was dead, and Elisa . . .

She tightened her chin. She was *fine*. Just fine. It wasn't like she was an untouched innocent, after all. Willis would have wanted her to keep trying. She thought he would, at least. She knew for certain *she* did. She had to, because sometimes when Leonidas looked at her the way Victor had, rage surged in her such that her fingers itched for a stake herself. Especially when he scented her fear, and she heard him snicker.

Deliberately, she turned her thoughts to Jeremiah, because he gave her hope, soothing her mind like the vision of that perfect dining room. Looking about nine years old when he was turned, he was a slim boy with blond hair and serious gray-green eyes. None of them communicated in words, making only inarticulate noises as they fought past the demand of their blood that roared up at the sight of anything resembling prey or food. However, they'd made the most headway with Jeremiah. He'd been the very first to reach out.

~

At the station, she'd discovered a predawn routine that helped ease the children's agitation. Dev's bedtime stories calmed them, perhaps his voice reminding them of parents they dimly remembered. He'd sit cross-legged within a few feet of the semicircle of cages. Since the children found adult vampires unsettling, Danny would stay at the barn entrance, but she usually came to hear what story he'd tell, a slight smile on her face even as her gaze remained watchful.

Though Elisa was sure Dev was equally alert, he'd appeared relaxed that night as he told the story of the Three Sisters rocks in the Blue Mountains. While some of the children were hissing and growling low in their throats, she thought a couple expressions flickered with sparks of curiosity. Nerida and Matthew, the two youngest, mimicked his cross-legged posture.

"They tell this story several ways. Legend has it there were three beautiful sisters among the Katoomba people. Three brothers of the Nepean people fell so deeply in love with them, they knew they'd never be whole until they had them. So they rebelled against tribal law that forbade the marriage and planned a battle to capture them. Sometimes you have to capture sheilas before you can work on winning their hearts," Dev added. At his broad wink, Danny gave him a raised brow that made Elisa hide a smile. "But as the day of the battle approached, a witch doctor of the Katoombas decided to turn the three sisters into rock to protect them. He figured he'd turn them back when the battle was over."

Dev's gaze flickered to the left. Jeremiah had put a hand through the bars. Just pressed his palm flat on the wooden slat floor, near one of the toys that Elisa had left close to his cage. None within reach, because the children shredded them, but it had been something pleasing for them to look at. This toy was a stuffed bear.

Leaning over, so he was on his hip and elbow, Dev pushed the bear closer, continuing the story even as the boy scuttled back. Dev kept that position, his shoulder propped near the bear. Danny tensed. He'd brought himself within reaching distance, and the boy's gaze was too focused on the artery in his throat. Even Elisa could see him fixate on it, and wondered at Dev's judgment.

"Unfortunately, the witch doctor was killed in the battle. So to this day, those three magnificent rocks stand in the Blue Mountains, the three sisters forever captured, because no one knows how to reverse the spell." He tilted his head back to eye Danny, humor and something else there, something that made Elisa's vampire mistress curl her hands

into balls and give him an exasperated look. "Course, I've always wondered; if those girls could do it over and had the choice—to become
three magnificent rocks for hundreds of years, or offer those three
blokes a chance to be their husbands, despite tribal laws—how would
they have decided?"

Danny pressed her lips together, about to move forward. Dev shook
his head, apparently quite aware the boy had reached through the bars.
With one hand, Jeremiah took the bear. With the other, he stretched
toward Dev's hair. One fingertip touched it, then another. A crooning
noise came from the boy's lips, garbled by the long fangs curved over
his lips. Then the hand retracted and Dev turned his head to watch the
boy pull the bear into the cage. As he held it against his belly, a curious
look crossed the boy's face. Jeremiah moved it back and forth, experiencing the soft sensation under his ratty T-shirt.

"There you go, mate," Dev said. "You go to bed now, and have sweet
dreams."

Elisa had swallowed, trying not to clap her hands in victory over this
small progress. In her joy, she of course had paid no attention to the
crimson flickering in Victor's gaze. The vampire who looked thirteen
years old would be the one who, a couple months later, would take her
and Willis by surprise in such a tragic way.

It was too bad Jeremiah wasn't stronger than Leonidas, because if he
had more authority with the others, it would go much better. Her most
"gentle" vampire had terrible moments himself, though. Elisa had seen
him fight the bars of his cage until he bloodied himself, his fangs dripping with saliva as he stared hungrily at any living thing. They all had
such episodes, though Jeremiah's and Leonidas's seemed more intense.
For no reason at all, they would become savage, as if they were going
insane in their own skins. Those were the hardest moments for Elisa.
She could sense their distress, their need to be touched and comforted,
but the bloodlust in them wanted only to destroy. It was like watching
paper dolls being torn in half.

It was also at those weak moments she wondered if Danny was right
in her first thinking, that they should have been put down.

Elisa closed her eyes. *No.* She couldn't bear to think that. It couldn't all be for nothing.

~

As Elisa got off of the plane, she looked for him, this Malachi. He was not a Region Master or even an overlord, so he bore no lord or ladyship title as did Lady Danny. Elisa decided she would address him as Mr. Malachi until he indicated otherwise. She wasn't unhappy about Thomas's presence with her, though. The weight he brought as Lady Lyssa's human servant—Lady Lyssa being Region Master of the southern United States, as well as a consultant to the current Vampire Council and the last royal blood of the vampire clans—would be helpful, even knowing Thomas would not stay long from Lyssa's side. Three days . . . She had to convince Malachi to let her stay, to convince Danny it was okay as well.

For one thing, she couldn't bear to go back to the station and see the empty spot that should have been Willis. Riding the stock in, or whittling in a chair leaned back against the barn. Tipping his hat to her with a lazy smile when she came out to beat the rugs. If she went back, she'd have nothing to do but be a maid. Having the children had filled her days *and* nights. It kept her from thinking so much.

Once being around vampires, it wasn't difficult to spot one. The exceptionally graceful, predatory way they moved, the intense focus of the eyes. And of course, every single one of them was beautiful beyond words. It should get tiresome, her senses unaffected by it. Perhaps because of his unexpected appearance, that wasn't the case when the island's owner strode toward the plane.

Even the untitled vampires she'd met took care to appear as aristocracy. Well dressed, well-groomed, well-spoken. Most had lived long enough to accumulate money, education, making themselves appealing to human prey if they didn't have a servant for a regular blood source. In contrast, Mr. Malachi wore jeans and work boots, an untucked and snug-fitting dark T-shirt. The outfit was no more formal than what Dev or Willis might have worn for their stockman duties. Black hair, unruly and brushing his shoulders, looked like a lion's mane. He had an aquiline nose, the features of a hawk. He was an *Indian*.

When Danny bought her a book about the United States, they'd compared Western Australia with the American Wild West. In the pictures of the natives whose tribes had once been scattered over the United States, the resemblance was unmistakable.

A black stone carving of a cat, threaded on a braided strip of leather and worn around his neck, only added to the impression, as well as some kind of tattoo on his biceps that involved a barbed wire pattern twined with feathers. When she at last focused on his dark brown eyes, she saw he possessed a predator's strength and authority in his focus, but it was far more . . . primal. None of the vampires was exactly what she'd call gentle or safe, but he had an untamed look that said he'd always be more at home among wild animals in a dense forest than among his own kind. A strange thought.

He stopped before them, gave Thomas a curt nod. "My greetings to your lady."

"And hers to you. She thanks you for assisting Danny." Thomas cleared his throat, his gaze flashing with amusement. "She says one of these days she expects you to stop playing with your kittens long enough to visit a cat with real claws."

"It may take me a century or two to find that kind of courage."

Elisa drew in a breath, not expecting the quick flash of a male grin that showed fang tips. But then Malachi's glance turned toward her, and the deceptively approachable expression was gone. "Where are the fledglings?"

"They're in the plane," she said. "We didn't wish to unload the children until—"

"They are not children, girl." He cut across her. "*You* are a child. They are vampires. For the *very* brief time you'll be here, you will not call them *children*."

"You haven't even met them yet," she retorted. "You don't know what they are or aren't."

"Elisa." Thomas put a quelling hand on her shoulder, but Malachi had already stepped forward, bumping her toes, moving her back a step with his greater height. He wasn't heavily muscled, but there was a lean, tensile strength to him that suggested he spent a great deal of time doing manual labor. Another thing vampires didn't do. But daring a brief look into his face, she revised her earlier opinion. He might be different, but she saw that full blast of dominant authority a vampire could quickly bring to bear in the face of a challenge by a weaker opponent. What was the matter with her? She'd been trained better than this, but they'd barely stepped foot off the plane and now he assumed—

He settled a strong hand on her throat, tipping her chin up. She froze all over. "In time, I will ask you questions, and I will hear your thoughts. But I'll make the decisions, and you'll follow them instantly. You will not question me. If you have difficulty with that, I'll stick you back on this plane and we'll cut our three-day ordeal two days shorter. Understood?"

"Mal," Thomas said. Malachi cocked his head toward him. Only a faint flicker showed in Thomas's face, but the vampire glanced back down at her. Then his hand was gone and he'd taken a step back. While his face remained implacable, she realized why Thomas had spoken. She was shaking, and there was a swirling panic in her chest threatening to cut off her air flow.

Damn it. Firming that chin he'd handled so familiarly, ignoring the quaver in her voice, she spoke. "Mr. Malachi, I've served vampires for a few years now. I'll have no problem being respectful and obedient to your wishes, but I also have a responsibility to these . . . young vampires. They're mine," she added with a determined stare that locked with his gaze, despite the breach of vampire-human etiquette. *I've paid in blood for the privilege.*

~

Danny had described Elisa as an obedient and efficient servant, naturally submissive. She was trembling like a leaf, her hands knotted together like a frayed rope. When he'd stepped into her space, she'd given every indication she'd bolt, but she'd dug in and stood fast under his touch. She had soft skin. Her curling dark brown hair might fall to her shoulders if she freed it from its pins. Those large jewel-blue eyes were drowning in emotions.

This was the one who had been violated. *Christ.* Her foolish defiance had driven it right from his mind. He took stock of the paleness from recent serious injury, the flash of automatic terror at an aggressive, unknown male. Danny was a fool for permitting her to come. She wasn't up for this. Grudgingly, though, he acknowledged the fortitude it had taken to make this kind of trip and to continue to champion them.

On the other hand, she could be a complete mental case. A smile tugged at his lips, unexpected. One could say the same of a vampire who chose to live away from his own kind and play nursemaid to "kittens," as Lyssa had taunted him.

How many scars had healed on his body from his missteps with his cats? At the beginning, while he was learning their ways, how often had he gone down under them? He could be considered prey with one wrong communication of body language or scent. It was unexpected to see that same history in her eyes, misguided though it was. A vast difference existed between a vampire's mind and a cat's. And a woman's was entirely incomprehensible.

"You're absolutely correct. I've not yet met them." Gesturing, he directed her toward the plane. "Take me to them."

2

As Elisa turned, drawing a steadying breath, she almost choked on it again as his hand grazed the small of her back. If a human male had done it, it would have meant nothing, a courtesy. However, with vampires, touch always conveyed sensual intent, exploration, no matter how dispassionate it seemed on its face.

The first time she'd met Lady Danny, the woman had kissed her. Though it was a mere brush of lips, it had been the way a man kissed a woman, and Elisa's Catholic background crackled up like paper being eaten by flame. Like getting poison ivy or having the sniffles during the blooming season, it was something a human couldn't control. She told herself that as a shiver of reaction spread out like teasing feathers all around that incidental touch.

Willis had been dead all of a few weeks, for Heaven's sake. Yes, they'd had just a couple kisses and all, but still, he'd been thinking about forever. For keeps. And so had she. A family, a home, maybe children of her own one day . . . Those thoughts proved her body's reaction didn't mean anything. She didn't even know why she was worrying about it, beyond the sensible concern Mr. Malachi might think that, because she was Danny's second-mark, he was allowed liberties. She couldn't let that fluster her right now, though.

They ascended the ramp to the cargo area, the efficient and well-armed crew nodding to Thomas, since this was of course his lady's plane. Malachi preceded her into the hold. She would have preferred to lead, reassure the children. Because of their experience with Lord Ruskin, male vampires could agitate them into full-blown hysteria. But Thomas gripped her elbow.

"Remember his warning, Elisa," the monk murmured. "He's in charge here. Trust Lady Danny's wisdom in this. Mal knows what he's about."

Mal strode into the cargo area and came to a halt, gazing about the silver semicircle of cages. The six reacted in myriad ways to his arrival. Three bolted to the backs of their cages, silent, skulking shadows. In contrast, the one who looked the oldest moved forward, baring fangs. Holy Christ, Ruskin had taught them nothing. Their fangs couldn't retract, were permanently locked like saber-toothed tigers. The sickness that twisted in his gut now was what Mal felt when a half-starved juvenile lion was brought in, some misguided idiot's pet or the whipped failure of some circus. He had an active dislike for humans, but before him was the reminder that malicious brutality and unforgivable ignorance weren't limited to them.

That didn't change what needed to be done here, though, so he made sure neither his scent nor his expression emanated such sympathy. Instead, he glanced at one of the handlers. "How do you open the cages?"

"A combination on this control, sir." The man pointed at it.

Mal nodded. "Open his cage." He gestured to the most aggressive fledgling.

"Sir?"

Mal cut a glance in the man's direction, but Thomas was already attending to it. "Obey him," he said. The monk put a reassuring hand on Elisa's quivering shoulder. Her eyes had moved to the young, snarling male, then skittered away, her skin paling further.

"Open it," Mal snapped.

As the cage door retracted, Elisa fully expected Leonidas to leap out. Anticipating that, her body refused all rational thought, going rigid with the desire to bolt. Instead, moving faster than she could follow, Malachi was already in the door, chest to chest with the gangling boy. Leonidas was a few inches shorter, but had the lanky length of a teenager who'd been starting his growth explosion when he was turned.

Baring his fangs, Mal snarled in a way that made Leonidas look like a house cat standing up to a fully grown lion. Leonidas attempted to snarl back, but fear suffused his expression. Malachi moved into him so the boy shuffled back, farther and farther, until he was in the corner. However, Malachi continued to lever the advantage until the boy was shrinking down onto his knees under his looming body, cowering.

"There's no reason to be that cruel," Elisa muttered, starting forward. Thomas clamped down on her arm anew, but then Mal spoke.

"Elisa, come here."

She'd intended to come a couple steps and admonish him. Faced with the actuality of coming into that cage, something happened to her feet, as if they were lodged in concrete.

Mal, his gaze still locked on Leonidas's bowed head, stretched out a hand in her direction. "Trust me, Elisa. You are coming to me, not to him. Nothing will happen to you. Look at me only. Do not make any eye contact with him."

Somehow, responding to the sure authority in his voice, her feet were moving, a blessed miracle. One step, two steps, and she kept her eyes locked on Malachi. Was his hair long enough to braid, she wondered. Did he put feathers in it? Of course, this was the 1950s and Indians did not run around half-naked on horseback with feathers in their hair, but she made herself imagine Malachi in such a way, anything to keep her mind away from what she was doing.

He'd be breathtakingly bare, on the back of a pinto. His bowstring drawn back to his ear, an arrow ready to fly. He'd be painted with symbols for a good hunt, wearing only that and the stone necklace on his upper body. Those brief leggings that showed the muscular curve of buttock would be his only clothing. The horse wouldn't have any tack, man and horse as one, which fit with her idea of Mal as more wild creature than vampire.

As distractions went, it was a good one. It wasn't the first time she'd used visual image to get her through a moment, but it was the first time since that terrible night she'd used imaginings like this. It made her want to scowl. Bloody vampires and their pheromones, as Danny called them. But if it did the trick, got her to him, then so be it.

She hesitated at the threshold, and then she was over it, placing her trembling hand in the grip of his. She tried hard to stare just at him, but then, nervously, her gaze skittered to Leonidas.

The boy struck. Elisa screamed. A flash of movement, a resounding thud and cry of pain. Not hers. Malachi was holding Leonidas against the bars of the cage. One long-fingered hand squeezed his throat, the boy's feet half a foot off the floor. She had somehow ended up against Malachi's chest, her face buried into it, his other arm curled protectively around her.

"Look at me, Elisa."

Taking a breath, Elisa managed to get to his throat, her eyes glued to that dark stone totem in the bronzed hollow. She was used to pale vampires. When his fingers tightened along her back, she felt that odd dichotomous shudder again. *Don't touch me. Please touch me.*

As Leonidas choked against his hold, she wanted to tell him to ease up, that he'd proven his point. But she did as Mal told her to do, at least for this volatile moment. They could argue about it later. Gathering her courage, she raised her gaze to his face. Without looking down, Malachi eased his hold on her, guided her around so she was facing Leonidas. She kept her head turned to stare only at Malachi. She wasn't sure if it was because he hadn't told her to do otherwise, or because she couldn't do anything else.

Mal let the fledgling's feet touch the ground. As he loosened his hold, he bared his fangs again, a rumble coming from his chest, unmistakably a warning growl. The young vampire capitulated to it, going down until he was crouched in the corner again on his knees, his eyes downcast.

"I will taste your blood tonight, every one of you." He swept his gaze over the room. "You will be marked by me as a sire, and I will have access to your minds. If you want to live, I will find *complete* submission to me there." As he moved his grip on Elisa, she tried not to shake harder. He curved his fingers in her hair, an easy, stroking touch that startled her, because it was unexpectedly soothing, despite his fierce, steel-muscled posture. "And this is mine."

When she would have jerked her head up, his hand tightened in her hair, warning her to stillness. Lifting a booted foot, he pressed it against Leonidas's chest, drawing the boy's attention and holding him against the cage wall.

"With one push, whelp, I can crush all your ribs. Rip them out of your chest and stake your heart a good dozen times. You'd live long enough to feel pain such as you've never felt from anyone. You ever even *look* at her in a way that displeases me, that will be your fate. She is mine, and that's the end of it." Malachi passed his attention over the assembled cages, making sure he had the acknowledgment he wanted from each. As he did, he gathered her hair in one hand, and tilted her head to the left.

"What—" But she had no time to react before he'd pierced her with his fangs, taking a draught of the blood she had to offer. Her gaze briefly locked with Jeremiah's, squatting in the middle of the cage, his eyes intent on her face. Then he looked away.

The shock of it rippled down to her toes as Mal marked her. Dropping his hand to her waist, he caressed her there, while her body warred between panic and something not like panic at all. Dizzy, she leaned into him, and the warmth of his arm came across her chest as the electric stimulus of a marking burned through her blood.

You'll be safe from them from here forward, fierce Irish flower. But you are still getting on that plane in three days.

Holy Mary. He'd given her the first and second marks, as smooth and easy as she'd ever seen it done, though she'd heard giving more than one mark at once could burn. Maybe it was different when the third mark wasn't involved. Regardless, he was in her mind now. She should have felt violated, and part of her perhaps did, but another part felt something she'd experienced for only a short time during Danny's employ. So short that the terrible incident with Victor had made her think everything before that night had been a lie, or something she'd never feel again.

She felt safe. Despite her mortification, it made her begin to cry again, but she pressed her face into his T-shirt that smelled like animals, grass and man, and let the tears absorb there.

He didn't seem to mind.

3

AFTER that dramatic beginning, the next few minutes were decidedly tame and efficient. Mal brought Elisa out of Leonidas's enclosure, had it resecured and then went to the opening of the cargo bay to wave at the driver of a small forklift. The piece of equipment had been taken off one of the four flatbed trucks that were going to be used to transport the cages. Elisa counted ten men and one woman. Back home in Australia, all the station hands knew Danny was a vampire. She'd second-marked them so she could be in their minds whenever she chose. Elisa wondered if these were the same, and expected they were, because they moved forward to do his bidding with very little obvious conversation. Of course, perhaps it was just familiarity, because Elisa had learned to serve her Mistress without much direction, anticipating her needs.

Mal escorted Elisa back to Thomas's side and indicated they would go in a Jeep to their guest quarters, where he would join them later.

"Mr. Malachi, I can help," Elisa protested. "I'm not your guest. I'm here to work, same as your people."

The vampire gave her a dismissive glance. The reassurance and patience he'd demonstrated when he'd held her against him were no longer evident. In fact, she sensed her very presence was irritating him.

"Duly noted. If you're working for me, then follow orders. Go to the house with Thomas."

"They don't know you."

"No, they don't. But they do know you. Which is an additional problem I don't need during this transfer." He gave her a look out of those dark eyes that held a clear warning. "Get in the Jeep; go to the house."

Danny had told her she could trust him. But he didn't see what she did. While Leonidas was predictably savage to everyone, the others had known only one kind of male vampire. The kind that tortured and starved them for his own purposes, everything from hunting to simple sadistic entertainment. When Ruskin had made four adult vampires to serve him, he'd also allowed them free use of the children, in whatever manner would entertain them best. When she looked toward Jeremiah, she saw the terrible apprehension in the tense line of his jaw, though he was trying to mask it. Nerida and Miah, the girls, had naked fear in their expressions. William was already on the side of his cage closest to Matthew's, as close as he could get to reassure him, though they both knew there was no reassurance. There was only getting as close to one another as possible, so that one didn't feel all alone in the suffering. She knew why that was so important.

When Victor had taken her down, Willis had been too weak to help her, his chest crushed, but he'd used that last precious spark of energy to drag himself a few inches. She'd fought, until Victor hit her in the face and broke her jaw, pinned her to the floor. After that, she couldn't fight him any longer. It was then she'd looked left and met Willis's pain-filled gray eyes, blood coming from a mouth that no longer could speak to her. He was trying, though, the lips working. His blood-soaked hand strained toward her. When she'd reached out, there'd been an inch between their fingertips. Then Victor had jammed himself into her, making her cry out, her body jerk in response. That had closed the distance. She'd managed to get her fingers underneath the callused surfaces of Willis's.

There'd been a slight twitch, a valiant effort to close them, to hold on to her. His eyes held hers to the very end. She'd seen the life die out of them, though his hand didn't slacken for some moments afterward. She held on to him anyway, believed that he was holding on to her from the other side. Maybe he was making sure she could step through death's door right after him, to get away from this terrible pain. When Victor had yanked her away like a rag doll, she'd cried out in anguish, even more than she'd felt when he slammed her up against his cage, breaking ribs. He'd forced her to stay in this world, with all this anger and hate, pain and suffering.

She knew this was the height of stupidity, that she should be cowering, running for that Jeep, but when she looked toward the girls, she couldn't. She met Malachi's eyes directly for the foolish second time of the night, took a deep breath. "No. I won't go back to the house. I can help you—"

She had more to say, but sucked it in on a gasp as Mal moved. Or she assumed he did, because she never saw it. All she had was the glimpse of dark, piercing eyes, a yank on her arm, and then, before she could do more than yelp, she was standing on the roadside nearly out of sight of the landing strip, a hundred yards away from where they had been, screened by foliage.

Great, giddy aunt. She blinked; her knees turned to water. She was gripping his forearm hard. He gave her time to steady, but his forbidding expression helped her with that. As soon as she thought she could manage without falling down, she released him, folding her hand against her flopping stomach.

He crossed his arms and scowled. "Say what you're going to say. Out of hearing of the fledglings."

She'd been ready to be chastised, to have to stick a word in here or there wherever she could manage it, knowing she was desperately close to going back on that plane. Put on the spot, she led with emotion, blurting out what was foremost in her mind.

"You can't frighten them. They've been afraid and alone, too much in their lives. The only thing they've known from male vampires is brutality. If I'm there, it helps. It helps calm them—"

"That's plenty." He silenced her with a raised hand and a look. "Elisa, Danny gave me the impression you are a reasonably intelligent girl. So prove it by listening to me."

"I can't stand for them to be afraid. I won't bear it. Do you understand? I won't."

She couldn't stop the words from pouring out of her mouth, rushing right over his. She'd *never* acted like this toward an employer. And a vampire . . . God in Heaven, humans didn't argue with vampires, unless they had little value for their own skins. Even Lady Danny could get that cold look in her eye, her line in the sand. Dev pushed over it more than anyone—or rather, he was the only one who could get away with it—and then only within limits.

But she couldn't take it back. She had enough sense left to keep her gaze on his T-shirt where it stretched across his chest, because vampires took it as a direct challenge if a human met their gaze head-on, and she'd already done that one too many times. Right now, she expected she'd find his expression more than a little intimidating. She noted an impression of blue and white feathers in the ridged pattern of that biceps tattoo, perhaps some kind of cat etched out by the ink, before it disappeared up his short sleeve. "Please," she whispered.

A sigh. When his hands descended, she flinched, but he was only settling his palms on her shoulders. She stilled beneath that touch, particularly when one finger touched her cheek, a mildly impatient but not ungentle tap that brought her eyes back to his face.

"Have you ever ridden a bicycle, girl?"

"No. I've ridden a horse." *Willis taught me.* She didn't say it. She couldn't risk what saying his name aloud would do to her.

"Were you afraid, the first time?"

"Yes." But only for a little while. Willis had been there, after all. Right behind her, guiding her hands on the reins.

"You got over it when you learned the way of it, right? It's learning the difference between fearing things you *should* fear, and being afraid of the ghosts that plague you." Seeing he had her full attention now, he nodded. "You have to step out of the way and let that happen for them."

She was nonplussed. He was talking to her, not at her, a complete flip from his high-handed treatment of a moment ago. However, he still looked stern and a bit annoyed. "They know you can't stop me from doing anything I want to them. Your agitation tells them there's a reason to be afraid. That's why I don't want you there right now. You're no good to them like that. But if you calmly go back to the house, get settled in the guest quarters, what does that say to them?"

He was right. That intelligence Danny had praised knew it. But her heart resisted it. Without them to occupy her mind and time, *her* ghosts might carry her away. Given how he was looking at her so intently, she wasn't so sure he didn't know that. Those eyes made her feel too vulnerable, as if he'd peeled back a scab to stare at the wound it hid.

A Jeep engine startled her, causing her to lurch into him, catch his forearm again. She immediately pulled away, flushing, especially since it deepened the bug-under-a-microscope look. As the vehicle rolled up next to them, she saw the female staff person driving it. Thomas was in the back. Malachi turned her toward the passenger side as the monk got out to help her into the vehicle.

They'd left her no choice. Suddenly she was tired. So tired. But she needed to tell him about William and Matthew. How Jeremiah was. What the girls would do if . . .

"Take them to the house, get them settled in guest quarters. And get her something to eat before she falls down," Mal told the driver. He glanced at Thomas, who gave him a nod, then brought his gaze back to Elisa. The vampire stepped closer, pressing a knee into the Jeep's running board so he could bend to eye level with her. "Remember what I told you. Once you've eaten a full meal and gotten eight hours' sleep, you can tell me everything you think is of importance."

"When can I come—"

"Once they're settled and I'm confident you're ready to follow some basic rules, you can see them."

"I don't need sleep and food. I—"

"That wasn't an offer." His voice was back to clipped, annoyed. "You may not be my servant, but while you're under my protection I'm well within my rights to do what I see fit to serve your Mistress's interests."

Maybe because her nerves were so raw and exhaustion had gripped her so unexpectedly, Elisa didn't think to mind her hands and feet, what they were doing. Her hand had settled on the front of his T-shirt, fingers curling into the cloth, feeling the hard male beneath. His gaze flickered to it, then back up to her face, his jaw tightening.

"They *are* children," she insisted. His expression could be uncompromising, but she saw something in those depths, something from a moment ago that she thought she could trust. "Children who've seen too much, been through too much. Please, I know I'm nothing to you, but please, please don't . . ."

Hurt them? Make them afraid? What wish would best match the trajectory of this falling star, make it come true? "Please." That was all she could say. Like praying, she hoped the need would be understood and heard.

Malachi curled his hand over hers. His lean strength covered her cold fingers. His penetrating gaze swept over her face, the set of her mouth, then up to her brow and the curls that had escaped her hair arrangement from her dozing on the plane. She must look a sight, she realized. How could he take someone seriously who looked like an exhausted child? He might be right about her not being worth a brass razoo to him without the food and sleep. Held by those strong fingers, she thought she might need to trust him, at least a little while. Danny trusted him, after all.

It was clear the man worked with difficult creatures, because despite his boorish attitude, he had an oddly calming touch. His fingers squeezed, a brief pressure; then he put her hand back in her lap. "Take them up to the house," he ordered. He glanced at Thomas. "And make certain she does as she's told."

$\sim$

Out of his sight, her worry spiraled back up and snagged in that fog of exhaustion, even as she tried to focus on Thomas and their driver, Chumani. Her Sioux name meant *dewdrops*, which Elisa found appropriately beautiful. The woman was tall and smoothly muscled, her thick dark hair plaited in a braid to her waist, the loose strands emphasizing her sculpted cheekbones and firm chin, the forest of dark lashes that framed her vibrant eyes.

As if the awkwardness at the tarmac had never occurred, Chumani directed their attention to the landscape like a seasoned tourist guide. Since it was nighttime for the comfort of the vampires, she couldn't see detailed features, but Elisa noted dark silhouettes of thick forests, as well as open plains whose grasses were highlighted white-gold by moonlight. That same moon caused tiny sparkles off rock facets along cliff banks. They passed over and through quite a few freshwater sources. Creeks, ponds, waterfalls. The Jeep windows were open, so the evening breeze helped cool her cheeks, which were still heated by her exchange with Malachi.

The more her nerves settled, the more appalled she was with herself. All her life she'd been docile, obedient. The proper servant, whether she was maid, housekeeper or convenient whore. She closed her fingers together in a ball in her lap, not wanting anyone to see the tremor. That memory shouldn't unsettle her. The two male employers who had used her that way might have been insistent, but they were unexpectedly kind about it, and she knew just how fortunate she'd been in that.

Why was it that what had happened in the barn that awful night seemed to be polluting not only her present, but flowing backward as well, a blood-colored paint changing the hue of her past?

Well, then, she'd just repaint it the way it should be. Mr. Collins, the first one, had been the most kind. She remembered his trim brown mustache, his grass green eyes and warm hands. He'd given her a bracing shot of brandy after he asked—he *asked*—if it was her first time. He'd seemed to even enjoy taking his time, touching her enough to get things slippery between her legs, and he hadn't jammed himself into her like a hammer driving a nail into wood. It had hurt, but he'd kissed her tears, even caught one in a tiny little rose-colored bottle, tied with her hair ribbon. He'd kept it in his desk drawers with some other mementoes until it dried up. He'd told her it wouldn't hurt like that again, particularly if they did it often. She'd been thirteen.

His wife had tolerated it. They already had three children and apparently Mrs. Collins had no interest in having more. Elisa hadn't conceived, thankfully, because an older girl in the household, Linda, had taught her the necessary herbs and methods to stay that way. She'd worried at first it was a sin, but the pragmatic Linda told her that starving to death in the street with a child to suckle and no way to feed it except whoring with far more dangerous strangers might be a bigger sin. Elisa had taken the herb packets and the little sponge.

His wife was no longer as tolerant when Elisa turned eighteen. But Mr. Collins had made sure she ended up with his friend Mr. Pearlmutton, who'd been less kind, but only because he expected her experience. He taught her to do the things he enjoyed, and sometimes she felt unexpected spirals of pleasure. Not because she found him appealing, but because sometimes his fingers and the movement of his cock did things to her. Those puzzling instances were nothing next to the few handfuls of times Willis had kissed her. Then she'd felt the true promise of something building in her lower extremities, a much stronger reaction that made her cling to him shamelessly those few times.

She hadn't known it was possible for women to enjoy rutting the way men did, all that grunting and heaving. She'd seen whores fake it in alleyways with their clients, but it wasn't until she came into a female vampire's employ that she'd seen what the act could be for a woman.

Lady Constance and Ian had shared a room, and she heard them a few times, but initially she assumed Lady Constance faked it, like the whores, to make Ian happy. After all, a girl had to give a man that to keep him around, and in return he took care of her and helped her do things. Lady Constance owned the station, though, and was the overlord for the territory. She didn't seem to need that kind of security from Ian.

Then Danny and Dev came to live in the station house and Elisa was given an eye-opening education. It wasn't like she'd popped in on them in their bedroom to get a front-row seat. It was a gradual thing, starting with how they were with each other. At night, she'd seen Danny press up behind Dev while he was bent over a table, reviewing the ledger books. The female vampire would get so close there was no space between their bodies, her breasts pressed tight against his broad back, hips firmly against his tight arse. Her lady's hand would slide down his muscular thigh, her knuckles teasing her way across the hard line of it. Though Elisa pretended she didn't see, Dev's cock would react, getting full and stiff in his trousers, and Lord, he was blessed far more in that department than most.

He'd smile that faint smile of his when Danny whispered she didn't want him to stop what he was doing, that she expected her station manager to keep her accounts up-to-date. As he tried to do her bidding, her hands would stroke and squeeze, wander until it was obvious he couldn't pay attention to anything but her.

As mesmerizing as it was to see a man as handsome as Dev get aroused, Elisa's fascination had been with Lady Danny. She was fully in charge of all of it. She didn't have to couple with Dev to keep him. He was her servant . . . He served her.

It had been confounding. One early dawn, she'd come to the kitchen to get a cup of bedtime tea, thinking she was the only one moving about. She'd heard murmuring, soft gasps, and paused at the library. The double doors had been open just a crack. It was wrong, but she'd looked. And then she couldn't tear her eyes away.

Danny was in one of the comfortable broad chairs, her long white legs draped wide over the arms but her ankles coming in like the shape of a heart to rest on the lower curve of Dev's broad, bare back. He'd had his mouth between her legs, teasing and suckling her there the way they often kissed, with tongue and deep penetration. As his head moved, Elisa saw the pink lips of Danny's sex, wet not just from his mouth, for she heard him murmur, "Ah, love, your cream is the sweetest treat I know."

Danny had arched up, her fingers spearing into his hair, and the flush that crossed her body was obviously not pretense, the way her muscles strained and her body both yearned and resisted his hold on her thighs. The climax that took her made her grip harder, and her head dropped forward and then snapped back as a cry split from her throat, a cry of pleasure she didn't care if anyone heard. Dev's back muscles rippled as he tightened his grip. He still wore his trousers, but he'd had them open and loose, so Elisa could see the upper rise of his buttocks, a glimpse of the seam between. He flexed rhythmically, as if he were already inside her. Holding on, he kept teasing and suckling, until that cry became a scream of absolute, undeniable pleasure.

Elisa had been surprised to find her own thighs damp with a thick response of her own. Thanks to Mr. Collins, she knew how to make herself slippery using her fingers, until the collywobbles were dancing in her stomach. That was how he'd told her to do it, but he hadn't said anything about keeping on with it until it reached the point Danny seemed to be experiencing. It made Elisa wonder if it was possible to do it to oneself. For the first time in her life, she had a yearning to try, but she slept in the housekeeper's room, Mrs. Pritchett, and there was no way she'd risk being discovered doing *that*. Seeking pleasure by oneself was definitely a sin. Right?

And why on earth had she gone down this road in her mind, far beyond where she'd intended to go to simply dispel a bad memory?

She started at Thomas's hand on her shoulder. "We're here, Elisa."

Focusing, she saw they were in a valley. A long field stretched away to the left, merging into a new set of rolling inclines that led up into higher, rockier terrain. It reminded her of the terrain surrounding Danny's station, a reassuring thought.

The house was a dark, sprawling smudge in the center of the field, but it wasn't some tall, opulent mansion. It was built much like the station itself, with a porch that wrapped all the way around, and open doors and spaces, welcoming the land around it. The sturdy post and wire fence built along the perimeter of the field and encompassing the house, vehicles and outbuildings didn't detract from the feeling. As they went through the gate and pulled up to the front of the house, she saw a pair of house cats on one of the wooden swings, their eyes gleaming off the Jeep headlights as Chumani killed the engine. At the bottom of the porch steps, a trellis thickly covered with vines showed off white, mysterious-looking flowers the size of Elisa's hands. The blooms had a light, haunting scent.

"Moonflowers," Thomas murmured. "My lady loves them. Unlike most flowers, they open at night and close during the day."

"Kohana cares for the house, does the gardening and upkeep around the place," Chumani offered. "He's got a way with greenery. He'll have heard us. Takes him just a minute to— Well, here he is."

As the door opened and a male figure filled it, she raised her voice. "About time you got off your lazy ass, *mato*. Need to come out and give Mal's guests a proper greeting."

"Well, they'll certainly not have gotten it from you, will they have, *pahin*?"

As the man moved forward out of the block of dim light behind him, Elisa saw he was limping. He had only one leg, the other amputated just above the knee, his pants tied in a convenient knot on that side. With the use of a carved crutch, he moved forward with practiced ease, however. He came down the steps by holding the crutch in one hand, and hopping without the aid of the banister, his other leg taking his considerable weight.

Elisa was used to everyone towering over her. Mal had probably been about six feet tall. However, this man had to be a foot higher, with a face scarred by three spaced lines on one side. His wide shoulders strained against a flannel shirt tucked into the workman's trousers. She noted he wore a pair of hunting knives strapped to his hip. Despite his infirmity, the shirt revealed well-defined forearms and hinted at muscular biceps. The flex of his body when he maneuvered down the stairs said that he was as fit as any man they'd left unloading the cages. He looked to be in his fifties, streaks of gray in his dark hair, tied back loose and unbraided.

When his gaze settled on her, Elisa realized she really *must* look quite tapped out, because everyone was giving her that assessing look.

All right, then, fine. So Mr. Malachi was right about the sleep. She'd get some sleep, she'd eat and then she'd talk to him again. And maybe she'd act much more sensibly.

Kohana came to her, leaned on his crutch and extended a hand to help her out. His dark eyes were deep-set over those prominent cheekbones Malachi and all the staff seemed to have, perhaps an Indian trait, though there were structural differences between the three that suggested different tribes. Had they left reservations? From what the book had said about those, she suspected this was a much nicer place, but there had to be a good story explaining their presence here. She'd have to find out, tell the children, since they'd gotten used to Dev telling them stories and she didn't want them to lack for it. Of course, she'd have to work on her storytelling skills, because Dev was raised in the Aboriginal tradition. He could tell stories with flare, making different voices and dramatic body movement.

When Kohana spoke, he had a good story voice himself. It was deep and slow, his accent suggesting his musical native language. She wanted to reach up and touch his face, just as she had when she first saw the pictures of Indians in the books. Trace the flare of the nose, those sharp cheekbones. Malachi had possessed thick, dark lashes and his nose had an uneven slope that indicated it had once been broken. She knew he was a made vampire, not a born one like Danny, so the break would have predated his making.

Being a made vampire meant he had a lower status among vampires, but it didn't appear relevant on this remote island. In fact, from what she'd seen so far, Elisa expected he'd have a few choice things to say to any highbrow vampire who wanted to talk down to him.

"You look as though you're already dreaming, miss."

Elisa snapped out of it, realized she had in fact been hazily staring at Kohana's face, lost in her thoughts. Heavens, if she'd been this addled and disoriented at the station, Mrs. Rupert, the cook, would have taken a switch to her arse, something she'd threatened once or twice when Elisa first came to work for Lady Constance, but had never done. A good thing, too, since Ian got dangerously worked up by that kind of thing. He'd have probably insisted on watching if he'd heard of it, his pledge to Lady Constance to keep his hands off Elisa notwithstanding.

She couldn't suppress the shiver and slight jerk to her hand. Kohana let her go, as if he thought he'd startled her. She wanted to apologize, but then decided she was just too tired to do it. She settled for a nod and slid out of the Jeep. Her boots hit the ground and her knees buckled. Fortunately Thomas was already there and he caught her elbow.

"When was the last time she slept?" Kohana murmured as if she weren't there.

"Too long ago," Thomas responded, but gave her a squeeze about the shoulders to include her. "The Master of the house wants her fed and put to bed, and kept there a good eight hours."

"We'll see to it." Chumani came around the nose of the Jeep then. Despite her gruff teasing of Kohana, they exchanged a look, in obvious accord. "I'll help her to her room and you can bring her some food."

Elisa didn't think she could eat anything, but her wishes didn't seem to matter. She was so used to that, she let herself be shepherded into the house, Thomas supporting her around the waist and Chumani on the other side, Kohana bringing up the rear.

She didn't remember the threshold, or even the interior. By the time she got to the top of the stairs, the light-headedness had taken over and she slumped against Thomas, spots on her eyes telling her the meal she should have eaten on the plane would have been a good idea.

"I'm okay," she tried to say, mortified to be the center of attention. She was a servant; she took care of others. But they didn't hear her, because Chumani was lifting her in strong arms. It was a remarkable thing to be carried by a woman, but that was a fleeting thought, for they were bearing her to a bed and oblivion. It was a place she shouldn't want to go, but her spirit was racing ahead, eager to take her there.

For just a while, she wanted to leave behind everything she knew she still had to face—including one implacable vampire who thought her children were better off dead.

4

"**W**OULD you like to explain what the hell you've gotten me into?"

"Would you like me to fly to that godforsaken island to teach you some manners?"

Mal knew it was midmorning on Danny's side of the world, but he'd informed the housing staff they needed to get their Mistress's ass out of bed to answer the damn phone before he came halfway around the world to drag her out of it. Therefore, when he heard her not entirely empty threat, delivered in a mix of Aussie and Brit temper, it helped him rein in his own a bit. She was above him on the feeding chain, and while she didn't go out of her way to emphasize it, her tone suggested he was pushing his luck this morning. After all, his present situation was the result of him owing her a tremendous favor. However, given his current frame of mind, he thought when this was over, she'd owe him.

"You didn't tell me everything about her."

"Yes, I did. I assumed you would know that someone who's endured what she has would present some challenges. Oh, I forgot. You're male and need it spelled out with a bloody crayon."

He winced. Yep, he'd chosen the wrong tack. Sometimes, living with his cats, he did forget how to play nice with others. He bit back a sigh. "I apologize, my lady. It has been an . . . unexpected few hours. My manners aren't what they should be."

She was silent; then he heard a matching sigh. "Apology accepted. Perhaps I could have prepared you better, but I wanted you to form your own impressions and see if they match my own. So tell me what they are so far."

"First, let's be sure we're still on the same page, because I'm not so sure we are. I was supposed to evaluate the fledglings, see if they have any meaningful chance of surviving in our world. If not, I have the discretion to give them a merciful end."

"That's correct."

He tightened his lips at the short answer. She knew there was more to it, damn it, but she wanted to see if he'd seen it. A blind man could have done so. "You didn't tell me the girl's life depends on theirs."

"She's not marked by them. There's no chance . . ."

"Lady Danny." Danny didn't particularly care for honorifics between them, so he used the title deliberately. "Are you blinding yourself out of sentiment for her, or are you testing me to see if I'm as clever as you remember?"

"You have the discretion to send her home as soon as you feel her presence is no longer necessary."

"Hedging, my lady. I'd have been happy to turn her pretty 'arse,' as you call it, right back onto that plane. But she wants to stay, and she's being fairly insistent about it."

"I'm glad you think she has a pretty arse. It means you've taken the stick out of yours long enough to notice something other than your cats."

"Danny."

The female vampire blew out a breath, so ferociously it sounded like a fitful gust of wind through the static-laden connection. "Damn it, *you* stop hedging. What do you think?"

"I think she's recovering from a severe trauma. Actually, no, she's not recovering. She's hiding from it, making the well-being of these fledglings her obsession. She looks like a ghost, barely able to stand on her own two feet from worry. Kohana says she fell asleep before she could eat. From those nicely shaped breasts of hers, I can tell she used to be a bit more of a handful. A good wind would blow her away."

"Yes, she was very appealing. A nice, generous arse and breasts that were more than a handful. Tiny feet and a waist you could put your hands around. A little hourglass. Your preferred type, right?" There was a trace of amusement in Danny's voice. "When Dev travels, she keeps me company like a favorite doll, gives me blood in bed at dawn. We had to keep a close eye on the hands to make the more thickheaded of them behave around her."

"She was a tease?" He wasn't seeing much of a flirt in the hollow-eyed child who'd gotten off that plane.

"Certainly not." The nearly maternal offense bemused him. "Just the contrary. Sweet and honest to a fault. That kind of freshness awakens all sorts of wickedness in a man's mind."

"Not this one."

Danny snorted. "Spare me. I've seen you around women. Though not for a long time. When was the last time you left that island?"

"I come and go as my cats need me. We're talking about her. What is it you're expecting me to do for her? Straight out, now." Though he knew asking a woman to come straight out with something was like asking a cow to jump over the moon, there were times Danny could be as direct as a man. Fortunately, this was one of those times.

"I want you to help her see what you see. You save lives all the time, Mal. You bring in souls from terrible, dark places, and give them a chance to embrace some semblance of the life they were supposed to have." She hesitated. "I'm not so certain she and the fledglings aren't in that same place. We weren't unloading her on you. She needed to get away. We're still figuring out how to scrub Willis's blood, and hers, off the barn floor. And the walls. The hands were creeping around, treating her like porcelain, and Mrs. Rupert could barely set a plate in front of her without bursting into tears."

When Danny paused, Mal was surprised that she herself seemed to be taking a steadying breath. But of course, she'd made the decision to take in the fledglings. Handling them while running a sheep station and a vampire territory had to have been more than a load. Then they'd lost control and Danny had lost one person, nearly lost Elisa. Mal was still surprised the girl had not shown more physical scars, but Victor had apparently taken out his brutality on her in the form of rape and broken bones. The second-mark healing ability had been able to handle the rest. The physical part at least.

On an earlier phone call, Dev had told Mal more details of what had happened. At the time Mal had thought Danny had merely delegated the call to him while she handled other matters. Now, hearing the emotion lashed down in her voice, he realized Danny had gotten closer to the situation than she'd let on. Dev said she'd handled Victor's execution personally.

Opened up his cage, and walked right in before I expected it. She'd told me to wait at the house, but of course I followed her. He tried to get past her, and I didn't even see her move. She was just suddenly holding him against her, that stake buried in his chest, body still twitching as he slid down and she let him go, watched him die. Then she told us to drag him out and let him burn. She didn't say a word to the others, but they're kind of afraid of adult vampires anyhow.

Christ, Mal, seeing the way they looked at us. The girls went back to sitting in their cages, rocking and whimpering to themselves, and Jeremiah turned to face the wall . . . It's a bad business. And Danny suffers the most over Elisa. She came up with the idea of letting the girl watch over them, but she never expected it to become so much a part of her. Or for it to come to this.

"I should have come with her." Danny had resumed talking, her voice steady again. "But I have a damnable meeting with my territory overlords, and I've got one causing problems in Perth. I would have said the hell with it and come anyway, but Dev pointed out she might do better with someone less emotionally close to what happened to her. I trust you to do right by her. I don't do that lightly, Mal."

"I know. My lady." He added the title, because it did touch him.

She took another breath. "All right, then. What I'm hoping is you can determine if survival's a possibility for these children. If it's not, and she's still on the island, she needs to understand that, too. Even if you put her on the plane before you finish your evaluation, you could still help her state of mind. Beneath that cranky exterior, you tap into the nature of other beings, four-legged or two-legged, better than anyone I know."

"Glad I have your trust on that, because I had to make a split-second decision. I second-marked her. I felt it was necessary, to stay in touch with her mind for what I'll be doing. I hope that doesn't offend you."

"You should have asked first, but you're right. I trust your judgment. Don't count on that too heavily. Wouldn't want you getting cocky."

His lips curved. "I would never be so foolish."

He wasn't surprised that it was Dev, a man close to the natural cycles and life of the bush, who'd realized Elisa needed objective eyes. Time and again, Mal had accepted cats that, because of past abuses, people had wanted to coddle and cocoon to excess. It turned the creature into a permanent victim. Through good intentions, the caretaker could trap the creature into that mind-set, such that they could never become like any other wild creature. A well-adjusted animal, even if it couldn't be fully rehabilitated, viewed the world the way a wild animal was intended to view it.

"So who am I supposed to really be helping here, Danny? Her or them?"

"I hope both. But she may be the only one you can truly save."

~

He thought about it for a while after hanging up. As he sat back in his chair, boots propped on the desk edge so he could tip the chair back, knees bent, fingers laced behind his head, he reviewed everything he'd learned while getting the fledglings settled. The ferocity in Leonidas's eyes was easy to interpret. He responded to intimidation, but he'd keep looking for any opportunity to strike. Mal had already told the hands no one was to come within ten feet of that cage without his presence, and he'd waited until every staff member acknowledged the order.

Whatever had been done to Leonidas had pushed him right into psychopathy. The chances of reaching him, of ever getting him to a point where he could be trusted to follow a code of behavior, were probably lost. His days were numbered. However, the others weren't as obvious a decision. Elisa thought he wasn't listening or paying attention, but Mal paid attention to every detail. In the work he did, it was essential, because every nuance of a cat's behavior told him something about the beast's state of mind, what he or she needed, whether they were progressing in rehabilitation, or if they were trapped in a dependent state where the preserve had to be their forever home.

His mind turned to the one she called Jeremiah. He considered the expressions he'd seen in the fledgling's face, particularly as he looked toward Elisa for his cues. There'd been a hunger in his gaze, a yearning for so many things that had been denied him, that Malachi felt a momentary empathy. An entirely dangerous feeling, as Elisa's current state showed.

Pushing it away, he took his feet down and opened the thick file that Thomas had brought with him from Australia. It was filled with Danny and Dev's meticulous notes. Because he'd second-marked all his staff so he could know their minds as well as communicate with them telepathically, it was second nature to toss out a request to Kohana. Instead of simply following it, however, Kohana appeared at his door a moment later. "You wanted the monk?"

"You deaf as well as one-legged?"

"Well, seeing as you spoke inside my head, being deaf would hardly keep me from hearing you. Else I would have faked that a long time ago."

Mal gave an absent grunt, still studying the paperwork. "Something you want to say? You wouldn't be darkening my door like a bear woken from hibernation otherwise."

"She's sleeping deep. I don't think she'll wake for some time. She wasn't interested in the food. Thomas said she threw up what she had on the plane. She's not well."

"Well, we'll just have to get her stronger. She has a lot to do over the next few days." Mal raised his gaze and met Kohana's. "Once she has a proper rest, I'll meet with her here. There are things I need to know from her."

"I think there are things she needs from you as well."

"Yeah, yeah." Mal waved him away irritably. "Danny said as much. Hell and damnation. Babysitter to a bunch of foul-tempered cats, fugitive Indians and now one puny Irish maid."

Kohana didn't smile, not technically. He never really did, but there was a rearrangement of the muscles of his face that gave away mirth. "I'll leave you to your reading, *Mr.* Malachi."

The thunk of the hunting knife sinking into the heavy paneling next to the doorframe was a familiar threat, one that Kohana ignored as he withdrew. Mal's accuracy was impeccable, a uniform pattern of slits up and down either side and along the top of the door.

Kohana wondered how good his employer's aim was going to be on this new lot of rescued "cubs." The large Lakota had an uneasy feeling and didn't like it, but he knew it was best to let time show where danger lay before one reacted too hastily to it.

However, Kohana suspected the greatest challenge to Mal lay in the bed upstairs. Maybe it was a good thing. Malachi had been on the preserve for a long spell now, turning down any offer to go with the others to the mainland for R & R. Might be time to remind him of the world outside. And it had been a remarkable moment, the way the little miss had stood toe-to-toe with him, trying to give him what for.

"Winds of change," he noted to himself. "Good or bad, only time will tell." Heading back to the kitchen, Kohana started mulling what he could scare up for a breakfast. At the end of this long work night, the hands were sure to be extra hungry.

5

SLEEP did help, but Elisa wasn't sure anything would truly prepare her for her meeting with Mr. Malachi that following evening. She was glad Kohana had woken her a few hours before, coaxed a couple bites of something into her, then let her go back to sleep. When she finally put her feet on the floor and stumbled into the small bathroom to splash herself awake, nervousness took away her appetite. She brushed her unruly dark brown curls back from her face and slipped a band over them, then ironed the modest dress she pulled from the suitcase Danny had bought for her. She should have done it when she arrived, but in truth, she remembered little once they'd gotten her to this room.

But that was yesterday. She checked herself in the mirror. She was ready to go to work, and it was best to think of Mr. Malachi as her new employer, meeting to discuss her duties. If she could remember that, stay calm, maybe he'd let her see the children today. The thought gave her courage as she made her way through the house.

The architecture was log cabin, so the walls were smooth-surface logs, fitted together and caulked. The gray-brown color was balanced by large windows that made it seem they were outdoors, or peering out from the cocoon of a cool forest. Several pairs of French doors led out to the wide wraparound porch. It was sunset, the sky red and gold with wisps of dove gray. One set of windows faced east, the other west, so it would lack for natural light only in the most heated noontime. There were electrical lights, but she saw enough lanterns they must use kerosene in the evenings to save the power source.

It was definitely a man's haven, very little indicating a woman's touch, though even Mrs. Pritchett would approve of the cleanliness. The wood floors were swept and the rugs, in interesting designs she expected were Indian, were bright and clean.

The main sitting area was an open layout with chess- and checkerboards. That and packs of cards, a left-behind coffee mug, suggested staff members might gather there during off-hours, which she found interesting since she recalled a bunkhouse outside. While Danny treated her men well, they weren't encouraged to come sprawl in her home, on her lovely mahogany furniture and needlepoint pillows.

The furniture was sturdy and natural-looking, the chair arms retaining the knotted appearance of the trees from which they'd been created. The back of the sofa was woven sapling branches. She wondered if they'd ever considered weaving fresh flowers into them, so whoever lay there could inhale their sweet scent. Despite the rustic appearance, thick, deep cushions scattered about made it all look appealing and comfortable. Warm fleece throws were tossed over the backs of a couple chairs.

The kitchen had a pass-through area and a radio. Currently, it played Big Band against a layer of static. Like on the station, the hands probably passed their leisure hours listening to the radio while mending, telling stories, playing cards and the like.

A stairwell led to a lower level, subterranean for vampire guests to sleep without worry of the sun. For capricious reasons of her own, Danny sometimes chose to sleep in an upstairs room, the curtains securely closed. Dev always slept with her then, refusing to leave her so near the damaging morning sun without his watchful guard. When Elisa brought in a breakfast tray near twilight, Dev's meal as well as a glass of juice to mix with his blood if Danny chose to take it that way, her lady would be lying across Dev and slumbering peacefully. Her blond hair would be a beautiful sweep of gold along immodestly bared shoulders, her naked breast concealed only where it was pressed against Dev's chest. He'd be stroking her hair to aid her sleep, and would nod at Elisa, giving her a faint smile and a gesture to show her where to put the tray. She'd never walked in on Dev asleep. He was alert as a cat.

Watching that large, capable hand soothe her lady's brow, stroke down the bare spine, Elisa hadn't wondered that Danny felt so secure that close to the sun, so safe. For some reason, Elisa remembered standing against Malachi in Leonidas's cage. Since that made no sense, she pushed it away as the product of an overstressed mind.

Just like humans, most vampires didn't have a Dev or a Willis. They looked after their own safety. Hence, most slept on lower levels where the sun couldn't be an immediate threat. Besides that, she knew from Dev that younger vampires had a harder time getting a good night's rest if they weren't deeper in the earth. Mal was younger than Danny was, and she was still considered young by vampire standards, at a little more than two hundred. So he likely slept in that subterranean level.

All in all, seeing a world similar to the one in which she'd lived for the past few years made Elisa feel a little better. No one was in the main room or visible out in the yard through the large windows, so the staff was either sleeping in the bunkhouse—there was no telling whether humans in a vampire's employ kept his hours or their own—or had risen long ago, going about their duties. She hastened her step. She hadn't meant to sleep the day away.

Though Mr. Malachi had ordered her to sleep eight hours, she knew how it was with vampires. They weren't that different from human employers. If one did a semblance of the more irrational things they wanted, they were fine. As long as they weren't paying too close attention.

When Lady Constance had been her Mistress, Elisa had been able to convince her that Ian was giving her no trouble, because she didn't want to worry the already troubled mistress of the house. Technically it was true, though it took the combined efforts of most of the staff to keep it that way, thwarting his clever and strategic attempts to get her off by herself. Of course, once he'd gotten involved with the poor housemaid Mary, she'd provided a distraction. She was living in Perth now, working as a seamstress in a dress shop.

Lady Danny had been much harder to pacify. It had been a new experience for Elisa, an employer who shouldered responsibility for everything that happened under her roof, considering the well-being of even her youngest maid to be of great importance. What she didn't catch, Dev did. Elisa didn't mind their care. Even admired it in some ways, but she hated to be a burden. Being a burden meant she wasn't doing her job properly, which was to be unnoticed and yet a great help, all at the same time.

Though she was more than a little homesick, she knew it was why she'd been glad to chaperone the fledglings, leave the station behind for a little while. Everyone had been spending far too much time noticing her.

Fortunately, from how gruff and impatient Mr. Malachi was, Elisa didn't doubt he'd be more along the lines of Lady Constance, happy to ignore her as long as she gave the appearance of obeying him and not getting in his way. He might even forget she was here and stop entertaining notions of sending her home until the children's fate was resolved.

All she had to do was get through this meeting. *Stay quiet; answer his questions. If you feel you must tell him something, do it in a calm, obedient manner that doesn't suggest you're challenging him in any way.* Every male did better when his ego was cosseted, like a cat having his fur stroked the right way. She wasn't a manipulative female, one who thought her wiles or other such nonsense would distract a man to stupidity, but these were simple facts about men that all women knew. Even if the man was a vampire.

She froze abruptly. *You daft thing. He marked you twice. He can read your mind.*

For several seconds she didn't breathe, but then slowly she let it out. Surely if he was listening, he'd have spoken by now, right? Even so, she needed to be more circumspect. Taking the lesson to heart, she drew a deep breath to balance the abrupt lack of oxygen, cleared her mind as much as possible, and turned down a short hallway off that main room. She could hear the rustle of paper, and her second-mark senses told her a vampire was waiting.

As she approached, she saw it was a library as well as his office, the walls full of books. Rapping on the panel before she stepped in, her eyes slid to the desk in the corner.

It was a heavy, impressive thing like a pirate's sea chest, only much larger. There were carvings of ships on the front panels, and hinges to the lid so things might be stored inside. Paperwork was scattered across the top, and several file cabinets provided drawers behind him. Among the papers was a bright red ball of string, currently trapped under the paw of one of the cats she'd seen last night. The enormous gray tabby was sprawled in limp repose over a crumpled portion of the paperwork.

Her gaze rose to the male sitting in a roomy but rickety metal-and-vinyl office chair, not quite a compatible match for the antique desk. Except for a slight variation in the T-shirt, not much had changed in his attire. His hair was carelessly yanked back and tied. He was reading a letter, one hiking boot braced on the worn edge of the desk to help him rock back and forth, explaining the rhythmic squeak she'd heard as she approached. The boot was crusted with red mud, telling her he was not responsible for the pristine cleanliness of the house. Only the person *not* responsible for the hard work of cleaning would be so careless of it. Which was why Mrs. Pritchett regularly chased the hands back on the porch until they wiped their feet.

At her appearance, he glanced up. "Who is William protecting?" he asked.

"Excuse me?" Whereas before he'd been harsh or deliberately gentle and calm—as if she were mentally impaired—now his tone was that of an employer asking a question of an employee. Good. That was what she wanted. Though in that brief second while he waited for her answer, his gaze covered her, from the nervous clasp of her hands, to the rise and fall of her bosom, up to her throat. He lingered there for a bare second before coming to her face. She ignored the reactive warming of her skin.

"I'm sorry, sir. I don't understand the question."

Putting the paperwork aside, he laced his fingers across his flat abdomen, pushing the chair back farther on its complaining stem. "You named them, didn't you?"

"Their ability to communicate is limited, sir. So far. We didn't have records of their names. With all they've been through, we think most don't remember them. Or they don't want to tell us, as if they're giving something precious away. We had to call them something."

He arched a brow. "Do you have difficulty answering a question with a yes or no, Elisa?"

She firmed her lips. "Yes, sir. I named them."

"I thought so. William means *protector*. Matthew, *gift of God*. Leonidas, *lionlike*." He paused. "For the eyes, I assume. You couldn't bring yourself to give him a name as gentle as the others."

"It didn't seem to suit."

"Yet you think the others do." Did his tone reflect a hint of scorn? She told herself she was going to hold her tongue this time even if she had to bite through it. He studied her for another uncomfortably long moment. "The girls are half-caste. Aboriginal and white."

She nodded. "We expect Lord Ruskin took them from their families through the government program."

"Nerida is *flower*. Miah is *the moon*."

Because a moon shone light through darkness, and Nerida looked at Miah like she was the moon. "Since it's likely they were taken from Aboriginal mothers, I wanted to give them names from the people they knew." She'd explained to each child why she was giving him or her the name she'd chosen. It was only until they felt like telling her their real names, of course. To her way of thinking, giving them a name told them they mattered, that they were unique and important.

"And Jeremiah." He glanced back down at the paperwork. "You imagine yourself closest to him."

"He reacts the best to me. To us."

Mal rocked forward, back. To entertain herself, trying to break the building tension, Elisa imagined what would happen if he overbalanced. Would he be so agile and quick he'd be up and clear of it before it fell, or would he sprawl on his arse like any other man too full of himself and in need of being taken down a peg or two?

"'God will raise him up,' or 'God will set him free.' That's what Jeremiah means," Malachi continued. "Which interpretation did you tell him?"

"Both. Mr. Malachi—"

He made an impatient gesture. "My name is Mal. Not Mr. Malachi. You'll use Mal."

She blinked. "But, sir, it doesn't seem proper or respectful to call—"

"Elisa, do you think I'll have any less difficulty commanding your obedience and respect if you call me Mal instead of Mr. Malachi?"

"No, sir. I—" She paused as his sardonic undertone hit her. She tightened her lips. "I didn't mean it that way. I meant, I would respect you either way, but it doesn't seem—"

"Let me say it another way." He pinned her with those dark eyes. "You will obey me, regardless of what you call me, won't you, Elisa?"

"Yes, sir."

He nodded. "*Sir* is an acceptable compromise, but if you address me by name, you will call me Mal."

"Yes, sir. I'm not sure why you want to know the background of their names."

"Because I need to know everything about them. There are things you've picked up about their behavior that will help me, things you may not recognize as useful. Which is why I need you to answer the questions I ask." When he brought his boots down with a decided thump, Elisa jumped. He scowled.

"Girl, put your ass in that chair and stop acting like I'm going to attack you. You're in no danger here. If you annoy me excessively—more than you're already doing—I'll simply send you home. Do you really think Lady Danny would send you anywhere she wasn't certain of your safety? She's very protective of you."

"Yes, sir. I apologize. It's . . ." Sitting down in a stiff perch on the edge of the guest chair, she tried to stop the nerves constantly jittering in her stomach like tiny electrified wires. Unfortunately, any arc could jolt her like this. "I'm ready for your questions."

"It says that, according to Ruskin's records, he took quite a few full-blooded Aboriginal children, but they had a higher death rate than the white children."

She nodded. "Dev says he expects it's because the Aboriginal children understood better, at a spiritual level, that what had been done to them was . . . wrong, not the way Nature is supposed to be. They let themselves die to escape."

When he paused again, she wondered if he thought that was nonsense. Something in the way his fingers tightened on the edge of the desk made her think he wished it was nonsense, but knew better. Then the curious moment passed. "Hmm. Your notes mention seizures."

"Danny calls them bloodlust episodes, but for Leonidas and Jeremiah, it's like nothing she's seen before. Victor was like that as well. The girls and William and Matthew have episodes, but they're less severe."

Mal grunted. "Tell me how often you've noted it in each one."

As she recalled those details, Mal scribbled on the pad in front of him, glancing at the open file as if comparing data. This was yet another version of the male she'd met last night. She marked the faint frown on his forehead, the way the earth brown eyes shifted back and forth between the two sets of paperwork. Delving into the behavior of a creature and ferreting out what was needed, that was his gift. Danny had said so. Only her vampires weren't cats, big or small, like the ones she'd yet to meet or those on his desk.

Sitting back, he braced his foot again and crossed his arms across his chest. "During the time I was in their compound last night, two of them had fits like you described. I wanted to be certain. They're likely caught in transition."

"What does that mean?" Too late, she realized she didn't know if she had permission to ask questions. Fortunately, he didn't seem offended.

"A normal adult vampire transition is over in several months. For some time after that, a fledgling deals with bloodlust, and is typically under the care of a sire for at least a year as he or she learns to manage it. What Danny gleaned from Ruskin's sparse files suggested he had Matthew and William for just over a year. There's no history on the others. You said they don't communicate. Do they verbalize at all? Talk, that is."

"They'll gesture, point, nod. Miah and Nerida will sometimes sing together, like chanting. I can't make out any words, though, and neither could the blackfellas at the station, more humming and made-up sounds than anything. All of them seem to understand everything we're saying, but it's as if their spoken language skills are gone."

"They're not." He pushed the file away from him, a frown on his face. "I marked them as a sire, as I said I would, but that won't give me much of an advantage. Ruskin wanted them to be savage animals, so he punished them for any behavior, outside of their hunting skills, that demonstrated reason, intelligence, gentler emotions. Their minds are a thicket of chaos, the best defense they could manage, though it only adds to their impulse-control problems."

She of course had suspected that, but to hear it confirmed made her heart hurt anew for them. She masked it, though, already well aware of Mr. Malachi's impatience with sentiment.

He gave her a sharp look. "While they've learned to mask emotion or rational thought, the ability to speak, I don't believe they are incapable of it. They've just done what brutalized slaves or prisoners have done for centuries. Figured out other ways to communicate. They use a subtle form of sign language in front of others, and likely talk to each other when they're alone. If they are capable of trust, they may become more interactive."

"I've . . . I've never noticed that."

"It's often done in movements too quick for human eyes to follow. And subtle enough to even be missed by a vampire who's not looking for it."

She thought about Jeremiah, how often she'd seen something she'd interpreted as a burning desire to communicate, to tell her something. Though she encouraged him to speak, he never would. He simply looked at the others and shook his head, shuffling to the back of his cage in the barn.

"How long will they be caught in transition?"

"It depends." He sighed, ran a hand over the back of his neck, an unexpected gesture of agitation, as if something bothered him. It sharpened Elisa's attention on him, though she was hanging on every word already. "Bloodlust seizures are like when you have too much energy to spare and can't sit still, magnified a hundred times, and coupled with an overwhelming desire to draw blood." His glance suggested he thought it unlikely she knew, at least of late, what it was like to have an overabundance of energy. Elisa couldn't deny it, but she sat up straighter in the chair. "Since we know at least William and Matthew should be getting past those now, something has gotten hung up, developmentally."

"Maybe your work with them will help them get past that."

He arched a brow at her forced, bright tone and Elisa told herself to be quiet. Fiercely.

"Victor was different," he continued. "From Danny's notes, it appeared the seizures became more and more violent, until he integrated that killer instinct into his personality. It was no longer an episode, but what he was. Leonidas appears to be on a similar track, according to what you've said about the frequency of the attacks. And Jeremiah—"

"He does it a lot less than Leonidas. When they happen, he fights it, trying to keep himself under control. Sometimes he manages it."

"If what happened to Victor is happening to Leonidas and Jeremiah, then it's fairly inevitable. Enduring it year after year will take its toll."

"You can't predict anything like that," she insisted. "The children are all different." At his warning look, she pressed her lips together. "The fledglings. They're so different in how they react to things, different levels of emotion . . ."

"Elisa, I know you wish to help—"

"I *can* help."

"Not if you keep interrupting me."

She'd been used to having her opinion counted for so much more with Danny and Dev. She didn't want to feel animosity toward Mal—she really didn't—and she knew he just needed to get to know her, but to do that, he had to give her the opportunity to prove her value, right?

"You are proving it, by following my direction. I expect when you entered Lady Danny's household, you had to do that for a while before she trusted your judgment, correct?"

Her cheeks burned. Apparently, he did sometimes listen in.

"Somewhat. Part of it is your face. You're pouting."

That burning became outright mortification. "I am not." But then she touched her mouth and found it had in fact shaped itself into such a disagreeable shape. She tucked her lips tightly together, surprised to see a faint trace of amusement cross his face. "I do take your point, sir," she said. "I will work to prove myself worthy of your trust."

He blinked at her. "You almost managed to keep the scorn out of your voice that time, Irish flower."

"Perhaps, with all due respect, Mr. Mal—sir, I have to learn to trust you as well."

"I don't have to prove myself to you." In a blink, his tone became a warning that straightened her spine with a snap again and made her stomach do a full somersault. His brown eyes cooled, and he put his feet flat on the floor, holding her gaze captive with his own. "Perhaps Danny gave you more latitude, but that was your home. This is a new, unfamiliar territory, and as any of my staff will tell you, if you do not take the time to learn it, under my direction, it can lead to tragic consequences."

Images swamped her as he pricked at that wound. She dug her nails into her palms hard enough to draw blood. It was intended to steady her, hold it together, but panic ran together with the pain as she imagined what losing her calm now could do to his opinion of her. Whether out of negligent cruelty or to study her like a lab rat, just like her children, he'd meant to do it. She was sure of it, and for an alarming second she felt genuine rage against him.

"I am familiar with . . . that," she managed. "There's no need to . . ." She rose from her chair abruptly. "Excuse me, I need to go . . . to the lavatory. I'll be right back."

Instead, he rose from his chair, and came around the desk in a graceful flow of movement that caught her in place before she could escape. "Please . . . don't touch me," she whispered. Her arm jerked under his touch when his fingers closed around it. Shudders ricocheted up from those muscles all the way to her tense neck. "Sir."

He eased her back into the chair but then took his hand away. "Elisa, breathe."

"I know . . . I'm fine."

She heard him sigh as she stared at the dark panel of the desk to the right of his lean hip. He wore a knife there, the size of the scabbard suggesting an impressive hunting blade. "Last night, you thought I was being cruel to Leonidas. I was teaching him. Have you ever seen two dogs squabble in the yard?"

The even timbre was unexpectedly reassuring, like the night before. She nodded. "We have several at the station."

"Who's top dog?"

"Rodney," she responded automatically. "Dev thinks he's part dingo, and Lady Danny thinks he's part Tasmanian devil." Pleating her fingers into her dress, she studied the folds. She gave Rodney extra scraps because he did whatever his mind told him to do, hang the consequences. But he'd sometimes lie on the hem of her dress when she was sitting on the porch, mending. Occasionally he'd look up at her in what she imagined was a fond way.

"When Rodney fights with another dog to teach him to mind, does he hurt the dog?"

She thought about that. The sporadic dog fights in the yard could be loud and startling, but they were usually brief things. Very little blood was ever taken. Most of the time, if it happened, it was only at the beginning, when a new dog arrived. "No. Not often."

"It's pretty scary to watch two dogs fight like that, but it's simply nature's law of dominance, and their way of working it out. As soon as one dog proves he's the leader, the others are fine falling in line, including the one he fought with."

"But the childr . . . fledglings, aren't dogs."

"No, more's the pity. It would be easier. Human and vampire blood makes things far more unpredictable. Plus, the fledglings' former master was like the humans who train dogs to fight to the death. He's messed up their proper sense of things, exploiting what nature intended. Did I hurt Leonidas last night?"

She shook her head. "No."

"But it was somewhat scary to watch, right? Just like the dogs."

Malachi took a knee then, brushing her thigh with it as his hands covered hers. The position put them at eye level. It was an unexpected thing for a vampire to do, and flustered her somewhat, to be so central to his attention that way. "I'm not telling you your job is over, Elisa. But I'm telling you that I'm going to shoulder a lot more of the load now. It belongs in my hands, because I'm the one who can handle it. I will need your insight, but there are things I already know about them that you don't. The same way Rodney knows things about the other dogs in the yard. There is a difference between the brutality of Lord Ruskin and merely a firm, dominant hand."

"Oh, I know." She didn't want him to think she was ignorant. "I've seen Lady Danny handle things. And with Dev . . ." Lord in Heaven, why did she open that cache of images in her head?

～

A light flush tinged her cheeks. Mal didn't need to take advantage of the window in her mind to know what she'd seen. He'd been around Danny and Dev himself, and knew Danny's feelings and desires for her unusual bushman servant.

However, given what had happened to Elisa, she'd still view a female's dominance like Danny's as "safer" than a male's. Testing, he cupped her face, bringing her startled gaze to him. Using his thumb, he traced her lips, exerting enough pressure she had to part them, then teased the sensitive interior flesh, creating a shiver along her nerves that made her eyes widen farther.

She was a natural submissive, so his intent had been instructional, a memorable example she'd remember. It was surprising to react to her response. He imagined her on her knees, that mouth put to a far different use . . .

"You haven't been around a dominant male vampire much, Irish flower." He cleared his throat. "It's different, but it shouldn't be capricious or cruel, no more than Danny's authority."

"Ian lived at the station. And . . . we've had a few males . . . visit. I-I've seen things."

But none of them had paid her direct attention, he was sure. Danny had made it crystal clear this one had been limited to household duties, as second marks often were. Even so, a riot of needs and emotions trembled from her, enough to spook every creature in a fifty-mile radius. It reminded him of his conversation with Danny. For good or ill, Elisa was a vital key to who the fledglings were, what they could be. In order to make a complete evaluation, he was going to have to understand her, draw out her emotions and responses. If what he believed was inevitable happened, it would be a critical step.

"All right." He dropped his hand and rose. "I have some more notes to review with you; then I'll head out to the fledglings' quarters before I attend to our usual routine with the cats. And before you ask, no, you won't go with me tonight. I want to observe them without your distraction."

She flinched, that innocent expression of desire she'd had under his touch disappearing. He ignored it. "You'll stay here for the time being. I don't want you wandering off and getting yourself in trouble."

"I may not know your world, sir, but I'm not a child. You don't have to treat me as one. Our station is in the Outback, and I understand about dangers in the environment."

"Then you understand why you'll stay put on this compound until someone can show you around." Reaching the other side of the desk, he gave her a look. "And I can promise you I don't think of you as a child. It might be good for you to remember that, for a variety of reasons."

6

WHAT did he mean by *that*? Under Danny and Dev's station management, Elisa had fallen out of the habit of staying so wary of males, but even after repeat reviews of that meeting in her head, she was still baffled. There'd been no warning signs, no lecherous light in his eye. Everything about his demeanor and tone suggested he *did* think of her as no more than a silly child, here to cause him irritation. He kept her under intent regard, but they all did that. Around vampires, one often felt like a sheep ambling past an interested pack of dingoes.

You're in no danger here. But a vampire's definition of harm and a human's could be quite different. Lady Danny had said she was to obey him as if he were her, and Danny had regularly touched her in such sensual ways. However, she'd never outright bedded Elisa, though Elisa had no doubt she could have seduced her into it, shocking though the thought was. Did Mr. Malachi have that right?

He'd left after their meeting, and, as if he thought saying it once wasn't enough, he'd taped a piece of paper to the front-door window glass. *Elisa, stay on the grounds and follow Kohana's direction. Thomas will join you for midnight tea.*

She'd known Thomas wasn't in the house, because his door had been open when she passed it in the hallway. Apparently, *he'd* been allowed to wander this dangerous jungle. Mal would probably take him to see the fledglings.

Oh, bollocks. Children, children, *children*. She knew it was petulant, to chant it in her mind so adamantly, but it helped her from screaming like a banshee. She wasn't worried Mal was listening. He'd probably forgotten her existence as soon as he taped the note to the door and got into the Jeep. In fact, she was surprised he'd even written the note, fully expecting her to stay where he'd dictated. Dutifully accepting of his edicts, not about to go stark, raving mad.

Bloody males.

Drawing a deep breath, she struggled for calm. The fledglings were all right. Thomas was going to come at midnight and tell her all about the proper place constructed for them. Mal had had a couple months' notice to prepare, after all. Just like at Danny's station, his staff would rotate responsibility with Elisa to donate fresh blood for their meals. But he didn't know that Miah and Nerida refused to drink as long as someone was looking at them. Or that Matthew preferred his warmed, such that Elisa put the packet inside her clothes before his feeding. That way it at least acquired her outside body temperature before she gave it to him.

She took another steadying breath. She'd been trusted with so much responsibility so young because she was even-tempered and eager to please, with a deep-seated need to serve her employer to the best of her ability. But since the incident with Victor, she wasn't entirely sure who was inhabiting her skin or how to predict her own behavior.

To keep herself from wild ideas of ignoring Mal's orders and setting after them on foot, which she was certain would win her a one-way ticket off the island, she went looking for a housekeeper. She understood Kohana handled the house upkeep and some butler duties like bringing meals to the room, but surely there was a woman in charge of laundry and cleaning.

Kohana was in the kitchen, his backside propped on a stool as he stood at the sink, washing the dishes left from the staff's latest meal. The stool gave him the support his missing leg could not as he performed the task. He was humming, something that sounded like a chant, reminding her of Miah and Nerida's quiet songs.

"Good evening," she said.

Kohana nodded without turning. "And to you, little miss. Did you sleep well?"

"Fine," she said, though in truth, despite the duration, she'd slept abysmally, with nightmares and starts into wakefulness, wondering where she was, and how the children were. It was why she'd overslept, because normally she was on her feet by early afternoon, preparing to care for Lady Danny's needs. The time difference might also be playing havoc with her.

He grunted. "There's hot water in the kettle over there. We have tea if you want it, though we prepare it in more of an instant fashion than you're probably used to. Sit down at the table and I'll scramble you an egg."

"Oh, no, I can do that. I'm not here for you to serve me. In fact, I came looking for the housekeeper so she can put me to work. Mr. Malachi says I have to stay at the house for the next little bit, and I want to make myself useful until he calls me to assist with the chil—fledglings." She almost snapped out the last word, gritting her teeth at Kohana's sidelong look. He'd likely read that note and already knew the master of the house thought she was a nuisance. However, his stern mouth lifted in a slight smile.

"You're looking at the housekeeper, little miss. As well as the cook and handyman."

"Oh. Well, then." Moving to the kettle to cover her surprise, she blanched at the idea of tea in individual *bags*. "When Chumani said you took care of the place, I thought she meant only the maintenance and the occasional help to the housekeeper."

"We're all here to help staff the sanctuary. Everything else is secondary. But since I can't work with the cats anymore, at least not out on the open preserve, I took on responsibility for the house and everything that goes with that. Mal sometimes gets visitors with deep pockets, vampire and human, so it's important to keep the house looking presentable. Despite his best efforts to the contrary."

Remembering the mud crusted on Mal's boots, propped on the desk edge, Elisa well understood the wry note in Kohana's voice.

"You do a fine job. I'd never have guessed this cleaning was done by a man's hand. Does he have a lot of vampire guests?"

"Not too many. There's a vampire on the mainland, Lady Resa, who used to come and stay on occasion, long time ago. She shared the blood of her female servant with Mal and liked hanging about here with him, in limited stretches. Then she'd miss the busy world and off she'd go. Most the time it was because he'd make her mad, usually for the same reasons she couldn't stay away from him. His obsession with his cats and this island fascinated her, and then the fact she couldn't take their place as the center of his universe didn't. Plus she was a pretty highbrow type of vampire and Mal's . . ."

"Not." Elisa finished that thought easily enough and Kohana grunted.

"Some women like the idea of something, but once they spend too much time with it, it's different."

This was at least familiar. Servant gossip, a vital resource to anticipate the Master or Mistress's needs. He dried his hands on a towel, hands so large they looked like they could be used as cricket bats. "I'm making you up a couple eggs and some toast. I think we even have some bacon and sausage."

"Really, I'll do that for myself," she insisted. "You just point me toward where things are. If you want to tell me what you usually do for the meals and housekeeping schedule, I'll be happy to take part of that load from you. No sense in wasting my idle hands. I intend to become a part of the schedule here, not a distraction from it."

The unspoken message being that she would do everything possible not to leave, not as long as the fledglings were here. Her resolve might be wasted on another servant, but it was good practice.

"Until he says otherwise, you're a guest, little miss. I—"

"Please put me to work before I go insane." *Another moment and I'll get on my knees and beg.* She didn't add that, but since she sounded like a morning bird whose tail had been goosed, all the usual rhythm of the syllables high and jumpy, she expected he figured it out.

"I'll make you a deal." Facing her, he crossed his arms over that massive chest. "You clean up every bite, and I'll let you help me. All right?"

"At my lady's station, I'm second to Mrs. Pritchett, the main housekeeper." She wanted to sound reasonable, but knew her blue eyes were snapping. "I've served as Lady Danny's personal maid and servant for nearly a year. I've been cooking and cleaning practically since I could walk. Why everyone is treating me like a half-wit who can't do for herself, I don't know. Just because . . ."

Just because she'd been torn open for the world to see, and everyone seemed to know about it. They all wanted to cradle that damaged part, when all she wanted was to close the door and leave it behind, never have it touched by prying, sympathetic eyes again.

Kohana reached out, closed a hand on her shoulder. Before she could ask what he was about, he'd moved her into the hallway with two hopping long strides for him, about four or five steps for her, and faced her toward the hall tree mirror.

"That's why," he said.

The face that peered back at her was hollow-eyed from stress and lack of sleep, her eyes dominating her face, the pupils dark and large. The work dress she wore was a neatly designed yellow one she'd had for several years. While she didn't intend to accent it, it had a pleasing fit over her curvy figure. Now it hung on her, the waist loose and too low because the bodice that once had strained a bit over her ample bosom was much looser in that area, her hips far less round.

"That isn't me." She firmed a chin determined to tremble. "The way I look isn't what's going on inside me. I want to see my children. I need to see them. Can you take me to where they are?" She knew her expression was abruptly pleading, not reserved and in control the way it should be. She just had to see them, to know they were okay.

"Not yet." Kohana's tone was firm, but gentle. At least he didn't correct her, tell her to call them *fledglings*. Instead, he settled both hands on her shoulders, a comforting mantle of strength. "He lacks tact, but Mal knows a lot more than it may seem, little miss. We've had animals brought here who were beat up in so many ways, most of us thought there'd be no teaching them about living under a wide sky and rolling against the warm earth, but he does it. He watches, and he listens until he finds the key to it. Sometimes he figures it out right away, sometimes it takes him days or weeks, but he always does."

Days or weeks?

Registering her alarm, Kohana pressed on. "I'm not saying that's how long it'll be before you see your young vampires. I'm just telling you what he does and how he does it."

"He thinks they're mistakes. That they should be dead."

"What do you think?"

It was the first time in a while anyone had asked her, such that it gave her a moment's pause. "I don't think God creates mistakes."

"Maybe not. But they aren't as God created them. From what I heard, they aren't even proper in the sense of a vampire-making."

"That may be so, but just because that's one truth doesn't make it the whole picture. Do you know that when William sleeps, sometimes he cries?" She turned under his hands, looked plaintively up into Kohana's creased face. "He won't talk when he's awake, but I was in the barn— that's where we had to keep the cages, because it was the only place big enough—and I was sitting there, not being idle, but Mrs. Pritchett said she had everything done that day, so I was reading, and I heard him.

"He wasn't crying like some savage monster. It was the way a young boy cries. Crying for something he's lost, something he can't even see or feel anymore when he's awake, but when he's asleep, he does. They've been hurt so bad, for so long, they don't know what's right. But there was this one day—"

She was talking too fast, the words too jumbled, but she pressed on, because he was listening. Kohana was a member of the household, and maybe he had Mr. Malachi's ear.

"That Dev, he's so clever. He had the cages put on wheels so they could be rolled out into the yard at night when it's pretty. For one brief second, Miah realized she didn't have to be afraid or quite so watchful. She was caught up in the way the clouds were rolling over the night sky, how the moon kept hiding and then coming back out. She lifted her hand toward it, as if she was trying to touch that light, every time it came out behind its curtain. Then she saw me looking and tucked everything back in again. Like a rock, all hard sides, so nothing's vulnerable.

"Willis said . . ." She bit her lip, unable to get that thought all the way out, though the words still went through her mind. Willis had said she'd become as attuned to their state of mind as if she'd birthed every one of them. She'd flushed, thinking he was telling her how good a mother she'd be. He'd seen it and stolen a kiss, murmuring against her hair. "Plenty of time for that, girl. And God help me if most of them come out little girls with their mother's eyes and smile."

They said time was supposed to blur memory, but sometimes it was as if he was still there, right beside her. She wanted that voice and those hands, that reassuring presence, so much. He'd stood with her, and now she stood alone against the whole world, it seemed. It made her feel trapped, all by herself with her fears.

But she also remembered Willis would have worry in his eyes when he made that observation, a worry similar to what she saw in Kohana's eyes now.

"I think you should sit down, little miss." Kohana steered her firmly back to the chair. He gave her a pointed look. "Do we have a deal? You eat; I put you to work."

She bit back a sigh, her fingers curling into her lap. "All right. But I really can help fix the breakfast."

"Are you saying a crippled man doing woman's work can't?"

Elisa's gaze flew up to his face, mortified that she might have caused him offense, but the twinkle in the eyes gave him away. It helped her find a flicker of her usual spirit. "I've not yet met a man, crippled or otherwise, who can handle a day's worth of woman's work, Mr. Kohana. They usually make up some nonsense about hunting or herding sheep and run for the hills."

He grinned then, patting her shoulder with a large hand. "I'll prove I'm the exception. Scrambled okay?"

A FTER consuming one scrambled egg, a piece of bacon and a bread
that impressed her with its softness and taste, as well as the fact it
was called a biscuit—what she thought of as biscuits Kohana called *cookies*, and wanted to know if she could bake them—she insisted she was
full. When she promised to nibble at the rest throughout the evening if
it was left under a cloth on the counter, they bartered again. She agreed
to eat one more item for each chore she performed.

She knew she was too thin, but it was so hard to have an appetite
when her stomach was upset so much. Willis had liked her fuller figure.
Most men did. Danny was tall and lean, and Dev liked her better than
any other, but Elisa had seen his gaze stray as much as the others to the
loose wobble of her heavy breasts when she was on her knees scrubbing
the porch boards, or his attention linger on the nice breadth of her arse,
though he was discreet and polite about it.

There was a difference in Dev's kind of looking. It was kind of like
the wildflowers growing out by the billabongs. He had no intention of
plucking them out of the ground or otherwise disturbing them, because
he already had the beautiful, greenhouse rose he wanted most. Regardless, he still appreciated the others.

Now Willis wasn't here, and for a long time she hadn't cared what
she looked like, to anyone. Kohana had made his point, though. It was

hard to take someone who looked like this seriously. So she tried to eat between dusting the front room and then sweeping the vast expanse of wraparound porch. The only task he gave her was the dusting, but she'd fallen into what she did at the station, noticing what needed to be done and doing it. After she swept, she persuaded him to show her where cleaning supplies were kept and tackled the porch windows, giving them a good shining.

She tried to focus on the tasks and not get lost in her head, where she'd shame herself with tears again. Fortunately, she found a distraction. As the night deepened, there was a plethora of animal noises she'd never heard before. A rough coughing, a rumbling grumble. Then a sudden sharp *cheep* sound, with needles all along the sound. Coming in behind that was a repetitive chirping, like crickets but far more spaced out.

While she was listening, Kohana stepped out, leaving his crutch leaning against the wall and balancing himself with obvious long practice at the railing as he shook dirt out of a rug. Noticing her attention, he nodded. "The chirp's one of the cougars. Mal's probably with her tonight. It's a sound of welcome. The coughing is the mating call of the leopard. He's trying to catch a female's attention."

"What's the sharp sound, like a screech, but not, because it's too short and prickly? Like an angry little girl."

Kohana gave her that grin again. "Good description. That's Lola, one of our female cheetahs."

"Good heavens, are they so close?"

"The habitat area for our non-rehabs or new arrivals is close by, enough that if the wind shifts, you'll get a faint whiff of them. However, what you're hearing are the ones on the open preserve. Sound carries a little differently here." Kohana busied himself with turning the rug. "Plus, your hearing's good. Second mark, remember?"

Having been second-marked by Danny, she knew it did improve her senses. She'd used them for detecting what might be going on in the yard with the stock hands. She could catch a plume of dust farther out on the horizon, an indication guests were coming, which gave her time to help Mrs. Pritchett make lemonade and set out biscuits for the arrivals, whoever they might be. A snippet of conversation caught from Danny—not eavesdropping, mind you—would let her warn Mrs. Rupert there might be more coming for dinner. But perhaps having two second marks made the effect even more pronounced, because she could swear the beasts were just beyond the tree line flanking the property.

She'd never seen a cheetah or leopard, not in person. Thomas had shown her a book of cats on the plane and she remembered the cheetah, a sleek, long-legged creature with a nipped waist and enormous amber eyes in a relatively small, dainty face.

"How about the barking noise? I heard that one a little while ago. It doesn't really sound like a dog, though."

"That's a jackal." Kohana shifted his hip to the rail, folding the carpet over his arm so he could cup his hands to his mouth. The imitation made her smile; then he shifted to the rumbling, hoarser cat call which earned a response, one of the cats echoing him.

"So does this mean the leopard who wants to mate will come find you?"

Kohana snorted. "For all that a cat in rut can be a bit brainless, I think he's got more sense than that."

"Do another one."

His eyes warmed on her, pleased with her enthusiasm, and he gave her a succession of calls. It worked like a dog howling, setting off a chain reaction. The catcalls from the night got more varied and diverse, a natural music that made her rise and put her hands on the rail, cocking her head to take in the song. As she did, she was amazed to feel the touch of the night close around her, a real sense of all the things moving and part of that darkness, the way nature was supposed to be. The simple pleasure gave her some reassurance. As well as laughter, when the radio at his hip beeped and Chumani's irritated voice came through.

"Do you mind, *mato*? You're getting everyone down here worked up with your racket."

"No man wants a shrew, *pahin*."

"Good thing I don't want the nuisance of a man, then. Shut it or I'll come make you sorry."

Kohana grunted. "You're all talk on the radio, skinny girl." But when he released the button, he cocked a brow at Elisa. "They're doing feeding and exams down at the enclosure."

"What's *m-mato*, and the other word?"

"*Mato* is bear, and *pahin* is porcupine. We'll call you *tuxmagha*. Bee."

Elisa smiled. "I'm sorry. I didn't mean to cause a problem."

"Far as I can tell, *you* didn't." He gave her a wink. "Keeps them on their toes."

"Does he rehabilitate jackals as well?"

"Not exactly. Mal and the people who helped him set up this place knew they needed an environment similar to that of the different cats, to help with their rehab. We have meat flown in for those in the habitat, and to supplement the ones learning to hunt, but we also have small herds of gazelle, wildebeest and other game. Since cats don't eat everything, and because we're trying to make it as close to what they'll experience in the wild, he also brought in the smaller scavengers. Jackals and the like. There's a zoologist on the mainland who spent a lot of time helping him know what would work and what wouldn't."

"Extraordinary." She thought about the drive. Hazy, tired and flustered as she'd been, she did remember some details. "The island has very different terrain. Last night, it was like crossing through entirely different countries."

"Mmm." Kohana's benign expression turned into a scowl. "Yeah. He worked that out with someone, too. Someone he shouldn't be tangling with."

Someone a *vampire* should avoid? Kohana didn't linger on that curious statement, though. He pointed to the sky instead. "Can you see that many stars back in Australia?"

"They're arranged a bit differently, but it's a lovely new view of it."

"We're in the Northern hemisphere," the Indian said. "Some things you see from one side, you don't see from the other."

Nodding, Elisa turned her face back up to the sky. "I guess I've been distracted by so many other things, I haven't appreciated what it is to be traveling half a world away from everything I've ever known. I've never been much of anywhere. Lady Constance met me in Perth, and sent me to school in Adelaide. And of course I went to Darwin to help Lady Danny and Dev when we first got the children."

"Fledglings," Kohana reminded her helpfully. "He's right about that part. Plus, it's best not to rile a vampire for no reason."

"No worries. That part I *do* know." She considered the sky again. "There's the Milky Way. We can see that one, though it looks a bit dimmer here."

"The Tsalagi, the Cherokee, call it 'the place where the dog ran.'" Kohana slanted her a glance. She wondered if he spent a lot of time here by himself, which made him so willing to talk to her, or if he'd been instructed to keep her distracted, though Mal hadn't really projected such sensitivity. He might be merely gathering impressions to share with Mal later, but if so, she could only be herself. Plus, she was doing just as much information gathering herself.

"Why do they call it that?"

"That's a Tsalagi story. I'll tell you a proper Lakota story, which is much better."

She gave a mock snort. "Oh really? Better than a story about the Milky Way?"

His eyes creased, showing his enjoyment of her. "Yes, young smart mouth. It's a story about the creation of the world. There was another world before this one." When Kohana looked out at the night, at the beauty of the darkened island, she saw something in his face that quieted her. "But people didn't act as they should in that world, so the Great Spirit sang and it rained. The more he sang, the harder it rained, until the whole earth was flooded and nearly everyone drowned, swept away by his disappointment. However, Crow came to the Great Spirit and asked to please give him a place to rest his feet. The Great Spirit relented and decided to create a new world. He sent four animals who could swim into deep water to get him creation clay. Three of them failed, but Turtle succeeded, bringing back the clay that became the land. The Great Spirit cried over what had been lost, and the rivers and streams formed from his tears. He populated the new earth with animals from his pipe bag, and then, after much deliberation, he took red, white, black and yellow earth and made people again. He gave the people his sacred pipe and told them all would be well if living things learned to live in harmony. But if they made it bad and ugly again, it would once again be destroyed."

As he glanced toward her, she showed her appreciation with a curve of her lips. "Dev would like you. He tells Aboriginal stories, because he has their blood. What kind of Indian is Mr. Malachi?"

"His mother was Cherokee; his father was a white trapper. But Mal doesn't tell Tsalagi stories, or speak the language."

"He's never learned?" she ventured.

"I never said that. I said he doesn't speak it. Doesn't tell the old stories."

Since Mal would hardly talk to her about the children, let alone something personal about himself, she wondered why she heard a warning in Kohana's voice.

"He hired all Indians to work here. So he must feel some connection."

Kohana made a rather irritable grunt. "That's a story for him to tell. Mal's put all of himself into this. Too much. You two may have more in common than you know."

Reclaiming his crutch, he hopped back toward the door. She noted he'd left a stack of bedding on the arm of the couch. "Is that for the guest quarters?"

"No. I expect you and Thomas don't need a linen change yet. Unlike some other people who live here, I assume you don't fall into your bed at dawn still wearing your dirty clothes, and get leaves and dirt on the sheets."

Elisa bit back a smile. "No, I try to wash off a bit before bedtime."

"We might as well give him a hole in the backyard," Kohana snorted. "He wouldn't notice the difference, and I wouldn't have to keep it clean."

"I'm about done with the windows. Would you like me to take it to his room and change them out?"

"Be happy to let you do that." He waved her in that direction. "Downstairs, last bedroom at the end of the hallway. I usually straighten up a little in there, but don't get too fussy about it. He won't be able to find anything and he'll bitch about it for half the night."

Nodding, she returned her window-cleaning supplies to the supply closet as he disappeared around the corner, headed back to the kitchen area. He'd told her he started cooking for the staff just before midnight to give them a good supper break, so she'd do the linens and then come back to help. She was pleased she'd worked hard enough that her muscles were aching. Fatigue dogged her all the time now, but this felt like a physical tiredness, not a stress-caused one, and that was an improvement, to her way of thinking. While she wished Mal had taken her with him, it was quiet here. She liked it, and Kohana's company. Liked not being the center of so many sympathetic or *tsk*ing countenances. She liked those new sounds in the night, the idea she might see things she'd never seen before.

Kohana seemed to trust her well enough, though it was probably because she'd come from Lady Danny's household versus any merit of her own. Still, she'd take the opening it provided. There were puzzles here to engage her interest, like Kohana's cryptic comments about the island and Mal's dedication to it.

The other doors along the wide corridor downstairs held guest bedrooms. They were a bit nicer than what was provided for the humans on the second level, but not by much. The walls were stone, as were the floors, giving a castle impression to her fanciful imagination. The gaslight sconces added to the feeling, casting dim, shadowed light across the rock. They illuminated drawings on the wall, or rather, one big drawing. A mural of cats.

They weren't polished, not like a painting in a museum, yet there was a rough realism to them, reminding her of the Aboriginal drawings one came upon in caves in the Outback. It was apparent the mural had been done over time, no real plan for it, as if the artist was merely idling away spare time, drawing what captured his imagination. For instance, there was a picture of a lion lying down, but a domestic cat's tail lay over one paw, the cat looking over his shoulder and up at the lion with typical feline disdain. Cats of myriad species played, hunted, leaped, slept . . .

It had to be Mal. She sensed his restless energy coupled with the intense focus in the drawings. It gave her yet another intriguing view of the master of the house. No matter his harsh worldview or practicality, down here he was willing to entertain a more fanciful view of his charges, of a wondrously playful and different kind of world. She thought the surroundings encouraged it, warm and dark like a mother's womb, where everything was still possible.

Now she was about to enter the intimate sleeping quarters of the unpredictable male vampire who was caretaker for her children. Most beings, even vampires, left clues to themselves in the places they slept, coupled and felt most secure. Mal didn't seem the type who knew what fear or insecurity was, though. Maybe Kohana was right—a coffin in the back would be just as appropriate, and she'd find nothing in here of note but a bed and a line of muddy boots.

He was hard to pin down, that was for certain, but she had to admit, not only from Kohana's grumbling, he was one of the more nonegalitarian of his kind she'd ever met. In some ways, he reminded her more of Dev than Danny. Except when those eyes sharpened on her. Then she felt that same thing Danny possessed, in spades, the quality that could fluster Elisa in such unexpected ways. He was right; she wasn't used to feeling it from a male vampire. As unsettling as it could be from Danny, when it came from him it made her knees buckle in a downright embarrassing fashion. She needed to get a handle on herself, and perhaps a greater familiarity with who he was would help with that.

Or make it worse, a sly voice in her subconscious suggested. Ignoring it, she pushed open the bedroom door.

The left corner of the room was a far messier version of his upstairs office. Papers, files and sketches scattered everywhere. As she wandered in, sheets in her arms, she glanced into open boxes that contained reference material and reports that looked like they came from universities, dealing with animal behavior, habitat studies and anatomy. The table in the corner was laden with mostly toppled wooden carvings, all different types of cats. She realized they had distinctive markings, added with markers. Names were scrawled on them, an aid to remembering which cat was which, she assumed.

He had a radio, though she wondered at the reception he might get down here. No pictures, just black-and-white photos of what looked like landscape features of the preserve. They were tacked up on wooden strips embedded in the stone. Turning in a full circle, she faced the right side of the room. And she discovered the most extraordinary bed she'd ever seen.

Carved of some type of black wood, the posts twisted in a natural treelike way up into a canopy of interlaced branches. She expected looking up into it would be like looking up in a forest during winter, when there were no leaves. But hanging from those different branches were sparkling things. Drawing closer, she saw they were crystals, rough-cut gems, strung together in beaded lengths and woven in and out of the branches, along with feathers, and braided lengths of what appeared to be animal hair. Golden, brown, black, white.

Thrown over the bed was something she also didn't expect. Animal skins. She recognized the tiger's pelt from pictures in Thomas's book, the strikingly rich black and gold markings. Underneath and offset from it was one that, from its size, looked like it should belong to a lion. It was tan with a dark, broad arrow of color forming a pattern upon it. Another coat looked black until she drew closer and saw it was a bitter chocolate brown, with a pattern of faint spots through it. A black leopard, maybe.

As she touched the foot rail, she realized she'd placed her hand over a string of animal teeth. Fangs. The string was mixed with feathers as well, some pretty beads, several stones with sparkling crystal sides. Perhaps the teeth had come from the cats that had belonged to these coats, though the size of these fangs gave her pause, as she realized these species were roaming loose on the island. But he protected cats. So why would Mal have their skins?

Putting down the linens, she crossed from the foot to the side of the large bed and closed her hand on the tiger skin. Pulling it back, she discovered it was heavier than she expected. However, the smoothness of it coaxed her to stroke the stripes. Following the pattern made her dizzy, so she closed her eyes, inhaled the animal odor. Not unpleasant, but with her eyes closed, it was as if she were inhaling the creature as it crossed her path, real . . . alive. She could almost feel its back brushing under her fingertips, the chuff of its breath as it passed into the camouflage of a jungle of tall green bamboo, using Nature's magic to become invisible to the human eye.

She realized then that she was humming. No, not humming. It was a wordless chant, like the Aborigines might craft. It had a soothing power that had her swaying along with it. But she didn't know any songs like this. It startled her enough to shake her out of the spell.

"Stop daydreaming," she chided herself, since Mrs. Pritchett wasn't here to do it. Folding back the skins, since she was reluctant to take them completely off the bed, she retrieved the clean linens.

Tucking the bottom sheet in, she smoothed it, circling around the bed to do the other side. As she worked it to the bottom corners underneath the heavy array of pelts, the fur tickled her forearms, the creases of her elbows. She pulled the sheets taut, since one should be able to bounce a coin on a properly made bed, but it was a wide bed, and the mattress was not the typical flat surface. The stuffing was thick and gave invitingly under hands. She didn't feel a hint of springs. Curious.

She wrestled the top sheet into place, but wasn't entirely satisfied with the look of it. The sheet had a faint stripe pattern, after all, and it needed to be straight. She didn't want Malachi to come to his bed thinking it hadn't been made up right. Of course, from what she'd seen of him, she thought it more likely a bedbug would notice and complain before Mal did. She tripped over the toes of several pairs of boots that had been carelessly deposited under the bed and grimaced. If she was Kohana, she'd chase him out of the house like Mrs. Pritchett until he learned to leave those muddy boots at the door, or clean them properly before coming in.

The idea of chasing the formidable vampire with a broom gave her a smile. Warmed by that, she put a knee on the bed and crawled her way to the middle of its vast expanse, using her hands to straighten and smooth.

She had to catch her breath, so she sat down on her hip, studying the skins as she pulled them forward enough that they lay on her lap. Tiger, lion, leopard. Giving in to her curiosity and desire, she bent her head, rubbed her cheek over the lion skin. She wondered if Mal's house cats came down here to sleep with him. The mousers at the station were wild as dingoes and not given to being petted or coddled the way it appeared Mal's were with their sprawling indolence. That fat lot definitely weren't mousers. Though with an island full of predators, she expected they didn't have much of a rodent problem.

Her eyes were closing again. It was ridiculous, how often she seemed to want to sleep. At home, she could resist it. Something about this room, deep in the earth, called a body straight into the arms of a nap. It was like the heartbeat of an old woman, sitting by a fire, rocking, that chant coming to her lips again. Elisa moved with it, swaying, her body sinking into the bedding, curling around the animal skins and gathering them in to her. Drowsily, she wondered what that old woman was chanting, and why it felt so natural to join her. It was a great comfort to be part of that rhythm, part of that heartbeat here, deep in the earth. She never had to leave. She could stay here, everything else stopping so that it didn't matter if she stayed here for eternity. Time would stop as long as she was in the center of this place, this moment.

Fanciful thoughts, nothing like her usual practical thinking. But then, nothing was usual anymore, was it? A young maid in a rich man's house, who worked hard and let him have his way to keep the job . . . That was usual. A maid who worked for a vampire and played babysitter to six vampire children . . . That required a different way of thinking, right? The world was a daft place, far more unexpected than it first seemed.

~

She was in a forest, the earth cool beneath her feet. The thin air told her she was higher up, in the mountains, only they were much greener than those in her part of Australia. Hearing a chirp, she looked up to see a large cat studying her from a tree. A beautiful grayish brown creature with enormous eyes like molten gold. She had long white whiskers and touches of white on her chin and face.

Cougar. Or mountain lion. Kohana had said they chirped, right? The female cat jumped down and stalked over to her, but Elisa felt no need to run. The creature rubbed her face on her skirts, marking, and Elisa heard her purr.

The cougar is the largest of the purring cats . . .

That was Thomas's voice, for he sat in a tree nearby, reading his book, the filtered sunlight flashing off his glasses and obscuring his eyes.

Elisa's hand fell naturally on the cougar's coat. It didn't seem right to pet a creature like this. Instead she offered homage through the respectful touch. Then the cat was moving and Elisa was following, no idea where they were going, just knowing she needed to follow. Thomas was gone. A walk became a lope and then a run. She wasn't in her skirts now. She was astounded to find herself wearing nothing but an animal's skin. Its head, or rather the top of its skull and a portion of its face, the ears and glittering eyes, formed a headdress for her. The rest cloaked her body and was pinned at her throat with a piece of carved bone to hold it in place. Her nakedness beneath didn't bother her, because she was coated in soil, cool and damp on her skin, making her smell like and be a part of the cougar's world.

She ran so sure and fast, right behind the cougar's ground-eating lope. They went up and up, until abruptly they emerged on a precipice. Elisa stopped, her breath catching in her throat. The moon hung low and heavy in the sky, so large that the cougar was outlined by it as she propped her feet on a knoll and settled down on her belly, letting out a long yowl.

"Oh my . . ." Elisa let out a delighted noise as that yowl was answered. From a hundred different throats came roars and grumbles, growls and high mewling calls like her companion. Looking down over the precipice, she saw the whole island stretching out below her, much larger and wider than it had appeared on the plane. A faint bluish light ran through the island like veins. She could feel the pulse of it like heat on her skin, and there was a pressure to it, a sense that it was aware of her, shaping itself to her form, learning her and making her part of it, tying her into it, so no matter where she went, that magic would always recognize her . . . or could call her back to it if she got lost.

She sat down on the cliff edge, unafraid as her legs dangled over the edge and she put her arm around the cougar's shoulders. She'd been a city girl until she came to Danny's station, and then the wide-open spaces, the very wildness of the world that pressed in on them on all sides, had become more of who she was than where she'd been born.

So perhaps it wasn't surprising that this was the next step. This was what home should feel like, a place she could come, no matter how empty she was, and she'd be filled. There were no questions here, so no need for answers. Her grief could become part of the fabric of this place, as could her laughter, if it ever came back to her again.

If it could find her anywhere, it would be here.

8

MALACHI showed his teeth as Kohana blocked him at the top of the porch. "You need to take off your shoes," the old Indian said. "They're covered in mud."

"They're always covered in mud."

"Which is why they need to be left out here."

Mal gave him a gimlet eye. "It would take two fingers for me to rip your throat out. Maybe just one."

"I expect you could do that with or without shoes on." Kohana sighed, made room as Mal ascended the porch with a near snarl. "Fine. Go on in, then. But the girl's worked herself to death to clean things up today."

Mal came to a stop. "She's not here to be manual labor."

"Well, you're not leaving her with much to do, and she's worked all her life. It's what she knows. It helps her. She doesn't go mad, thinking about how much she wants to see those young vampires. Look at how pretty and shiny those windows are. I hate doing windows."

Mal scowled, pivoted and thumped down in one of the porch rockers. Kohana cocked his head as he began to tug the laces loose. From his employer's expression, he could tell the night's work had not gone well, and it didn't take much of a leap to figure what had caused the problem. "How are they?"

"Damaged."

"Irreparably?"

Mal grunted. "Pointless either way. If I can fix the damage done to them, they have nowhere to go, nowhere they'll fit where they won't end up in a situation that might actually be worse. In the vampire world, they'd be viewed as circus freaks. Or worse. Plenty would take advantage of it."

"But not all. Could some of them stay here, permanently? We could surely use a few more with vampire speed and quickness, like yourself."

"These aren't animals." Mal sighed, rubbed a hand over his face. "They have intellect, the root of all human mischief. It's what makes us discontent with our lot in life, seeking higher meaning and purpose. If these fledglings had a mortal life span, say sixty or seventy years, fine, but they're immortal, Kohana. Do you think they'd like to stay on this island for the next four or five hundred years or more?"

"I know I would. Nothing out there better than this. You see enough bad stuff, get your heart broken, you know why an animal is smarter than us, without that intellect. Maybe you learn to accept it, want that for yourself."

"Don't be talking to her like this. I mean it, Kohana." Mal lifted his head. "Don't give her false hope. Each of these fledglings is fucked-up twelve ways to Sunday. The chance any of them could reach a decent level of self-determination and stability is right up there with biblical miracle."

"I've seen you pull off miracles."

"You're like talking to a stump. Only a stump has the good sense to keep its thickheaded opinions to itself. Where is she?"

"Probably asleep in your room. I sent her that way an hour ago to put on clean sheets."

"What?" Malachi frowned. "You didn't tell her—"

"Of course not." Kohana looked offended. "I made an oath to you, Mal. You think I'd break it?"

"No." Mal rose, put a hand on his shoulder. "It was a gut reaction. But you sent her down there. What if she screws something up?"

"You think while she's changing out the sheets she might catch a thread of your devil-spawned universe and accidentally unravel the whole thing?" Kohana grunted. "Room's peaceful, quiet. I knew it might coax her to sleep some. She needs more rest. I wasn't going to disturb her until she came back, and then I was going to act like I hadn't even noticed how long she'd been gone."

"You probably have the right instinct, putting her to work." Darkness settled back over Mal's features. Leaving his socks and shoes behind, he moved to the threshold in his dusty cargo pants and T-shirt. "We won't help by coddling her, Kohana. Nobody gets past something like she's been through by being treated like glass. You have to convince them they're flesh and blood, as they've always been. The earth keeps turning, no matter what happens."

"You might follow your own advice," Kohana noted. "You've been hiding out here for some time yourself, ignoring the outside world."

"Not ignoring. Mindful of it. Mindful enough to know this is where I belong, just as you said. I'll take my blood when I come back up. Just set it out on the counter. Everyone else is about ten minutes behind me and I know they'll be hungry. They had to handle the cats without me while I worked with those fledglings. Thomas helped some, but I'm not comfortable having even a third-mark near them. Not until we figure out what's going on in their heads."

"The girl could probably help with that."

"She's concocted all sorts of sentimental notions about it." Mal snorted. "I'll have to wade through that claptrap to get to the useful things she knows. But stop your scowling. I plan to take her to see them soon. Don't tell her that, either. I may very well change my mind."

Moving into the house, Mal headed toward the lower level.

～

Elisa started awake. She'd been staring out over that beautiful puzzle of light and earth, and then there'd been a fog rolling in, a darkness. She hadn't felt fear, just a need to come back to herself, a sense that someone was calling for her, and she needed to answer.

She pushed herself up on one arm, orienting herself. The precipice and the cougar were still so close, it was difficult at first to realize she was in a bedroom, an unfamiliar one.

Oh, Lord in Heaven, had she really fallen asleep on his bed? What was the matter with her? She galvanized her sluggish limbs into motion and then, on top of that mortification, she realized she wasn't alone.

Mal leaned in the doorway, arms crossed, thumbs hooked at his armpits. He was barefoot, which somehow suited him, made him look more wild and untamed. Or maybe it was just the lingering effect of her dream. In a sudden spurt of panic, she clapped her hands to her body, and confirmed she was still wearing her work dress, and not an animal skin. However, looking down, she felt a little faint when she noticed there was dirt caked under her fingernails that hadn't been there before.

In her dream, she'd dug her hands into the soil, to smear more of it on her. Lying flat out on the ground, looking up at the sky, she'd liked the way earth felt across her abdomen, over her breasts, the tops of her thighs. The cougar had lain on her legs, a heavy, solid warmth.

Don't be silly. You just didn't wash your hands properly after cleaning the windows and porch.

Despite her reeling head, she managed to get off the bed and began to smooth it. "I'm so sorry, sir. I just . . . I don't know what happened. Must be the jet lag. I didn't mean to nod off like that. I got on the bed to make it, and I was touching the animal skins, and next thing . . . Anyhow, it won't happen again. I'll just go see if Kohana needs anything . . ."

She'd been gathering up the old sheets while she babbled. That was another mistake in judgment, because the sheets smelled like him. For some reason, her mind was flooded with a detailed image of him standing before her if she *had* been wearing only an animal skin. Not the one in her dream, but the tiger skin, gathered around her, her hand clasping it loosely just above her breasts as she knelt in the center of his bed. What if he'd crossed the room, closed his hand over hers, loosened those fingers and pushed it away, so it coiled around her like the actual beast? He'd bear her down against the pelt and put his mouth on her flesh . . .

Scurrying around the bed, she caught her toe on the heavy wood frame. Jesus, Mary and Joseph, God forgive her, a toe stubbing hurt like a son of a bitch, and on top of that it was an embarrassing reminder that she'd slipped off her shoes to get on the bed. She hopped, biting back the curse, and gathered up the tails of the sheets that were trying to unravel from her grasp. He was watching her with unfathomable fascination. Then, before she could rattle off something else, he spoke.

"I didn't take their lives."

She stopped, trying to push her mind past the throbbing. "Excuse me?" He nodded toward the bed, the pelts. "I didn't kill them."

"No, of course not. I didn't think you did." She knew hunters who respected their prey, even as they had to hunt them for food. Dev was one of those, as were most of the men on the station. But cats were predators, not food, and it wouldn't have made sense, no matter what kind of hunter Mal was.

"Their spirits help protect the island. They were poached by men, so they know the dangers, and that adds to the strength of their protection." He pushed off the doorframe then, moved across the room toward her. She stayed frozen by that bedpost, toe aching and mind confused. He stopped at the side of the bed, catty-corner from her, and laid his hand on the skins. She realized now the one she'd been lying upon most squarely was the cougar's. That grayish brown color with touches of white.

"Still warm," he murmured; then he glanced at her. "The cougar is sometimes the gentlest of the large cats. They even purr. Which doesn't mean much. She'll still disembowel you if you do the wrong thing around her."

Elisa remembered that throaty rumble as the cat sat beside her on the precipice. She'd thought she'd merely merged her own fancy with the house cats she'd seen earlier, and maybe she had been, but apparently a cougar did purr.

He moved again, this time toward her. It was instinct to step back, to clutch the sheets tighter. She was in his bedroom, alone with him, a male far more powerful than her. And she'd been thinking unseemly things. He would have seen it.

"I didn't mean it," she burst out, trying to step around him. "I don't . . . It doesn't mean . . . I need to get back to Kohana, get these sheets to him."

Mal shook his head, took the sheets from her arms, dropped them to the side. Putting his hands to her waist, he boosted her onto the high mattress. She clutched his forearms. She wouldn't beg. She wouldn't make a fool of herself.

"Stop your shaking," he said quietly, a firm rebuke that perversely reassured her because of the familiar irritation in his voice. It was his form of growling, and apparently a regular feature of their conversations. Not really the sound of a man about to be overcome with a fit of lust. Or so she thought.

"The thought was mine, not yours, Elisa. I let it slide into your head. It was a picture too pretty not to share." He gave her an absent smile that made the bottom of her world drop about two feet, her stomach with it. Lifting her left foot, the one she'd stubbed, he studied the toe, which had an extra pink tone from the agitated blood vessels. There was also a small cut in the cuticle, since the bedposts were unfinished wood.

He squatted onto his heels, which drew the fabric of his trousers taut along his haunches, and bent his head over her toes. His hair fell forward, teasing the top of her foot, and he flipped it back impatiently to see whatever it was he was trying to see.

She was going to protest, tell him it was fine and pull her foot away, but instead, maybe because the natural impulse that had taken her over in that dream was still with her, she leaned forward, folding her body over her knees, and reached toward his face. He stilled but didn't glance up, and she wondered if he'd learned that from dealing with shy, uncertain animals. Appear as if what she was doing was unremarkable, so that she'd have the courage to follow through with it. It worked for her.

Gathering up his hair on both sides, she handed it off to her other hand so she could pull the majority of it to his left shoulder, her knuckles resting there as she held the shoulder-length locks out of his way. Like all vampires, his hair was a treasure of thick silk that made a woman want to bury her fingers in it, like those pelts. There was something fascinating in touching a wild creature so intimately, wasn't there? Only this one still inhabited his skin. Of course, after her dream, she thought the ones on the bed did, too, a magical notion.

He looked up at her then. It increased tension on the strands, tightening them over her fingers. "So you can see what you're doing," she managed. Just being helpful, because that was what she did. It didn't mean anything.

That regard continued for a long moment; then he bent his head again. This time he brought her foot to his mouth and she drew in a breath as the heat of his mouth closed over that smallest toe. His tongue swirled over the cut, tasting the tiny revelation of blood, and soothing the pain at once. Since the capacity of his mouth was far greater than her littlest toe, he was able to include the pad of her sole and the toes next to the injured one in that sensation of heat and moisture, though he kept his focus on the one that needed his attention.

Her fingers had curled inward, holding the hair tighter. She was also conscious of his hand supporting her ankle and heel, holding her fast. As he licked the cut and teased her flesh, his own grip increased, so that sensation rippled up her leg, toward the inner thigh and higher.

Just like the image of her on the bed, in nothing but one of those skins, now she saw him commanding her to lie back on her elbows, the skirt of her dress slipping back to her thighs because he would rise, lifting her leg higher, continuing to hold it. Only now his heated palm would move from her ankle to behind the knee, his fingers caressing that sensitive part. His gaze would travel down the length of the leg to the shadowed folds of the dress, pulled back enough to reveal her undergarments, the panel of her panties, which were . . . She swallowed. They were actually, truly damp, not just in her vision. He was doing this to her, with nothing but his mind, but she couldn't tell if it was his imagination or hers.

"Does it matter?" He lifted his head at last. "You're calmer now, aren't you? Less afraid. There's nothing to fear from pleasure, Elisa. Your body still responds to arousal, as it should."

It made her stiffen. She let go of his hair so it fell back down over his shoulders. Slowly, she exerted pressure to bring her foot back into her own care. Sitting back on his heels again, he let her go. She didn't look at him as she slid off the bed, somewhat awkwardly since she had to maneuver around him, and circled to gather up the sheets again.

Once she did, she faced him. He'd stood up, one hand high on the bedpost. "Mr. Malachi, sir, I don't want you to play such games with me. That's not why I'm here. What happened to me . . . that's mine to deal with, and Lady Danny sent me here to be of use with the fledglings, and your household, when they aren't occupying me."

"I don't need a house servant."

"Kohana is a man with one leg. As capable as he is, there are things that are harder for him to do. You might as well let me be useful while I'm here. I can't keep you out of my mind." She spoke carefully now, staring a hole in his chest. "But I'm asking you, as a courtesy, not to do what you've been doing here."

"It helped."

"I'm not here to be helped." She snapped it, ducking her chin into the sheets, hugging them to her body. "Don't play with my mind, Mr. Malachi. I can't handle that. I truly can't."

Darting forward, she ducked under his arm, giving the edge of the bed a straightening tug where the cougar skin had flipped back and wrinkled. Then she spun and headed for the door. Once she reached the upper level, reality and the dawn would clear this nonsense from her head.

"Elisa."

She stopped. For just one second, she thought of pretending she hadn't heard him, but of course that would be unwise and unlikely. She couldn't turn and face him, though. She just waited, afraid of what he might say, her heart pounding in her ears. He didn't have to listen to anything she wanted. She had no idea what hold Danny had on him, but for all she knew, he could do as he liked. She needed to talk to Thomas. And oh, God in Heaven, Thomas would be leaving after those three days.

He sighed, that impatient sound as if she were a bug he'd prefer to squash and dismiss from his existence. "Tomorrow night I'm going to handle your orientation of the preserve personally. You'll learn what rules you need to observe if you go off the compound."

Did that mean he was already considering letting her stay longer? Why would he teach her the rules for such a short time, otherwise?

"Whether you're off the compound once or a hundred times, you still need to know the rules. And I told Danny I'd show you our setup, so you know what kind of place this is for the fledglings. Don't read more into it than that."

She nodded, swallowing her disappointment. "Will I see the chil—fledglings?"

"We'll see how it goes. Be ready at dusk. I'll have Kohana scare you up some trousers and boots. You can't go out there in a dress."

She nodded, dug her fingers into the sheets and fled with as much grace as she could muster. Her body was still throbbing and her mind a confused tangle from that dream, and though she'd been here a day, she felt mired in all the mysteries and puzzles of this place, the most dangerous of which was going to spend tomorrow evening with her.

9

THANK heavens, after she dropped the sheets in the laundry, Kohana seemed to have meal preparations in hand and had merely shooed her away, knowing she wanted to speak to the monk. Grateful, she'd headed toward Thomas's room.

When she knocked, he bade her enter. He was in trousers only but drying his hair, apparently having taken advantage of one of the showers to wash off the night's work with Malachi. Work she hadn't been allowed to join. She tried to push down that resentment and instead focus on the item of greatest importance.

"How are they?"

Thomas set the towel aside and shrugged into a loose linen shirt. She was always surprised at how fit the lean monk was. She associated men of God with soft paleness. But of course, most monks hadn't consigned themselves to the service of a vampire queen.

He nodded to the small sitting area in his guest room, a side table and two chairs that would allow tea to be taken in front of the windows. They overlooked the front of the compound and the green, rolling terrain beyond, visible during daylight hours. "Why don't you take a seat? You look like you've been on your feet most of the night." He glanced down at her bare toes, and she winced, curling them into the throw rug. "Without shoes, no less."

Darn it, she'd left those in Malachi's room. Well, she'd figure out how to go get them between now and dusk. That was a problem for another moment.

"I wish everyone would stop telling me to sit, sleep, eat or . . ." She had a flash of the images Malachi had put in her mind to "calm" her, and bit back the desire to scream. "I would be fine if everyone would stop treating me like I am some kind of pampered invalid."

"We're just concerned that's where you'll get, if you don't take better care of yourself," Thomas said with his quiet firmness. "Elisa, when a man is hurt at the station, he has to take time to recuperate."

"But I'm *not* hurt. My injuries healed rather quickly and it was weeks ago. I can do a cartwheel to demonstrate, if everyone would like."

"Probably not advisable in a dress." Thomas's mouth quirked.

"I helped Kohana most of the day. I—" With an irritated sigh that she realized sounded a bit like the master of the house, she flopped into one of the chairs. "There, I'm sitting. Now will you please tell me how the children are doing? Fledglings, whatever. I will call them cows, chickens, trolls or gnats if it will get someone to tell me *something*."

Thomas's amusement deepened, though it was laced with some bolstering sympathy. "They're frightened, of course, but they're settling in. Each one took a pint of blood. Their facilities are actually an improvement on what they had. He's set up their cells like small cabins, with a private walled area for sleeping. They're locked into a wheel formation with a large center area where each one can get out and move around more. In fact, when it's not feeding time, all the cell doors can be opened and they can share that communal area with one another, going back to those shelters when they want their own privacy."

"And it's secure."

He nodded. "Remember, Danny lent her not-inconsiderable funds to help him do this. The materials weren't hard for him to get, this close to the U.S. mainland. Probably easier than it is to get things back at the station."

"Is there anything for them to do?" They liked it when she read to them, but they hadn't had much luck with giving them books or toys, except for Jeremiah's bear. They tended to destroy them.

"The communal area is a natural area. Large stones, trees, even a small pond." Thomas sat down in the chair across from her and took her hands. "They're safe and cared for, Elisa. He may grumble, but he's lived up to everything Lady Daniela said he would do so far. You can trust him."

She nodded, then bit her lip. "Can I really? Thomas . . . what is he allowed to do to me?"

She couldn't put it plainer than that, though she didn't want to sound like a sniveling ninny. His brow creased in concern. Of a sudden, there was a look in his eye that made him seem far less like a mild, unassuming monk. "Why do you ask, Elisa? Has something happened?"

Yes. "No." She shook her head. "I know how vampires are, Thomas. They're so different about bedroom things, and I know sometimes they just . . . ooze that feeling, right? They tease us poor humans as an afterthought. It's like breathing to them. Even Danny, she was always sliding a hand along my neck, or stroking my hair . . ."

"So he hasn't forced you to do anything."

Except make her confront the disturbing fact that her body hadn't died with Willis. She hadn't had enough time with him, such that his memory could be swept aside by a vampire with a clever mouth.

That was the crux of it. She was ashamed. Knowing that, she shook her head. As Thomas's shoulders eased, she added, "But *can* I say no to him, if he wants something like that from me? Even if I . . . I mean, they know how to make you feel and want things that a person shouldn't. I'm sorry; I don't mean like you, you being a monk and all. And the thing about Danny, I don't know how you feel about that."

"I'm a man, same as any other," Thomas assured her with a wry smile. "While Lady Lyssa doesn't require me to serve her carnal needs, as vampires usually do from their servants, it doesn't mean she reins in her considerable ability to make me feel and want things I shouldn't. I take it as a continuing, lifelong test of my faith to God, Heaven help me."

She smiled, because his eyes were twinkling. But then he sobered, obviously mulling it over. "It's difficult to say, Elisa. I know that doesn't reassure you. I can tell you with complete certainty that Danny would not send you into anyone's keeping she didn't trust implicitly. But a vampire has a different notion of what's permissible to do to a servant, even a second mark like yourself. She certainly wouldn't countenance any violence toward you, or having you forced against your will.

"There are vampires who feed on human fear and torture." His eyes darkened. "But there are vampires, like Lady Danny and my lady, who are a different turn on that dial. What intrigues them are those doors inside a human being that we ourselves have not opened, through fear of our own desires, or societal constraints. Sometimes we don't realize the door is there, but their gift—and our curse—is how clearly *they* see it."

She thought of Mal, of how he'd looked up at her after he'd had his mouth on her foot, as if he could see everything, all the tangle of emotions and physical responses, a tapestry as complex as the interwoven branches above his bed. He likely could see the light that connected and threaded all of her lines, just like the lights of the island she'd seen in her dream.

"It's cruel, when they do that," she said low, with great feeling. "They're not doing it for love. Or any real caring. It's like we're puzzle boxes, and they like figuring out how the box opens. They feed off of what spills out after they open it, but then they don't care that they've left that door open, everything private out there, like being naked during a sandstorm. Blast the skin right off you."

"Yes, sometimes it feels that way." A grim smile touched the monk's lips. "But I think those feelings that spill out somehow nourish their hearts and souls, not just their ego or lust. It doesn't work that way for all of them, but some. Mal strikes me as a male who does things for very specific reasons. Unlike most vampires, he is driven by an intuition that taps into the very earth. If he's turned his attention to you, Elisa, I expect there's a good reason for it."

"So he feels I'm his project. Like the children."

"I think we all know, at this point, you both go together. Mal surely knows that." He straightened, tapped the top of her hand. "I'd say trust Danny's faith that he won't do anything to you personally that you can't bear, and in fact it may just make things better. Don't be afraid to stand up for who and what you are, though. Vampires like ours respect that. The ones that don't . . . Well, you're not with one of those, I promise. No matter how he's acted thus far. And you can always call Danny and talk to her if you're truly concerned."

Not likely. She didn't want Danny worrying about her at all, because that might win her a ticket back even faster than Mal wanted it to happen. She gave him a studied look. "You're talking like you're leaving."

"I am. In a few hours." He nodded toward his bag. She thought he hadn't unpacked, because of how few belongings he had, but she saw everything was neatly folded in the top.

"You were supposed to stay three days."

"I know, but my lady needs me back on some business right away. The supply plane comes about once every two weeks, though."

As he examined his teacup in such a deliberately casual way, light dawned. "With your plane gone, I get that much longer with the fledglings."

"Why, Elisa, that sounds very manipulative and deceitful. My motives are purely to serve my lady, as always. It's unfortunate that she has an emergency that requires my immediate attendance."

So there *was* a reason Mal was teaching her the rules tomorrow. Perhaps that was why he'd been so surly about it, though she had a feeling he didn't need much of an excuse. Regardless, she was staying longer. That was the most important thing.

"Thank you," she whispered. "I mean that. But another part of me . . . I don't want you to leave."

"I know." Rising, he drew her up into a hug. She leaned into his strength, tried not to cling, but it was hard. Thomas spoke into her hair, cupping the back of her skull with a reassuring hand. "From what I've seen, you're a very strong young woman. You'll be fine here. Just have faith. That's all any of us can do."

~

As she left his room and headed back to her own, she realized he hadn't been terribly comforting, at least on the issue of Mal's intentions. Well, she could hardly fault him. In the vampire world, human fate could be tossed around like a child's marbles and yet they were supposed to keep rolling along. Until the nicks and dings made it impossible to maintain a straight line. Of course, far as she could tell, all life was like that, with or without vampires to muck it up.

She slowed as she approached her room. Her shoes were there, neatly placed side by side in the hallway. At first, she assumed Malachi had sent them with Kohana, but two things suggested otherwise. One was that one of his carved figures, the cougar, was placed in the cup of one sneaker. The other was that the white canvas had been drawn upon, each shoe now bearing a whimsical depiction of the female cougar's head, her eyes molten gold.

He was certainly a curious vampire. Still, picking up the shoes and looking at them, she couldn't help but feel like he'd given her a totem, a protection symbol. An actual reassurance, though she would have been hard put to explain why she felt that way. Hugging the shoes to her chest, she slipped into her room, hoping that tomorrow she'd get to see her children.

~

Mal lay in his bed, staring up at that starry canopy, the glitter of the crystals as they turned. The magic that traced through those branches twined around him, as if he lay inside a living thing. It drew on his life energy each day as he slept, bolstering the protections and sorcery that had created this sanctuary. Even though he'd learned to moderate its effect on him, he was well aware of the kind of journey Elisa had taken in her dreams. There'd been peace and contentment on her face as she slept, her mouth eased, her body loose and relaxed. In his bed.

Any male, let alone a male vampire, would feel a ripple of lust at such a picture. He imagined her again, sitting in the center of the mattress with nothing but a tiger's pelt wrapped around her bare shoulders. Her curly hair would be loose and rumpled, her mouth swollen from kisses and other uses.

It had been a long, long time since he'd gone to the mainland. When Lady Resa had been a regular visitor, years ago, she'd always brought her curvy servant Magdalena with her, and shared her with Mal. He could have his fill of both women, take them countless times over the few days they stayed. Though a vampire's libido could recharge within hours, he'd always been sated enough that he didn't give such needs too much attention between their visits. But then it became clear he was replaying history. Lady Resa viewed him the same way his sire, Lady Diana, had. Even now, the dulled hurt of the realization made something in his gut churn.

Emotions were the problem, though, weren't they? He wasn't looking at this girl and merely seeing a receptacle for his lust. If that was all it was, he and Chumani had gone a round on occasion, fulfilling a mutual need. No, Elisa and her fledglings tripped off other things inside of him, things he knew he shouldn't be ignoring.

He'd wanted to know how she reacted to the shoes, so he'd waited, following the geographical first mark until he knew she'd left Thomas's room and headed for her own. When he dipped into her mind then, he read how she took the shoes as a reassurance. He wasn't sure how to interpret that, any more than he understood why he'd done it for her.

He didn't much care for lurking around in a human's mind like a constant spy, so he mostly used his second markings in a functional manner. Besides which, his particular gift was intuition, developed to the point he almost didn't need a second-mark. But this girl . . . she was a wild mixture of things.

He understood her distress at responding to his mouth on her foot. Willis had been her first true lover, and they'd barely discovered that love, not even past the kissing-and-holding-hands stage. Having him torn apart in front of her, however, had elevated that nascent relationship, imbuing every memory with forever-and-all-eternity promises. Willis had had a mere blink of time to introduce her to the idea of how deeply she could yearn for a man, emotionally and physically, and then he was taken away. That torment was all over her. As was her deep investment in these fledglings. Behind all of it, screaming in the dark, were her nightmares, capable of dragging her down and making her feel isolated.

That sense of isolation would have developed in her childhood, fighting to survive without a parent's protection. It was something that never left the consciousness, waiting like a dormant virus and raising its head when life became unbearable. His fingers curled as he recalled Danny's intel about her former employers, as well as snatches of what he'd seen in Elisa's mind.

Remarkably, none of it had broken her . . . yet. She'd clung to the good, to the hopeful, with an optimism that would have been irritating if it weren't so genuine and heartfelt. But now it had a desperate tone to it. In the vampire world, there were many glittering, charismatic and strong personalities, not only among the vampires but among their servants as well. Elisa was not glittering or charismatic. She was a servant, from every perspective of the word—vampire, human, sexual. On top of that, she had a core of steel. It had been twisted, dinged up, even melted with the flames of her own personal hell, but it was still holding.

He found her . . . fascinating, even as he knew that might not be such a good thing. What right did he have to add to her distress and conflict? Yet tonight, when he'd found her in his bed, he'd felt that intuitive click that told him something was going to happen. The vampire nature had stirred, strongly, and he'd felt a desire to claim, to take what was his by right.

He closed his eyes. He'd long ago stopped denying such things, because it was the nature of the species he was now, and he knew better than anyone that nature would not be denied.

The cheetah he'd visited tonight, Lola, was almost ready to return to the wild, where he might lose her to a poacher's bullet. But he couldn't deny her the chance to be what Nature had intended. He should take the same tack with Elisa.

It sounded good, but still, it might need a different approach. Because, unlike with Lola, in the case of the wounded Irish maid, he was all too aware that he was the one holding the gun.

10

S HE was on the front porch promptly at dusk. Kohana had insisted she eat first, so she'd abandoned all table manners to wolf her meal down, afraid Malachi might change his mind and go without her. Her anticipation helped her not dwell on the fact that Thomas was gone and she was by herself.

No, not by herself. She'd always had good luck making friends in new places. For instance, Chumani had loaned her a pair of dungarees. Since she was shorter than Chumani, she'd had to roll up the cuffs twice and put a dart in them for their outing. She was also a bit flustered by how snug they were over her bum, since even with her weight loss she was rounder than Chumani in that area, but she put a serviceable cotton blouse over it and managed to pull it down a few inches past the waistband.

She'd donned her decorated sneakers, of course. Kohana had glanced at them while she ate, made a noncommittal grunting noise, and shoveled another layer of eggs at her. She expected herself to grow feathers and start squawking before long.

Her self-consciousness about her appearance was wasted, because Mal barely gave her a look as he emerged from the downstairs, obviously ready to go in cargo pants, usual long-sleeved T-shirt and boots, his knife at his belt. He didn't slow his stride toward the front door, just jerked his chin toward the waiting Jeep. She scrambled to follow him, giving Kohana a hasty thanks and apology for leaving the dirty dish. Mal seated himself in the Jeep with a ripple of biceps and a flex of lean thigh.

"The rest of the crew is already out doing their jobs," he said, as if she was keeping him from his, or she was shirking hers. She bit down on her retort, though, and said nothing. She'd do nothing to jeopardize the chance to see Jeremiah and the rest today.

He glanced at her with an arched brow. "You do know I heard, 'Well, I'm sorry to inconvenience Your High and Mightiness'?"

She pressed her lips together. "But I didn't say it. I can't help my thoughts, but I always try to be respectful when it comes to what I say, Mr. Malachi. Kohana said you don't normally listen in much, even though they're all second-marked." So why was he listening to *her* mind? Perhaps he felt he needed to babysit her more closely. She tightened her chin. "With all due respect, if you eavesdrop less, we'll get along better."

"I think we're getting along just the way we should." He grunted. "Hold on to the bar there so I don't throw you out on the turns. If you call me Mr. Malachi one more time, you'll walk to where we're going tonight."

"Yes, sir."

He gave her a look, but put the Jeep into gear. She did take a firm hold as the Jeep lurched off the drive onto the bumpy incline that would take them out of the valley.

"You're one of the first vampires I've seen that prefers to drive himself," she ventured. "Danny prefers Dev or another of the hands drive. The vampires who visit the station are the same." There. She'd attempted civil conversation, though she knew vampires didn't always encourage chitchat with servants. But if he would strike up a conversation with her, maybe he would talk about the fledglings.

"Still listening."

She counted to ten. She would remain calm. If he would act more like a lordly vampire, instead of like one of the station boys, teasing her until she went after him with a cooking spoon . . . "Fine, then. Are you going to tell me anything about how the fledglings are doing? Though it's obvious you're very good at what you do, there may be a few things you haven't figured out."

"Does Danny listen in on your thoughts? It's fascinating, your inability to stifle them. And on that note, I'm sure there *are* actually a few things God has figured out that I haven't."

Elisa tightened her hand on the bar. "You don't need to pick at me to get me to shut up. You merely need to say so."

He sighed. "It limits our focus."

She cocked her head. "What?"

"Why so many vampires don't drive. We're used to being alert to our surroundings, above, below and all the way around. When you're driving, you have to give a larger portion of your attention to one direction." He nodded through the windshield. "Out here, I'm not as worried about that. Plus, I think a vehicle makes a fine weapon, being two tons or so."

"Oh. Well, that's very sensible."

"I have my moments." He gave her a sidelong look as he downshifted, and though she met his gaze for a second, she couldn't hold it. She looked out at the nighttime terrain even as his regard lingered, like a trail of heat over her bare forearm, the crease of her elbow, the line of her neck.

"I've spent one-on-one time with each of them in the communal enclosure."

That brought her attention back to him. He was navigating the tight turns over the hills now, so his eyes were back on the road, his hands sure and capable on the wheel. "What I've learned about their personalities thus far suggests at some point we need to separate them. They've meshed into a highly dysfunctional pack."

Separate them? She thought of Miah and Nerida, and William and Matthew, both obvious couplings for mutual protection and reassurance, flimsy though it was.

"They reinforce one another's fears and negative influences. Vampires are not pack animals. In fact, they're far more like cats. With the notable exception of the lion, most feline species are solitary, only coming together for mating or breeding. They hunt alone, mate briefly, raise their cubs and then send them on their way. They maintain distinct territories."

Elisa gripped the bar tighter as the Jeep rocked over a depression in the faint road. He continued, "The fledglings were all made vampires, children kidnapped and brought together by a common enemy, Lord

Ruskin. That made them a pack by necessity, for survival. It's the reason Leonidas, while likely to tear apart anything that wanders too close to him, is still bonded into the group. He won't harm the others, not mortally, if not provoked. Would you agree?"

He was a pendulum, making wide sweeps between annoyance with her and barbed teasing, with the occasional stop right in the still middle to discuss the things that mattered. She scrambled mentally to keep up. "Yes. He and Jeremiah don't get along at all, but Matthew and William don't bother him. He ignores the girls, but they do everything not to be noticed by him."

"He notices them; don't mistake that. An even better reason to keep them apart."

She'd missed that entirely. Her brow creased. It made her all the more certain she should be with him when he observed her fledglings. What they might see together . . . And how had they reacted to him?

"I don't disagree, but the first couple of times, I needed to see how they reacted without you there. It's important to know that the tree really does make a sound when it falls in the woods, if you're not around to hear it." The quirk of his mouth was almost Dev-like. "As to how they reacted, not as badly as I expected, with the exception of Leonidas. He still has reasoning skills, but they're honed in one direction, for the hunt and kill." His mouth tightened, eyes darkening. "The only thing he respects is greater strength, and the lesson has to be constantly reinforced."

She'd seen that herself, but it didn't make it easier to hear, because it left little room for hope. "How about the others?"

"The rest are very cautious of me. When I opened his cell, Matthew didn't come out at first. I played cards on a stool and table in the communal area for quite a while. When he came out, he explored the furthest points away from me. He did pass by William's cell, and eventually squatted there, watching me. William stayed close to his cell wall, right behind him."

"Yes. Miah acts in a similar way with Nerida. I think the two pairings were taken about the same time, so maybe they bonded during their transition. I'm afraid what Ruskin may have done to exploit that protectiveness."

"Actually, the fact William openly shows it suggests Ruskin was too much of a bastard to ever notice it. To him they were things, not living beings. He assigned no sentiment or sentience to them, except for their ability to serve his purpose. He didn't register the compassion, since he had none of his own."

The longer she'd spent with the fledglings, the more she hoped the man responsible for their state was rotting in Hell.

"But that can't be a factor when you interact with them." Mal glanced over at her again, then back to the road as he started a winding, downward slope that offered a changing view of the forest line, the headlights more necessary as they dipped lower and the early moonlight slid behind the trees. "You remember the way you hated everyone at the station tiptoeing around you, suggesting you sit down, take a rest, rather than letting you work?"

"You're doing it here, too."

"Kohana was. I set him straight on that. When we tell you to rest here, or to eat more, it's because you're physically not up to the level of work you're pushing yourself to do, and you won't be any use to anyone if you break yourself down, make yourself sick. Take the rests you need, eat and build yourself back up to your work. We'll give you the space to do that, and believe me, when you're up to something, I won't hold back on making you pull your weight."

Was he suggesting that she might be staying? That he might consider—

"Not even close to that yet," he said shortly. "But part of it is proving to me you have sense enough to take care of yourself. I have over a hundred cats here, and now six fledglings that need attention in various ways. I don't have time for my staff to need my nursemaiding, physically or emotionally. But back to the original point, that's the kind of pragmatic feeling the fledglings need aimed at them. No coddling, no pity."

He pulled into an open gravel area then. From Kohana's description, she realized they were at the vast maze of habitats for the cats that weren't able to go onto the open preserve, or not yet ready for it. In their discussion of the fledglings, she'd forgotten they were coming here first. She'd have to bite back her impatience.

Mal switched off the Jeep and closed a hand over her elbow before she could get out. "Part of it is keeping your focus where I tell you to keep it. This is an orientation, not a tour. It's to teach you things that are important for your safety as well as my staff's. If you mess up because you haven't paid attention, they're the ones who risk themselves to get you out of harm's way. You said you want to work, to be a help. Well, if that's the case, you need to understand the operation and rules around here. The better you demonstrate your understanding of that, the more likely it is you'll have more freedom to move around the island."

He knew what kind of carrot to dangle in front of her, for certain. Still, his reasoning was sound, so she nodded, making a monumental effort to push the fledglings out of her mind, at least for now.

This area was a sprawling compound of wire enclosures. There was no artificial lighting, because Malachi could see at night, and second marks could see in the darkness passably well, no worse than the gray hours of dusk. The lack of man-made light made it seem an even wilder place, the enclosed cats calling out, everything from low rumbles to huffing chuffs of breath or sudden shrieks. Things she'd heard last night had seemed close, but these noises were far more pronounced. Remembering the pictures, the sizes of some of the cats, she felt a moment of trepidation, but a sliver of amusement from the vampire at her side disrupted it.

There is nothing here that's more dangerous than a fledgling vampire. And you want to cuddle those like kittens.

She pressed her lips together. *Bloody galah.*

"Not *bastard*? I would have thought that would be the first that came to your mind." He lifted his brow. "Not sure what *galah* means."

She thought Lady Constance's education had driven such vernacular out of her head. While she could blame Dev's influence for letting it come so readily to her mind, it apparently took Mal to bring it to the forefront.

"*Bastard* is an affectionate term in Oz," she said stiffly. "If someone is your mate, you might call him a right bastard. It's one mostly used by men."

"Hmm. Chumani uses *arrogant prick*. She also claims it's a term of affection." He gestured ahead of them, ignoring her startled glance. "This whole section is for our new cats, where we evaluate their condition or get them back into shape. It's also for our cats that can never return to the wild and wouldn't be safe if we let them roam the island with the ones that are being rehabilitated. On the western end of the island is a large running area, separated from the open preserve. Once or twice a month, we take different groups from here to spend a night out there, really stretch their legs. I camp out with them to make sure they come to no harm."

He surprised her when he came around and offered her a hand out. His long fingers were warm and strong, and though the contact was brief, when he released her, his palm slid along her forearm, his other hand touching her back to guide her.

Fortunately, she was distracted from that by something going on at one of the nearer fences. She'd met Tokala yesterday, a tall, handsome Indian with a thick braid that fell to his waist. He had a WWII battalion tattoo on his biceps, which told her he'd been a soldier, like Dev. Now the tall man had his arm raised above his head. On the other side of the fence, a tiger had his paws against the mesh, stretching up toward the hand.

"That's Shira," Mal said. "Tokala's doing what's called operant training with him. We need to do cursory physical exams periodically to make sure everything's fine. So we teach them that maneuver, reaching up toward the top of the enclosure, so we can do a visual check of the belly and genital regions, verify the skin and fur look healthy and his weight looks good. We make sure there are no signs of stress, like over-grooming or tail biting."

"How do you help him, if he is stressed?"

"Various things. If we think he's truly sick, we bring in the vet from the mainland, though Chumani has pretty good training as a technician. Sometimes he just needs more stimulation. We do enrichment activities, which is a fancy term for giving them different toys and stimuli. Cardboard boxes, dead tree limbs, water pools for the tigers since they love to swim." He nodded toward a water hole in Shira's large enclosure. "At Easter, we paint eggs and let them roll them around and play. They eat them raw. It's fun for the staff, too."

"Easter eggs?" She was intrigued at the thought. "Is it fun for *you*?"

Mal grunted. "We compete to see who can decorate the prettiest egg before the cats mash them. Bidzil usually wins, but I've come in second a couple times."

She blinked at the remarkable statement, then looked back toward the cage as Tokala gave another command. The tiger dropped down to all four massive paws. The man put what appeared to be raw meat in a smaller cage attached to the enclosure and then pulled a lever, giving Shira access to that cage to retrieve his reward.

"We limit direct contact between humans and the cats," Mal said. "When he was merely an adolescent, Shira could have broken a toddler's neck with a playful swipe of his paw. These are wild animals, even if they've never been outside of captivity, and we want to maintain that as much as possible. If contact is encouraged, it also encourages the natural human tendency to treat them like pets. Then someone gets badly hurt."

Since she wanted to get closer and see the tiger, Mal showed her the single-strand wire that was the three-foot barrier between the fence and all visitors or those not working with the creatures. The fine stripes along the tiger's flanks and sides were like that pelt in Mal's bedroom, and it made her think of Thomas's book. There'd been a photograph of a tiger running through a jungle, light playing over those stripes.

"So he can never be free?" she asked softly.

"He was bred to be a white tiger for movies and entertainment, which didn't pan out, because white tigers are mutations; they're almost nonexistent in their native environment, and when they happen, the mothers kill them pretty quickly. She can't hide the cub from predators, so he endangers the other cubs, and even if he grew up, he couldn't conceal himself to hunt effectively. Because they wanted a white tiger, and he wasn't, they didn't know what to do with him. He was kept in a small carrier when he was young. They kept him in it for too long, didn't give him proper nutrition or exercise, so his back legs never strengthened as they should. He enjoys our nights at the open preserve here, though, and he's happy."

"You know that for certain."

He shrugged. "I'm simply assuming."

"You don't do that." She considered him. "You've marked him. I didn't know that was even possible. How did you do it?"

She saw a gratifying flash of surprise at her intuition, then he rewarded it with an image in her head. It unfolded as vividly as her dream in his bed. Mal had spent hours interacting with the tiger on the western area, letting him learn who and what Mal was, and letting Shira have a freedom he'd never had before. When the tiger finally sank down for a rest, obviously tired but like a child at the fair, still too amazed with his new surroundings to sleep, Mal squatted behind him. As he laid a hand on the mighty flank, the tiger made a loud moaning noise. Even in the midst of the memory, it made Elisa smile, because it was as if he were talking to Mal. At length, when the tiger laid his head down on the ground, Mal bent. He gave the mark through the shoulder as the tiger made another moaning noise. A brief sip, and the tiger was panting, eyes glazed and staring straight ahead as if somewhat entranced.

When Mal drew back, his hand sliding away, the tiger stayed on his side, eyes closing in a nap, but it didn't last long. Within minutes, a swarm of nighttime moths caught his attention and the beast was up again, chasing them through the grass. Since it was Mal's viewpoint, she couldn't see him, but she imagined that crimson gaze that came upon vampires when they took blood dying away to dark brown again. As he wiped his mouth with the back of his hand, a slight smile crossed his lips.

Elisa swallowed. The memory had taken over her mind so clearly it had unbalanced her, such that she was leaning against Mal's side. He clasped her waist, keeping her steady until she lifted her head and looked up into his face. It was entirely intimate, as close as two people would be before they kissed, and she jerked back, taking a couple unsteady steps that brought her up against that dividing wire and would have had her falling over it if he didn't close the gap again, steadying her further.

"I'm fine." She pushed away, putting more space between them. "Well, that was something, wasn't it?" She brushed at her hair, straightened her shirt. "So that means you can talk to them, and they to you."

"No. Vampires aren't any more capable of understanding animal language than humans. But it does give me the sense of their state of mind, which supplements the operant training, and helps build trust between me and them. Since I have a different scent from a human, there's less risk in me having more direct interaction with both the rehabilitating cats as well as these."

Shira gave her a brief glance, whuffed and backed out of the smaller cage, taking his piece of meat with him.

"I guess he doesn't think much of me."

Mal made a noncommittal noise. "Don't be offended. Cats don't like to meet your eyes."

She noted the top of the enclosure was open, though it appeared there was a strand of electrified fencing at the top. "Aren't you worried about him getting out?"

"No. Tigers aren't climbers, unless extremely provoked. Now, others . . ." He pointed out another enclosure, this time one that was screened at the top. She was just in time to see a medium-sized cat with tawny pelt and long ears with black markings and tufts dart out of a nest of foliage and rocks. The feline leaped dramatically in the air, catching a flying pigeon in her paws.

"Wow." Elisa blinked as the cat vanished back into the undergrowth.

"That's a caracal," Mal said. "And there's her mate up there. Watch—he's going to get another."

Elisa drew in a breath, catching his arm unconsciously as the cat launched himself off the rock, knocking another bird right out of the air. Locking his jaws around it, he carried the creature back to the rock formation that served as his cave. "Oh my. He's so fast."

"They used to train caracals in India to do that for show. They'd release pigeons in the ring with them and take bets on how many they could knock down."

He pointed to a chute system that had been rigged to their enclosure. "Since these two are being rehabilitated for eventual release, we send the birds and small rodents down through the chute."

She looked at the mesh fencing. "Aren't the holes big enough for their prey to escape?"

"Sometimes. That's part of it. We're training them to watch and be ready, just as they'd have to do in the wild. When they first get here, if they're malnourished or ill, as they often are, we give them meat, however much they need to get them back in good health. The amount of cats we have here consume about three hundred pounds a day. We get in whole slabs of cow ribs from a supplier on the mainland that ships to us once every couple weeks. We breed rabbits and mice in the compound, as well as the birds. We start with dead rodents, humanely killed, to introduce them to whole prey, and then move them on to live ones. Once they're out on the preserve, we've of course populated it with a variety of animals they hunt for food, big and small."

Taking her arm, he guided her onward. Maybe he hadn't intended to take her through more than one or two habitats, but she was so enthralled with all of it, his willingness to tell her more seemed to expand with her enthusiasm.

"Do any zoos ever offer to take them off your hands? So you could have room for others?"

"They did at first, but we turned them down. They're not all bad, but the primary purpose of a zoo is entertaining humans. That's how they raise money. They take animals bred or captured specifically for their facility. An animal may live a longer, less dangerous life in a zoo, but that's like saying human children are better off being locked in their rooms all their lives."

"Well, they seem happy here." She studied a bobcat lying on her side, washing. "That's something, right?"

"Yes." She sensed a hesitation, as if he was considering his next words carefully. "There's another vital reason I mark the cats, Elisa. It tells me who can never find any contentment here, the ones who are too damaged and we have to let go. End their suffering."

She swallowed. He'd marked all the fledglings, that first night. "You said their minds are all chaotic, that you can't tell much. So it's best not to be too hasty."

"What's interesting to me is that you leaped to defense, rather than a question. You didn't want to know if I saw that kind of resignation and permanent despair in any of them." His hand tightened on her elbow. "Why is that, Elisa? Do you already know?"

"No, I don't, not really. And neither do you, no disrespect intended. Sir. The way any one of them feels today may not be the way they feel a few months from now. When terrible things happen, we all have despairing thoughts for a while. We get past it. They just need time. Are those ocelots over there?"

He gave her an even look, but gestured her toward the habitat for the smaller cats. He held her elbow, though, and bent his head, a quick breath of heat against her ear. "I'll let you get away with it right now, but if you're going to be any good to them, you're going to have to learn to face this head-on, Elisa. You hear me?"

She nodded. Just not today.

She liked the distinctive array of markings along the ocelots' bodies, like tabby cats only in bolder lines and designs. It launched her into another litany of questions about everything, even how the enclosures were cleaned of animal waste if the humans couldn't go in. She found they used long rakelike devices that helped them take out the waste. Plus the enclosures were set up in a pod system that allowed rotation of the cats from one area to another if there was a need to go into an enclosure for a more thorough cleaning. She observed it was like one of those hand puzzles, where one square was always left empty.

That coaxed a smile back out of him, loosening the tension inside of her further. Then she jumped into him as a deafening roar split the air behind her, so loud her hands clapped over her ears. It was automatic to press into Mal's chest to help blot out the sound. His hands came down over hers, increasing the soundproofing, and when she tilted her head up, he was still smiling. He spoke to her then, and she thought she'd gone deaf indeed, because she didn't understand a word he said.

"What?"

"That's the expression the Africans use to describe what the lion is saying when he roars. He's saying, 'Whose land is this? It's mine, mine, mine!' "

She was a little too aware of the fact his hands remained over hers, sliding down to curl around her wrists, something that tripped her pulse up higher. He noticed, because his grip tightened perceptibly, a hint of restraint that shortened her breath further. "Males are always so concerned about their territory," she managed. "Doesn't matter what species they are."

"Well, we tend to recognize what's valuable to us and want to keep others away from it." Mal nodded to a dead tree that had been planted in the large enclosure. "Notice all the claw marks? That's one of the ways lions send messages to one another, mark their territory."

"It reminds me of all those knife marks around your door in the study," she said.

Chayton, another nearby staff member, chuckled outright. When Elisa glanced his way, she caught him looking at the way Mal was holding her. He had a bemused *and* amused look on his face. Mal apparently noticed as well, because he scowled and stepped back from her. "We're on a schedule. Let's keep moving."

11

A⊤ the next enclosure, Elisa stared for a good minute at the fuzzy, black slothlike creature. "That's not a cat," she said emphatically.

"Yes, it is. It's a binturong. When he passes gas, it smells like fresh popcorn."

"You are making that up."

"Wait a few minutes and see. They have chronic flatulence."

They passed several more staff members. The staff worked on two shifts, and the first part of this shift was apparently spent here, since the open-preserve cats needed less direct attention. As they moved through the maze of pod enclosures, those staff greeted her or sometimes added to Mal's information, demonstrating their specific knowledge of their charges. But she also caught their speculative glances, much like Chayton's, when Mal laughed or smiled or expanded on something, as if they weren't used to him acting that way. Whatever the reason, she was glad to see him in a good mood. It boded well for her being able to see the fledglings.

Of course, as soon as she had the thought, she wished she hadn't, because a shadow crossed his gaze and he got more succinct again. She felt a pang, wondering if he thought it was all an act, that she was appearing interested only to secure her own goals, but of course he could read her mind and knew that wasn't true. Right?

"Yes," he said abruptly. "I know that, Elisa. But there are times you are like a dog on a chain. You might explore the area as much as that chain allows, but eventually you always go back to the anchor holding you, obsessing over what has you tethered, so you are incapable of truly focusing on anything else."

She bit back her reply to that, because she knew there was no way she could pretend that everything in her wasn't yearning toward that anchor. If he didn't understand or approve of that, there was nothing that she could do to change it. Seeing all this, how it consumed his life, she wondered why he didn't understand how she felt.

They'd reached the edge of the habitats, and now he brought her to a higher point, where she could look down at it. Seeing the winding lines of the silver fences, she remembered the lines of the island from her dream. Fishing for something to turn the conversation from the darker path, it seemed as good a choice as any.

"Kohana said someone helped you set all this up."

"Mmm. Someone he didn't like, I'll bet."

"I did get that impression," she said cautiously. "And when we were driving earlier, when we got up to the top of the hill . . . I thought I could see lines. Bluish, glowing. I know it sounds . . . odd."

He squared off with her, the dark eyes intent. "*You* can see the fault lines."

"In your bed"—her cheeks heated at the words, at the flicker in his gaze—"I dreamed of them. It may be none of my business, but it seems that they mark the places the terrain changes. Is it . . . some kind of spell or boundary?"

He blinked at her. "Have much experience with magic in Western Australia, do you?"

"No." She shook her head, feeling a bit foolish at his expression. "I guess, working for a vampire, I've learned not to consider certain things as impossible as I once did, and magic makes the most sense, doesn't it? In my dream, the island looked nothing like it looked from the plane. From that knoll, it's the same as the dream."

"That's true." He considered something for a time, then spoke. "A lot of things went into the creation of this island, and the price was dear. For now that's all you need to know."

She gave an accepting nod. "Anything truly important like this comes at a dear cost. I expect whatever it cost, it was worth it."

"Like the fledglings are worth everything you've sacrificed for them?" His thumb moved across her palm in a casual caress that felt anything but casual.

"Yes. They're worth it." *They have to be.*

He studied her an extra moment, then nodded. "Yes, I guess that's true enough."

She had an uneasy feeling he was responding to her thought, rather than her statement. "Where did all your cats come from?"

"Various places. Sideshow zoos, circuses, criminal seizures. Though we get most of them from people who got them as cubs, thinking they'd be good pets."

"So I guess it's not obvious to everyone they're not house cats?"

His lips tugged, appreciating her dry humor. "Dogs and cats have thousands of years of domestication behind them. When these cats get into the one- to three-years-of-age range, they get territorial. Spraying, aggression, things that don't make them suitable to human cohabitation. Like what I said about the tiger breaking a child's neck."

"So they give them to you?"

"Most of them." He lifted a shoulder. "Depending on the circumstances, some of them I take, and leave a strong message that they won't be purchasing any more, or they'll wish they hadn't." He briefly showed fangs. "The advantage to being outside the range of human law."

"You let them see you . . . as you are?"

"No. But I make it clear that their desire to have an exotic pet should be far outweighed by their fear of me."

Elisa digested that. "Why does this matter to you?" At his look, she added hastily, "It's just, most vampires seem concerned about things inside the vampire world. They don't really get involved in the human world so much."

"I'm a made vampire, so I was part of the human world. I know what it's like to be treated like an exotic pet. You let yourself be locked in a cage, no matter what it's made of, you become something that was never meant to be, and that goes against the natural order of things. The natural order of things matters to me. If I can no longer be part of it myself, then I can help make it happen for them."

Dropping her hand, he walked with her on the path that would take them back to the Jeep. There was bitterness and pain in his voice, though it was subtle, a very old wound. The path had narrowed, so it seemed natural to put her hand on his forearm. "I don't believe that. That you're something that was never meant to be."

"No?" He stopped, looked down at her. "Why not?"

"Because it's like a caterpillar becoming a butterfly. God could have just made caterpillars and butterflies. Why'd he make one become the other? When someone makes someone else into a vampire, that's an ability God gave vampires, right? Like anything else we do, maybe the power isn't always used the way it should be, but that doesn't mean the person who became a vampire isn't something just as right as a born vampire."

"Do you really have that kind of faith?"

From the sudden dispassion in his tone, she was sure he was thinking she was a simpleton again. Why did she feel it necessary to babble on like this sometimes? Mrs. Rupert had always said it was charming; Mrs. Pritchett said it was a recipe for trouble. Under the scrutiny of her current vampire guardian, she was ready to believe Mrs. Pritchett. Still, she closed her hands into balls. "I'm here, aren't I?"

Of course, the real answer was she needed the children as much as they needed her. But it was more than that. "I haven't been able to go to church much in my life, and my mother wasn't much for practicing it, but I was born Catholic. And I've seen things that tell me that something bigger than ourselves is out there, even if we don't always understand it."

She could still see the enclosures through the trees. Shira was prowling, playing with a cardboard box. "You believe in something, or you wouldn't be doing this. You'd think they were better off dead. You probably sometimes do think that, but seeing him like that helps, doesn't it? I don't have your connection to him, but I can feel his contentment." She made a frustrated sound, gripping the loose tails of her cotton shirt and yanking them down just to give her hands something to do. "It makes me cry to think of what was done to turn him from what he was meant to be. But here he is, still something beautiful and amazing in his very own way, and sharing that with us. That matters."

He didn't follow her direction, didn't look toward the cat. Instead, he gazed at her as if she were an entirely new species he hadn't seen before. It made her cheeks color, but she stood firm, waiting for whatever caustic thing he was going to say.

Instead, he dipped his head, and kissed her.

The settling of his lips over hers was like the landing of a butterfly, such a light creature, but at the gift of that touch, suddenly it was a palpable, significant weight, holding her still and awestruck. The animal and earth scents he carried on him surrounded her, so that when his arms circled her body, pulling her in closer, it felt natural, like sun and sky itself. He'd done things to taunt her mind, mildly arouse her body, but this was far more devastating. His hand cupped her jaw and throat, tipping her head back so he could insinuate himself more deeply into her senses and her mouth. His tongue made a teasing caress on the bridge of her teeth, then against her own tongue, which shyly quivered beneath it.

Her employers had not been interested in kissing, and once she met Willis she'd been grateful for that, because it was something she could keep for herself. Kissing Willis was one of the favorite things she relived about him in her mind. But this was not Willis.

In fact, she was having a hard time holding on to her memory, because it was replaced by the very immediate, real-life impression of Mal, the way his tall, lean body curved over her. She was folded tight in his arms as he took her on a winding journey through a hazy, pleasurable fog. His mouth seduced hers into welcoming submission, and she knew she'd surrender to his desire to kiss her as long as he wanted.

When he raised his head, she was leaning on him because she couldn't stand.

"Why'd you do that?" Her voice was a throaty whisper.

"Because you deserved it." With the return of his irascible tone, he made it sound like an accusation. Nudging her upright, he jerked his head. "Come on. It's time to show you the open preserve."

~

Damn it, damn it, damn it. Mrs. Pritchett was right. It was best not to be noticed by vampires. If they made a move like Mal had just done, it wasn't courting. It was sampling, a thought as unsettling as her own melting response had been. She had to figure out how to make him listen, so he'd know, despite how her body responded, she really didn't want that. And hope to Heaven Thomas was right, that Mal wouldn't push the issue. Even trickier, she had to do it in a way that wouldn't ruffle vampire or male pride, both sizeable things.

Maybe he'd read all this from her mind and save her the trouble of a fumbling explanation. Of course, he was back to being broody and uncommunicative, so the one time she might have wanted him to scour her mind, he'd turned into a badger, shut up in his hole.

Because her mind was churning, she wasn't immediately delighted with the open preserve. However, as Mal brought the Jeep to a stop in an open field, she saw a female cheetah carrying an impala fawn across the field. Elisa was enchanted by the sleek beauty of the female, her large amber eyes, but then the impala twitched violently beneath the cheetah's grip on her throat. Elisa sucked in a breath. "The baby's still alive."

Mal stretched his arm out across the Jeep seat behind her. "Watch."

Two cubs came out of a tumble of rocks along the slope. As the mother patiently held the impala above them, they played with the twitching legs, batting at them like string, and then took tentative nips at them.

Elisa closed her eyes. "What are they doing?"

"It won't last long," Mal said quietly. "The cubs are old enough to start understanding how to take down live prey. Up until now, their mother has brought them their food already dead. They have to learn to hunt, and this is part of doing that. She'll finish the kill in a few moments, just tighten her grip on the neck and take the young one's life."

"Tell me when, and I'll look again." Elisa stared out the front windshield. "I can't look at that, Mr. Malachi. I just can't."

Whether or not the cheetah had intelligent, sensible, God-given motives, it was too close to other, darker things she didn't want swirling through her mind. Victor, dragging her across the barn floor, knowing she was alive and not caring . . .

Mal touched her shoulder then, and she looked toward him. "She's done," he said. "You can look."

She nodded, set her jaw, expecting him to patronize or chide, but he did neither. The babies were all tugging at their now mercifully inert dinner, joining their mother in tearing back the fur to get to the meat they needed.

"Even when the cubs play, they are learning how to survive, developing hunting skills. You see something similar with humans, particularly poorer parents who rely on the children's help to run the household. More well-off parents sometimes forget the point of parenthood is to create successful, independent adults, not forever children. They must learn to hunt what they need, survive and prosper on their own. If they can't, they won't know how to fit in our world. They'll only have a life of unhappiness and discontent because they've never truly learned or been given the skills to take control of their own destiny. They won't understand that their happiness rests squarely in their own hands."

He'd successfully turned her mind from her own memories, but it was clear where he was pointing the compass now. She pressed her lips together, hard. "If we can help them learn control, the fledglings can learn those skills."

"Hmm." Putting the vehicle in gear, he took her across the field, saying nothing further. Earlier she'd felt so good, but now she was in turmoil again. Why was he trying at all? Was it just an empty favor to Danny? No, she didn't believe that. He was a variety of things, but she didn't think he'd be spending time with the fledglings if he thought there was no hope. He wasn't the type to waste time on sentiment or a perceived favor to a female vampire.

Which meant he thought something was possible. She just didn't know what.

~

"All right, we'll lay down here."

They were behind a half-buried tree trunk, over which they could look down the slope of a shallow plain. The meadow rolled off into rocky slopes and denser forest beyond that. He'd parked the Jeep a few hundred yards away on a road that passed through the trees. She'd noted that the Jeeps didn't really startle the creatures. Mal told her there were times the cats would even jump up on them for a hunting vantage point, indifferent to the humans. She imagined her cougar crouching on the dusty hood, thick tail twitching over the powerful haunches before she leaped. It made her shiver, remembering another point he'd made.

Normally, you'd never leave the Jeep when surveying the cats, because once you're on foot, you look entirely different to them. But I thought you'd appreciate this vantage point, at least this one time.

She didn't see any cats at all, but his senses were sharper than hers. She wondered what he was seeing. Mal stretched out beside her, but instead of being side by side, shoulder to shoulder, he put one arm over her, his body canted so it overlapped hers, his hip bone pressed into her buttock, his chest against her shoulder blade, and spoke into her ear, his lips close.

His mind-voice was unsettling, but merciful heavens. Her blood went right back to hot, because of that warm breath on her skin. Her earlier resolve scattered in twenty different directions. *Please stop doing this.* It was an internal plea, so weak it was likely directed more to her errant mind and body than at him. That kiss hadn't seemed to affect him in a lingering way at all, unless being cranky was a reaction. She tried to calm her mind and body, because even if he didn't choose to read her mind, he could certainly sense arousal. If nothing else, she didn't want to embarrass herself.

She'd once thought arousal was something a woman had to summon up with concentrated effort, like pumping up water from a well. It took some effort to make it happen, but it had an important function that helped everything go smoothly so she could handle the man's needs and then move on to the next thing. Now she knew that slick and secret moisture would come forth spontaneously when her body was drawn toward a certain edge.

As Malachi's hand settled on her opposite hip, his fingers curved over her right buttock. That was their way, wasn't it? They played with their food like the cheetah cubs, with as much concern for their feelings.

"What do you see?" she whispered, determined to get out of her head.

"You can use your senses almost as effectively as I can. You just haven't been doing it to their full potential. Close your eyes now, and listen. Have you tried to use the enhanced ability for your ears, your sense of smell and taste? Your sense of touch?"

Though she'd used them, she hadn't thought of using them like this. Full potential, indeed. She could feel the heat of his hand through the thin fabric, his steady heartbeat behind her back, even the whisper of his hair falling along her neck, for she'd bundled her hair up.

"Not me, daft girl. The world around you."

The flush of blood in her face was altogether uncomfortable and humiliating, but it also pricked her shortening temper. "It's a little hard to notice anything when you're not giving me much space, Mr. Malachi."

"You can do it," he said, unimpressed by her tart tone. In fact, his fingers on her buttock tightened into a grip that was an admonishment, strong enough to make her bite back a yelp, a reminder of her place in the world. It helped her focus . . . somewhat.

Closing her eyes, she told herself it was like seeing a big shiny diamond—she might *ooh* and *aah* over seeing it on the Queen's neck or under glass in one of those traveling exhibits, but in the long run it had nothing to do with her. Like that diamond, he was unaffected, as if it was tiresomely expected that human females would trip over their tongues around him.

Ironically, that helped her push past the hurt pride, because it meant he considered it an involuntary, chemical reaction, like a sneeze or hiccup. Though one usually did say, "God bless you," for a sneeze. She wondered why.

"Because technically the heart stops, which means you're close to dead for about a second. Historically, it was also believed a person was more open to demon possession in that moment, your foot in two worlds. *Focus*, girl."

A demon possession might be closer to the truth. She had an entirely uncomplimentary response to his impatient command, one that she prudently kept to herself. At least, that was her intention.

"Stick that tongue out at me, and I'll find a use for it," he said in that rumbling murmur against her ear, his hand smoothing over the curve of her bottom as if he had every right to do that. She wasn't stopping him, because of course she couldn't, could she? Yet it was more than that. It didn't feel . . . wrong. It was almost nice to be touched in such an absently intimate way. At bedtime, she'd take the memory and replace his indifferent expression with Willis's face and hand. She'd imagine them on a picnic blanket beneath a Boab tree, watching the birds and flowers during the wet, when everything was pretty and green . . .

Mal shifted, now no longer touching her. "Think about what you're hearing now," he ordered curtly. "Then try to reach a little further with it. Don't push. It's like opening a door. Put your hand on it and let it give way."

It took several moments, but as she did as he suggested, she marveled at it. The rustling of the wind in the grasses became more than just rustling. It was music, with notes and shifts of melody, up and down. For a moment, she thought she would actually see the various wind currents meet and veer off, tangle and cyclone, then curl and uncurl. They'd drift onward in their play with the leaves and tree branches, making notes among the trunks like strumming a harp's strings. Or a child with a stick, clattering along a picket fence. Her lips curved at the thought.

More instruments and voices joined in. A *drip*, *drip*, *drip* told her nighttime dew was falling off the eaves of the tiny supply shack hidden in the trees. Those shacks were scattered across the island, putting medical and maintenance supplies within ready reach.

Birds called back and forth in the night. Not as many as those during sunrise, of course. Tomorrow she'd stay up late enough that she could come out and listen like this during the dawn, appreciate how different the resonances were between the calls. How many times had she noted Dev doing something like that? She'd thought he was enjoying his coffee and a passing interest in the scenery, but sometimes he'd close his eyes. As a third mark, with senses even more expanded than hers, was he allowing himself time to get lost in the miracle of hearing things the way one of God's creatures did, so much more possible with enhanced senses?

"Now." Malachi's arm was back over her, his masculine voice resonating through her chest, her throat. "Open your eyes and do the same with your sight. You'll discover treasure in the field in front of you. Don't strain to look for it. Just *see*."

Slowly, she lifted her lashes and took in the scene. Each blade of grass in the field was lit up, turning what was golden brown under a sunny sky into silver-white strands under the moon. Moths, dancing between the blades, spiraled upward into a night sky, competing with the stars. The tree silhouettes, their shapes looking like women in various poses, bent and danced, their arms out, swaying with the rhythm of the night.

Mindful of his promise, she lowered her gaze back to the field. That was when she saw them. She drew in a breath. "Oh my," she whispered.

12

THREE leopards, lying in the grass. They'd obviously been there all along. Yet she never would have seen them if he hadn't told her to take full advantage of her eyes.

Sitting up, they can be seen as easily as a sunflower, but lying down, their pelts blend and make it hard for prey to see them.

"So they hunt by hiding until the last possible moment?"

"Only cheetahs hunt using their speed," Mal agreed. "Most cats are pouncers, not runners." The biggest leopard's ears flickered, but she didn't appear alarmed. It was as if the cats knew humans weren't really a part of their world and, as such, were simply ignored.

Then Mal slid his hand down her back again. This time, when he explored the roundness of her buttock, cupping and weighing it in his hand, his fingers teased lower, at the inseam of the dungarees, in a way that had her breath drawing in again.

Elisa, part your legs for me.

The simple command shocked her, issued with an unruffled mind-voice that said he expected to be obeyed. Even more remarkably, her legs loosened instantly. Was it because she'd always obeyed such a command? Such a thing would make her cry if it was true, because she remembered Willis's gentle rebuke. *Value yourself more than that, girl.*

But it wasn't only that. Even if Malachi wasn't in charge of her, she wasn't sure if she could say no. Her body reached for his touch like a child for candy, ignoring the admonishments of her parental mind. She didn't know what that said, but it made a mess of her feelings, for sure.

"Easy," he murmured. "I won't say I'm not getting pleasure from it, but this is for you, Elisa. To show you something else about your expanded senses. See what you can do with them, what gifts you can give to yourself, like finding those leopards."

He stroked between her parted legs, finding the soft flesh even with the barrier of the denim fabric. The heel of his hand pressed against the base of her buttocks as he kneaded her, slow and easy, like she'd seen Dev fondling a dog's nape. Only whereas the dog had half closed his eyes, lulled into a near doze, her body was doing something entirely different.

"These pants are so tight across your ass it makes a man want to do unspeakable things to it."

She swallowed as he bent, pressed his mouth to her collarbone, his forehead brushing her cheek. When a fang grazed against her flesh, her stomach clenched. He nuzzled her, his touch now becoming less provocative, more reassuring, bracing her for his next question.

"He bit you, didn't he? Victor."

She shuddered, unable to stop herself, and he made a quiet noise. *You're safe here, Elisa. He's far beyond where he can hurt you.*

"Lady Danny . . ." She couldn't speak in her mind, way too intimate with him already doing personal things she was having difficulty processing. "She was afraid he'd third-marked me, but said I would have remembered it, because if he'd done it all at once, it would have been like I was scalded, inside out. But . . . after, I couldn't remember. At first it all hurt so terribly, and then . . . I went numb. Pain was all I was, so one was no different from the other. Willis . . . that was the worst pain of all. I kept holding his hand, even though he was gone, until Victor pulled me away. I'm glad he was already gone, so he didn't have to see . . . so that there was someone holding his hand at the end."

His hand had stilled, moved back to her buttock, resting there in a light caress. "Lady Danny, she did something to make sure that he hadn't marked me, before she went and . . . ended it."

"Wise Mistress." He spoke after a long moment. "If he'd marked you three times, she would have killed you when she killed him."

At the time, she'd wished for exactly that. She knew that was a terrible thing, a sin beyond God's forgiveness. But for quite a while afterward, even during those days in the upper bedroom that had the most sunshine—and yet never felt warm or bright enough—during changes of clean sheets and people coming and going, she kept wanting to go into oblivion. Her body felt like rotted garbage, a huge suppurating wound, with a massive, aching hole in the center where Willis had been. The image of his murder played over and over in her mind until she wanted to scream with it.

What finally got her out of bed were the children. She'd overheard Tilda, one of the day maids. *That young one, the one they called Jeremiah. He's been going crazy since it happened, won't hardly eat. Cal thought he actually heard the little fella say Elisa's name through those long teeth of his.*

When Victor had dragged her past Jeremiah's cage, Jeremiah had tried to grab hold of him. Victor snarled, and Jeremiah responded with a wild, shrieking cry, like a banshee screaming anguish straight from the bowels of hell. Victor had ignored him, pulled her onward . . .

She placed her forehead down on folded hands, the grass tickling her nose. The longer strands fluttered around her head, like a curious crowd studying something unexpected that had fallen in their midst. She thought of Dorothy's house, all its black-and-white darkness dropping out of the sky into the colorful beauty of Oz. That was what she was.

His chest was pressed even farther over her left shoulder blade, his hand braced to the grass on the other side of her, forming a shelter. For just a moment, purely out of necessity, she put aside that he was a vampire with no particular liking for her. "What would the leopards do if I stayed here like this, for hours and hours?"

"Eventually they'd come sniff you, roll you over, maybe take a nibble to see if you're good eating." There was a tightness to his voice, as if the attempt at humor was a trifle strained. Probably tired of nursemaiding her, just as he'd said. But she still couldn't move yet, and so was shameful but glad when he continued to speak.

"Of course, it might take them a while to find you. Cats see by motion. That's why a gazelle teaches her fawn to sit very still. A cat might walk within a few feet of the little fellow, and if he manages not to move a muscle, they'll likely miss him altogether. But often, when they get that close, he panics and bolts."

She knew about that. Sometimes she tried to stay so still inside her heart that the memories might pass by without noticing her, without latching on like vultures on a half-dead carcass. Sometimes they got so close, though, she had to twitch, to bolt. Then they had her.

Malachi turned her over so she was looking up into his face. In the darkness, many of the features were shadowed, but his hair fell on her knuckles as she rested them on his shoulder. She turned her fingers into it, twisting. With her words out there in the air, a dark gift to him, it felt natural. All she had right now was honesty.

"Do you feel like bolting from me, Irish flower?"

The way he said it in that low voice unfurled warmth in her belly. "I wish I could be afraid of you touching me," she admitted. "Men don't scare me all that much, because Victor was something altogether different. When you get . . . intense, I see his intensity. But you don't scare me that way. I wish you would. I don't want to like the things you're doing."

Because I've been with a man when it really meant something, and I don't think I can go back to lying still and letting a man do that because I'm supposed to let him, rather than because he loves me.

He paused, his dark eyes flickering on her face. "That's not about Victor. That's about the others."

It was difficult to say it, with his face so close. "If the master of the house comes around at night and he's not too cruel or slobbery about it, you let him in. It's like having to make lye soap. It might be your least favorite chore, because it can burn and be hot and tedious, but in the end, it's just a chore like any other."

That hand on her face changed its shape. Instead of cupping her jaw, the fingers spread out, followed one another along her cheek, under the crescent of her eye, then trailed down the bridge of her nose. Her mouth trembled a bare second before he reached it, traced the bottom curve. "Is that what this feels like?"

If she was braver, if it didn't feel so good, if his touch didn't seem to hold her so still inside herself, she might have bitten him. His eyes gleamed, registering it, but she sighed. "You know it doesn't. Please don't taunt me."

"I'm not." His mouth tightened then. "Don't assume you know everything about me, girl. I know what being subject to another's whim is like." His thumb resumed its tease across her mouth, dipping in to spread moisture across her bottom lip and making the sensitive inner flesh tingle. "But your pleasure can belong to you. It's an escape all its own. Not just from your body's response but from your mind. You respond to me, because you're on the cusp of discovering that. And you sure as hell need it."

He bent, pressed his mouth to the corner of hers. Her body quivered, her hand closing over his forearm despite herself. "It was already high in your mind, not only because of your relationship with Willis, but because of the things you've seen between Danny and her servant. When your mind is idle, or you sleep, what you've seen them do laps at your mind. You imagine how it might have been with Willis, if his mouth had been between your legs, making you cry out in pleasure. If he'd taken you to the same place that Dev took Danny that night by the fire, where you get completely lost in your own pleasure, rather than worrying about the pleasure you're giving another."

Get lost in your pleasure, rather than worrying about the pleasure of others. Such a thing was beyond her comprehension.

Mal shook his head. "When it comes to a woman's pleasure, a wise man knows it's one and the same." He dipped his head, inhaling her flesh. "Watching a woman get aroused, smelling it, gets a man hard. When she feels it, knows what it might be able to do for her, there's an answering response between her legs, a contraction, as if she's already squeezing him there, taking him in and rippling along his cock, encouraging him in every way to sink deep and thrust, take them to that place they'll both be mindless."

He wasn't the only one affected by what his nose could detect. Underneath the musk of his animals, the grass, the soil, everything of earth, she could scent *him*, the hardness pressed against her thigh already secreting that glistening moisture that sometimes happened when a male became aroused.

"You've been listening in my mind when I didn't know you were there." *A lot*. Her voice came out shaky. She didn't know whether to be terrified . . . or something else.

"It's not my usual way. Kohana was right about that. But your mind has been going to so many interesting places, and you are part of what I need to understand to determine what's best for the fledglings. So I thought it would be best to use *my* expanded senses to follow you."

Somehow, that didn't seem like the whole truth to her, but he had no reason to tell her less than the truth, right? She was his, for whatever he wanted in this moment, as if he'd cast a spell over her in truth. As he'd spoken, touched her, she'd wound her fingers tighter into that loose fall of hair, and found his neck. She trailed along the artery there, the one she'd drink from if she were his third-mark servant, in need of strength. Or just for his pleasure. She'd seen that, too. Sometimes, even if he didn't need it, Danny liked it if Dev drank a few drops of her blood, licking them from her throat, reaffirming that connection with her.

Stiffening at her astounding train of thought, she saw a flash of intensity in Mal's eyes she wasn't sure was warning or a fierce reaction to the way she'd touched his throat like that.

He shifted, the grass making a rustling noise beneath his body. She heard one of the leopards chuff, then make a questioning growl noise. "Being in your mind, even at the level of a second-mark, I know what your body wants, regardless of your conscious inhibitions and reservations. A human male without that advantage might back off, appalled at what you've had to accept, or he might worry that he'd bring back what Victor did to you." He held her in the clasp of that gaze. Those dark brown eyes had flecks of gold, she realized. And glimmers of crimson. "But I'm not human."

He followed the curve of her chin with his knuckles. Just like one of his cats, she lifted it, so he could stroke down the line of her throat. At the base, he reversed his direction, his fingers spreading out and moving back in toward her so there was the startling pressure of his hand collaring her throat, tightening enough that she had to hold her chin up, held fast by his strength and the mesmerizing power of those earth-colored eyes. It should have stoked fear, as he'd said, but it didn't. Her body recognized the dominant move for what it was. Her thighs, uncaring of her principles or baggage, trembled, shifted, telling her she was fast moving beyond damp, straight into slick-and-willing-for-entry.

"As a vampire," he continued, his voice as effective as fingertips down the center of her body, trailing over bare sternum, midriff, to the mound of her sex, "I read your desire and your arousal. When one of these cats feels hunger stir in his belly and sees that impala taunting him with the challenge of escape, he must hunt. My instincts won't deny me the chase, the need to answer that hunger. The nourishment I want is your cry of pleasure. You may resist it, may try to tell yourself I'm taking from you as they did, but it's your chance to take, too. You've fought so hard for these fledglings. You're fighting your memories, your fears of the future. Surrendering to me is the one place you can let go and act on your instinct, like a wild animal. Once you do that, you'll bring the strength of a lioness to what you face as a woman."

He drew his touch back then, diabolically making the ache intensify. "So what will it be, Elisa? A woman, or a wild animal? If you choose the woman, remember you back away from a predator slowly, one step at a time. No running, no taking your eyes off him. If you run, I will take you down."

The challenge weighted the air between them, a challenge she didn't know how to answer. She'd never "taken" in her life, never had the aggressive instincts of the wild animal he was referencing. It coiled inside of her, the things she wanted, the things she'd lost, the things that confused her still. She knew she had no answer for him. But perhaps she could test herself in another way.

Slowly, she drew her arms down, her hands slipping away from his neck as she folded her limbs against herself, staring up at him. "You told me I don't need to know more. You were surprised I could see those bluish lights. You talked about the protection of the skins, but you didn't say it like it was a wishful thing, the way we wear crosses and hope someone is listening when you pray. It *is* magic, isn't it? Will you tell me?"

She didn't expect him to answer. In fact, she was counting on it. It would confirm there was no real connection between them, the physical lust as temporal as an animal coupling and as emotionally empty. However, after following her brow with a fingertip, then tracing it down her nose, a brief touch on her lips again, he sat up, bringing her with him. She was inside the span of his arm as they sat, legs bent, gazing down on that meadow where the leopards were.

"The cheetah and cubs we saw tonight aren't here, on the island. When we drove through that open plain, we were actually in Africa. For just a moment or two."

"Of course. That's what I would have suspected." She blinked at him. "I don't think you need to worry that I'll give away your secret. Not sure anyone would believe that."

His lips curved, but the serious set of his eyes remained. "There is a sizeable island here, and the house sits in the center of it. However"—he drew several lines in the dirt banked against the fallen tree—"these sections, when you move into them, you're not actually *here*. These are pieces of land elsewhere in the world, that have been patched here by magical fault lines. You can't wander past them into larger territories. And it's . . . off-kilter with the reality there. Those actually in those places can't see or hear us or our cats. Our lions on the open preserve are walking in the environment they'd have in Africa, a shadow of it, without the danger of the poachers. When the island was first formed, a certain number of prey animals—impala, zebra, wildebeest—enough that we could maintain a herd, wandered across that protected fault line before the man who created it sealed it and . . . off-centered it. I'm sure he'd laugh at my rather nontechnical explanation, but that's the bare bones of it."

She was more than a little amazed. "I don't know anything about magic, but that sounds extremely complicated."

"It was. Just about depleted him. Had to nurse him here for a week before he was back to standing strength again. He's a little too sure of his own talents. Course, I don't really know what *will* kill him." Mal grimaced.

"And the bed?"

He shrugged. "The canopy over the bed is the focal point for the magic. All the interwoven branches, the charms and sigils, hold it all together. If you tried to unravel it, or break it, you'd simply . . . incinerate. If you merely touch it, you're fine," he added at her startled look. "When the pelts came into my keeping, Derek said they would make a vital part of the casting and protection. The spirits of the cats that used to belong to those coats helped strengthen the connections and the overall protection on the island."

"Derek. Does he live here?"

Malachi shook his head. "I don't know where Derek Stormwind lives. Sometimes I'm not quite sure *what* he is. A sorcerer is probably the best definition. He looks about thirty years old, has since I first heard of him, back in the eighteen hundreds. He came through here years back, when I was setting this place up and trying to decide how I would make it work to rehabilitate cats from different environments."

"He sounds a bit frightening." Now Elisa understood Kohana's darkly ominous comment.

"He's a lot like one of these cats. You respect his power, have confidence when you deal with him, but you never forget he can be dangerous. I think Derek belongs more to the mysteries of nature than things of man, and it's a part of nature far darker and more twisted than most of us get to see or comprehend."

She thought about that, thought in his current disarming state he wasn't much different from the unpredictable Derek. "So when you sleep in the bed . . . does it do anything to you?"

"Sometimes I just sleep, but there's always the sense of cat spirits in my dreams, their bodies pressed up to me. And no, it's not my house cats. They don't like the bed. They prefer my desk upstairs. I think the magic unsettles them."

"So much for cats being familiars."

"Well, I expect there are familiars who are cats, but not all cats are familiars. Some of them are just basic folk." He gave her a half smile.

It was alarming, how her heart skipped a beat at that expression. She needn't have worried, however. In a blink, his mien became stern once again and he rose, offering her a fairly impersonal hand up. "I brought you out here so you know what the open preserve is like. I or one of the others will bring you again if you'd like, but you leave the grounds only in my company or others of the staff. If, on the unlikely chance you're here long enough to be trusted to run errands off the compound, you will get out of the Jeep only where Kohana tells you to get out, and then you come right back. If the Jeep breaks down, you stay inside of it, with the windows rolled up, until we come find you. You'll have a radio at all times if you're off the property. Understood?"

She nodded. "Yes, sir."

"Do you want to go see the fledglings now?"

Her heart leaped. She couldn't contain her joy, even though his voice became even colder and more authoritative. "While you're there, you'll obey everything I tell you to do or not to do, immediately and without question."

"Yes, sir." *Just please take me to them.* She didn't intend it as a direct plea to him, but she expected he heard it. On their walk back to the Jeep, he didn't try to touch her again.

She knew how to pick up information from nuances, things unspoken and physical evidence—things on a bedside table, dropped carelessly under a bed or left between the sheets. Looking at his unrelenting profile, she knew he thought her feelings toward them were a problem to be solved. Was it possible these brief moments of consideration and seduction, when she felt a surprisingly compelling connection to him, were merely ways to do what she suspected Danny had asked him to do? Brace her maid for the worst.

Since Danny's motives were based on affection, she couldn't fault her much for that. But his motives still felt unclear to her. The fact she was sure he heard her thought, and didn't care to confirm or deny, only made her uneasiness that much worse.

13

She wasn't one to waste a good moment on worry. She was going to see her fledglings. As they drove through the hills, she held on to that thought. Since Mal wasn't talking much, she focused on the scenery with new eyes, particularly at the elevated points open enough that she could look down and see that puzzle piecing of different terrains, the magic glue like a dim line of blue fireflies. During daylight, she was sure each crest gave her a panoramic view of the ocean, the sunlight glittering off the waves. She hoped she'd eventually have the freedom Mal suggested to see that. She'd love to walk barefoot along the sandy shore, wade in the water.

Of course, first she had to learn how to drive. She'd coax one of the staff to teach her, in exchange for mending or cooking or other skills she had to trade. They'd done that at the station, one man whittling her a new stirring spoon in exchange for sewing his shirts, or Mrs. Rupert knitting her a cap while Elisa took over the baking for a day, giving the older woman rest for her swollen legs. That type of companionable bartering had to exist on an island where supplies were flown in and things weren't readily at hand. While she was still perceived as a guest, and a temporary one at that, if that changed, she'd become part of that fabric.

She stole a glance at Malachi. Wanting to reclaim the earlier ease they'd had, she ventured forth with a question that seemed relatively safe, particularly since she already knew the answer. "There's a council-person named Lord Malachi. That's not you, I assume?"

When Mal cocked his head toward her, the dark wing of his hair, the aquiline line of his nose, the way the dim light caught his dark eye, made the likeness to a bird of prey even more arresting. "Do I strike you as good at politics, Irish flower?"

My fat aunt jumped into her head before she could stop it. At his quizzical expression, she cleared her throat. "It's an Aussie expression. It means . . . not really."

He snorted. He turned off the main road, such that it was, onto something that looked like a deer track, the trees closing in so that palm fronds slid over the windshield and tickled the elbow she had braced on the open window. A trio of birds flushed just ahead, their crimson feathers and snow-white heads a splash of color against the greenery.

"Lord Belizar, the head of the Council, also has a full servant named Malachi," Mal said. "There being so few vampires, they've considered changing the servant's name to save confusion."

"But that's his name. I know they're powerful vampires and all that, but taking away the name your mother gave you, that seems too much. Sometimes that's all you have of yourself."

Mal missed a gear. The Jeep jerked such that Elisa caught the dash with her free hand. She didn't miss the look on her driver's face, though. In that one brief second, his expression altered. It reminded her of how, sometimes, when her day was going along just fine, someone came up on her sudden-like, startling her. A dark well opened inside and things supposed to be in the past were all too present. His expression became inscrutable again in a flash, but she'd seen stark pain, overlaid by a rage so deep it was impossible to ignore.

"I'm sorry," she said, suddenly terrified that she'd angered him beyond immediate repair. "I wasn't trying to be insolent. I—"

He stopped the Jeep so abruptly she was glad she was still holding the dash, but his advice about standing fast before a charging predator came to mind when he turned toward her. "Elisa, short of you spitting in my face, you are going to get to see these damn vampires tonight. All right? So stop walking on eggshells and making everything about that. And for fuck's sake, be quiet until we get there."

The savagery took her aback, such that she had to force herself not to shrink into a corner. She sensed the anger wasn't at her, not directly. She'd simply been a messenger carrying a missive he hadn't wanted to receive. Taking a steadying breath, she tried to fold her hands in her lap and sit in dignified silence as he put the Jeep back in gear. After several tense seconds, she glanced at him through the gray darkness, the hard set of his mouth.

She wanted to apologize, and not because she was afraid of not seeing her fledglings. She hadn't intended to hurt or upset him. She didn't like to do that to anyone, not without cause, and she'd really thought it a safe line of conversation. But since he seemed to prefer her silence, she swallowed the compulsion and hoped to have a chance to offer her regrets later.

He navigated one final turn that slid them into a clearing, which gave her a first glimpse at the enclosures Thomas described. Eagerly, she sat forward, straining for a better look. She could see movement, and thought it might be William. Another small figure stepped out of a walled shelter inside his cell and turned toward the oncoming Jeep. Unmistakably Jeremiah.

Though it had been only a couple days, she'd thought about them with every inhale, worried with every exhale. She'd treated that rhythm like a clock, counting down to this moment so she wouldn't go mad. Perhaps she had gone a little wobbly. But now, so close to her goal and not wanting to do a single wrong thing, she forced herself to stay seated in the Jeep, waiting for Mal's direction.

She admitted being impressed by what she was seeing. The enclosure area was large, each individual cell enough to house a small cabin and patch of yard. The yard area wasn't just gravel or dirt. Small trees had been planted there, flowers, bushes. Like the cats, there was a box-sized cage attached to the larger cell, through which she suspected the staff could leave their blood donations so the fledglings could retrieve it without contact.

The individual cabins were joined to one large communal enclosure, the place Mal had let them interact with him. That area was likewise landscaped, with a birdbath to attract small feathered creatures through the gleaming silver fencing that completely enclosed the area, including the top. That gleam made it like no type of fencing she'd seen. She wondered if Mal had somehow used an extra wisp of Derek's magic to reinforce this area, ensure it was strong enough to keep vampires from tearing, digging or climbing out.

Danny had contacted Mal several months ago. Despite that length of time, this was far more than his attitude had led her to expect. She was a bit shamed by her doubts.

"This is all just for show. They were actually yanked out of a dank hole in the ground, hosed down and cleaned up, then put here to ease your mind," Mal observed acidly. "That's why I've been wasting your time and boring you with the rest. They weren't quite ready."

"It wasn't a waste—"

"Here are the ground rules. You stay four feet away from the cells at all times. I'll open up the communal space inside and you can walk around. You can leave them things in the lockdown cages. I'll show you how to open those so they can take the trinkets and tidbits you've brought them. You'll always be accompanied here, but once you know the system you can operate the controls under supervision, and that way my person can do paperwork and other useful things while babysitting you."

"I thought I'd be helping you . . . with your evaluation."

"You will be. Doesn't mean I trust you here alone."

He was impossible to understand. As if to add to her confusion, he came around the Jeep to help her out again. Maybe his bark was worse than his bite, and she just had to figure him out. She accepted his hand with a brief hesitation, but when she placed her fingers in his he tightened his grip enough to snap her gaze to his face. "Repeat what I said to you, Elisa."

"I don't see how—"

"Now. Or you get back in this Jeep."

"Fine." She blew out a breath. "No closer than four feet to the cells. Always supervised. You'll show me how the cage system works so I can leave them things."

"Good. You forget to do this right, and one of them may rip you to pieces in bloodlust, whether or not they want to do so. Or they could do it quite intentionally. I expect you remember that, don't you?"

His tone held the mildest touch of sarcasm, but it lanced across her belly like a knife wound. For a moment, she wasn't sure he'd said some-thing so unspeakably cruel, but then she wrenched her hand away, backing into the Jeep. "You bastard."

Immediately, she sucked in a breath, appalled at herself. But before she could admonish herself or stammer an apology, he'd recaptured her arm in one swift movement. Drawing her resisting body close again, she realized he thought she was going to storm away.

Elisa, calm down. You can't be emotional here. They feel everything. Look at me. Look up at my face.

Apparently, he didn't consider his sarcastic barb emotion. She set her jaw mutinously, and heard him sigh. He touched her chin. "Yes, I was being a bastard. I'm sorry."

That surprised her enough to look up. She saw genuine regret in his eyes. *You touched a nerve, Elisa. It wasn't your fault; you didn't know. You don't know my past the way I know yours. Which only makes what I said that much more unforgivable.*

Vampires never apologized to humans. Dev often joked about it, the backhanded way Danny would make amends for being catty, anything short of a verbal apology. The fact Mal did so now, so straightforward, turned everything around in her, as quick and easy as she'd been hurt. Simple. Reaching up, she touched his face, because he looked like he'd made himself sad, and she didn't want that. "Nothing is unforgivable," she murmured.

Realizing how forward she must seem, she took her hand away, but he caught her wrist, holding her still, her fingers brushing his cheek-bone. "I think you believe that." *And I guess* bastard *sometimes isn't an affectionate term, hmm?* Before she could respond to that, he lifted her palm to his mouth and took a tiny nip, enough to cause pain but not break the skin.

My bite is far worse than my bark, Elisa. Never doubt it. You break one of my rules here, and you'll find out.

She wasn't sure how to explain the shiver that went through her at that. She honestly couldn't keep up with her emotions any better than she could his. Next to that, dealing with the fledglings would be a breath of fresh air. Almost.

Mal showed the girl how to use the cage system, and then went to the Jeep to stretch out on the hood, his back against the windshield. The fledglings were far more wary when he was inside the communal area, and Elisa far more self-conscious, at least this first time. Being a contrary prick hadn't helped, and he knew she was right. He needed to get a grip on his emotions as much as she did. But Christ, she had a way of innocently yanking a scab right off a wound best not disturbed, ever.

As he watched, she went to Jeremiah first, taking the two inexpensive dime-store books she'd brought, along with some treat morsels she'd gotten from Kohana. Laying them down on the concrete pad of the lockdown cage, she backed out and secured it again. He approved of how she looked toward him the first time she did it, making sure she'd followed the process right. She waited for his nod before she opened the interior door so Jeremiah could retrieve it. Mal tensed, though, when the young vampire retrieved the items but reached through the bars toward her. He saw her yearn toward that hand, but a blink before he would have intervened, her shoulders squared.

"It's not allowed, Jeremiah. Not right now. I'm so sorry. I'm very glad to see you, though. I've missed you. I've missed all of you so much. You need to look at that top book. Remember how I was teaching you your letters? This book will help you remember some more of the schooling you had . . . before."

He kept reaching, his expression becoming more agitated. Elisa looked over her shoulder at Mal. He made sure he appeared relaxed, dispassionate, as he shook his head, but every muscle was ready to move if she disobeyed him. Jeremiah's grip could break her arm with barely a flex. He could yank her up to the bars and take out her throat, and he was far too worked up. Fledglings got frustrated as a normal matter of course, but stirring them up meant they were far more likely to have a bloodlust episode, which could come upon them like quicksilver.

All those emotions she'd been bottling were welling up. She was obeying Mal's direction, but it was tearing her apart, seeing the fledgling's need to touch her and having to deny him. And Jeremiah knew it, would push it until she couldn't help herself.

Mal stood up then, immediately drawing the young male's attention. He made sure there was no doubting his expression or the thought he sent into the boy's chaotic mind. *Cut it the hell out.* Jeremiah made a plaintive noise, then withdrew his hand. His gaze dropped, surrendering. Stepping back, he took a seat inside his cell. Elisa glanced toward Mal, then back at the boy. He could feel her weighing his actions, determining how to respond, but then she turned, sat herself down on a stump in the center of the communal area where she could easily turn and see each of them. Drawing up her legs, bracing her heels on the edge of the stump, she locked her hands around her knees. "This is a really nice place, isn't it? Remember I said it was a cat sanctuary? You won't believe the things I've seen today. Tigers and lions, and cats that can jump ten feet in the air and catch a pigeon . . ."

Her voice strengthened as she spoke, and it carried to all of them, as if she was used to talking to them this way, like a storyteller in a hall with a listening audience. He watched, interested, as warily and in their own time, they each moved to the portion of their cells closest to her. All except Leonidas. That one continued to prowl, occasionally hissing to himself, but he'd remembered the lesson of the first night. He kept his gaze down or elsewhere, anywhere other than on Elisa, but Malachi could feel his intent toward her like a simmering volcano.

It intrigued him. Their minds grew no clearer, but there was a definite slowing of those chaotic whorls of activity, a singular focus on her. Was it like what the Easter eggs provided his cats? Something different to do, stimuli that kept at bay what they longed for more than anything? Wide-open space, lazy days under trees, and the thrill of the hunt, the power of sustaining one's own survival. Except the fledglings' instincts toward their natural state had been twisted, and not just because they'd been turned far too young. At the whim of a brutal vampire, the only outlet they'd been given from his torture was hunting human prey. Now, draining a human corpse was an unrelenting thirst. Like those rare instances of lions who'd become man-killers, the easier, more plentiful prey was an irresistible drug.

A nine-year-old boy reached toward her and she saw a lonely child, grasping at the memory of a mother. Mal saw the traces of red in his eyes, the mindless strain behind that grasp.

When they were turned, they'd had the undeveloped emotional maturity expected of young humans. Children saw things differently from adults, and were far more impulse-driven. The base savagery of the vampire nature, as well as its carnality, had given them a confusing soup nigh impossible for a child's brain to process. Victor and Leonidas, being teenagers when they were turned, would have had it worse because their bodies had been changing, puberty's hormonal flood.

His gaze strayed to Leonidas. Though they might be physically trapped in the age they'd been turned, how it affected the aging brain was the troublesome unknown. Was there any chance they could ever have any meaningful self-control, enough to live their lives outside of a cell, without a jailer always attending their every movement? As he'd implied to Kohana, even if they could, their future would still be bleak. They'd never be as strong or mentally agile as an adult vampire.

He sent another mild curse Danny's way, for saddling him with this, but that was water under the bridge. He brought his focus back to Elisa.

She was balanced on the point of her lovely buttocks and rocking back and forth on the stump as she told them all about the cats. The animated way she was relaying every minute detail of what he'd shown her said how closely she'd paid attention. She was right; he had known her enthusiasm was genuine, but he'd gotten caught up in his own past. He wasn't wrong about the fledglings; he knew it. But he was doing something wrong, because this agitation wasn't like him. He of all people understood how essential calm was to correctly anticipate the needs of the creatures here.

Ah, the hell with it. He was thinking too much at this point. Pushing all that away, he watched her leave the stump and begin to pace. Gesturing with her hands, she gave a sudden, dramatic jump to demonstrate how the caracal had caught the pigeon. It made her curls bounce, and she smiled at her own play. Another item she'd brought was a small ball, and she approached William's enclosure, close enough that she could toss it through the bars. She warned him it was coming, encouraging him to catch it. When he did, her smile became brilliant. She coaxed him to toss it back.

Interactive play. He was impressed with her intuitive understanding of their development, unschooled though it was. They had the agility and speed to do things far more exceptional than catch the ball, but what she was doing was teaching them how to control it, dial it down a notch so the ball didn't get thrown halfway across the island. Ruskin had always kept them whipped to a fever pitch, to the height of their bloodlust. In order to truly defuse that, they would need regular outlets for that energy, more than what could be accomplished in their cells, playing catch. He gave that some thought as William threw it back to her. He shot it wide, and it rolled over to Miah and Nerida's cells. Elisa ran after it.

Mal nearly came off the Jeep, but caught himself just in time to avoid notice as she stopped a good number of feet away from Nerida's cell. Like a gazelle herd, all of the vampires would still instantly if he shifted in any way, and he wanted to avoid disruption. The little girl, who appeared all of six years old, reached through her bars and got it, then winged it to Jeremiah. Elisa laughed as they continued their game of keep-away, now obvious from the direction and height of the ball. She grinned, took a seat on the grass by the fountain now. Leaning back on her arms, she watched them take over the game.

After a while, she got her drawing pad from her pack, made a few sketches. Keeping up her idle chatter, she asked the fledglings to do things for her. Asked Nerida to do a somersault, Matthew a handstand. She was doing what they did with operant training, verifying that they were responsive, healthy. Eventually, she rose and circled to each lockdown, leaving a picture she'd done for each child, as well as some markers and more paper if they wished to do their own drawing.

Despite the fact a game of catch couldn't meet their energy needs, there was no denying they were now calmer. Most of them. It troubled his mind, the energy between her and Leonidas. She didn't have the same open and relaxed body language toward him she had with the others. In fact, there was a reluctance to it that suggested she had to make herself turn toward him, go to his lockdown and offer him things. He registered her fear, even as he kept his eyes down and prowled, making those warning noises like an aggressive cat about to pounce on a rival.

Perhaps he should move Leonidas to a different part of the island. As he became more agitated, it stirred up the others. The entire time she was near his lockdown cage, Jeremiah and William focused more intently on him. Miah, Matthew and Nerida moved to the backs of their cells, even into the doorways of their cabin shelters.

No wonder they'd been calmer before that disruption, though. Interestingly, Mal realized he'd been as absorbed by watching her as they were. He didn't yet have the key to resolve this situation, couldn't see how it would be anything other than a Greek tragedy, but he was clear on one thing. He wanted her. The lust didn't surprise him, because a curvy female *was* his preferred type, as Danny had slyly suggested. But his interest in the twists and turns of her mind intrigued him.

Elisa Farraday. Daughter of an Irish prostitute who died with her throat cut in an alley. A street child picked up by fate to be trained as a maidservant. Used like a whore by her employers until Lady Constance. It made his jaw tighten. Yes, human servants were required to submit to the sexual demands of their vampires, but as he'd made clear to Elisa, human servants submitted willingly, if the vampire followed the generally accepted guidelines for taking a full servant. A vampire, deep in his servant's mind, knew that willingness was true.

Her inability to say no to a man's desire had been the practical reality of her life, enough that the violence of Victor's attack lingered more with her than the violation, the only real blessing of that wretched affair. But it bothered Mal that she'd never had the right to choose, not until the brief taste of it with Willis.

Yet he also saw a strong core of faith, built on a kernel of innocence she refused to relinquish. When she'd so simply forgiven him for such a heinous barb, it touched things inside of him he couldn't explain, couldn't shake. It made him uncomfortably aware that he was starting to entertain the idea of letting her stay here longer.

Maybe Kohana and Danny were right. Maybe he really needed to get off this island more often, particularly if one guileless Irish house servant could tie up his mind like this. He scowled, hoping the expression was lost in the darkness and the fledglings' absorption with her.

~

He hadn't said how long they could visit, though of course she was sure they would need to go by dawn, unless she wanted to see him fried like an egg on the hood of the Jeep. Because Miah opened the door of her small cabin wide enough so she could see from the proper distance, Elisa saw they had a bed and other comforts. A floor trap led down into a concrete reinforced subterranean space. Mal perfunctorily explained in her mind they could choose to go down there for coolness and complete protection from the island sun during the height of the day. There was a cot there as well.

Other than that explanation, however, he remained silent, and his closed expression from where he sat didn't encourage further conversation.

Fine, he could be surly. She was too pleased with seeing the fledglings to let him irritate her. When Jeremiah took one of the books and slid it to her, making sure it had the momentum to go beyond those four feet, she knew he wanted her to read to them. The others immediately settled down, anticipating. As always, she noticed how Nerida and Miah stayed at the adjacent corners of their cells, as close as they could get to each other. They even put their hands through the bars, flattening the palms on the grass, fingers pointing toward each other like arrows. Though they were separated by a good six feet, it was as if their palms were connecting through the earth's energy.

"What story would you like?" she asked Jeremiah.

When he held up three fingers, she went to the third story in the book, an excerpt from *Treasure Island*. "A boy's story for sure." She sent him a teasing look. "We'll have to let Miah and Nerida choose next. A story of princesses, maybe. Or one day they'll tell us their stories."

From Dev and the blackfellas on the station, she knew their race had a rich history of storytelling, reciting them to their young ones practically from the time they came out of the womb, and probably within it. She wondered what amazing tales of their world still drifted through Miah and Nerida's heads, or had Ruskin driven them out entirely?

Nerida made a chirp like a bird and then she was flapping around her cell in a graceful emulation of flight. Elisa paused, watching with the others as the girl came to rest on her haunches. She cocked her head just like a bird might, studying the world out of the wide-set eyes.

It was the most outgoing she'd ever been, though Elisa managed to keep from leaping to her feet and cheering. Instead she settled for a broad smile and a nod. "Bird stories. I'd like to hear some of them. Would you like to tell me one?"

Nerida shook her head, glancing at Miah, then up the hill at the Jeep and the figure slouched lazily on it, though Elisa had no doubt he was as attentive as a hungry lion.

"He won't harm you. He's here to help you, help all of you. I can tell this is a better place for you all, and he's responsible for that. Plus, he comes from a people that did a lot of storytelling as well. I read a book about it on the way here, on the plane. I bet he knows a lot of stories and would share some as well." Then, remembering Kohana's warning, she bit her lip, cursing her overeagerness. "Well, not today, but perhaps another time."

Why not today?

Glancing up, she saw him straighten from the Jeep and slide off it in that ripple of smooth muscle and deadly vampire grace. As he came down the hill, though, his attitude and body language altered. Surliness gone, now he reminded her of Dev, the way he moved around the animals at the station, sending out a signal that not only calmed them, but told them he was completely in charge. Dev had told her animals liked knowing the pecking order, because it was reassuring, cut down on a lot of uncertainty. She couldn't deny it reassured her.

Mal came into the main enclosure and matter-of-factly took a seat on the stump she had her back against now, so his calf was pressed against her side. They were all gazing at him with varying levels of wariness and distrust, but none of them moved from their positions at the fronts of their cells, an encouraging sign. As he sat down, she had a thought, looked up at him. "Will you tell us how the Milky Way came to be?"

His lips curved slightly. "That old bastard," he muttered, but he gave her a slight nod before he turned his attention to the fledglings. "Most Cherokee stories are simple and straightforward. It's the way they're told that are entertaining. This is one my mother told me. Do you know what the Milky Way is?" At their lack of response, he tilted his head back, lifted an arm to point. Enchanted, she saw the fledglings tilt their heads back with him. "That crescent of stars there, like a faint brush of white paint across the sky. That's part of it.

"Tonight you look up and see thousands upon thousands of stars. But at one time, there were not very many at all. Probably because the Creator hadn't had time to attend to it, the world still being young and all. At that time, the People depended a lot on corn for their food. They made it into cornmeal and stored it during wintertime to carry them through the Windy Moon, a time when winter stores are almost depleted. But one morning, an older couple found that something had been in their meal. They found dog prints, but it was no ordinary dog. These prints were the largest they'd ever seen, and it appeared as if feathers had swept the ground around it, leaving large swirling patterns in the meal the beast had wasted, gobbling out of the sacks."

Mal made a face then, stretching his mouth wide, and sweeping his arms around him the way a dog with wings might. Elisa saw Miah's eyes widen. Matthew was studying him like he was an entirely new animal. Elisa wasn't sure if she wasn't doing the same.

"The people of the village knew this had to be a spirit dog, and they had to keep it from coming to their village. So that next night they gathered together drums, turtle-shell rattles, and whatever noisemakers they had. They lay in hiding around the storehouse. It got very late, and some of the young ones had fallen asleep against their mothers, but they were all awoken by the flap of mighty wings. Out of that darkness, that middle time of night, came a tremendous dog. The spread of his wings was so large they weren't sure how he'd fit in the storeroom, but since he was a spirit dog he could go where he wished, couldn't he? As they watched, he landed among the cornmeal and began to gobble it down."

He made the motion with both hands, a gulping noise, his eyes darting about like a wild animal's might, conveying both danger and hunger at once. Elisa felt a shiver go over her skin.

"They were afraid, but that was all the food they had to survive the winter. So they leaped up and began to make a tremendous noise. Rattles, drums, shouting, like a mighty thunderstorm. That dog bolted out of there like there were cans tied to his tail, which of course would have been a funny sight, such a large dog with cans tied to his tail. But the people chased him, all the way to the top of a hill. Then he leaped into the sky, the cornmeal spilling out of his mouth. Since he ran across the sky to get away, the cornmeal trail he left became a series of stars, so thickly laid together they're what white people call the Milky Way. The Tsalagi call it 'the place where the dog ran.'"

"How do you say it, in Cherokee?" Elisa asked softly, looking up at his face.

That shadow appeared across his face. But then his eyes met hers and he spoke, the syllables like a warm stroke across her skin. *"Gi li' ut sun stan un' yi."*

14

When they got back, just after two in the morning, her mind was churning with all of it. The children had listened to his story, even Leonidas. For that moment, leaning against his leg and a bit amazed at how comfortable she was doing that, Elisa had felt settled, balanced. She treasured those moments, because they didn't happen often, but this time it had happened because of him. One moment she doubted his commitment and had no idea if she could trust him. The next, he did something like that. It was getting hard to believe she'd been here only two days and her world was already so off-kilter.

While he told the story, his hand had fallen on her shoulder, his thumb sliding back and forth over her collarbone, bared by the neckline of her blouse. As she got ready for bed, putting on her thin white nightgown, she stopped in front of the mirror, put her hand there and felt that compression, the heat, bring back the memory of his touch.

Though she should be going over everything that had happened with the fledglings, and how she could help him see them the way she did, she kept coming back to that touch. The earlier kiss. His words. *Your chance to take, too . . . be a wild animal . . .*

It went against everything she had been taught. Submitting, surrendering had always been about sacrifice. Yet she recalled that moment in Mr. Pearlmutton's dining room, seeing what she'd done to give him and his guests pleasure. She'd been serving, but such service had given her something. Peace, fulfillment. Like when the priest said to surrender oneself to God and let that peace fill your heart. Though to think of that in this context seemed more than a trifle sinful.

Sitting at Mal's knee, looking up at his face, trusting him fully in that one moment as he took her and all of them on a journey with words, she'd had a hint of what surrendering to him, even just once, might mean. He'd pointed out she was all too aware of that element between Danny and Dev. Lord, Dev was a man's man, and no woman's fool, but there was something he gave Danny that resonated in a matching chord in Elisa. She'd called it something different with Willis, imagining all the ways she'd be a good wife and make him happy. Mal touched on darker aspects of it, aspects that had to do with what Elisa sensed in herself, a wild, untamed thing that could scare her with its ferocity when she felt it.

She slid into her bed, shaking her head at herself. Mal had told her to go to bed despite the "early hour," but maybe she should have helped Kohana with chores, worked herself into exhaustion. She was going off in odd directions tonight. What she was feeling now was hardly what that priest had envisioned, she was sure. The pulse between her legs was beating hard, such that when she laid her fingers over it she drew in a breath. Her flesh inside contracted, just as Mal had said. She wondered, and her fingers passed over those petals, the tight bud of flesh at the top. A shudder went through her lower belly, tightening her thighs, even though she'd only touched herself through the thin night rail.

Trying not to think, at least not like a rational human being, she slid off her very practical underwear, deciding she liked the way the cotton of the gown felt, whispering over her indecently bare flesh beneath.

She realized then she was trembling. Victor had brutalized her. Mr. Collins and Mr. Pearlmutton . . . they had stolen from her. They had. She wouldn't have known that without Willis. He'd persuaded her to offer her body, wooed her with a firm, pleasurable insistence. Mal . . . He was a whole different animal, but one that seemed to understand the dark, violent need that she carried over her heart. When he touched her, he took that firm insistence to a different level.

Danny had always touched her in passing, a flirtation, an indulgence. When Mal touched her, his attention was fully riveted on her, and to be the center of a vampire's sensual intentions . . . It was a dangerous magic, wasn't it?

Remember, you back away from a predator slowly . . . If you run, I will take you down.

Pushing back the covers, she put her bare feet to the floor, ran her hands through her hair so the tie on it loosened. The strands fell past her shoulders in brown curls, brushing her neck, the exposed part of her collarbone, like Mal's fingers. She remembered how his hand had gripped her there before, that collared hold, keeping her still, making her breathing constrict, and not because he was compressing her airway.

She'd always been given to romantic notions, but she had lived in a very real world that kept the wishful child and the grown-up servant separate. Daydreaming was fine as long as it wasn't slowing down your work or making you inattentive to your mistress or master. She swallowed, and then in the quiet of her room, where no one could hear, she spoke it aloud, though as a whisper.

"Master."

When they'd had visitors at the station, she'd heard female servants address their male vampires that way. He'd heard Dev call Danny *Mistress* a few times, and when he did, there was always a certain light in his eye, a tone to his voice that sparked an answering fire in Danny's expression. As if he taunted her with it, only it was the kind of taunting that stirred a woman's blood. A woman like Danny.

Was Mal the kind of vampire to be stirred by a woman calling him *Master*, and all it implied? And did she have a good grasp on what it truly meant? Of course not, which was why she was playing such silly games in the dark where it was safe and did no harm.

It was odd, to have a room all to herself like this. Since she'd been with Danny, she'd shared a room with an older woman. Danny had intended it that way, to keep her out of trouble. But here, Elisa was the only human guest. She was the only one on this hallway that would receive the sun in the morning, a few hours hence. In a new place, being so isolated from the rest of the household might have made her nervous, yet he'd given her that second mark. Though she didn't know when he was or wasn't in her mind, she sensed that if she was in true distress, she could call out and he would come and help.

He would come because she was Danny's servant, his guest. *Don't be daft, thinking romantic nonsense.* She needed a glass of milk to settle herself, make her go to sleep. Rising from the bed, she moved to the door and slipped into the hallway. There'd be no staff in the house at this hour. They rotated shifts, some working through the night hours with Mal, some working in daylight, but at this time the nightworkers were still out or at the bunkhouses. Kohana had gone with Chumani to help her with a construction project at the habitats. Mal had likely gone back out after dropping her off. Kohana had said he would take blood at dinner, but then he'd head to the open preserve and usually didn't come in until just before dawn. She made a face. He'd probably grumble about how "babysitting" her had put him behind.

She padded down the hallway, her footfalls silent in the plush of the runner, then moved down the stairs. There might be a little bit of that bread Kohana had made, and perhaps she'd have that with some butter and the milk. Even as she had the practical thought, she was way too aware she hadn't put her underwear back on or even donned a wrap over the thin gown, her mind entirely too absorbed in the way it felt. The feathery glide of the gown over her bare arse, the way her thighs brushed together with no panties to muffle the way those folds between her legs touched, tiny kisses against moistening secret flesh.

She clutched a handful of fabric in one hand, the banister in the other. Alone in the house or not, she needed to keep her head on straight, and these were decidedly not wise thoughts. It wasn't entirely her fault, of course. Serving in a vampire's household, carnal thoughts were barely a breath away, since they didn't bother to restrain themselves when they had such desires. Mal . . . Mr. Malachi—she firmly made herself return to the formal use, suspecting it was safer that way—had certainly not curbed himself when he was lying in the grass with her, watching the leopards. Or when he'd kissed her. Or touched her collarbone with the fledglings.

When she got to the bottom of the stairs, she intended to turn toward the kitchen, but a light to the left drew her attention. She paused, her heart accelerating. Those senses he'd had her open wide today told her she wasn't alone. Mal was decidedly not at the open preserve.

The French doors across the hall from his study were open, letting in the sounds of the night. Using those same enhanced senses, she heard the distant grunts and snuffles, and realized the lion pride had come closer to the house tonight. She imagined one sauntering through that open door and giving her a curious once-over, wondering if she was dinner or something to be dismissed.

She wasn't thinking of the four-legged kind of cat, and she knew it. Particularly when her feet turned toward the library, not the kitchen. She moved silently, though he could easily hear her, scent her, plumb her mind. She wondered what he would find there, because she wasn't quite sure herself. Barely two days. She'd been here barely two days. What was she thinking?

But she'd spent the past months mired in fear, grief, guilt, longing. During her orientation, he'd said that animals didn't do that. They lived in the moment, because every moment was about survival, an instinct even domestic animals didn't seem to completely lose. They made the most out of that nap in the sun, a good meal, play with siblings. They didn't know what would come after, and whatever had happened before was done and gone.

Done and gone. If she believed in such a heathenish thing as coming back and being something else, like the people from India did, she'd want to be one of those sleek female cheetahs. So fast and strong, and living in the moment. Everything in the past done and gone. She wasn't sure she could do that thing with the baby impala, though.

The hallway grew shadowed as she moved away from the living area and the stairwell. She stopped at that dividing line between darkness and the block of light thrown out from the study area. She could almost sense his head lifting from whatever he was doing, knew that he was waiting, seeing what she would do. That only sharpened the feeling arrowing down her sternum, spreading out across her flesh in goose bumps. Could she trust him, this vampire she barely knew? *Yes.* Because she remembered that first moment, when he held her against his chest in front of Leonidas. Somehow she knew the more important question was whether she could trust herself. She should back away, pivot and go back to the kitchen, but she didn't want to do so. This was a place for wild animals, and wild animals did as their instincts told them.

She stepped into the light.

He was at his desk and, as she anticipated, he had his attention on the door. He had a pen caught between two fingers, yet he was idly tapping it back and forth against the desk, like a slow seesaw, or the ticking of a clock. And, glory be, he'd shrugged off the T-shirt against the evening's heat, the cool brush of air from the open doors touching that bronzed skin.

She'd been aware he had a tattoo on one arm, but this was the first time she'd had the opportunity to take a good look at it. It had a ridged appearance, because it had to be scarred with his own blood to make it indelible. Otherwise she expected a vampire's regenerative ability would simply swallow it. A barbed-wire design circled his biceps, white and blue feathers printed through the dark ink and in a twisting pattern below. A sinuous female lion batted a large paw at the feathers, golden eyes narrowed, her tail wrapped around the bend of his elbow and ending where his forearm began.

His hair was loose, brushing the broad shoulders. Tas, his large striped tom, had fallen asleep with one paw stretched out toward the pen, as if he'd been playing with its movement before he got bored and went into nap mode.

Elisa merely stood there and stared at him for long moments. He let her do so, not saying anything, either, a decision that made the strands of need tighten between them. When she met his dark gaze, she wondered what he saw, and realized, with her being in the thin night rail, he might be seeing a great deal.

"What are you doing, Elisa?" he asked. Caught between thrilling anticipation and abject terror, she heard the male interest behind the question, read the heat in his gaze that said he might know the answer better than she did herself.

She didn't care. She wanted to touch his hair, bury her fingers in it, hold it tightly to draw him to her. She wanted to stroke the lines of that tattoo. Put her mouth against his throat, and feel the heat and life beating there, feel his hands on her as he took away any fear, burned it away with what he could do to her body. She saw a rapid montage of so many images—Willis's stirring kisses, Danny and Dev's carnal embraces in the firelight, Mal's hand on her throat, eyes so close . . . Victor's viciousness.

Mal had given her permission to take, but it was more than that. He'd approved her *desire* to take. No one had ever done that. She could choose.

She made another visual pass over his upper body, wondered if he was already aroused in the jeans he wore, if his arse and thighs beneath the denim would be as taut and muscled as what she was seeing, bare to her avid gaze.

"Elisa." The one word was a near growl, so like his cats she almost smiled. It shot pleasure through her, enough that she shivered with it. "What are you doing?" he repeated.

She met his predator's gaze, and answered his question.

"Running," she whispered. And bolted out the French doors.

15

MAL had heard her on the stairs, of course. Figured she was coming down for a snack, and forced himself to stay where he was, not go sniffing out what she was doing. She'd been wrong, earlier today. She thought he was unaffected by her aroused state, when entirely the opposite was true. But he knew enough to curb unwise desires. Danny had sent her to him for protection and guidance, and the girl was messed up in too many ways, too much like the cats that came to him.

But then he'd heard her steps turn in his direction. He'd expected the quick, efficient step of the dutiful servant, coming to ask him if he needed anything. Though of course the dutiful servant hadn't gone to bed like he'd told her to do.

Instead, her approach had been like that of the bobcat, stalking small game while remaining wary of rear attack by a larger beast. Then she'd paused at that demarcation line, before she stepped into his line of sight. He'd smelled her arousal, strong and unmistakable. Heard the increased pounding of her heart, the hitch of her breath, and his blood had run hot.

Now she gave him that one word, a deliberate reminder of his warning earlier in the day. *If you run, I will take you down.* He didn't have to think. Before his accelerated heart could beat more than twice, the cadence of a full-out pursuit, he was over the desk and after her.

~

She made it almost twelve steps into the yard, and then he'd caught her about the waist. Elisa let out a startled yelp, a little amazed at how quick he'd been, as well as at the unyielding strength of that one arm. Then she was turning into him, practically crawling up his body to reach his mouth, to tangle her hands in the hair at his nape as she sought his lips with clumsy fervency. He cupped the back of her head, slowing her down, steadying her so their mouths could meet. Before she could decide how best to go about things, he took over.

The heat of his mouth was an inexorable, tempting pressure that had her lips parting, inviting him in before she even had the thought to do so. She strained on her toes to reach him, but then he dropped his grip around her back and waist to cradle her buttocks. He hitched her up so her bare feet left the tops of his and curled around his thighs, her heels hooking there. Digging his long fingers into her curls, he pulled her head back, broke the contact between their mouths so he could explore her face with his lips and tongue, a curiously intimate feeling as she went still and tremulous. Nuzzling the length of her nose, he passed over each of her brows, kissed her eyes and traced his tongue along her cheekbone, the shell of her ear.

Her fingers dug into his back, her thighs tightening, and his voice was as tactile as his mouth, rubbing them together, mind to mind.

Tell me, sweet Irish flower. Is your cunt weeping for me to fill it? Have you been dreaming of my cock inside of you?

She nodded against his mouth, her eyes closing. *Yes, yes, yes.* She needed his gentle fierceness, the raw language. Her body had been aching for what he'd shown her with Shira's marking. His strength reined in, but no less able to pin her beneath him if he wished, make her submit.

"It's been growing in you for a while, hasn't it?" His voice was a hot wind, coursing through her body. He intensified it by speaking in her mind. *Groomed from birth to serve, but the feeling you have now, it would have been there whether you were born a maid or a princess. It's grown to a hard hunger, ever since you came into the service of a vampire. You crave a Master's touch, don't you, Elisa?*

She didn't know how to answer that. She knew only that tonight, she wanted, needed, to belong to him. As she always had, she'd take the joy of the moment, move forward and demand nothing more of the past than what was necessary to get through tomorrow.

Thankfully he didn't demand an answer. Instead, he moved them to a stretch of lawn adjacent to the house. Laying her down upon it, he knelt between her knees so her legs had to be parted for him. His attention moved over her breasts, the nipples shamelessly hard and pushing against the fabric, then down to the tender curve of her stomach. When he placed a hand on her upper thigh, even through the nightgown, she felt the heat and strength. A tiny noise escaped her lips, a needy sound.

"Took off your panties, did you? Came down without your wrap, knowing a man would see your body through this thin thing, be teased by it. Did you think of someone seeing you, like Kohana, or one of the others? One who might get the wrong idea?"

"No. I . . . I thought I was alone. I didn't even know you were here. I just needed to feel . . ." Suddenly she was uncertain of him, and herself, and what he might think, and cold invaded the heat. "I wasn't trying . . . I don't. I'm not like that."

"Shhh. I see that. I feel it. Easy." His knuckles turned, stroked down her leg. "I was just unsheathing my claws, Irish flower. You bring that out in me." His lip lifted in a brief, feral smile that brought the heat back. Then he leaned over her, his dark hair falling forward, so it brushed over her nipple. She arched to that faint touch and his expression intensified. "You thought I might take you like this, just slide that thin gown up and sheathe myself deep inside of you. But I want more than that. We're taking this off now. I'll see you naked to me."

The neckline had several buttons down the front amid a tiny bit of embroidery of dainty roses. He flicked them open, slid a corner back enough to reveal a collarbone, and then bent closer. She closed her eyes as his hair whispered over her face and his mouth pressed to that bone. The sharp drag of a fang made her draw in a breath, tightened her stomach further. He eased the gown off one shoulder, then the other, and began to pay close attention to them, moving out of the shallow valley of the collarbone to the curve of her right shoulder, nuzzling and nipping at it, while his hand tugged the gown down even farther on the right side.

"You taste like the grass we were lying in today. The sunshine you absorbed earlier in the day, before I rose. The food you helped Kohana prepare. You baked a chocolate cake for them." There was a trace of amusement in his voice. "With icing."

"They . . . they liked it."

"I'm sure they did. They'll refuse to let you leave. Did you have any icing left?"

"I . . . I did. But Tokala . . . licked the bowl . . . and spoon." He'd enjoyed it so much she'd thought about making another batch the next day and perhaps asking Mal if she could take a taste to the children. Jeremiah had shown a liking for chocolate before, at the station.

"You're starting to think about asking my permission for things. I like that." *It shows you think you might be able to trust me.*

Or I just don't want you yelling at me.

He muffled a chuckle against her, and the vibration sent out a composition of reactions from her nerve endings along the top of her breast and upper arm. *I don't yell. My punishments are far different from that, sweet Elisa.* "Maybe you'll make me a batch of that icing and bring it to me here tomorrow night. Do you know what I'll do with it?"

She didn't, but she was having a hard time thinking, for now his mouth was cruising over the top of her breast, following the path of his breath from his chuckle. When his lip settled on the upper curve, so close to her nipple it was pressing against his jaw, she felt that contraction between her legs again. He was between them, so she couldn't squeeze down on the feeling.

"No, you can't close them," he whispered. "Just like you won't be able to do so if I choose to take you to my bed at dawn, tie your legs so they're spread, each ankle hooked to a bedpost, your arms tied above your head. I'd lay down next to you so I can touch you as I sleep, my dreams haunted by the perfume of your cunt, soaked for me, your mind begging me to wake, to come inside of you."

She'd expected the wild animal. She hadn't expected this skilled mastery from a male who stayed cloistered on his island. Apparently he was better traveled than she'd believed. It frightened and thrilled her at once. Perhaps a sophisticated woman would know how to play this game, but she was close to begging now. Her eyes were almost as ready to weep as much as the other parts of her body were. *Please . . .*

There was a stillness to him as he paused over her breast, drew the nightgown down another few inches so her breasts emerged, the cloth tucking in under their rise, framing them for his gaze. "Keep begging, Irish flower. You've no idea how hard that makes me. You've got beautiful breasts. You'll eat some of that cake yourself so they'll get as full as they once were. Understand?"

She nodded, willing to agree to anything. "What were you going to do with the icing?" She couldn't take too much more. Her body was overloading with need, and her deeper emotions were too close. *Please* . . .

Sliding down her body a few inches, he settled his mouth above the nipple, and began to trace the areola, all around that stiff point, as if he were licking away icing in truth, in lazy circles and brief, sucking bites.

His body was pressed down on her pubic mound, and when he began doing that, she lost all control. She would have arched against him, writhed and rubbed, anything to get closer, to get more of what she wanted, but he was too clever for that. He used his hands to press down on her shoulders, keeping her immobilized for his ministrations.

Please, please, please . . .

"Please what, Elisa?" He spoke against her this time, and she shuddered at the way the words added to the stimulation.

"I need you . . . inside me. Please."

"Hmm." And he went back to what he was doing. She struggled; she cried out with every lash of his tongue, and outright screamed when his mouth closed over the nipple thoroughly, finally pulling on her in deep, dragging rhythms. She was trying hard to move her lower body against him, to get some type of friction. She was so wet, her fluids dampened that pocket between her sex and thigh, trickling down onto her buttocks.

She heard the various calls, growls and huffs of the nighttime hunters. The sawing notes of the leopards were closest. Even if they were in the very front yard, she wasn't afraid. She knew Mal was aware of their proximity as well, and it was a titillating thought, to think the creatures could smell what they were doing and knew it for what it was. Animals mated out for all the world to see, and why not? God saw everything, no matter the curtains and closed doors. He'd seen what Mr. Collins had done to her, just the same as what Victor had done.

She squeezed her eyes shut, and those frustrated tears ran down the sides of her cheeks.

"Easy." Mal cradled her face, and she pressed her mouth into his palm, willing it away. Then she bit, hard.

"Fierce cub." He'd moved the nightgown to her hips, his other hand exploring her navel, the rise of her belly, the flare of her hips, fingers tracing the edge of the gown, inches above her pubic bone. "I think it's time I unsheathe my claws a bit more, mark you with my scent."

She knew it was merely the intensity of the moment, that the words probably didn't mean anything special to him, but she couldn't say the same. What had started as a peculiar stirring with Lady Danny, elevated to a romantic yearning with Willis, had been goaded to full blazing life by Mal in two days. He was right; she'd been thinking about it for a while, somewhere deep and hidden. He'd just opened the door to it, discovered her secret, showed it to her.

In her bedroom she'd said it in such a soft whisper. *Master.* God help her, she wanted to embrace what she'd seen other vampires' servants accept, cloaking them with a confidence and surety, the knowledge that their Master or Mistress's ownership was something nothing could tear away from them, because the choice to accept it had been all theirs.

His eyes were on fire, full of crimson. Rising onto his knees, he slid the gown all the way free. Cupping her under her hips, his fingers molded her arse as he pulled the fabric down. She watched the play of muscles along his abdomen and shoulders, the way the lioness on his arm rippled with golden strength as she played with those feathers. He'd chosen to put a female on his arm, acknowledging her strength and beauty.

He bent again, and as a picture of Dev and Danny flashed in her head, she knew what he was going to do. It was something no one ever had done to her. The others . . . they wanted her to do that to them, but never . . .

His mouth cruised over her pubic bone, circling that thatch of wet curls; then he found her damp entrance. He didn't seal over it right away; he was far more diabolical than that. Instead he used the tip of his tongue again, teasing at that bud of flesh, the one that seemed to harbor such tremendous sensation, despite its small size. She moaned, her head thrashing back and forth on the grass, her hands gripping the blades, the earth, anything to hold herself down as he pushed down on her thighs, keeping her lower body captive to his desires. She couldn't buck against him, and that made the sensations that much more excruciating.

In some vague section of her mind she knew she should be mortally embarrassed because there was no way the second-marked hands in the bunkhouse couldn't hear her, her cries rising and falling, an erratic continual plea that only made him want to tease her more, a craving she knew she was feeding. It felt as if she was being drawn up far above herself, and in a moment, something was going to let go, and she was going to fly . . .

It's possible for women, too. She saw Danny in the library, her head thrown back, upper body flushed as Dev did this to her. It was a quick, near-incoherent flash in her mind, for Mal knew the precipice on which she teetered, and he had control of it all.

Lifting his head, he balanced his upper body over her, his mouth a firm line, lips glistening with her response. The rigid line of his shoulders and that glittering, intent gaze, as well as the size of his arousal pressing against her, told her he wasn't indifferent to her responses.

I'll fuck you into next week, Irish flower. That's how indifferent I am. I want them to hear. Want them to know I've had you.

The blunt words only made her tremble, long even more for him. *Please. Do it.* She would lie here for hours and days, take him into her body again and again to feel this way, this mindless, astonishing pleasure. It was the best she'd felt in so long.

He pulled open the front of his trousers in one efficient jerk; then he was lying down upon her, capturing her whole world by bracing his elbows on either side of her head. She turned her face into his forearm, inhaling that same earth and grass smell he'd scented on her.

No. Look me in the face. I want to see your eyes as I take you.

It was difficult, because she was learning how vulnerable a woman on the cusp of climax was, everything laid bare and unhidden. But she did it, locking gazes with him like a lifeline over raging whitewater. If that connection broke, she might be swept away in a storm where she'd never find her way home again. If she ever figured out where home was.

At the first touch of his cock to her entrance, a frisson of terrible memory went through her, making her shiver, but then he did something extraordinary. Like a picture show where everything went from very fast to very slow, he cupped her face, passing a thumb over her lips, a gesture fast becoming familiar. His eyes were so close, holding her in a still blink of time, where there was only the thundering of their hearts, their bodies trembling on the edge, so close, every part of her against every part of him. Connected, together. She wasn't alone. They were in this together. Then he closed the distance, put his mouth against hers, that light butterfly landing again, his tongue teasing her lips.

She let out a plaintive sound against his mouth, but she stayed still as that broad head pushed inside of her. He was thicker than the others had been, and longer, but as he sank deep into soaked flesh, that fullness became a deep, savage pleasure in the pit of her belly, the aching of her breasts, pressed against his hard chest.

All mine. The words came on a wind gusting through her as he withdrew enough to surge back in and stroke that part of her waiting for one electric touch of friction, a detonator.

"Oh . . ." Her mouth convulsed against his, as a similar involuntary reaction took over her body. "Mal . . ."

"Come for me, Elisa. Let me hear you scream. Grip my cock as hard as you can."

Without thinking, she did, muscles spasming around him as he went to a long thrust and retreat, something that dragged against that part of her that was overtaking all the rest, making her nails dig into his bare shoulders, her upper body coming off the ground to bury her face into his throat. She sank her teeth into his pectoral as he palmed the back of her head in one large hand and rocked with her, pumping deep and hard, making her feel the strength of every thrust, muscles rippling under her hands.

It was astounding, incredible, a taste of what Heaven had to be, this divine euphoria, yet so close to the earth, so visceral she wanted to taste his blood and flesh as she experienced it.

She also wanted him to release, wanted to feel the flood of his seed inside of her. It was something she'd never thought about wanting. She wanted to feel his heat and life coming into her. Vampire babies were so rare, vampires never used protection, because if a baby was conceived, it was always a treasured miracle. So she could feel him come into her without serious worry of that. Not that anything was worrying her at the moment.

In fact, all thought deserted her as he did climax, and the pressure of him jetting against still-spasming tissues sent her over another precipice, even higher than what she'd been experiencing. She did scream, over and over, the feeling too much for her to have any restraint. When she caught a glimpse of his face, it was rigid with his own pleasure . . . and the fierce satisfaction of pure male possession.

≈

She didn't quite know what to say when they'd caught their breath, or what to do, but he helped her on both counts. Sliding next to her on the grass, he turned her so she was spooned inside the shape of his body, his breath on her neck. She folded both her hands around his one, a loose tangle of fingers against her breasts, his thumb idly tracing the curve within his range. Nothing really needed to be said, right? It wasn't a moment to profess undying love. She had no expectations. Things inside of her were quiet, exhausted, girlish yearnings and romantic ideas muted by pure physical satiation. She found it wasn't an unpleasant place to be.

What girlish yearnings would those be, Irish flower? He pressed his mouth to her throat, and she let the thrill of it unfold lazily inside of her, the promise of more desire, more mindlessness.

"Don't," she whispered. "Just let this moment be . . . what it is. Please?"

He held his mouth there, his arms tightening around her, but he said nothing more, inside or out. At length, though, he rose, pulling his trousers back on. She was modest enough to lie curled on her side, but hungry enough to tilt her head to watch him, the play of muscle and limb, the gleam of moonlight on his skin. The way his genitals looked, cupped briefly in his hand before he tucked them back into the jeans. He hadn't been wearing underwear, either.

He retrieved her nightgown, which was good, because she wasn't sure where to start looking, and was a bit shy about getting up in the altogether and striding about to look for it. A smile touched his firm mouth, but he dropped to one knee and slid an arm beneath her, keeping the nightgown slung over his shoulder as he lifted her.

"Leave it," he said, as she tried to pull the edge of the gown over her. "I want to look at you."

He did, all the way back into the house, down the halls and then up the steps to her bedroom. Laying her on the mattress, he took a seat next to her, placing a hand on her thigh.

"Part them for me, Elisa," he commanded, and she obeyed, with a tremor that darkened those beautiful, long-lashed eyes as they gazed upon her. Threading his fingers in the damp curls, he made an idle pass over the sensitized flesh beneath, registering her indrawn breath, the additional quiver in her limbs.

"Did you like this? What we did?"

"You know I did. You're in my mind, after all."

"I'm in your mind. Not in your heart. When it comes to this, for women it's in the heart."

"But not for men. God's cruel joke."

He looked up at her then, but she didn't want to be sad. Didn't want to feel empty and alone after something so magnificent and overwhelming. So she pushed down whatever was trying to rear its ugly head and rose on her elbows. Gathering her courage, she curled her arm around his neck and pressed her mouth to his, perhaps a little too strongly, too fast, but she was afraid she'd appear stupid or be rebuffed.

Instead, his arm slid around her waist, tightening her against him so she could feel his bare chest against her breasts, the lean hardness of him. He persuaded her mouth to open, teaching her, and engaged in a complex choreography with her tongue, tangling with his until she was pressing harder, more insistently, against him. She wanted him inside again. When he was there, lying upon her, his cock deep between her legs, she felt sheltered against storms she'd never truly feared until that one terrible night. Tonight underscored how that one incident had changed how she viewed everything in her life. Made her angry and afraid, restless and needy at once. When he'd taken her down, she'd given it all to him, and he'd used it, used her up. Left her quiet. She liked quiet.

He eased her back, going with her until her head touched the pillow; then he broke contact, though he did it gently, cradling her face in strong hands, holding her there. "You need to sleep, *atsilusgi*. Sleep. Tomorrow is the same as any other day."

"Wh-what does that mean? What you just called me." His very command lifted her exhaustion up like a wave that immersed the burgeoning desire, taking her down into a pleasant lassitude. He kept stroking her a long time without answering, such that she finally started drifting off to sleep.

However, her last memory was of his fingers slipping reluctantly away from hers, and his answer in her head, this man who Kohana said never spoke his mother's language, yet had spoken it to her twice in the same day.

Flower.

16

SHE wasn't entirely sure how things would go on the following night, and was already telling herself not to act like a ninny. But as she cut tomatoes at the kitchen counter, helping Kohana handle the fixings for the meal planned later in the evening, she kept listening for his voice. Some of the staff were in the front room, but several were in the kitchen, grazing on the things that they were able to snatch from Kohana. When she wasn't worrying and flustered over Mal's arrival, she was enjoying the close quarters, the way the men picked on one another and her as they jostled around to snatch bits of bread and roast beef off the counter. Chumani sat on the center island, trying to distract Kohana with her usual vinegar-and-sugar barbs. Elisa could tell Kohana was fully aware of the ploy, and thwarted some of the more aggressive attempts easily.

They were a family. Of course, unlike a family, when they'd all come in earlier, there'd been no speculative looks, nothing that indicated they knew what had transpired on the grass outside, though there was no way no one had heard or seen. At first, their apparent courtesy soothed her, but then she started thinking about it. Was it so usual for Mal to ravish a human guest out on the lawn that it wasn't worth one mortifying sidelong glance?

See, she was acting like a ninny already. *For Heaven's sake, he's known you for two days. How do you think he's going to act?* Vampire, human. Capital Vampire, lowercase human. He wasn't a lover, a beau or anything else. Just like the staff, he likely wouldn't act any differently around her. Except that he might decide to ravish her again, which she already knew she'd embrace, no matter how ashamed it made her.

Hearing his voice in the front room, she jerked, her cheeks flushing before she could prevent the reaction. She kept her head ducked down, her eyes on the tomatoes, telling herself to act completely normal, never mind he could certainly sense the turmoil in her mind.

Fortunately, he was busy. He laid out the night's work schedule, mentioned that they had two lions being flown in tonight. They would be checked over and then put in the western area to stretch their legs. After he sent the hands on their way, he turned to Kohana. Realizing it would look peculiar if she kept her gaze so studiously averted, she raised her head, holding the knife at rest.

He wore the usual khaki cargo trousers and a close-fitting T-shirt tonight, but now she was hyperaware of the body beneath the clothes. Her hand had clasped the hard biceps, small fingers overlaying the barbed wire and feather design of his tattoo. His hair was brushed back into a short queue, emphasizing the precise line of his jaw, the hawklike nose and defined cheekbones. But she'd dug her fingers into that wild mane, held on as he shattered her. Had he bathed at dawn, rubbing the damp stickiness of her body from his cock?

She had no idea what he'd just said to Kohana, but now those dark brown eyes shifted to her. "You'll stay in the house with Kohana for the first part of the night, while we deal with the lions. If that goes well, I'll be back to get you later. I'll radio in."

He was . . . the way he'd always been toward her. Unpredictable. Grumpy or showing her a glimpse of humor. One moment distant, the next not even a breath between their bodies. Only now, distant or far, her body was singing for that touch, taut with anticipation. She managed a nod. "Yes, sir."

He lifted a brow, then turned, headed out the front. A few moments later, she heard the Jeep start up and leave the yard. When it did, she let out a shuddering breath, turned back to the tomatoes. She was cognizant of Kohana's scrutiny, his grunt, a commentary hard to interpret.

Ninny. She was a total ninny.

~

She attacked the job of scrubbing all the wood floors in the house, something that hadn't been done in some time. As she did that, she gave herself a far sterner lecture about vampires. They took when they wanted to take, and when they didn't, you waited on their pleasure. She'd begged him to take last night, and he had. It would be up to him to set the pace of what this was.

She closed her eyes, pushing a damp curl from her sweaty face. God in Heaven, did he know how hungry she was for more, so ravenous that she felt dizzy with it if she thought too long or hard upon it? As she pushed the brush back and forth, both hands clasped on it, all she could think about was the movement of her body. What if he came up behind her, and her jerking rhythm was caused by something else, his thrusting into her?

If love wasn't part of it, then so much the better. Her cracked heart couldn't handle that yet. While she knew she wanted a family, home and babies, vampires didn't do that. In his world, her shameless behavior wasn't condemned, and maybe what he gave her would help her heal, so she could pursue that domestic dream once more. While she'd be here until things were resolved with the fledglings, she wouldn't be here forever. Eventually she'd go back to the station, another reason there was no point to imagining this as far more than it was.

"You're going to strip the finish off those floors, you keep doing that."

She jumped, then gave a nervous half laugh. Sitting back on her heels, she swiped at her forehead with the point of her wrist, and eyed Kohana, feeling the ache in her shoulders. "That's not finish; that's grime. I think these were originally bleached pine wood."

He grunted. "Just took some bread out of the oven. Come get a piece with some cheese. You've earned it."

"I was hoping you'd offer. It smells marvelous. Every crumb will be gone ten seconds after they all come back. I'll finish this spot and then come."

Kohana shook his head. "Might want to finish up now. Mal radioed and said he'd be here in about fifteen minutes. Wants you ready to go."

"Oh." She brightened, though she couldn't say if it was because she was going to see the fledglings, or because Mal was the one taking her. At Kohana's scowl, she reached out, hooking both of her hands over his one large one to help her off her protesting knees. "You shouldn't worry, you know. I'm not a child. It's not like I think it's love or anything."

She didn't see any reason to pretend that she didn't understand the reason behind his scowl, but at her words, it only deepened. "To him, you're a child *and* a woman. It's a dangerous combination to any male. Makes us think we can act like children ourselves while we take what a man wants. Don't go convincing yourself you can be a vampire's full servant, Elisa."

Her mouth almost dropped open. "He hasn't even offered—"

Kohana waved a hand, cutting her off. "You need love. A family. Don't fool yourself into believing you can settle for less than that just because you got hurt. And no, I don't want to hear anything else about it. I have laundry to do. Go away."

She lifted her brows, but obediently headed for the kitchen, carrying her bucket and brush. However, as she passed him, she bumped his hip with it, giving him a reassuring smile. "I know all that, Kohana. I'm okay. Really."

From his skeptical snort, she guessed only time would convince him. She decided to ignore the fact that his words had been uncomfortably close to her own uneasy rationalizations.

She'd put away her cleaning supplies and was eating the bread and cheese when Mal arrived in the Jeep. He hit the horn once to summon her out to join him. Not in a gentlemanly mood today, she thought wryly, but picked up her basket of things for the children and headed out.

He looked a little less relaxed than he had earlier. The arm of the shirt had been ripped and his khakis were stained with dirt. "Everything okay?" she ventured.

As soon as she got settled, he put the Jeep in gear, but he gave her a brief shrug. "The new lion pair were a bit tricky to handle. One of them was wearing a harness that had been put on him as an adolescent. It had grown into his skin and needed to be removed. They don't respond well to tranquilizers, but we put him under for a few minutes to get it free and treated. Just a busy evening so far."

She was sure he'd been calm during all that, but now, away from

them, she picked up his anger at the treatment of the animals, and the
settling of nerves that came in the aftermath of handling two dangerous
creatures. Plus the tension of overseeing staff members who were far
more vulnerable to maiming.

She shifted around on her hip so she could look at him, because she
might as well not deny she liked looking at him, imagining the way that
lean body had curved over hers only hours before. "We had a stockman
with a mean streak to him. Kicked one of the dogs one day when the
poor thing was doing nothing more than sleeping in the sun. Broke a
rib or two. Willis gave that man a thrashing within an inch of his life
and sent him off with no back pay, telling him he could consider the
fact he could still walk payment enough." She nodded with firm convic-
tion. "Some people need a foot up the backside; that's the truth. And
the larger the foot, the better."

Mal's jaw eased, amusement crossing his face. "That's about the size
of it."

"And here you are, after such a busy night already, having to chaperone me."

"You're a pain in my ass," he agreed. He dropped his gearshift hand
onto her thigh just above her knee, his fingers resting with casual intimacy in the seam between her legs. She stilled all over as his gaze flickered to her. "Did you bring my blood?"

She nodded. "After a fashion. I thought you might want to drink
from me. I know vampires prefer that to refrigerated blood. I'm here,
and a girl, and second-marked, so you might as well, right?"

He was on a curve, so his startled glance stayed on her a beat too
long. Mal cursed, correcting the course with a protesting squeal of tires.
Branches of the roadside foliage slapped and squeaked against the hood
as he brought the Jeep to a halt.

She was pretty certain he wasn't stopping to take her up on the offer,
but her pulse pounded at the mere thought. She didn't think she'd offered anything inappropriate, but maybe she was wrong. Part of the
reason she suspected vampires had such a distracting effect on human
sensibilities was that one saw them only at night. During daylight, a
person had a lot less fanciful ideas. Ideas that, in hindsight, might make
him think she had kangaroos loose in her top paddock.

He turned toward her, his scrutiny uncomfortably shrewd. "Since I was able to help scald the top layer off one bad memory, letting me drink from your throat might scald away another? Is that about the size of it?"

The moment he said it, there it was, bright as the harsh glare of full sun in the desert. Victor gulping at her throat, a wet, sickening suction she couldn't break because she was helpless against him. Just like that baby impala, still alive and kicking as the cubs played with its legs.

Her hands convulsed on the basket, but he wasn't of a mind to ease off or be reassuring. "I asked you a question, Elisa. And I want the answer out loud, not from your mind."

"Yes," she said shortly. She turned her face away from him. They were in the plains region right now, so she could see the swaying meadow grass, the lonely outline of the few craggy trees dotting the expanse. A small wildebeest herd was nearby, at the watering area. She could hear their lowing and their grunts. If the wind shifted, she was sure she'd get their overpowering musky aroma. Would any lose their lives to the cats tonight?

"In Africa, their saliva and waste stimulates grass growth. Since they follow the rains, they don't stay long in any one place. It's very beneficial, ecologically."

She glanced at him, a brow raising at the unexpected change of topic. "During a drought," he continued, holding her gaze, "they become absolutely fearless in their pursuit of food. They might jump a dangerous riverbank, risking broken limbs and certain death to get to another food source. Because at that point the only thing they fear is starvation. Much like a person who will make extremely foolish decisions when the only thing she fears is her memories."

She turned her face away again, tightening the grip on the basket. He sighed. "Yes, I am patronizing. But I'm not wrong."

"Why is it foolish?" She glared at him. "You're hungry; I have a neck. It seems rather practical. I was just offering. If you don't want it, then fine. There's no reason to turn it into more than it is. No reason to turn *anything* into more than it is."

She really had turned a corner if she was snapping at a vampire like a fishwife. He surprised her by making another noncommittal grunt, much like Kohana, and put the Jeep back in drive. Only instead of turning down the road that led to the enclosures, he kept going.

Elisa's heart leaped into her throat, but then she realized they weren't returning to the house, unless they were taking a much longer route to do it. She wanted to ask, but instead she rummaged in the basket to withdraw the bottle of blood. Unscrewing the cap, she extended the offering ungraciously, catching his attention with the movement. Once he took it, brushing her fingers in a purely utilitarian way, she turned her eyes back toward the terrain, not wanting to see him drink it, not after her offer had been so summarily rejected.

"Are we going somewhere else first?" she asked at last.

"We're going somewhere else. Hold on to the bar. It gets bumpy through here."

She complied and passed the rest of the ride in silence, because it was what he seemed to prefer as well. Was he regretting last night? She'd never observed regret in a vampire, whereas humans seemed plagued by it. Perhaps because of those foolish things they did. Like getting out of bed in the middle of the night for milk. The silence that had been comfortable right after their lovemaking was definitely no longer.

She took a steadying breath. "You know, I have a right to make my own decisions. You gave me the choice and I made it last night. I'd make the same decision again in a heartbeat, and I'd do it full well knowing that it means something different to you than it does to me. Just like giving you my blood. I don't expect anything from that. I just wanted to offer."

There, she'd said it. She suspected she'd get further by saying it to a barn wall, but she wasn't going to be a sniveling coward about it. A few minutes later, in the lengthening silence, Mal brought the Jeep to a halt at the edge of a field. They were underneath the spreading branches of a gnarled tree that looked like an old, knotted woman. As they rolled under it, she felt that shimmer she was beginning to recognize as passage through another energy field set by the sorcerer.

Getting out of the Jeep, he came around to her side before she could get out on her own. He placed the basket on the hood, grasped her by the elbows and brought her out. He didn't move back, so she pressed against his body. Her hands had lifted, unsure of his intent, but his closed over her wrists, guided her arms down to her sides, holding them there. Bending for the difference in their heights, he nudged her head into a tilt, bringing his mouth to her throat.

She went still, except for a leaping pulse. He didn't bite, though. Just held her like that for a long, charged moment, letting her feel the heat of his breath. "I can't drink from you right now, Elisa. Not right before you see the fledglings. It leaves a trace scent of fresh blood on your throat, and they're not stable enough to handle that." He pressed his lips against her racing artery, though, and she shuddered, knowing her whole body went tight and liquid in all the right places, a mere heart-beat afterward.

"Of course, the scent of your arousal is capable of doing the same. It makes me want to bend you over the front of this Jeep and take you quick and hard, because my cock has been aching for that sweet wet pussy of yours since yesterday."

Her fingers flexed in his unrelenting grip, wanting the same thing, wanting it fiercely. Too soon, he let her go, stepped back, but he tilted her face up to his. "Later, Elisa. I will take blood from you later. And anything else I want."

Well, so much for thinking she could tone down her reaction before she saw—

She snapped back to that one point. "The fledglings are *here*?"

"They're over that rise there. Three of them. Jeremiah, Matthew and Miah. They were transported in a secure vehicle and Tokala is waiting for me to take over. Remember how I told you we use this western area for the caged cats, because it's cordoned off magically from the others?" At her nod, he continued. "They'll have it to themselves tonight, except for Thai and Bello, two of our older circus lions. The two new ones were too wrought up to bring them here tonight."

She imagined Jeremiah seeing a lion for the first time in his life. "They can't hurt each other, right?"

He shook his head. "The lions pretty much romp when they get out. I'll try to make sure the fledglings get to see them, but Thai and Bello will probably be fairly indifferent to them."

The fledglings were going to run, be free. Even on the miles and miles of land that made up Danny's station, they hadn't been able to give them that. Joy bloomed in her heart, twining with the lingering arousal to give her a surge of delightful anticipation.

"It does have a practical purpose, other than to exercise my generous and affable nature," Mal said dryly. Taking her hand, he guided her across the field, walking up toward the rise. "They need to exhaust themselves, run until the muscles are burning, the lungs are straining and the heart is pumping like mad, to burn off the demons in their minds. It may help them feel less antsy, help them control their physical reactions like the bloodlust better. We'll see."

His sudden even glance drew her attention from the fact he was holding her hand, so easy and natural. "You're here as a test, Elisa. To see how they do around a human who isn't supposed to be their prey. I've purposely chosen those three because of the way they act around you. Even so, you'll stay at my side at all times. If I go run with them, you'll stay with Tokala. I'll keep them drawn away from the both of you. The same rules apply here. You obey anything Tokala or I tell you to do, without question. Understood?"

"Understood." In pure delight, she seized both his hands and spun around him, taking him in the spin with her. She finished by teetering up on her sneaker toes to brush his cheek with her lips. "This is wonderful. Thank you. They've never had this."

He gave her a look of wry exasperation, but shook his head and tugged her onward. The grass was high and whispered against her trouser legs. Mal carried her basket and kept a steady grip on her to help her maintain her footing, reminding her there was a practical reason he'd taken her hand. Still, she couldn't entirely get her head out of the clouds.

"Were you . . . ? Did you ever wear real Indian clothing, like you see in the books?"

"Hush." But after a second, he slanted her another glance. "Why?"

"When I have dreams of the island, you're wearing things like in the history books. Leggings, loincloth, beads."

"You're still having dreams like you did in my bed?"

The phrasing made her cheeks pinken, but his speculative glance made her realize he was thinking it was related to the mystery of why she could see his fault lines. She cleared her throat. "They seem just as vivid. Did you ever . . . wear things like that?"

He grunted. "No, I never did. By the time I was born, the Tsalagi were participating in a Westernization effort, trying to fit in with white society." His lip curled, and those storm clouds scudded across his face. "But I remember seeing the elders in traditional clothing. They looked better that way."

As they crested the top slope of the hill, she saw the vehicle he'd indicated. The boxlike structure on the trailer bed held the three fledglings, because she saw their movement through the openings as they moved to each of the few windows, rotating their view.

"Do they know why they're here?" Fear gripped her as she remembered the only time Ruskin transported them was to play his sick, brutal games with human prey.

"Yes, they do. Which is why they're bouncing around in there like they're on a hot tin plate." However, even Mal sounded like he was anticipating how they would react to this. Seeing something meant to be free experiencing it for the first time couldn't help but affect him, she was sure. For the first time since their capture, they were being allowed out for their own pleasure, not Ruskin's.

Wistfully, she jumped ahead in her imaginings. Thought of them as working members of the sanctuary, Jeremiah helping Mal with the cats, Miah curled up with a book in the front room, reading aloud to Kohana . . .

He said nothing to that, but took her down the slope where Tokala waited, leaning against the truck. At the sight of Elisa, he gave her a nod and smile, but his manner was far more serious than when she saw him taking meals or relaxing around the bunkhouse with the others. In the front seat, she saw a shotgun as well as a crossbow. Despite her trepidation, she understood it was a necessary precaution even the fledglings would expect.

Jeremiah was looking out the trailer opening closest to her. Because of the height, she could see only the top portion of his face, not the unnaturally protruded fangs, so she saw serious gray-green eyes and blond hair, a sprinkle of freckles across the nose. When she looked at the eyes, she saw the unusual vibrancy there, the intent focus of a predatory animal, but otherwise it was the face of a young boy. She had to suppress the desire to put her fingers up there, let them overlap his. He disappeared again, and Miah and Matthew took his place, each craning to see her.

"Hello, all of you." She smiled at them. "I'm glad you're going to get out tonight."

"I've already run down the rules with them," Mal spoke. "Same as the enclosures, Elisa. Not within four feet of you, all right? Go sit on the hood of the truck."

She instantly moved to scramble up onto it. Mal put her basket next to her and squeezed her leg. Whether it was a reassurance or an admonishment to stay like an obedient dog, she didn't know, but she'd accept both. Clasping her hands together, she looked up toward the stars, too excited to watch while Mal and Tokala opened the truck. She needed to be calm. As she drew deep breaths, she studied that thick, jeweled, dark velvet curtain and felt like she could reach up, put her hand through it to touch whatever lay beyond. *The place the dog ran.* Perhaps someone on the other side of that curtain would clasp her hand, draw her up to show off the wonders.

For tonight, however, the wonders she wanted to see were earthbound. She didn't know exactly how she knew when they were out, because they all moved so silently, but she slowly lowered her chin to look right at Jeremiah. He stood what she was sure was precisely four feet away from her. He gazed at her with those gray-green eyes, no bars between them. For the very first time.

"Hello, Jeremiah," she said softly. She was aware of Mal to her left, so close and watchful. She wasn't afraid, though. Whether it was foolishness or not, she had never been afraid of Jeremiah. She'd fear Nerida before she would fear him. In Oz it was customary to give people with long names nicknames, so he should have been called Jez, but she wanted him to have the whole thing. Something weighty that was his own, though she wondered if he'd ever give her the gift of his real name. It didn't matter. He could be whatever he needed to be tonight.

He tilted his head up toward the sky like she had, only he kept doing it, until his neck strained and his back arched. As he did, he lifted his arms like a bird, stretching out far to either side. He straightened enough to turn a circle, then another, becoming a slowly spinning top.

Her heart was swelling painfully in her chest. His eyes closed as he did it, as if he was embracing the whole world. Looking left, she saw

Miah watching him bemusedly. Matthew was trying the same thing, though he was far more interested in looking at every single thing he could at once, like a puppy let off a lead for the first time, overcome with everything he wanted to do and see. The two fledglings were a few feet away from Jeremiah. A sidelong glance showed Tokala was to her right, holding the crossbow. She didn't see Mal now, but she knew he was there, his presence a physical, living thing inside of her. Whether or not he thought the fledglings were doomed, tonight he'd let them out, expecting them to follow his rules without threat of whips, violence or emotional manipulation. It was the first breath of fresh air they'd had in a long time, in more ways than one.

Miah and Matthew needed Jeremiah's lead, though, because one mere moment could not build trust or eradicate fear. They were looking behind her now, even as Jeremiah continued to spin. Twisting around, she found Mal on top of the truck, legs crossed in a relaxed fashion, hands lying on his knees.

She turned her gaze back to Jeremiah as he came to a stop, swaying. As he looked at her again, she saw that brilliance in his eyes had migrated to his expression. Just a minute tightening of facial muscles here and there, not a broad open smile of course, but it was transformation. The face of someone who'd been trudging through hellfire so long his skin had peeled off, leaving him as nothing but bone and lost soul, changing as he saw a tiny window to Heaven open right in front of him.

His arms were still straight out from his body, but when he stopped his spinning, he was facing more toward Tokala than her. Though he still stood four feet away, that arm was within a foot of her. Mal hadn't said anything, and though she might be rebuffed, she asked anyway, in her mind, showing him what she wanted.

Yes. Briefly.

She nodded, showing Jeremiah she'd gotten agreement, that he wasn't breaking any rules, and slowly lifted her hand from her lap. He latched onto that motion, but kept his hand motionless, poised in the air. She had to bend forward from the hood, but it was still easy enough to let her fingertips approach his. Jeremiah made an odd sound in his throat. Maybe it was a growl, but to her ears it sounded like a caught sob. His fingers quivered, and then the pads of hers met his, one, two, three. He lifted his palm so she could do the same with thumb and small finger,

four and five. She smiled, but her eyes were brimming. He tracked the
tear that rolled down her face.

All right, draw back now, Elisa. Don't tempt fate.

She closed her eyes, then opened them to give Jeremiah a reassuring
look. "Go play now," she murmured. "Go run with Mal. Feel what it's
like to be free."

He gave her that long, penetrating look again; then he glanced up at
Mal. Mal rose from his seated position, tall against the night sky, gesturing toward the open plain. "Go do as you like. You can't cause any
harm. I'll be near."

Matthew and Miah looked to their self-appointed leader. Jeremiah
pivoted toward the field. There was a moment of breathless anticipation, when Elisa thought all of them might be holding their breath;
then all of a sudden, Jeremiah took off. A vampire like Mal could move
swifter than the eye could follow. Jeremiah might be a bit slower, but he
was still faster than any car or train she'd ever experienced. She was
only able to track him for a few seconds across the field, the other two
following, before they disappeared over the rise. The thrill of it tingled
through her, all the way to her toes.

Jumping down off the Jeep, Mal directed his words to Tokala. "Keep
her near and safe."

Tokala nodded. "I've brought cards and some coffee. We're good as
long as you need. And I'm sure the little miss won't be itching for you
to put them back in that box until they've run themselves down."

Mal looked toward her then, shifting so his lower abdomen was
pressed against her knees, propped up by her feet braced on the front
bumper. "You asked me," he noted.

"I always ask you."

"Yes, but usually only because you're afraid I won't let you do what
you want to do if you disobey. You don't obey me instinctively. You did
this time."

"Oh. Well." A bit unsettled by his look, she dropped her gaze and
smoothed the legs of her trousers fastidiously. The one thing that
jumped into her mind came purely from nervousness, since she wasn't
sure what else to say, but of course he had to choose that moment to
read it. It elicited a smile of pure wickedness, those curved, sensual lips

taking her breath away and giving her an altogether different kind of tingle.

"Don't worry," he responded. "I won't let it go to my head."

Then he, too, was off. She didn't see his passage, only the movement of the grasses in his wake.

"They really are too much for the senses," she complained.

Tokala gave her a grin. "Best not to say so. Hearing that from a pretty girl will make him all the more full of himself."

17

SHE wondered if the second mark would give her the ability to see what was happening through his eyes, or if that was a third-mark thing only. Dev had tried to explain the differences between the second and third marks to her, and there seemed to be quite a bit of overlap, with the exception of the third-mark's extended life span and soulbinding. She wasn't sure she believed that last part, though. A third-mark died when their vampire died; that was true enough. But the theory was that the human's soul had to follow the vampire wherever it went in the afterlife. To her, that sounded like something vampires had made up to prop up their sense of self-importance, because no one knew for sure that was true, and she didn't think they could overrule God's opinion in the matter.

Maybe the story meant something far different, like Bible stories that sounded unlikely, but when a person really got to thinking about them, they made logical sense. If a servant became a vampire's third-mark willingly, they served them with everything they were, meshing their fates, consciences, morality, everything. Not all vampire pairings were like Danny and Dev. There were those who visited the station who obeyed their vampire without question, doing whatever he or she was told. In those cases, the third-mark might be an abdication of one's right to choose right and wrong. The servant's sins were linked to the vampire's, and that was why the afterlife fates were the same.

Or maybe the third-mark bond was so close the servant couldn't bear to lose it, even to the promise of Heaven, so he or she chose to follow the vampire wherever they went after death. Even if his mortality wasn't bound to his lady's, Elisa couldn't imagine Dev taking one additional breath after Danny did.

"You're going to crack your face, you're thinking so hard," Tokala observed. He was rooting through her basket, working through the sweet biscuits—cookies—she'd baked. She'd brought a few morsels for the children, but now she was glad Kohana had told her to bring the whole batch along. He'd apparently anticipated Tokala's appetite. And hers, because she accepted two when he offered. Her appetite had been better lately. The parts of her Mal wanted more plump were going to be obliging soon.

Elisa?

His voice gave her an additional rush of blood. It was intriguing—as well as a bit annoying—how the erotic richness of his tone didn't dilute a bit when it was a thought in her head. If anything, it intensified it.

I want you to open your senses the way I showed you, but instead of focusing on your immediate surroundings, focus on me. I'm opening a track in my mind for you to see something, but you have to imagine stepping inside of me, seeing through my eyes. Just like before, don't get in the way of it. Just let it happen.

She was ready for it to be a struggle, something hard, but maybe she was already used to focusing so well with Danny in her head. It was as easy as the click of a door, stepping over a threshold and going down a narrow passageway that had light at the end. If she put her hands on those walls, she'd sense his other thoughts moving behind them. It was like he was Moses, and he'd cut a swath through the ocean of his mind, leading her to a picture, a front-row seat to see through his eyes.

She drew in a delighted breath. The fledglings had found a water hole, a tributary off the main river that ran through the island. Vampires didn't swim because they had no buoyancy, but they could certainly wade. And Jeremiah was, his pants rolled up to his knees. Miah was holding the skirt of her dress, and Matthew . . .

In her physical body, Elisa closed her hands into knots of painful joy as Matthew snuck up on Jeremiah and splashed him, starting off a substantial water fight. The three sent sheets of water spattering at one another, then chased one another up and down the banks like squirrels. Whenever they paused, one might submerge entirely, just to marvel at how they could walk beneath the water's surface without floating. Then they were off and running again.

Thought you'd like to see that. Need to close down now. A little tough holding this open for a second-mark.

Yes, of course . . . Thank you, Mal. Thank you so much.

Realizing it was the first time she'd called him by his given name without prompting, she hastily added the honorific. *Sir.*

His inner smile was like the touch of sunlight on her hair, and then that tunnel went dark again. But she still felt surrounded by his awareness of her, even though he was not within sight. It made her smile, too.

Tokala was giving her a look, and she cleared her throat, explained what she'd been seeing. The Indian grunted, but his eyes danced. "They're at the water hole, three miles from here. I expect if I'd had the chance to see that, my eyes would be sparkling like blue flowers, too. And my cheeks would be all rosy from blushing."

"Oh, shut it."

He laughed at her then, offered her another biscuit. She played a few hands of poker with him, betting the last of the biscuits, and then decided she'd gather up some of the wildflowers to put in vases in the house, since there were some varieties here that weren't readily accessible in the yard. She found a bucket in the back of the Jeep, a stream within sight to fill it with water and keep the wildflowers fresh. She usually carried a penknife with her, as there was often a need for such a thing for a stray thread or other trifles, such as flower cutting.

Tokala stretched out on the hood, his long form easy in the pose, one knee crooked up as he kept an eye on her and watched the stars. Enjoying their companionable silence, she moved slowly through the long grasses, considering her choices. She realized she was almost happy tonight. It gave her a sharp pang, thinking of Willis dead in that barn, and her happy here.

Don't matter if the sun shines for me or not, girl. Long as you're smiling.

She blinked back the tears, remembering he'd said that to her, one morning when she'd complained it was overcast. It wasn't that she didn't miss him. Things were just going better now with the fledglings. The weight of worry she carried on her heart about their future seemed to be lessening, as if Mal was shouldering some of it in truth. He wouldn't be going to these lengths if he truly believed they were a lost cause, right?

She chided herself. That man was so thorough, even if he thought the fledglings were beyond hope, he'd want to make good and sure of it. But oh, how could anyone with a heart and soul feel that way, seeing them playing in the water like that? Monsters didn't have water fights, didn't have the beginnings of laughter on their faces, experiencing it as if for the very first time. In truth, they might not remember the last time they laughed, or if they'd ever laughed at all.

"Bugger." Her bucket bobbled on her arm as her ankle twisted abruptly in a soft depression. When she yelped, she lost hold of her penknife. "Oh, *bother*." She knew the sharp jab of pain that heralded a sprain. And damnation, even with the second-mark accelerated healing, if it was a bad one, she'd be hobbling at least until sometime tomorrow. Only third-marks healed within minutes, and sometimes they needed the Master's blood to do it. Vampire blood didn't do that much to accelerate second-mark healing; otherwise, this would be a gift instead of a pain in the arse, because it was a perfect excuse to get close to Mal's tempting throat.

Tokala sat up quickly at her cry, but she waved at him. "Just turned my ankle, is all. Clumsy. Let me get these last purple ones, and then I'll come that way."

Moving to the edge of the hood, he propped his boots on the bumper and gave her a grin, spitting out the wad of grass he'd been chewing. "Won't get you out of cleaning and cooking. Kohana'll say you did it on purpose and figure out things much worse you can do sitting down."

She chuckled. Three days ago, Kohana wouldn't have let her do anything if she hadn't insisted, but now he was starting to welcome her help. It made her feel good, another thing that added to her happiness quotient. It really was remarkable. It'd been so long since she actually felt . . . good. Willis wouldn't begrudge her feeling better. He'd cross his arms and say, "'Bout time, girl. Been wallowing long enough." Then he'd give her that wink. She'd swat at him and he'd pull her over to rub his whiskers against her cheek until she was helplessly giggling and pushing him away.

Ah, blimey, she *was* moving like a hobbled horse, limping her way to that last clutch of flowers. Maybe she'd ask Tokala to come cut them for her. She could sit here for a minute and—

She'd kept her senses wide-open, so if Mal contacted her again, she'd have her engine running and foot on the gas pedal, so to speak. But she also found she really liked taking in so much more of what was happening around her. The sigh of the wind, the various smells of flowers, the way the long grasses felt, brushing her hips. However, now those senses gave her something else. An imminent sense of danger.

When she spun, the animal smell hit her, strong and immediate, as well as the huffing breath, the rumble of a growl in a deep, wide chest. Her bones liquefied into pure terror as she saw the lion charging toward her. That rumble was because he was closing in for a kill, his amber eyes so intent, his mane a swirling riot of rust color around the smooth face. The second mark gave her every vivid detail, amplified by her absolute certainty that her life was about to end.

It was so sudden, she had no time to think or act. Her heart caught in her throat as the creature leaped, its powerful haunches propelling him up and out, his speed mesmerizing. Almost as mesmerizing as the vampire who hit him midbody.

The lion's roar was a deafening explosion of surprise, but before Elisa could draw breath, she was seized in hard hands that flung her painfully over a shoulder. A jolting run across the ground; then she was dumped into the Jeep's backseat. Tokala slammed the door closed, then ran a few yards from the Jeep, bringing the rifle to his shoulder.

Elisa scrambled up to the open window, a cry catching in her throat. The grasses were a tornado of motion as the two beings struggled. There was a flash as they surfaced, and she saw Mal grappling with the lion, then ducking under the swipe of a paw, avoiding wide, fang-filled jaws that could have crunched down on her skull like shellfish. The lion had more than one set of claws, however, and as they rolled, the powerful back legs raked, tearing open the jeans and flesh covering Mal's left leg. A geyser of blood erupted and Elisa cried out.

"Mal."

Tokala fired into the air. It might have worked if the creature didn't have blood in his nose, but he was as gripped in bloodlust as one of the fledglings. As fast as they were grappling, the Indian had no clear shot, though Elisa knew he could shoot through the vampire if needed, since a bullet wouldn't kill Mal. She wondered why he didn't, shouted in panic at Tokala to take the shot, and then realized Mal wouldn't want the lion harmed unless absolutely necessary.

Tokala cursed and leaped forward. As Elisa watched in amazement, he darted in, seized the lion's tail and twisted it, hard. At the same time, he yanked on it, using his second-mark strength to haul the lion back several feet. *By his tail.* The creature howled in pain, turned like a whipping snake.

"No!" But Tokala was already backpedaling and fired directly into the ground between him and the lion, spraying up dirt and grass and startling the creature. It gave Mal the moment he needed. He threw himself on the lion, pulling the beast onto his haunches and locking his fists around the maddened creature's neck, a wrestler's headlock.

Get her out of here. Elisa heard the thundering command in her mind and Tokala was already in motion. She scrambled to the front, shoved open the door. Tossing the rifle in the back, Tokala slammed into the driver's seat, turned the engine over, fishtailing the vehicle to get up the slope and back toward the service road. She twisted around in the seat in time to see Mal release the lion, thrust him away, and then the vampire was no longer there, moving out of the animal's range faster than she could follow, despite that grievous injury.

Less than two minutes, and it was all over. As they reached the top of the hill and the road, she looked back and saw the lion at the abandoned trailer. Mal's blood had sprayed against it, such that the beast was hitting the metal side with his body, roaring, as if he thought his prey had escaped in there. She noted he was trampling the flowers she'd dropped when Tokala had been running with her.

Her mind was pinwheeling, panicked. *Mal? Mal?*

I'm here, Irish flower. I'm well outside of Thai's range now. He'll calm down in a bit. I'll meet you on that next ridge.

She glanced toward Tokala, whose face was tense, lips pressed tight. "It's okay; they're all right."

He gave her a half nod, and she realized he was listening to someone else. Someone giving him what for, because he looked like he was being beaten with a tire iron sitting still.

This wasn't his fault. Sir? Mr. Malachi?

He ignored her, making her jaw clench. How could Tokala have known the lion would come out of nowhere like that? The western section had miles of area, after all. Even Mal hadn't expected them to be around. They'd be *indifferent*, he'd said. When they pulled up to the ridge, though, her worried irritation over that was eclipsed. Mal was sitting on the ground, that frightening tear in his jeans soaked with blood, and he was pale.

As the Jeep slowed, Elisa was all set to jump out, but Tokala clamped down on her arm. "Wait." He nodded, and then she saw what he did. Jeremiah, standing at the edge of the forest.

Mal managed to get to his feet, and though he didn't look toward Jeremiah, she could tell by the set of his shoulders he was well aware of the young vampire's proximity. Their bloodlust could be set off by violence, weakness, the smell of blood itself, and this moment was rife with all three.

However, that didn't appear to be Mal's primary concern. He was pure vampire now, the one who commanded all of them, his expression devoid of emotion or familiarity. Tokala got out of the Jeep to face his employer, his eyes anguished and smooth face tight.

"You want me to get my stuff and leave, I will, Mal. No excuse for it. Just plain stupid, in so many ways."

"No." Elisa got out, though the fact she was having to hop took some of the dignified determination away from it. "You can't fire him. The lion came out of nowhere."

"No, he didn't." Tokala turned toward her, since Mal said nothing. "I knew there were two of them wandering the preserve. I should have been keeping my senses tuned to it. They likely wouldn't have bothered us, even if they saw us, because they're familiar with humans, but it was your limping that drew him. Sets off a prey radar and he pretty much has to run you down. The moment you twisted your ankle I should have told you to stop where you were, not move until I scouted the area or brought the Jeep to you."

"So you made a mistake. It happens. I'm fine. We're all fine." Though she'd feel far more certain of that if she could get a closer look at Mal's leg, see if it was healing up already. Offer him blood if he needed it. She sidled, just a discreet hop, and Mal's gaze twitched wholly onto her.

"Stay by the Jeep, Elisa."

Jeremiah straightened then, and when Mal glanced toward him, his throat worked. Elisa stilled as she heard a coherent sound come from him, such a remarkable occurrence that everyone's attention turned. He squared his shoulders and spoke. "Go . . . I'll go."

"You spoke." She let the joy of it fill her, keeping the trauma of the past few minutes at bay.

Jeremiah nodded, ducked his head. She heard the next words clearly enough. "Different . . . here."

Mal studied his bent profile. "Join the others back at the water hole. I'll be there shortly."

Jeremiah gave Elisa one more look and then disappeared into the trees. Mal waited, obviously confirming the boy was well out of range before he turned his attention back to Tokala. Elisa could see the man's pain. This was his home. It wasn't a matter of being fired from a job. If Mal told him to go, he was being expulsed from a family. She wanted to argue or plead with Mal, whichever might work, but she was afraid either one might push him in the wrong direction. After a long moment, the vampire shifted.

"Take Elisa back to the house. You and I will talk in my office later tonight."

She let out an unsteady breath. Tokala might not be able to tell, but she could. He was going to get a serious thrashing in some manner, but Mal wasn't going to send him away. Only then did she notice she'd started to shake, her knees weakening at an alarmingly fast rate.

Of course she didn't fall or faint; she'd never own up to that. She just lost a few minutes, after which she found herself being placed in the passenger seat of the Jeep. Mal slid his arms from beneath her. She guessed he'd caught her before she could hit the ground. Which would have happened if she'd done something like fainting, which of course she hadn't.

"Of course not." He pushed one of her curls off her cheek, the irritable look at odds with the gentle touch. "You'll go back to the house now. If you so much as lift a finger to clean, cook, iron, scrub or whatever domestic verb applies, you'll regret it. Take a bath and go to bed for the next few hours. Tell Kohana to make one of his herbal teas to help you sleep."

"I'm fine. It wasn't any more terrifying than being in the way of a cattle stampede. Which *is* bloody awful, but in the end, it's over and done with. That happened when I was a cook on a cattle drive for a short stint. You need blood, though. He *spoke*, Mal."

"Tokala will give me some if I need it before dawn." Mal leaned in then, rubbed his mouth along the line of her cheekbone. "And if you're in bed, I'll know just where to find some more, won't I?"

When Tokala turned over the engine, Mal stepped back without further comment. However, watching him recede in the rearview mirror, Elisa thought she'd do better with whiskey than tea, if she wanted to sleep after *that* comment.

18

DESPITE that, by the time she reached the house, she was dozing in the seat. The sudden surge of fear, the pleasure of seeing the children run, the wonder of Jeremiah talking, it all washed through her, taking the evening's energy with it. Vaguely, she was aware of Tokala radioing ahead to Kohana. Probably letting him know what happened, giving him Mal's instructions. She was aware of a barking response from Kohana, and realized that everyone was going to have their turn pummeling the man verbally. But no one would be harder on him than Tokala himself. So as she bumped along in her pleasant haze, it was natural to reach out, find his hand on the gear shifter and close on it briefly, then move up to his forearm to stroke.

"'S okay," she mumbled. "I'm fine, Tokala. It's all good. No worries."

She wasn't sure what he replied, but she was aware he let go of the shifter to squeeze her hand, hard enough to cause her bones to complain, but it was okay. Men were so funny. They couldn't cry about it like girls could, or simply be thankful it hadn't been worse. They had to get mad at someone, like Mal or Kohana did, or be all silent like Tokala, afraid to let it out. It was all right. He'd be fine. They'd work it out in their own way. Just like the children were starting to do, now that they were in a safe place. She cherished those few words Jeremiah had spoken, reliving them again and again. Especially the last two. *Different here.* Yes, it was.

She knew her mind was wandering, but that was okay. When Tokala lifted her out of the Jeep, cradling her like a child in his long arms, she was aware of Kohana at his shoulder, peering down at her to make sure she was all right.

"Just my ankle." Her mouth felt full of marbles. "'S okay. Already feeling better. Second-mark . . . heal in no . . ." And she was somewhere else again.

She was distantly aware of taking some tea, but then she was put to bed. It took her a while to realize it wasn't her upstairs bed. She was in Mal's bed, under that beautiful twisting canopy. Had he told Kohana to put her there? Made it clear that she was providing his breakfast, and so he expected her to be there? It gave her all sorts of disquieting feelings she wasn't up to examining. At the same time, the bed did its magic, filling her with a warm and delicious comfort that unfurled and stretched to all parts of her, soothing her nerves. As she burrowed down under the covers like a cub in a warm den, she wondered if the way Mal's scent and the imagined heat of his body filled her senses was the bed's magic, or his.

She was drifting over the island, wading through the waters, splashing with the children, laughing with them, then moving onward. She passed the new lions, Solomon and Signet. As if she were seeing the future, they were watching a pride of lionesses crossing an African plain. The two rehabilitated males would soon try to become the male leaders of that group. She was glad to see there were no cubs.

On her habitat orientation, Mal had said the more experienced males would run off young males, but they would kill babies outright, to bring the mother into heat and create their own offspring. If they came into the pride now, there need be no such fatalities. A peaceful takeover, welcomed by the females.

She wondered if the same applied to her and Mal. A peaceful takeover. As if her thoughts had drawn her to him, she found him then. He was with a group of cubs in the habitat area, past or present, she didn't know. Leopards, three of them, probably a year old, and then a younger one, perhaps no more than a few months. She held her breath at how the older ones wrestled. They were rough, but if one got pinned and found it unpleasant, he'd let out a yowling protest that would make his siblings back off. For a moment, at least; then they were at it again.

They flung themselves exuberantly at Mal as well. She smiled over it, how he handled them with such firm strength, like an older leopard would. When he played with the younger one, he toned it down, yet still challenged the cub's strength, teaching him to lunge, claw and bite. Unlike domestic house cats, where people encouraged them to sheathe their claws with their human playmates, he was teaching them what their mother would have.

She drifted back to Jeremiah and the others. He'd spoken. It had to be getting better, right? Was there hope at the end of this rainbow, or was this a rainbow at all? Maybe it was only the eye of a storm, a moment of peace before things got worse.

Her dreams took her into darkness, and she was afraid there. Afraid of the black loneliness, the scent of blood and fear, and anger. Screams, and Victor dragging her. Elisa struggled to get away from the memory, but it sucked her in. In this veiled world, she was a ghost doomed to endure the same act, again and again.

Her fear was Victor's entertainment, a toy that made sounds if pressed certain ways. She would never forget that feeling, and she wanted to forget it more than she'd ever wanted anything in her life. He'd made her believe she was completely insignificant. There was no God, no devil, no real meaning to all of it. She was a dust mote, swept up in a pan with other dirt and tossed into the yard. Things were getting so very dark . . .

"Elisa." *Elisa. Come back to me. Come out of there.*

Were there places one wasn't supposed to go in the dreams offered by this bed? Shadowed, fearful places? Turning, she wasn't sure what way to go, but in the end she followed his voice, crawling out of blood and death toward a room lit by candles. A concerned, strong face was poised over hers, his features familiar and yet new, different, something she could explore with her fingertips over and over and find them amazing. "Make me matter," she whispered. "Bring me back. Make me forget."

Mal bent, his hip pressing against her. Turning her face away, she gave him her throat, and when she felt his mouth and then his fangs, she wanted to weep and hold on to him. She did both, her fingers curled hard into his biceps as his arm slid beneath her, drew her close. He drank from her, letting her nourish him, give him life. As he did, she let those tears fall among the soft furs, the animal totems that protected his island.

"Am I supposed to be in your bed?" The words came out thick as she lifted a heavy, logy hand, tangled it in his hair as he continued to tease blood from her throat.

I told them to put you here, Elisa.

"I saw you playing with the cubs." She closed her eyes, tightening her grip as he slid his hand down to her breast, stroking and kneading in a soothing way, those capable hands. She stilled, remembering. Her fingers found the leg he had crooked on the bed. He'd changed trousers, of course, because if he'd continued with his duties, he wouldn't want the other cats spooked or agitated by the scent of his blood. But she remembered the swipe of that big cat's paw, how Mal had twisted beneath the lion, contorting to break the hold, get on top.

He'd saved her. She'd been terrified, seeing him go down under hundreds of pounds of muscled feline flesh. Yes, unless the lion had somehow ripped off his head, Mal couldn't be killed, but if he'd been forced to unconsciousness and dragged off, beyond where she and Tokala could find him in time, Thai might have eaten him. She expected having his heart and other internal organs digested might be as effective as a stake. And she would have lost another man who made her feel . . . significant.

"If you give the pants to me, I'll sew them." Her voice had that detestable tremor again, no help for it. "Thank you for saving my life."

Shhh, girl. Just hush and feel.

Her eyes closed tighter, two men overlapping in her mind at the endearment that linked the past with the present. You weren't supposed to think about one man while you were with another, but this didn't really seem like that. She wasn't preferring one over the other. It was as if one was a continuation of the other, a strangeness she couldn't really explain.

When his lips moved on her neck, his fangs retracting, it shuddered through her body like he'd withdrawn from her after a more carnal penetration. As he straightened, his hand slipped to her hip. She'd been too tired or Kohana had been too respectful, so she was still wearing her trousers. His touch skirted that area the pants delineated so precisely. Some of the churchgoers in Perth thought a decent woman didn't wear pants, probably for that reason. Of course, it delineated that same part of men, but good girls didn't look at that. She'd challenge any of those wowsers not to look at what Mal had to offer in his daks, though.

He blinked at her. "Wowsers?"

"People who . . . Prudes?"

He nodded. "It's a unique thing, to be in your mind and not understand half of what you're saying."

"A bad thing?"

A smile touched his lips as his hand continued to wander, down over her knees, giving her a tickle that made her squirm. The smile faded as he watched the way her body moved. "No. Not a bad thing. Your fledglings are safely back in their enclosures and Jeremiah is fine."

"They did well, didn't they? Did . . . I?"

He regarded her, his face settling into those more remote lines she knew too well. She was chattel to him, but she also knew if he told her he wasn't going to take her back to see them for a while, she might not be able to hold it all in. Seeing them tonight, being part of what happened, had meant so much to her that almost being mauled by a lion couldn't overshadow it.

"Elisa." He looked toward the wall, obviously pushing back a sigh. She waited, her hands closing into tense balls. One rested by her side, but the other had naturally followed the line of his biceps to his thigh when he straightened. It now waited there, a closed knot reflecting her bated emotions.

"Starting tomorrow, a staff member will take you to the fledglings' area for a couple hours each night. You'll interact with them there, and provide me information on how our outings seem to be impacting their behavior with you. I will continue taking them out in small groups every other night, and we'll reassess in two weeks. All right?"

She nodded, a quick jerk. Rising, he pulled the covers over her more securely. "Sleep now. You need more rest."

"Aren't you going to stay?" Lord, what was she doing? And what must he think of her for even implying such a forward thing? She straightened then, sliding out the other side of the bed before he could stop her. It was reassuring to find the ankle was tender but able to bear weight as she snatched up the sneakers Kohana had left for her there. "This is your bed, sir. Nice as it was to give you breakfast, I'll sleep upstairs so I won't be a bother. And thank you. I'll be a big help to you, I will . . ."

Whoa. She'd forgotten she'd just fed him. The room spun alarmingly as she straightened with the shoes in her hand. But in the next blink, she was against his chest, hands curled in the fabric of his shirt, his hands steadying her. "Wow, you move fast." She blinked, trying to focus. "Like with that lion. Is he okay? Was the dream true?"

That she'd asked after the lion seemed to surprise him, but he nodded when she dropped her head back on her shoulders to look at him. "Good. Wasn't his fault that I looked like good eating. Doing all that limping." She frowned, thinking. "That's what Kohana meant, when he said he can't work on the open preserve anymore. Because of his limp. I kept wondering, because he's so strong and capable."

"Yes. It's why birds sometimes fake having a broken wing to draw a cat from a nest. A predator can't resist something that seems weak or injured, particularly when they're seeking a meal. And it's why anything that is less than what it needs to be rarely survives in the wild."

"Don't do that." Pushing back from him then, she took a couple steps away to stand on her own two feet. "You say I'm obsessed with being with them, but you're obsessed with making me believe they have no future."

"I'm preparing you for a reality that may be unavoidable."

"Reality's going to come, no matter what. That kind of reality, there's no preparing for it." She met his gaze. "There was no preparing for what happened with Victor. Nothing I could have done to make it less horrible in my memory, or give me less nightmares. Or make losing Willis hurt less. Except maybe not love him, not want to be with him, not cherish every brief moment we had. But if I had done that, I would never have had those moments.

"People who say 'prepare for reality' are just guarding their hearts, is all. To keep them from loving and giving, because everyone knows those things can hurt worse than being trampled by cattle." She managed a smile then, a quiet thing in the darkness that gave her comfort where he couldn't, standing on the other side of that gulf of belief about her children. "But it also feels better than anything else, when you have it."

He said nothing, and she knew there was no help for it, not tonight. But everything in the world changed if you worked hard enough at it. Even a vampire who thought he knew everything and who—sometimes— she was afraid actually did. She swallowed that thought and the fear that came with it and let her gaze skitter over the dark eyes and unrelenting features.

"Thank you again, sir. Good night."

"Elisa."

She turned at the door, trying to look anywhere but directly at him. "Yes, sir?"

"Did I say you could leave?"

She swallowed again, met his eyes. Briefly. "No, sir. What can I . . . Do you need something?"

He nodded. "I want you to undress in front of me."

"Oh. Well." She set the shoes aside, arranging them tidily on the floor, next to a pair of his boots that had been dropped there haphazardly. She straightened them, too. Her fingers were shaking and her body felt hot all over, and when she stood up, he was right up against her back, but she didn't jump. Instead, her breath caught in the back of her throat as he gripped her biceps.

"Are you truly good at sewing, Elisa?"

"Yes, sir, very good. Small stitches and—"

She gasped as he ripped the front of her blouse, sending the buttons clattering away across the floor. His thumbs found the tops of the bra cups, sliding down to tease areola and then nipple, making her arch into him, pressing her buttocks into the hardness of his cock and feeling an answering spear of wetness between her legs, readying herself for him.

Of a sudden, she was ravenous. She'd almost been killed tonight, but she hadn't been. She was alive, alive. When she would have twisted in his arms, he pressed her hard against the wall, cold stone against her hot flesh. He kept her pinned there as his hands wandered down, opening her trousers and sliding into them to verify that wetness for himself.

"That's it, *atsilusgi*," he murmured as she cried out under his clever ministrations, coating his fingers with her slickness so that he slid three fingers right into her, almost up to the second knuckle. His groan as she instinctively rubbed her backside into his cock fueled her desire. She wanted him inside, needed him to roar and rut upon her like one of the lions, because she was alive, alive, *alive*.

"You're eating more," he observed in that husky voice, one hand traveling back up to caress the breast. He'd worked the strap off her shoulder so it was exposed, a wanton dishabille. "I like that."

He was rubbing her, slow, slow circles between her legs. Her hips were working back against him, erratic, the feeling in her lower belly needy, going straight toward mindless. Good Lord, who knew a male could touch a woman like this?

"You will continue to eat more. And at dawn, every night, you will be here. You will take off all your clothes so I can see these gorgeous breasts of yours, your delectable ass. And I will determine if you are filling out properly. If I'm not here yet, you will lie in my bed and wait for me." His voice dropped, became even huskier, as stunning a stroke upon her sex as his hands. "And perhaps I will use the second mark to speak in your mind, tell you to touch yourself the way you've thought about doing in your own bed. You won't do that unless I'm watching you, unless I command you to do it. I'd like to see you bring yourself to orgasm the way I'll do it now, fingers inside your cunt, your body flushed and throat working, crying out."

She let out a guttural moan. Vampires weren't like human males, so distracted by their own lust they couldn't form coherent sentences. His ability to talk in or out of her mind, driving her to insanity, didn't seem to diminish his lust one centigrade as he lifted his head, cupped her face and drew her head back to a straining angle to look at him.

"What do you say to me, Elisa? How do you answer me?"

"Y-yes . . . sir." She stared up into his face, the craving need to say it greater than her fear. "Yes . . . Master."

His eyes flamed then and he had his mouth on hers, letting her taste him and the remnants of the blood he'd taken from her. He still didn't let her turn, kissing her thoroughly until she was writhing between him and that wall, all but begging for his fingers to take her where they were teasing her to go. Instead, he told her to stay where she was, facing the wall, and divested her of every scrap of clothing, putting them all to the side as she trembled, experiencing him only through the feel of his hands trailing down her shoulders, her back, over her buttocks.

"Spread your legs for me, Elisa," he said. "And don't move another muscle." She did, holding that position, her hands pressed flat on the rock above her, toes gripping the smooth stone tile floor beneath as the heel of his palm made solid contact with her pussy, sealing over it. She held still, even as a tremulous wail, a soft, short cry, came from her throat at the intensity of feeling that went through her. There was a light sheen of perspiration on her body. He worked his palm on her, a slow back-and-forth as she quivered.

"Are you wanton enough to do my bidding, Irish flower? Or will you be shy?"

She couldn't speak over a dry throat. "I'll do anything you wish, Master."

She was alone suddenly, standing there stretched out against the wall, but she stayed there, didn't look around until he spoke. "Then come here."

Turning, she found he was on the bed now, as gloriously naked as herself, his clothes kicked away. He had his hand out. "Walk across the floor toward me, let me see how beautiful you are, the way your body moves. Then I'm going to put you on my cock and make you ride me until you climax hard."

On top of him? Like experiencing his mouth between her legs, she'd never done that. She walked toward him then, trying not to be self-conscious. Faith, but vampires didn't have any sense of modesty, no sense of making love in the dark or hiding under sheets.

What point would there be in that, when what I want to see is the way your curls shine in the firelight, the way your breasts move as you walk, the juices from your cunt damp on your thighs?

She trembled so hard she wasn't sure she would make it, but then her fingers closed over that extended hand. She focused on his face, his mouth, then reached those burning, implacable eyes that wanted everything from her and wouldn't take no as an answer. *No* didn't exist anywhere inside her when he looked at her like this. This beautiful, amazing, wild and savage creature.

"You all are such a strange lot," she whispered as he brought her alongside of him. "So decadent and frightening, but so hard to resist. It makes things hurt inside me."

"Where?" His voice was soft, his eyes like one of his cats, so deep and dark.

She pressed the heel of her hand on her sternum, where all that pressure seemed to be building. He sat up then, keeping her between his thighs, his aroused cock brushing her lower belly. When he put his arm around her waist, brought her closer, tears burned in the back of her throat as he laid his lips lightly, so lightly on that column of bone that descended between her breasts. He turned his head, brushing his hair across her skin, and nuzzled.

"A vampire likes fear, Elisa," he whispered, "but the only kind I want you to experience right now has to do with pleasure. You understand me?"

"Yes, sir. I know you won't hurt me."

Cupping her head in one broad hand, he met her eye to eye. "What about you? Will you hurt me?"

It was so unexpected, the gleam in his eyes, a nervous chuckle sputtered from her lips. "I'll do my best not to cause you any permanent damage."

"On the contrary"—now his mouth was back at her jaw, cruising and making her mind wobble on its axis again—"I want to drive you to mindless savagery. I want to feel your claws dig into my flesh, your teeth snap at my throat. I want you to squeeze me inside of you as if you want to trap me there forever."

"Oh," she breathed, and then she caught his shoulders as he lifted her effortlessly onto his lap, holding her just above his groin.

"Put me inside of you, Elisa. Let me see your hand grip me."

It was all new territory. Mechanically, she'd done some things like this, but in truth, it was all so very different. She gripped the thick base, marveling at how the wetness at the head kissed her wrist, and took a moment touching him, running her grip up that length, then back down again.

Elisa, I gave you a very specific command. But his mind-voice held a strain that told her he liked what she was doing, so she did it again, her gaze flicking up to him to see it register in his face, wry acceptance, enduring her innocence, and growing ferocity, held back only by a thread. Then, in one smooth motion, he shifted his grip to her hips so he brought her forward and sheathed himself to the hilt, dislodging her hands.

The feeling was like a bolt of lightning straight up through her. She sucked in another breath at the tight spiral of pain and lust that spun through her torso as he held her down, wouldn't let her move on him yet. Bringing her fingers to her lips, she tasted him while he watched. But when she would have done it with the other hand, he shook his head.

"Rub that one over your nipple. I want my scent upon you there."

She did, discovering the decadent pleasure in that, such that she cupped the curve before his avid gaze and became bolder, passing her fingers over the hardened tip.

As she watched him watching her, something in his gaze changed. "Sir?"

He passed his fingers over where hers were, making her quiver a bit under his touch, but then he rested them on top of her knuckles, holding them both there as she breathed, her heart pounding, matching the pulse in her sex where he was lodged so deeply.

Mal followed the pulse up to her throat, then to those large blue eyes, the fringe of lashes, the tightening of her mouth against her passion. Many of the female third-marked servants he'd met were polished creatures, who never would have had the slightly chapped pink lips or callused hands of someone who did manual labor. But Elisa suited him in that regard. His hands had never been without calluses, before he became a vampire. Over time, because a vampire with his regenerative abilities couldn't reflect wear and tear on the body, the calluses had faded away. He missed them sometimes.

He wasn't polished. His sire had taught him all manner of ways to exercise his sexual dominance, and so he knew all sorts of ways to give a woman pleasure. But he'd never unleashed his carnal nature like this. She wasn't his third-marked servant, but he was acting the way he'd been told all vampires acted toward their first one. He, who understood animal behavior so well, had discarded tales of such unbridled sexual aggression as a generalization. Yet here he was, taking her over, commanding her to his will. Obsessed with owning her every reaction, every caught breath, the dazed light in her eyes, the trembling in her thighs.

"Ride me, Elisa. Do it now. Push yourself beyond what you know."

He helped, letting his hands settle on her hips as she made the first move, sliding up his length, biting her lip as her attention turned inward, eyes widening and lips parting as she experienced the feeling, then down, a moaning sigh coming from her throat as his ridged head teased those tender tissues, pushing back into her pussy's wet heat.

"Again. Harder. Faster."

She obeyed, and that fired him as well, as much as her earlier disobedience when she gripped him had done. She'd been prepared to leave his bed, stay out of his way, not be a bother to him. He didn't want her to leave his bed at all. Not this day, nor any in the foreseeable future.

Her tongue raked her teeth as she caught the rhythm, began to ride him like a dolphin riding storm waves, with pleasure and exuberance, embracing the wildness.

Tease your breasts with your fingers, Elisa. Pretend it's my mouth suckling the nipples. After this first climax, it will be. I'm going to pin you under my body, and suckle them until you come around my cock once again.

She moaned once more, cupped her breasts and began pinching, stroking and pulling at herself. He watched, imagined his brown fingers overlaying her pale ones, doing it together as those points became more and more stiff, until her cunt gushed from the stimulation. He was so hard inside of her he knew he wouldn't hold back much longer, but he wanted her to go over. He was fascinated watching her, the different expressions flying over her face, the way she was getting rougher with herself, with bruising pinches and hard squeezes of those pale curves.

He wondered how she'd respond to having clamps on her nipples like he'd seen in his more exotic travels. He'd make her wear them under her practical clothing while she cleaned and scrubbed, the chain feathering against her breasts, its movement tugging and keeping her nipples erect, pressing against a much thinner, sexier bra. He would get her something like that.

Let me hear you scream, Elisa.

He took over at last, driving into her with hard, fast strokes that took smoke to fire. She caught hold of him for balance as the orgasm rolled her, took her down deep inside herself and then flung her out into a silver moonlit sky, tumbling her over and over in the clouds as she shrieked out the pleasure of it. It took him with her, and he reared up, putting his mouth on the sensually abused right nipple, latching on to lash it fiercely as his cock spurted. She flung her arms around his shoulders and held on, her cries a sound he knew he'd want to hear again and again, long past the sun's rising.

19

SHE couldn't believe he'd agreed to let her have a schedule of daily visits, but in truth, she was glad, because her focus on that kept her away from making too much of the things he compelled her to do in the hours near dawn over the next couple weeks. It was how vampires were, she reminded herself. Again.

Before Danny had come, it wasn't unusual for Lady Constance or Ian to enjoy various marked humans in such ways. It was no more to them than sitting down and enjoying a fine meal. There wasn't even a contempt to it, for they valued the humans for that and other things. It was simply the way it was.

But she no longer entertained any comparison of this with past human employers. If there had been, she was pretty certain she might have been willing to do all manner of unspeakable things to stay in Perth instead of going with Lady Constance.

There was a disquieting element to this, however. She'd once worked in a laundry, and there'd been a widow there who'd had an ongoing assignation with the baker's assistant down the street. The widow told her that a woman who'd lost her man welcomed the right man's touch as a comfort, and it need be nothing more than that. That might be true enough, but the fact was how she responded to Mal had nothing to do with Willis. There were times Mal touched her that she couldn't even see Willis's face in her mind. She didn't like what that might say about her.

When she'd had such a thought around Mal, he'd said it made her human and left it at that. Given that vampires didn't always think so highly of humans, she wasn't sure that was a compliment. It all confused her, particularly the grin he'd given her for that parting thought.

All in all, it didn't matter. For now it was what it was. Since she couldn't really make heads or tails of how she felt about all of it, she set it aside and settled into a routine. Upon rising, she would run through the chores with Kohana, and then she'd collect the things she wanted to bring to the fledglings. Their blood allotment, of course, as well as a bite-sized variety of foods from the kitchen. She'd also pack things she'd found on her short walks in approved areas, and a couple books from Mal's library to read to them. Promptly at nine p.m., she'd be on the porch, expectantly waiting for Chumani to arrive from her first round of duties at the preserve.

She enjoyed her drives with the Indian woman. Chumani not only gave her more anecdotes about the island's residents, two- and four-legged, but she also had an uncanny way of determining Elisa's state of mind and helping her to arrive at the fledgling's area in the proper frame. Tonight was a prime example of that.

"Mal's right," the woman told her as they navigated the curves of the barely there dirt road. "Animals pick up on agitation or fear in a heartbeat, and it makes them look around for trouble or—worse—consider you the cause of it. Those little ones of yours, they're more dangerous than that. They use it to catch you off guard, take advantage. So what's got you worked up tonight? You came out of the house with that nervous energy sparking off you like fireflies gone berserk."

Elisa gave her a wry smile. "Nothing. Just . . . Mr. Malachi, he sometimes makes me unsettled." He'd been doing some work in the study when she left, had come in the kitchen for his blood. He'd told her he'd take it from the reserves Kohana kept for him. She'd absurdly felt a bit disappointed by that, even though she knew he wasn't using her as his sole blood source. But she was the only one from whom he was getting it fresh.

She'd fixed him a glass from the refrigerator stores, the same as she'd fix a meal for any of them. But when he came to the counter for it, he trapped her with an arm on either side of her, then dipped his finger in the blood and painted it on her bare wrist, lifting that taste to his mouth and suckling there. "Just warm enough," he'd said after a moment. "Thank you, Elisa." Then he'd picked up the glass and off he went, leaving her torn between the desire to put a foot up his backside or simply stand there and tremble with the feeling. The practically edible smile he tossed over his shoulder only made it worse.

"Mal can do that." Chumani snorted. "Lately he seems to have you in his sights."

"Have you . . . ever been in his sights?"

Though she told herself not to react like a child, she felt a sharp pain at Chumani's nod. "When he wants his blood fresh from the vein, he prefers a woman for that. I was willing to donate, and as you know, that can lead to the other things. I didn't mind it. It wasn't like he made me. Mal doesn't do that. If you don't want him, he doesn't pull that vampire routine on you. He just shrugs it off and goes on. But a woman has needs as strong as a man's, and he's more than equipped to take care of them." Chumani tossed her a grin. "Though most of the time he takes his blood from a glass. Doesn't seem to get the itch as much as most vampires, or maybe he just channels it into all this. Like that monk who brought you here, channeling energy to God."

Elisa thought Mal must have decided to split off from his usual channel, because she'd been getting her fair share of that rush of energy. In fact, his sexual intensity bathed her like a steam bath when he merely stepped into a room.

As if reading her mind, Chumani gave her a small smile. "With you he's a little different. You're all innocent and earnest, yet you're not innocent. From what I've put together, it should have been beaten out of you, but it hasn't been. There's a foolhardy strength to you that stands up to anything. It interests him. Here." She pressed a brief palm over her heart. "As much as his kind feels things that way, of course. I'm thinking that something about you may remind him of his life before."

"Before?"

"When he was a human." Chumani considered her. "He's never told me it's a secret, and he told me straight enough when I asked. Pillow talk, you know."

Elisa nodded, trying not to get distracted by the intimate idea of Chumani lying in Mal's arms, with him making "pillow talk" against that shining wing of ebony hair. Chumani currently had it braided, but Elisa had seen it loose and flowing in the dawn hours, right before they turned in. The other men teased her, but the woman's sculpted face and pouty lips, as well as dark, thickly lashed eyes, were any man's ideal of beauty, no matter her six-foot height and the fact she'd obviously been strong as an ox even before being given two marks. Maybe because Elisa ran up against so many obstacles with her not-overly intimidating stature, she saw everything to admire in the smooth muscles in Chumani's arms, the architecture of her shoulders and proud bosom. She emanated a warrior's confidence.

Because of that, despite her sour reaction to Chumani being Mal's lover, her compliments flattered Elisa deeply. It amazed her that the woman could see such admirable things. It must have shown in her face, for Chumani gave her a pinch. "You don't value yourself enough. You don't see anything remarkable in convincing your vampire Mistress to let you bring six vampire fledglings across an ocean, particularly after one of them damn near killed you? Or that you've stood up to Mal every different direction, even when he's set you back on your heels, time and again? You don't intimidate. Your jaw wasn't the only one that about dropped on the table when he agreed to let you do this. You just tunnel under, around and wear holes through your opposition until it gives way out of pure resignation."

Elisa found a smile. "It's not the first time I've heard that." Dev had said it once when she'd insisted on something to the point he'd given her a smart slap on the buttocks with his hat . . . before going to do as she'd asked.

"Well, it's impressive. I'm not sure anyone other than Kohana would go up against Mal like that. And that includes me."

"You could take on any of these blokes one-armed."

Chumani chuckled. "Not Mal. But I admit, I've beaten a couple of the others arm wrestling. Male pride is a tricky thing. I don't get caught up in it, but every once in a while, I wouldn't mind being short and cuddly like you."

"Cuddly?" Elisa echoed.

"Cuddly." Chumani gave her a poke in the belly and pinched her cheek before Elisa slapped her away good-naturedly. "Sometimes a tall, strong girl would like to have that advantage. You know, ask a man to get her something out of a cabinet because she can't stretch far enough." She batted her eyes, making Elisa bark with laughter. "You ever see the way a man looks when you do that? For just a minute, he's your hero, and he likes that. Not saying I want to tease or put on feminine wiles." Chumani shrugged. "But it's hard to convince a man you're interested in him if he thinks you can wrestle him to the ground."

"I think Kohana could take you in a fair fight."

Elisa bit back a smile as Chumani jerked the wheel in surprise. She gave Elisa a narrow look, made that noncommittal Indian grunt. "That one doesn't see the forest for the trees, for all his putting on airs that he's some great shaman's son. Old coot."

Kohana covered it well under his gruff teasing, taking her barbs and cracks about him being an old man, but in truth Elisa didn't think there was more than about a decade between them. Willis had been nearly ten years older than her, and Mal . . .

She stopped herself with a fierce shake. That wasn't the same at all, and no good would come from her mooning about it that way. She cleared her throat. "I think you *should* challenge him to a wrestling match one night. You know, there's that pretty glade near the house. Private, and lots of soft ground if he puts you down hard."

Chumani's eyes narrowed further, the long lashes becoming a bristling frame for glittering coal. "So confident of that, are you?"

"Just depends on how much you're hoping that you'll lose." Elisa slanted her a grin.

After a weighted silence, where Chumani made an obvious effort to hold her aloof expression, she relented, letting out a snort. "You are one *hell* of a maid."

"I was second to Mrs. Pritchett," Elisa said proudly. "When she retired, I was going to . . . Well, I guess I still can." Clearing her throat, she changed the subject. She wasn't able to imagine herself on the station, wanting the things she'd wanted before, so it would be too difficult to paint that picture for another. "What did you mean about Mal . . . before?"

"I know he's told you some basics. He's Cherokee, and his people were getting Westernized, even had a newspaper and a church. Then the settlers got greedy for their land and figured out ways to steal it from them. He was part of the thousands forced to walk the Trail of Tears. Did you read about that in your history book?"

Elisa shook her head, and Chumani's lips tightened. "They took most of them out of their homes at gunpoint, with little more than the clothes on their backs. Put them in camps where a bunch died of disease. Then they walked them over a thousand miles to a new reservation. Nobody knows for sure how many of the sixteen thousand died; probably about three or four thousand."

Elisa thought of the things in her own history, the Aborigines fed poisoned bread by settlers or hunted down like vermin, and closed her eyes. "Mal was six," Chumani continued. "His white father died in a hunting accident a year before, else he might have been able to give them an option to go elsewhere. Instead, they were forced to go. His mother died on the trail, and something happened after that where Mal got separated from the others. Ended up on a farm."

She came to a stop on one of the elevations that provided an ocean view, whitecaps and rushing noise coming through the night. It was a steadying reminder of where Mal had ended up, what he'd built. It helped Elisa remember she was in the present, not Mal's past. But there was still a cold feeling in her stomach as Chumani pressed on. "A few decades later there would be a real hard-core attempt to 'whitewash' Indian children." Chumani's voice tightened with sadness, a history she'd not experienced but that connected to her blood. "Unfortunately, Mal became one of the early experiments. They put him in a mission school with a bunch of orphans.

"The guy who ran it was a real fire-and-brimstone kind of bastard. They cut his hair, gave him the name Malachi, wouldn't let him speak his language. He was young, but he was rebellious. They had to beat him a lot, and they'd tie him to his bed at night like a prisoner to keep him from running away. Eventually he was broken, trained to do manual labor, gardening. As he got older, he was sent back East as an indentured servant to serve in the house of a rich Boston woman. Filthy streets, noise, too many people. That's how he remembers it.

"He couldn't figure out how to leave all that maze of streets, so he ended up being there for ten years, until he was a young man. Then another woman bought his contract to serve in her house. She was a vampire. He won't say more than that. That's always the way of things. The things that don't matter, you spit those out right fast. They're the unpleasant truths, straightforward. But the things it made him, he doesn't talk about that. This is what he is now."

Elisa gazed out over the night terrain. "So he does know what it's like to be a servant," she said quietly. *To be insignificant.* "I did him an injustice."

"He's a long way from that, and sometimes we have a tendency to put the painful past behind a heavy door, to the point we forget some of the things it teaches us. But he's definitely different than the few vampires who've visited this place. Maybe that's because he's 'young,' or maybe he'll always be that way. I'm hoping he'll always be that way."

Elisa couldn't help but agree, and she understood better now why he and Danny were linked. With her Outback frankness and practicality, Danny, too, was hard to define within vampire standards.

"Tomorrow, you be ready an hour early," Chumani said abruptly. "I'll show you how to handle this rig. We can practice on the straightaways and maybe even some hills. That'll give you something to be really nervous about, holding a clutch on these hairpin drop-offs." Giving Elisa a tight smile, she put the Jeep in gear and rolled on down the hill.

Elisa was glad the darkness hid her face, because it gave her the courage to speak her next words. "He confuses my heart. I know that's stupid, because I'm just a human to him. I like what he does to me, but it hurts, too. Like it's supposed to mean more, like I'm supposed to want it to mean more, and yet, since I can't have that, it's pointless. Which sometimes makes everything seem pointless. But I don't want him to stop. I can't stop him. I'm not strong enough to resist what he is, what he does to me, no matter what it turns me into."

Chumani pulled into the enclosure area and cut the lights. Elisa saw William, in the cell nearest the Jeep, step out of his small cabin.

"You need to tell him that," Chumani said quietly. "He's a vampire, but Mal has a good heart. He wouldn't want to hurt yours."

"Well, he can read all that from my mind, can't he?" Sadness swept her. Her feelings never really mattered, did they? It was senseless to indulge in thoughts otherwise, because she could trap herself in a melancholy that served no purpose. It merely took the joy out of the other blessings in her life.

The woman gave a laugh that cut short Elisa's self-pity. "He may be a vampire, he may be able to read your mind, but child, he's a man. Sometimes they don't understand anything unless you spell it out like one of those alphabet books you have. Maybe you could take those plastic letters you give to the fledglings and make him a sign."

Elisa smiled, despite herself. Then, because it was just how she was, she leaned over and surprised Chumani with a hug. "Thank you. I like our drives."

The Indian woman gave her a pat, tugged her hair like an exasperated older sister. "Little woodchuck. All cute, round and irresistible. Go on; do your thing. I'll be over here taking a nap in the car, if you need me."

20

MAL had said only one vampire could be let in the communal area at a time, with the exception of the girls, who actually did better as a pair. If any wouldn't go back in to his or her cell when Elisa asked, Chumani would radio Mal to come and handle it. If Mal had to be called, the fledgling was forbidden time in the communal or open-preserve areas for the next three days, an effective punishment Elisa hated but realized worked, because even Leonidas would now return to his cell when she told him it was time.

The desire to reach out to Jeremiah or one of the girls when they looked particularly lonely or distressed, to give them the gift of touch, was an aching need. But she lectured herself fiercely, and explained it to them as well, in kinder terms. It wasn't that she didn't want to touch them. If a rule was broken, she'd also be banned from the area for three days, no exceptions or arguments.

Though tonight had gone well, she'd had to explain it all over again, which gave her a tight ache in her chest when she finally got in the Jeep at midnight for Chumani to take her back to the house. On the way, the Indian woman was able to give her some comfort by explaining that Elisa wasn't being singled out.

"Mal's just as uncompromising in his staff training," she said. "He might give you a real dressing down if an honest mistake is made with the cats, but if one of us is careless or, even worse, deliberately ignores the rules, he'll fire that staff member on the spot and ship him off the island right away, in a leaky boat if needed."

Apparently they'd only had a couple cases of that, because Mal chose his people carefully. But it explained Tokala's reaction to the lion incident.

What also helped her feel better about his rules were the meetings Mal had with her each night when she returned to the station. He'd bring her into his study and quiz her on the observations she'd had. His questions always drew out far more information than she thought she'd seen. Sometimes after those interrogations, he'd take her for a drive through the open preserve. Safely in the Jeep, she could witness him with the cats, and that helped her learn as well. It was a true science, studying the behavior of others, whether vampire, human or cat.

"You've been an exceptional servant all your life," he'd noted one night. "Which means you've cultivated the common sense and intuition to pick up many things that others miss. All you need are the cues to hone that, to know what it means, what you're looking at. It's usually far more than what you see on the surface."

She'd been inordinately flattered by the praise, but her admiration for him had increased as well. From Chumani she'd learned that in the past twenty years, he'd studied a variety of behavioral sciences, as well as traveled the world to investigate and see the work of others. Such direct interaction with the human world, taking the risk of questions or exposure, was unusual for a vampire, but as Chumani had noted, he wasn't the usual kind of vampire.

She was beginning to see her fledglings through Mal's trained eyes, understanding the interplay of dominance and submission between them. But with that understanding came the unsettling realization of just how dysfunctional they were, their behaviors often similar to the most severely abused and unsocialized cats brought into the sanctuary.

Camaraderie helped deal with such worries, and Mal seemed to know that as well. Directly after their meetings, before she did chores or Mal took her to the open preserve, the entire staff would sit down to the "dinner" meal, around two in the morning. If it was nice, they'd have it under the stars, gathering around the large picnic table and assorted benches scattered in the grassy yard. There was usually a good breeze, filtering into their valley from the ocean. Though Mal usually sat by himself on a bench propped against a nearby tree, he was close enough he could prop his booted foot on the edge of Chumani's chair, because she sat at the end closest to him.

He was more relaxed with the hands at that moment than any other, discussing the day's work. Which cats were improving in their rehabilitation, the amusing antics of the permanent residents in the habitats. Foolish mistakes each of the staff had made and survived. As Chumani had stated, each had received the sharp edge of Mal's temper for it, but now the retelling of such war stories was a way to reinforce the lessons and accept the dangers of their work with good humor. Elisa found it comforting to hear that all of them had apparently made such missteps at one time or another.

Even Mal.

~

Tonight it was hard to stay melancholy, because everyone was in particularly good spirits. Lola had been shepherded through the fault line to the African preserve. She was now ready to hunt and live free, no longer part of the island system. A toast was made to her long life with a special iced tea recipe Kohana made to celebrate the mixed blessing of such events.

As part of the festivities, each hand was now trying to best the others in tales of humiliation. The latest story had been about Bidzil, who'd made the mistake of thinking a tiger they'd lured into a transport cage with meat could be nudged in the rear to get him to move along.

"He thought he was a cattle drover," Tokala chuckled.

"Well, his name means *strong*, not *smart*." Chumani ducked the chunk of bread Bidzil shot at her.

"I forgot, what does *your* name mean? Woman-with-Too-Big-a-Mouth?"

"Didn't think there could be one of those." Tokala gave a mock leer and Chumani retaliated with a healthy smack along his ear.

"I think I'd stay quiet before we name you Idiot-Who-Grabs-a-Lion-by-the-Tail."

"What happened to Bidzil?" Elisa asked. It was the first time since the lion incident that Tokala had seemed more himself, less subdued, and she didn't want him to be knocked back on his heels.

"Tiger turned, of course, and went after him with all claws extended. Fortunately Mal anticipated his mistake about a second before it happened and was already in motion. Knocked the tiger off center and threw Bidzil out of the way; then we were able to get Alexei back into his enclosure until he calmed down a bit and we could try again."

"Bidzil got by with a little bit of a chest swipe," Mal commented. "Though for a few minutes he lost all his red pigment. We called him Snowman for about three days."

Mal rose enough to give the man's shoulder a shove, an unexpectedly affectionate gesture, though he settled back on his bench directly afterward. Elisa thought he set himself apart for a couple reasons. Since he took his meal now as well, perhaps he knew the fresh blood smell could interfere with the cooked food humans preferred. But she suspected the main reason was the difficulty of being close to that many human bodies, pulsing with life and blood. She'd noted that about Danny as well. When she met with the hands, there was always a circumspect distance between her and them. Though Elisa understood part of it was respect to the owner of the station, she understood the other part.

Like most of the big cats, vampires were solitary predators. While they didn't have to take human life except for one annual kill, humans were still prey in one form or another. It might be difficult to simply "hang out" with them, rubbing elbows and knees at a table like this. People reaching past them for the rolls, the noise of laughter and banter filling the ear and closing in on a creature that did better with open space, the ability to move quickly if needed.

However, Mal seemed to do better than most. Even now, through the laughter, Kohana was shaking his head. He pointed a finger at his vampire employer. "Don't cast any stones, Mal. At least Bidzil knows nuts aren't the only things that fall out of trees."

"Oh, no." Mal shook his head. "You're not going to embarrass me with that one, old man."

"I will, then." Chumani jumped in. "Mal's less mean to us girls."

"You're a girl? Since when? Turn her over, Chayton. I don't believe it."

She made a suitable retort to that, one that would have done any male station hand proud. She turned to Elisa then, putting another biscuit on both their plates.

"We had a new pride of lions on the open preserve. Three of them, a male and two females we'd been rehabilitating. They came from one of those hideous traveling sideshow zoos. Used to being poked at by sticks, stuff thrown at them through the bars, no supervision on the patrons at all beyond a cord to keep them out of range of the claws. Lights on day and night, because they set up next to highways. No shelter."

"Drongos," Elisa observed, with great feeling.

"Drongos. I like that. No translation needed. Anyhow, Mal's gliding along with that oh-so-confident vampire speed of his." Chumani rose then, straddling Mal's leg to get free and offer a sexy saunter that increased the laughter.

Times like these, Elisa could close her eyes and believe she was surrounded by the station staff, the hands carrying on as she brought food to the table. Only in this scenario, she couldn't lay a hand on Willis's shoulder as she leaned over to put the meat on the table, or feel the brief brush of his hand against her knee through her skirt, that fond and discreet intimacy, a form of possessive marking she didn't mind anyone noticing.

She blinked back the moisture pressing at the back of her eyes. Damn it, she wasn't going to draw attention to herself because of her erratic emotions. She focused on the story and ignored Mal's scrutiny in her peripheral vision. He always seemed to tune in to her state of mind when she least wanted to be noticed.

"Anyhow," Chumani continued. "He's checking out the pride from a distance, making sure they're adjusting well. He stops under a tree, looking down the hill toward them, and that's when it happened. Apparently those finely honed vampire senses were jammed that night. One of the leopards was up in a tree over his head. Dropped down on him like a falling melon, rolled him down that steep hillside so he landed flat on his back right in the middle of the pride, the leopard still wrapped around him."

"The lions were thrilled to know that dinner was delivered so fresh here," Chayton tossed in over the rising laughter.

"The poor leopard, Susie, was just playing, as she always does when she sees him. But of course, she caught him by surprise, and as they rolled and she realized where they were going, she dug her claws in and panicked so he couldn't immediately loosen her."

Bidzil picked up the thread in his smooth storyteller's voice, his pale green eyes dancing. "Now, he could have gotten away if he'd needed only a blink to get his thrusters beneath him and charge away to preserve his pretty face. But he still had that leopard wrapped around him and the lions would tear her apart in a heartbeat. So he tossed her free, like he was hurling a rock, and launched himself onto the head lion."

At Elisa's wide eyes and horrified indrawn breath, Kohana leaned in, elbowed her. "I don't want to give away the ending, little miss, but he survived. I promise." He jerked his head in Mal's direction, who looked affronted by the whole production, though she saw a faint curve to his beautiful mouth.

This was when he came closest to happiness, she realized. When it was all about what they were doing here, their bonding together over it. The beauty of the night enclosed them, the wind singing through the mesh fencing that surrounded the house. Dispersed on that wind were the sounds of the cats, every call a distinct voice to these people, and especially Mal. If she had a place where she felt at peace like this, she wouldn't ever leave, either. She'd never wander far, at least. She'd felt that way about the station, until . . . what had happened.

His gaze shifted to her, and that smile left his face. It wasn't irritation, however. She saw that intensity he displayed with her in more private moments, as if he wanted to give her something, something beyond just a physical caress.

She looked away, unsettled. "So did he pin the head lion and tell him to give over?" Taking a bite of the biscuit, she cradled it in both hands. Still in the trousers she was beginning to like wearing, she propped her feet up on the edge of the bench, balancing her elbows on her knees as she ate.

"Oh, he got ripped up pretty good, just like the other day, but he rolled free and was off and running. Of course he left a blood trail that kept them snarling and agitated half the night. Took them a few days to get over it."

"Not to mention, he brought home a shirt he insisted on having mended, though it would have been better to use it for the scrap bag, after I washed out the blood."

"Waste not, want not," Mal commented.

"It was a waste of my time to spend two hours fixing it," Kohana grumbled.

"I'd be happy to do any sewing around the place," Elisa offered. "I'm a fair hand with a needle. That goes for the lot of you."

She was immediately regaled with a variety of thanks, and a hint she'd have a pile of mending by dawn. Oh, well. It was something else she could take with her to the fledglings tomorrow. Perhaps she could put needle and thread and a scrap of fabric in the communal area and get the girls to emulate what she was doing outside of it. Teach them some needlework, if they could sit still long enough. Even the boys might try. Most single men had to know the way of it until they found a wife to do for them.

As if reading the direction of her thoughts, Chumani gave her a regretful look. "Little sister, tomorrow I'm going to have to cut your time short. I have to get some fencing set up with Tokala during the day, and it will put me far behind in my night work. I've already talked to the others, and no one has a couple hours to spare tomorrow."

She pressed Elisa's arm, acknowledging how much the girl looked forward to her visits, but then lightened her tone. "Of course, if you do all these lazy louts' mending, you'll be like Cinderella, too many things to do to go to the ball anyhow. If Kohana wasn't so clumsy with those big hands of his, they wouldn't be so eager to take you up on it."

"If you knew what being a woman was all about, you'd have taken it over long ago," Kohana retorted.

"You're enough of a woman for both of us," she returned sweetly, and set off a round of guffaws as the big Indian lobbed a metal pot at her. The speed and strength was such it took Chumani's second-mark reflexes to dodge it. It winged past her and Mal caught it with barely a blink. Elisa saw they were both grinning, though, and realized such rough play was normal.

"What if I drove myself?" She blurted it out quickly. "You've let me drive with you in the passenger seat a couple times now. I've been there plenty of times, and know how to operate the gates, after all. There's no danger as long as I follow the rules."

The commotion at the table stilled, and all eyes went to Mal. He set aside his cup, wiping the blood residue off his lips with the back of his hand, showing a flash of fang as he did it. "I'll be fine," she repeated staunchly. "It's silly to keep sending someone with me when you know it's unnecessary. Your people have enough to do. You can trust me."

He put his feet down, sitting up straight on his bench against the tree. "Come over here."

She rose, a little nervous at the tone, her stomach wobbling for more reasons than one, but she skirted around the edge of the table. When she stopped in front of him, he rose and cupped her face, tilting her chin up and holding her steady and firm, a reminder of who had a handle on everything here. She didn't know if he intended that reminder or it was just how it looked while he plumbed her mind for her sincerity. She wasn't afraid of that scrutiny.

He released her, his chest and fine shoulders filling her view as she lowered her chin. "You take a radio. If anything comes up, you call Kohana. I don't care how minor a problem it is; you don't handle it yourself." He mortified her, as well as snapped her gaze back up, when his hand closed over her right buttock.

"You step over the line one inch, I'll blister your ass until you can't move, and then I'll take you to my bed and really remind you why it's wise to obey me."

Her face flushed. She wasn't unused to public chastising, because it was always a possibility for a servant, but this was decidedly different. She was entirely certain that wasn't the kind of punishment he'd dished out for Tokala.

That possessive look, and the proximity of his body, were doing what they always seemed to do to her. It was impossible to act simply like an employee receiving instruction from an employer. Especially when his grip eased so he could trace his knuckles along the curve of her arse, a far more provocative and teasing touch, indulging his own desires. Mal didn't care that the others saw, though she noted that the hands were kind enough to be studiously eating and talking among themselves. What unnerved her, however, was it didn't matter. She'd stand there as long as he wanted to touch her.

Bloody vampires.

A smile touched his firm lips and he released her. However, before he stepped back, he caressed her cheek, tugged one of her curls in what would have passed for affection if anyone else was doing it. "All right, then. Chumani, tomorrow night make sure she has a radio and knows how to use it."

21

SHE told herself to act as calm and efficient as she would be in the company of one of the island staff, as if there was nothing unexpected about her showing up alone. There really was no difference in procedure, except that when she went through the two-gate system to put things in the communal enclosure, she had to keep the outer gate wedged open until she came back out the inner gate. The inner gate controls were at the outer gate, and the outer gate controls were positioned on a pole embedded next to a stump for sitting. The outer gate controls also had the release buttons to the individual cell doors. It was a two-man system, designed to make sure there was always at least one locked gate between the inhabitants and staff. However, Mal had agreed it would still be quite safe as long as no fledglings were in the communal area until she had both gates securely locked between herself and them.

She further reassured herself with that thought, decidedly ignoring the hair-raising sensation that Leonidas was staring a hole into her when she wasn't looking toward him. Distributing blood in the small lockdown cages, she let everyone drink. They had discovered it was rare for any of the children to experience a bloodlust attack in the first hour or two after feeding, unless there was an unexpected stressor.

Jeremiah took his turn first in the communal enclosure, followed by William. She hoped Mal would eventually decide to let William and

Matthew out together, the way he did Miah and Nerida. When William was let into the communal area, he always went to Matthew's cell first, reaching through to touch the boy's shoulder or head. Despite what Mal said about vampires being more like the solitary cat species, she saw something of his lions in the way they used tactile gestures for affirmation. Likewise, during his time in the communal area, Matthew would eventually settle with his back against the gate to William's cell.

When his time was up, Jeremiah of course returned to his cell when she asked him to do so. Matthew and William did so more reluctantly, but mostly because they didn't want to be parted. It made her heartstrings tighten, but she was firm and reassuring at once. Given how well Matthew, Jeremiah and Miah had done on the open preserve together, Elisa nursed a hope that one day the cells might be needed very little, period. She liked to imagine William and Matthew living in a house, sharing a bedroom as brothers might.

Reminding herself there were two gates between her and him, and that Leonidas knew the consequences if he didn't go back in when told to do so, she let him out next. He had gulped his blood, watching her through his lashes with those narrowed red eyes. The other children had the crimson iris only when in bloodlust. Leonidas always had it. Whatever his original eye color had been was now a distant memory. She tried to imagine him with blue eyes or brown, settled on green as he prowled around the perimeter. He hissed at the others, who wisely stayed away from their cell doors, except for Jeremiah.

Jeremiah stayed within several feet of his door, arms crossed, feet spread, watching the vampire like a hawk. It was an oddly adult posture for a boy who appeared nine years old, the slim body braced and gray-green eyes intent. His fangs dug into his chin as if he was holding his jaw more rigidly than usual.

She dearly wished they could figure out how to get those fangs to retract. It had to make the fledglings more self-conscious around mature vampires, the constant problems with spittle, or flecks of blood and temporary scars where the fangs punctured the lip and chin.

"All right, then. It's time for you to go in so the girls can have their time." She said it reasonably enough, hoping that Leonidas wouldn't give her trouble and have to be forced back in by a call to Malachi. While she liked Chumani considerably, it was the first time she'd really been able to be alone with them since they'd arrived, and she liked having that uninterrupted time to talk to them without any self-consciousness of her own.

Leonidas gave her a sneer, a blatant defiance of the warning Mal had issued on the plane, but sauntered back to his cell. He knew he frightened her. Like all animals, whether human, vampire or otherwise, fear incited dangerous attention and, in his case, contempt. She could do little about it, though, except stay calm on the outside while continuing to struggle for it inside.

He went into his cell, closed it with a resounding clang, then shook it to show her it was locked. When he tossed her that derisive look again, it said clearly that, if he wasn't held in the cell, he would tear her to pieces. Beyond the fear, it made her sad, realizing Mal might be right, that there was less than Buckley's chance they could dissipate his rage or make his life better. Unlike the others, he'd never shown any interest in books, gadgets—anything that would prove he could be engaged by something other than the chance to kill.

She kept thinking she'd figure out the secret to him, though. Something that would change the tide of such thinking. She wondered what he'd been before. It was a game she played, like imagining his green eyes. At times she'd turned her game into stories for them, saying aloud what she thought they'd been like before. What sports they'd played, what their families might have been like. Miah and Nerida might be the only ones who really knew, since they'd been taken from their mothers, whereas the boys probably had come from orphanages.

Still, not remembering a family was all the more reason to imagine a variety of them. A father who was a famous traveler, carrying his son on his shoulders. A mother who was gentle and beautiful and could sing like a nightingale. Who never hit her daughter in the face with whatever object came to hand—her own personal fantasy. A grandmother who made pies and offered comforting, sage advice.

She supposed those were hardly original ideas, but every child who'd had no family—or one that might be worse than none at all—was comforted by such fantasies. She always allowed for significant pauses, and encouraged them to interrupt her if they wanted to give her the true version and correct hers. But they hadn't, not so far. They listened to the stories like a child listened to a fairy tale, seeing no real connection to their own lives. Ruskin may have erased all memory of such things, but eventually something she said might strike a spark.

Until then, she guessed she'd have to hope and fantasize for all of them.

She pressed the control to let out the two girls. Watching the way Nerida immediately ran to Miah, hugged her, she wondered if they'd been half sisters, sharing a mother and two different white fathers, perhaps coming through the area to work on the railway or fence lines.

Nerida brought the pieces of chocolate Elisa had left in her lockdown cage with the blood, offering Miah some. Though Elisa had given them an equal amount, and they both liked the sweets, Miah liked them even more and Nerida knew it. That was something the boys never did. They didn't share.

Elisa glanced down at the two books she'd brought to read by the lantern light. One had colorful pictures, a photography book of exotic places, but she thought she might read the poetry. They liked the singsong cadence of it, and Walt Whitman gave such beautiful descriptions of the world around them. It keyed into the desire to be free, soothing it in some odd way, as if the words could help transcend the cell bars. At least that was what she thought, because when Lady Constance had sent her to school and she'd discovered the book of Whitman poetry, it had made her feel that way about the more nebulous bars of her own life.

She wondered what Mal was doing. He'd intended to be in the leopard part of the range today, helping the adolescents learn to hunt. From Kohana, she understood that to mean he ran down game for the orphans, showing them by example how to do it. Chumani had said they were old enough that they would likely join in the hunt, jumping onto the creature to help bring it down, such that Mal would likely be able to pull back and let them do most of it except for the final kill, which was apparently the part that initially confused them, that clamp on the throat that would end the prey's life quickly.

Today's lesson likely wouldn't be quick *or* easy, so she was glad not to be there for that. She understood the point of it all, but she was just too softhearted to watch it.

Jeremiah cried out, a harsh shout. Elisa's head jerked up from the books, just in time to see Jeremiah leap forward and slam against his locked cell door, his hands clamping on the unyielding bars. Whipping her head around, she saw Leonidas shove open the door of his cell with a resounding clang. A glint of metal shot out of the locking mechanism, a shard she realized with horror he'd maneuvered into it to keep the locks from fully engaging.

He was in the communal enclosure with the two girls.

$\sim$

Nerida shrieked, darting behind Miah and grabbing the skirt of her dress, even as Miah tried to snatch her up and run back toward her cell, the closer of the two. She didn't make it. Leonidas was on her in an instant, knocking her to the ground, Nerida underneath her body. He had his hand clamped on the back of the older girl's neck, his knee in her back.

Elisa was on her feet, reaching for the control panel, but then she realized there was nothing she could do to help. She couldn't open the enclosure. Spinning on her toe, she grabbed for the radio instead.

"*No.*"

Kohana had said a lion's roar could carry as much as five or six miles. Leonidas's command shattered the calm of the clearing just that way. His crimson eyes burned into Elisa.

"Put . . . it . . . down. Or I tear . . . her head . . . off. Then . . . the other."

Put it down, Elisa. I know you're in trouble.

Lord in Heaven, how could she have forgotten? She didn't need the radio. Mal's voice was calm and deadly. It was peculiar—she hadn't thought he ever really listened in on what happened here, except for occasional babysitting checks. Now she wondered if he listened in more often. If he liked hearing poetry.

Strewth, what was she going on about? Her mind was splitting in half, refusing to see this was happening, wanting to prattle on about poetry. Shoving aside that dizzying sensation, she dug her nails fiercely into her palms. She refused to let past and present overlap and shut down her mind. They needed her. She needed to be fully here, no matter what.

Even now, since she'd appeared to hesitate, Leonidas had caught

Miah's hair, shifting his other hand around to the front of her throat. He could twist her head off with one wrenching motion, and he would do it in one blink to prove his threat. Then use Nerida for leverage.

"All right," she snapped. She laid the radio on the stump. The tranquil cover of *Leaves of Grass* mocked her. That day in the barn, one of the toys she'd given the children, a train engine, had been splattered liberally with Willis's blood. During Victor's rampage, it had gotten knocked into Matthew's reach. She remembered turning her head, watching out of glazed eyes as Matthew nervously sucked off the blood while Victor did what he was doing to her. She pressed her fingers down on the cover of the book, hard enough her bones protested. She hoped no blood got on it. She didn't want Walt Whitman to be ruined forever by whatever was about to happen.

God help me. Focus.

Nerida made a bleating cry as Leonidas shifted his grip. Nerida was buried beneath Miah, clinging like a baby roo inside her mother's pouch, her face hidden, body shaking enough to make Miah shake, or perhaps that was Miah shaking. Then Elisa realized Leonidas was rucking up Miah's skirt in the back, yanking her up to her knees as he tore open the front of his trousers. A skirt and trousers Elisa had made for them.

He notices them . . . Mal's words rang in her head. *Oh God.*

"No." She ran to the outside gate, gripped the links. Leonidas ignored her, slamming an engorged cock into Miah, no preamble, the way Elisa had seen cattle branded. The girl shrieked, but bit down on her lip ferociously, as if she'd realized long ago it just made the attacker enjoy it more. Victor had reveled in Elisa's tears and cries.

Elisa, I'm coming. We're all coming. Hold fast.

She was heeding him, she was, but she had to be closer, had to let the girls know she was as close as she could dare to be. So she released the outer gate, wedged it open a crack. The inner gate still stood between her and them. It was made of a type of steel Mal said the vampires couldn't tear open. "Stop it, Leonidas. *Stop!*"

He kept pummeling the girl, grunting like a hog, spittle gathering on his chin. But his eyes, those satanic red eyes, were focused on Elisa. In triumph, contempt . . . daring. She hated him then. Hated him with every ounce of her being and wanted him dead, wanted him staked and torn apart by animals. She didn't care what he'd been or what he could have been. This was all he was, this monster making a girl scream and cry and try to get away from him.

He turned his back on her, buttocks flexing obscenely as Miah wheelbarrowed on the ground, trying to escape his grip, but he had her fast. It freed Nerida, but instead of running to Miah's cell where she could have shut herself in, she scuttled in wide-eyed panic across the compound, toward Elisa. She landed against the interior gate, making it shudder.

As the child curled up in a ball against the fencing, whimpering, her frightened eyes fastened in pleading appeal upon Elisa. She knew she'd be next. He'd rape her next; then he'd kill them both. He'd been smart enough to engineer his escape, but he was all demonic beast, with no care that this would be the end of him. His only intent was to unleash the blood and rage that had been building inside of him.

Elisa, no. Mal's voice was thunder in her head, but his vehemence told her he might as well be off in the Never Never, because he was obviously too far away to stop whatever was going to happen for the next few minutes. All they had was her.

Jeremiah and William were both up against the bars of their cells, snarling, though she couldn't tell if it was bloodlust stirred by the violence or they were protesting Leonidas's behavior. Matthew was curled in a ball at the back of his cell, ears covered and rocking.

"No, stop it. Stop it!" Still screaming at him, she didn't let herself think or hesitate, anything that would give Leonidas a vital second of forewarning. She punched open the control to unlock the inner gate, yanked it open, reached down and caught the little girl by the arm, jerking her through.

Though she'd done all in one unbroken series of motion, Leonidas slammed against the inner gate just as she slammed it, the lock catching and holding, thank God. He'd moved like lightning, pulling out of Miah, dragging the girl with him. As his arm punched through the mesh opening of the inner gate, Elisa flung herself backward, Nerida wrapped around her. The wedged outer gate gave under the thrust of their combined weight. Nerida clawed her way out of Elisa's arms and was gone, disappearing like a ghost into the woods. Her kicking feet hit the swinging gate as she scrambled away and before Elisa could lunge and stop it, the outer gate clanged to a closing position. Nerida had locked her in the small space between the outer and inner gates.

Of all of them, Nerida was least likely to harm anyone before they could bring her back. Cutting her losses there, Elisa rose. As long as she kept her back against the outer gate, she was out of Leonidas's reach. And now, with her locked in, he had no way of blackmailing her with Miah's well-being to let him out of the enclosure entirely. Of course, she would have happily opened the gate to get him to release Miah, because Mal would have run him down like a cheetah on a turtle. But now it wasn't an option.

Leonidas howled, realizing it as well. Elisa pivoted, jutting her chin at him, despite the fact every muscle in her body was shaking, including those that controlled her vocal cords. "Now you're trapped, same as me. And the only thing that will save your life is if you let her go, let her go back to her cell and shut herself in."

"The only thing . . . save *her* life is you . . . in here. He kill me anyway. Don't command vampire . . . bitch."

Despite the lisp caused by the fangs, the spray of spittle, he was clear enough. So was Mal.

You tell that bastard letting her go is the difference between a long, slow death or a quick one. That's a promise.

Elisa spoke the words, feeling their strength, feeling the heat of a mature male vampire fill her, his rage and intent focusing on what was before her. She didn't mind feeling that bloodlust now. It was similar to what was going through her veins.

Leonidas spat, something horridly like a laugh strangling out of his throat. "This *is* slow . . . death. Stupid. At least Master . . . let us kill." The last three words were slurred in his long fangs, making a foam of his saliva. He didn't look like anything human anymore, not that he'd ever made that much of a pretense of it.

He held Miah in one arm, his hand fisted in her hair. The girl had tears on her face, her nose running with blood and phlegm, drool leaking from her mouth around the fangs. Elisa wondered if she'd been as grotesque after her rape, everything slack and lifeless, eyes dead like that, no dignity or modesty left. Everything ripped open raw. Neither victim nor perpetrator could hold on to a mask of humanity during such a thing, perhaps suggesting something deep and terrible about them all.

Elisa. Mal's voice, strained, telling her he was coming as fast as he could, such that even conveying a thought took precious effort. *You will not go into that cell.*

You're not close enough yet. He'll kill her before you get here.

He'll kill her anyway. Elisa—

Just after her rape, when someone was talking to her, sometimes a part of her stepped away, leaving her attentive face, dutifully appearing to record the words, a vague, meaningless acknowledgment of the person speaking. The rest of her went somewhere else, where it was just her, alone with the turmoil she was facing and the odd, disjointed thoughts that came with it.

Would Miah let her wash her face, her body? The way Mrs. Pritchett and Mrs. Rupert had done for her? Their quiet cluckings and silent tears had been a soothing lullaby that had let her stay in a stupor for a while, avoiding the stark reality of what had happened. Or, if Mal wouldn't let her be that close to Miah, would he do it for the girl? She thought he might. Which was good, because she might not be in any kind of shape to give Miah a bath after this.

There were several stakes and a crossbow hooked on one side of the square area, just in case they were needed. Picking up the stake, she estimated it would give her the extra arm length she needed. She looked toward Leonidas.

"Here's how it's going to be." Her voice had gone from shaking to eerily calm, almost hoarse. "I'll put my arm through this gate so you can hold on to me. You'll let her go, and when she gets in her cell and closes it, I'll use this stake to reach back and push the button behind me. The inner gate will open, and I'll come inside with you."

Mal had gone silent, probably because he knew he couldn't stop her. Or he was close. Either way, she wouldn't think. She couldn't. She just had to buy time. Leonidas would want to torture her, violate her. He wouldn't want to kill her immediately. He'd waited too long to have her at his mercy. She *would* survive this. She'd survived it before and no worthless, raping piece-of-cursed-garbage vampire was going to end things for her. She was stronger than that, and so was Miah. She met the girl's gaze, and that link helped her still her trembling hand on the stake.

So be it.

Leonidas stared at her as she extended her arm through the gate. The single limb was undeniably pale and fragile under that violent gaze. She let her fingers brush Miah's hair. The girl's dark eyes stayed on hers, and whatever Elisa could give her in that single exchange, she did. It helped her not think of what was ahead. Even without a blood-link between them, she hoped the girl understood the most important thing Elisa was thinking at her, hard enough that if will alone was all it took, it should be scrolling across Miah's brain in bright lights.

Run like the devil, the second he lets you go.

"There's your offer," Elisa said, shifting to hold those red eyes in the grip of her own. Her fear had gone, buried beneath that numbness. She wondered if it had worked the same for Miah, rape after rape, when she knew she couldn't stop it. But this wasn't the same. Elisa wasn't going to let go of control. She was making the choice. That made all the difference. She knew Mal would be angry with her, but some things a person had to do. There were too many bad things in the world to stop them all, so when one was laid before you like this, you had no choice. She suspected he probably knew that as well as she did.

Summoning up something black and dreadful in herself, as fearsome as what lay in a vampire's heart, whether it was the one before her or the one she sensed coming to their aid like a streak of dark lightning, she spoke again. "You know you've wanted human meat ever since Victor took me down under your nose and didn't share. Prove you're even more of a monster than he is. Let go of her, you bludger."

Before she could flinch, his hand clamped over her arm. He could tear it from the socket, break her bones like twigs. Yank her forward and crush her windpipe. But to do that last one, he had to let go of Miah. Plus, everything he wanted had narrowed to getting Elisa inside the enclosure with him, all his rage and violence culminating into one summary act.

What had Mal said? You never run from a predator; you never look away. He might kill you anyway, but he would for sure do so if you ran. She wasn't going down as prey; that was for damn sure.

Leonidas dropped his hold on Miah, and the girl was gone. Elisa had a brief impression of her flashing into her cell. Metal vibrated under her arm as Miah slammed the cell door.

Jeremiah was shouting something unintelligible through those interfering fangs. William was still snarling, further garbling any communications. Bloodlust had seized them fully, she was sure, the noises a pack's brutal encouragement. She understood. Mal had taught her a few things these past couple weeks. When instinct was involved, there was no fault or blame. It was simply the way life was. Like her instinct to save Miah and Nerida now.

It was then she heard Mal. No longer trying to stop her, as if he knew that was futile, but giving her something else.

Hold on, Elisa. I'll get there.

I know.

She pushed the button with the stake and the door buzzed its release. In the next blink, Leonidas had yanked the gate forward and ripped her away from it like a shred of ribbon. The stake skittered away on the ground as he punched her brutally in the face.

~

It hurt like bloody hell, but she was hazily sure he'd pulled the punch, because otherwise he would have broken her neck. Her head was reeling so much from the blow, she was barely conscious of him tearing at her flesh, the painful puncture of his fangs above her nipple as he shredded her clothes away from her. It was odd, but that was where Victor had bit her first as well. Was it a buried need, some twisted need to reconnect to the mothers they'd lost?

The disjointed thought sparked with lightning flashes of pain. Though she felt all of it, heard the scream that tore from her throat as a bone broke somewhere on her, perhaps at her thigh as he wrenched her leg outward, she was somehow floating as well. There was a noise, a short buzzing sound, like the gate releasing, and she wondered if he'd somehow rocked the inner gate door so hard it had slammed back against its own controls, bouncing there so it was depressing it in those irregular rhythms.

She was yanked up from the ground, shaken like a rag doll, but now it was more than Leonidas. She tried to blink through the blood in her eyes, to make sense of the whirling dervish going on above her. William . . . Yes, William was on Leonidas's back, his arm around the older boy's throat. Jeremiah was between her and Leonidas, freeing the lock of his hands on her, which explained the rag-doll effect before she was freed, thudding to the ground. She was being dragged back by two sets of hands, and got a momentary glimpse of Miah and Matthew leaving her to join the fray.

The noise was incredible, like the fighting dogs Mal had told her about. But this wasn't Rodney's calm pack logic, establishing dominance without real damage. This was a primal melee, as the others tore at Leonidas, pummeling him as he'd done to her.

But he was fighting them, and Elisa knew he was much stronger. Picking up Jeremiah, he spun the boy away from him with a snap of popping shoulder bone and shoved him nearly twenty feet away, sending him tumbling across the grass. He clawed at William's face, caught his collar and started to flip him over his head, but Miah launched herself at his front, taking Jeremiah's place. The girl was screaming, not the pitiful, fearful mewls of earlier. This was a shrill scream like the ferocious cheetah, sending out a call to warn others away from her territory.

Elisa tried to move, but things weren't cooperating. She couldn't even seem to move her arms without spears of blinding pain shooting through her sides and neck. Everything felt wet with blood. It was as if she'd fallen into some terrible, rank billabong and come out coated in viscous red mud, the sand turning it into grit.

Leonidas seized Miah by the throat. When he plunged his fist forward, Elisa saw it hit her midbody. She wished she could have looked away fast enough, because that fist exploded from Miah's back, splitting flesh and bone, the image forever seared across Elisa's mind.

"No . . ." Despite the pain, Elisa tried to reach out, tried to do something. Miah was tossed away from him. The girl landed near her, her loose arm flung above her head, fingers brushing Elisa's bloody calf. In that second, the second when Leonidas's eyes followed her track, Jeremiah returned. The boy plowed into Leonidas's chest and abdomen, his torso tucked in a bullish charge, head down, arms close to the body.

William let go, jumping back. Elisa cried out, not understanding why William would leave the fight, knowing Jeremiah couldn't take Leonidas toe-to-toe. But then she saw why.

Leonidas spun around, trying to dislodge Jeremiah, a howl bursting from his lips. As he did, she saw the stake he'd knocked out of her hand earlier. The point of it was jutting out of his back.

Jeremiah's arms and legs were wrapped hard around him, holding that stake in place between them. Leonidas roared, beating the boy's back so that she could see the ribs caving in like a matchstick creation.

Jeremiah, no . . . She was able to roll to her side, and peeled her lips back in a feral snarl, fighting the pain, daring it to stop her as she crawled forward, touching Miah's twitching arm. She couldn't get farther than the girl's bare foot, her vision starting to blacken and gray. She'd pass out if she tried to get to Jeremiah. While some part of her suggested that unconsciousness would be a blessing, she couldn't leave them alone to face this. She pushed her forehead into the torn-up ground, gripping Miah's ankle with her blood-smeared hand, fighting for awareness.

She lifted her head again when Leonidas hit the fence with a harsh clang and started to slide down it. Jeremiah still clung like a burr to the larger boy. He lifted his head, locking gazes with Leonidas. Jeremiah's face held a terrible expression as the life died out of Leonidas's. His lips formed words; then he was falling, dropping to the ground, back still propped up against the fence.

That ringing tone of impacted metal died to a hum, then was gone, leaving silence. A silence broken by Miah's wheezing, William's faint growling and what she realized were Jeremiah's sobs. He had the one hand so firmly locked on the stake it was halfway into Leonidas's chest cavity. The boy leaned into Leonidas's dead body, such that it looked like he was curled in his lap, his temple against Leonidas's shoulder as his own narrow ones shook.

His head turned, though, his eyes finding her. The starkness in that gaze pierced Elisa to the core, hurt her more deeply than anything had ever hurt her in her life, even Willis's death.

Chumani was wrong. She wasn't all that brave, because she couldn't find the strength to do anything now. Not think, or move, or hope or feel. Not to face terrible, desolate truths. She could only look at Jeremiah's face and think this kind of blood would never, ever wash away.

22

S HE'D placed the radio on the stump, and when she had, the weight of the books alongside had kept the receiver depressed. Kohana had been listening to gospel spirituals, but he'd deliberately kept them turned down below his preferred blasting volume, just in case Elisa needed something. Or Chumani wanted to banter with him. When the static crackled on the walkie-talkie at his hip and he'd heard the maid's voice, Mal's command came through his mind, through all their minds, at the very same moment.

Kohana wasn't surprised to find the vampire already on the move. They all knew his growing bond with the pretty miss. But his own reaction—all of them, felt through that shared bond—was the same. The girl was impossible not to love. *Please, Great Spirit, let nothing happen to her.*

Kohana lurched through the house, snatching up his shotgun and making it down the steps and to his ATV faster than he'd moved in a long time. He took the walkie-talkie with him, though hearing what was happening, the screams and growls, he damn near ran off the mountain, pushing the small vehicle past safe speeds. But they needed to get there as soon as they could, for Mal. In a situation like this, a man was likely to do all sorts of crazed things. An enraged vampire, protecting what he considered his, would leave a swath of death in his wake.

~

Mal cut a path across the leopard's territory, streaked over a corner of the cheetah's base, heard his shrieking cry. He was scenting blood and danger on the wind, just like Mal. Elisa's thoughts and the quick images he was seeing only made him push himself faster. The rest of his mind tracked the staff. Kohana's race up the slopes in his ATV, Chumani, Tokala and the others coming from the habitat area and open preserve, already preparing their weapons.

It didn't matter. They were all going to be too late. That stubborn core of steel of hers had come forward, poured itself over every fear, every lick of sense and self-preservation she had. He'd thought he could hold her back, but Leonidas, the conniving little monster, had known he couldn't. The fledgling had signed his own death warrant, but with his warped bloodlust fully unleashed now, he didn't care about that, any more than Victor had.

Leonidas had likely been plotting this, looking for his chance every moment, just as Mal had suspected. With that chaos as well as blood-lust always clouding the forefront of his mind, there'd been no way Mal could decipher it until it came to fruition. He hadn't anticipated the vampire having one singular focus, Elisa, but it made perfect sense. Leonidas was a combination of vampire and psychopath, a damaged child betrayed by all the parental figures in his life. Focusing on the latest person who'd tried to step into those shoes, he'd destroy her as the symbol of all the rest.

Mal emerged from the woods, the cuts from whipping tree branches healing under his torn shirt even as he moved in ground-eating leaps down the steep slope to the fledglings' compound. The maelstrom reached his ears now. Cries and growls, screams and roaring. As he came into the open clearing, he saw Miah tossed aside, a bloody mess that landed near Elisa. The maid's clothes were torn and blood-soaked, her leg at an odd angle. Black rage coated his mind, momentarily making him as insensible and blood-driven as Leonidas, but then Jeremiah's hoarse yell yanked his mind back.

It was a challenge, roared in his thin, young voice as he launched himself into Leonidas. The stake drove in, carried by sheer will through

Leonidas's body as Jeremiah clasped him in a bone-breaking hold. William, holding the older boy back, jumped away and rolled free, his job done.

There was that terrible struggle, the death moment hanging on the edge of a precipice; then Jeremiah and Leonidas were against the fence. Leonidas slid down, life going from him.

Mal had harshly trained his staff not to respond to emotional imperatives in a crisis, but even now he waged a brief, painful war with his own gut reaction. Forcing himself to slow and evaluate what threats remained was one of the hardest things he'd done in a very long time. He grappled with the need to tear apart everything between him and Elisa.

Nerida was curled in a ball on the stump. She hugged the pole that held the controls to the outer gate and the fledglings' cell doors. Her hand was still resting below those release buttons, making it clear who'd let the others out of their cells. She was vibrating so hard her small buttocks were quivering against the rough wood.

An eerie silence had descended upon the group, a quiet that seemed to connect and bind them. Jeremiah was still huddled in Leonidas's lap. Matthew had crept out of his cell, gone to Miah's side. He was stroking her hair, making a quiet noise Mal recognized as grief, held hard inside the boy's throat, as if he feared letting it out. William moved to him then and stood at his back, watching to see what Mal would do. He was the lone sentry, for Jeremiah had his eyes closed, head bowed. His hand, still fastened on that stake, was coated with blood and gore from Leonidas's insides.

"Nerida. You need to go back inside now." Mal spoke quietly, dialing back the lethal fury coating him that could add to the mix of an already volatile situation. He wanted to get into that enclosure area, to touch, to reassure, more than he wanted anything else. But she was alive; she would survive. He *had* to handle this first.

Nerida slowly uncurled, stepped off the stump and to the ground. Looking at his wet and muddy boots, coated with torn grass, she held her ground to speak one word in that fanged slur.

"Help?" Her dark eyes shifted to the blood-soaked ground around Miah and Elisa. "Miah. Leesa."

"Yes. We'll help them." His jaw tightening, he reached out.

She dropped, covering her head and bringing her legs up. He stopped in midmotion. Something turned over hard inside Mal's chest. Something that was deepest sorrow and hell-born rage, all at once. He swallowed.

"I've changed my mind. Stay right here instead." He spoke when he could trust his voice to be calm, as if nothing unusual had happened. "When we determine how she is, I'll let you come see her."

She crawled back over to the stump, scooching down with her back against it. Her eyes never left the mangled form of the other Aboriginal girl, twitching in the sand.

Mal entered the enclosure. Elisa's hand was on the girl's ankle, her head turned toward Jeremiah. Her breath was labored, suggesting critical injury that would soon become excruciating pain. Still, it was a deep, soul-shuddering relief to see her eyes were open, though glazed with shock. Right before she'd challenged Leonidas, he'd seen her gripped by the post-traumatic stress of what had happened to her before, and he'd hoped it would freeze her in place, hold her there. Instead, she'd handed herself over to Leonidas. When her fledglings had come to her defense, she'd registered every blow given and taken, gripped with fear that she was going to see Leonidas tear them apart in front of her.

Only a mother thought like this. Only a mother could have managed to get past what had been done to her, shove it aside as if it were nothing more important than yesterday's dirty laundry, and throw herself right in the middle of it for them. Only a mother could divide her mind that way, because nothing was more important to her than her children.

His mind went back to miles of dusty track, his mother's back bowed under his weight when he couldn't walk anymore, his feet frozen and bleeding. Scientists could call it what they wanted, a reproductive or biological imperative, but to anyone with a sense of God or a heart, it was love, pure and simple. Theories of obsession or misplaced guilt could be argued. Self-righteous do-goodery could be assigned to self-interest with little effort. But nothing could dismiss true love.

He closed his eyes, something he'd never have done in the presence of a group of unpredictable fledgling vampires, but the power of that memory, one he hadn't unlocked in so long, had the ability to knock him off his axis. *Focus. Breathe, even though you don't need to.* Tightening his jaw, he opened his eyes, and resumed his assessment.

William was pretty banged up, whereas Jeremiah and Miah's injuries were most severe. William had the wild, fierce look that male vampires had who'd been engaged in a mortal combat. His hands were still half-closed into fists, his stance more aggressive than he'd ever dared around Mal.

Don't . . . hurt them. Please, Mal.

Unfortunately, a mother's love could be so overwhelming she didn't believe anyone else saw the truth that she did. Still, he felt another hard, shuddering wave of relief at the sound of her mind-voice, weak though it was. *Be at ease,* atsilusgi. As he moved across the compound, he gave William a nod, male to male. "You did well. Take Matthew to your room and close the door. The staff is coming to help and I need you out of the way."

He didn't say it unkindly. The boy nodded. Grasping Matthew's arm, he brought him to his feet, murmuring something. Keeping his arm wrapped around him, he moved them to his cell. Mal knew it was a risk, but he was seeing some things with new eyes. He'd be willing to bet money that, even in bloodlust, William wouldn't harm the smaller boy. And he was strong enough to handle Matthew if he had an attack.

Keeping an eye toward Nerida and Jeremiah, Mal knelt between the two females. Elisa was shaking, repeating that pleading mantra in her mind. She was terrified he would dispatch them when she lost consciousness, thinking they were all somehow responsible for this. The effort she was putting into it was monumental, given how little strength she had. It wasn't misplaced. Anger filled him anew at the sight of her torn clothes, all the blood.

Moments before, he wouldn't have trusted himself not to do exactly as she feared. But he was looking at five fledglings who'd undeniably risked their own lives to come to her defense.

Do you think I'm so heartless, Irish flower, that I can't see what happened here?

Not heartless. Just . . . chronically practical.

"You are far too well educated for a maid," he murmured in a gentle voice as his hands moved over her, confirming the damage. Two broken ribs. Her thighbone hadn't snapped as he feared, only badly wrenched, so the ribs were the worst of it, though she had a number of open wounds, and her face was already swelling where Leonidas had first hit her.

A second-mark didn't have the healing ability of the third-mark, but it was still considerable. If they had the ribs taped and the leg reset by a process he would make sure she wasn't awake to experience, she should be herself again in a week or so. If she were his third-mark, he could give her blood, make it easier . . .

"Miah," she rasped. "I'm all right, but check . . ."

"You won't tell me what to do, or the order in which I do it." But he couldn't deny the raw look in those blue eyes. "I'm here, Elisa. Everything will be taken care of. All right?"

"Is she . . . going to make it? Her heart . . ."

He nodded. "Easy, girl." Still, under her worried gaze, he laid a hand on the wounded female vampire. Leonidas had put his fist through the chest wall, and it was ugly and gaping, oozing blood. He'd been able to compress the heart with a battery of broken ribs, but he'd mainly punctured the lung. It explained her wheezing. It was not a pleasant injury for a vampire, and she'd need blood and recuperation time, but she'd be all right. Unfortunately, she'd be in excruciating pain for the hours of the mending. He hoped she remained unconscious as long as possible. She was going to need a great deal of fresh blood to expedite the healing, though he expected when the hands understood what had happened here, they'd all willingly donate. He already heard the three Jeeps pulling up, as well as Kohana's ATV.

"I'll give her my blood." Still disoriented, she was trying to reach toward the girl. He caught her shoulders, holding her down as her face screwed up from the pain.

"No, you won't. Elisa, you're not thinking clearly. Lie still."

"If I'm dying, what does it matter if I give them blood or not?"

"You are not going to die. Elisa, I mean it. Lie still." He forced himself to sound like his irritable self and tapped her cheek, making sure her eyes riveted to his face. As they did, he stroked the tear tracks from the corners of her eyes. "You're worse than a deaf hound."

"Suppose that's because I'm not a dog," she mumbled with some of her usual spirit. The kind that usually bubbled around in her head, calling him a bloody galah, telling him to rack off, even as she stayed polite-as-you-pleased to his face. It almost made him smile. Or do something worse and far less manly.

In point of fact, she was as loyal and courageous as any dog he'd ever met. Despite that, he frowned. "You're forgetting which things you need to say to me in your head, and which you need to say with your mouth."

Her limbs twitched, and a small cry forced its way out her stiff lips. "Mal, this hurts."

"I know." Putting his forehead against hers, he framed her face, closing his eyes. Her small hand brushed against his elbow, her soft, ragged sigh passing over the bridge of his nose, taking his comfort. "We're going to take care of that. I'll take care of everything. The fledglings will be cared for. You have my word. Sleep now, while we do that."

She nodded. However, as her eyes closed and he reluctantly began to rise, she murmured something. He squatted again. "What?"

"Not your fault. You had to do it. So brave. It's okay."

Mal cocked his head. "Do what?"

She opened her eyes with obvious effort. "Jeremiah. He's hurting . . . upset that he had to kill Leonidas. He said he was sorry."

She gave a harrowing jerk then, a small spurt of blood seeping from her nose. Mal clasped her shoulders, holding her steady, his heart in his throat when consciousness left her. For a moment he thought he was wrong, that her wounds had been mortal and she was dying right in front of him. Reassuring himself, he tracked her pulse a moment more. When he stroked a matted curl from her face, passed a thumb over her lips, he noticed a tremor. In his own arm.

It startled him enough to rock him onto his heels. He gave himself a mental shake. There were things to do. Even so, it took a surprising amount of effort to rise, move toward the gate.

Kohana had the shotgun shouldered. The others were similarly armed with weapons, including crossbows. Not yet knowing what had happened, they were ready to shoot the lot of them like fish in a barrel. Every fledgling in the enclosure knew it. Nerida's eyes were wide, her face mostly hidden in her knees as Chumani kept her crossbow trained on her. In his cell, William had shifted Matthew behind him.

What struck Mal was that the three vampires were braced for it. They recognized he might do what he'd thought best from the beginning, exterminate the lot of them. They had no expectation that he'd tell his staff the truth of what had occurred, or if that would even count for anything.

Jesus, Ruskin had been a bastard.

"They saved her life," Mal said. "Took out Leonidas, all together."

When it sank in, there were surprised looks, an easing of shoulders. He nodded, shifting to brisk efficiency, which he knew everyone would handle better than a riot of emotions right now. Particularly himself. He'd hired them for their pragmatic natures, after all, though perhaps Elisa would call it a contagious condition they'd caught from him. *Chronically practical.* Instead of the thought making him smile, it made his gut hurt worse.

"We'll need a stretcher to take Elisa out of here. Kohana, she needs heavy sedation to keep her under while we set that leg and tape her ribs. Miah requires several quarts of blood, so get to the nearest supply shack for transfusion equipment and set up a triage here. I'll carry her back into her enclosure and get everyone secured. Kohana, pull those extra blankets out of the back of Tokala's Jeep we use as slings to transport sedated cats. Put a couple on Miah's bed so we don't bloody her sheets. Once she stabilizes, she'll need a bath and a change of clothes . . ."

As he issued further directives, he turned his attention to Jeremiah. The boy hadn't moved, though he'd stopped shaking. Now he was so still, they could pour mud over the two of them there and let them bake, a macabre piece of curious statuary.

"You all start working on that. I'll go talk to Jeremiah, and see what's to be done there. Tokala, Bidzil, once I get him back in his cell, take Leonidas out to the point so the morning sun can have him." He paused, glanced back at Elisa, though he hardly needed the visual. He hadn't let go of her mind, holding it practically in the cupped palm of his soul even in its unconscious state. "Say a prayer over him. He wasn't always this, and she'd want that honored."

Tokala nodded, understanding. Kohana spoke then, tersely. "Will she be all right?"

Mal grunted. "Not after I wring her neck."

It was the right thing to say, obviously, because expressions eased further. As the others began to disperse to do his bidding, he touched Chumani's arm. "Are you comfortable sitting with Elisa and Miah while I deal with Jeremiah?"

Chumani put her hand over his, squeezed. "Couldn't keep me away," she said quietly. Her grip was shaky. It was going to take some time for them all to settle down. A night like this made him regret not allowing alcohol on the island.

Before going to Jeremiah, he returned to Nerida. He stopped three feet away from her, watched the small chin adjust to stare at his boots again. "She's going to be okay, but she's going to hurt for a while. We're going to move her back to her cell and give her blood, tend to her. She'll need you with her. Are you willing to help?"

Her thin fingers laced and unlaced. She wasn't brave enough to speak again, but she nodded, a quick jerk.

"Very well, then. Go and get the blankets from Kohana. You can help him spread them on Miah's bed so she doesn't get blood on it."

Nerida got to her feet, slunk over to the Jeep. Mal watched as the child held out sticklike arms. Kohana met his gaze, but then gave Nerida a bundle of blankets, which the girl managed to get back into the enclosure, repeatedly gathering the bundle up so the corners wouldn't drag the ground, though the blankets bounced against her knees. Thinking of how devoted the two girls were, how often they exchanged touch, he thought he'd let Nerida sleep in Miah's cell tonight. Along the same line as his thoughts about William and Matthew, and after seeing what had happened here, he knew Nerida would be safe with the bigger girl, even in bloodlust. And tonight particularly, he wasn't going to make anyone be alone.

Chumani sent him a wan smile where she knelt between the two injured females. Squaring his shoulders, pushing away the pointless yet almost overwhelming urge to take Chumani's place, Mal turned his attention to the next matter.

~

He strode across the enclosure, toward Jeremiah. Leonidas was well and truly gone, the boy's eyes staring glasslike down on Jeremiah's bent head. Mal went to a squat, studying the two. Jeremiah was coiled inside the spread of Leonidas's thighs, bracing himself on one with a blood-stained hand. He lifted his head when Mal appeared in the corner of his vision, though Mal was sure he'd heard his approach. Or maybe not. The boy's expression looked distant, his mind obviously sunk deep into somewhere else.

"She's going to be fine," Mal said. "They both are, thanks to you. Thanks to you all."

Jeremiah's expression didn't change, but Mal didn't think that was because the boy didn't hear him. Elisa's words were replaying in his mind, and he was quite certain Jeremiah already knew she was going to be all right. How that was possible, he didn't know, but he wouldn't address that now, and not just because the fledgling was in no shape to answer pointed questions. Mal didn't trust himself to keep a handle on what was simmering in his own mind.

The possessiveness he was feeling was all animal instinct, but he of all people knew the dangers of vampire and human alike denying their animalistic natures. Mal's vampire nature was seething, wanting to take something apart. He was still young enough, in vampire terms, to have to deal with the ragged edge of his own bloodlust in an environment saturated with this kind of violence. And this young vampire had removed the one justified outlet to deal with that, while inadvertently moving himself into the bull's-eye range.

"You . . . kill us?" The question was asked in a dull mutter, as if the words had no real meaning or interest to the boy.

"Not today," Mal said. Reaching out, he closed his hand over the boy's wrist, attached to the hand that was mired in Leonidas's chest with the stake. "Let go, boy. It's all right. He's gone."

Jeremiah blinked. In the end, Mal had to loosen his fingers, staining his own with the clotting and cooling blood. "Go back to your cell; shut the gate. The staff are going to come in and treat Miah. We'll get Elisa back to the house and tend her there. I'll leave Chumani and Tokala here to watch over you all tonight. In case you need anything."

Jeremiah stared at his bloodied hand, limp in Mal's grip. Slowly, he drew it away, cradled it as if it were something fragile, his eyes shifting to the shaft of wood still protruding from the dead fledgling. Rising slowly, he swayed. Mal rose as well, ready to brace him, but Jeremiah stepped back, making it clear touch wasn't welcome. His legs steadied. Though the boy was quite a bit shorter, when he lifted his gaze to Mal's, it felt as if the power of the pain he carried had them meeting eye to eye.

"We . . . won't need anything," Jeremiah said, slowly enough to make it distinct. "We'll watch over ourselves."

23

SHE swam in her dreams, languid, too heavy to surface into the world of the living. If she was dead, this was not too bad, because she floated past things she liked. The wildflowers blooming after the wet. The way the land around the station went on and on, like God's promise of eternity. Mal's hair, rippling over his bare shoulders as he squatted in nothing more than jeans, watching his cats with patient eyes. Long, bronze fingers pressed into the grass, connecting him to the earth. When they touched her, they connected her to him, to the earth, to everything.

Willis had her in his arms and they were dancing at one of the picnic races. Turning on a wooden floor covered with sawdust, with the music twirling with them. Then Mal was there and she was between them both, past and present, with no idea of her future. But Willis's hands slipped away, and there was only Mal's touch, a mixture of pain and loss, pleasure and hope. They knotted together in her heart, making it hurt.

It was the first sign she was coming back to reality. She wanted to fight it, but she didn't fight duty. A servant rose at dawn's first light—or, in a vampire's household, at three in the afternoon—making sure everything was in order. There were the children . . . fledglings, to check on. But Leonidas was gone. Now there were only five.

Instead of floating, now she appeared to be on murky ground. When her toes curled, it felt like warm sand on the beach, or the grass of a lushly manicured lawn. The Collins family had such a lawn. Once, she'd snuck out at night and run through it barefoot, terrified of getting caught, but unable to resist. She was there now, standing in darkness, her feet in that grass, bugs chirping. Then it faded away and she was looking far down a beach. A distant figure appeared, a boy close to becoming a man, with brown hair and a gangly stride. He wore trousers with suspenders and no shirt, carrying his fishing gear and a healthy brace of fish. When he got close enough to her, he stopped, looked toward her with eyes as green as the grass on which she stood.

"My name was John," Leonidas told her. "I'd forgotten, till now." Then, with a smile that wasn't quite a smile, he turned and kept walking down the beach, until he disappeared into a fog rolling in off the crashing waves, a storm building.

That storm was in her, because she surfaced with tears on her face, sobs making her chest ache with a thousand shards of pain. Wide hands were spread over a bandage that had been wrapped around her rib cage, giving her support. "It's okay," Mal murmured in that rumble of calm she needed with all her heart. "It's all right, Elisa. I'm here. It's just a dream."

Oh, I hope not. I hope it's real. May it be the most real thing ever . . .

She thought he heard her, because his brow lifted. She saw it as she opened her eyes and focused on the world around her, her present world.

She was in her bedroom, and it was perhaps an hour until dawn, because the sky had that dark gray tinge. His hip pressed near hers, he sat on the edge of her bed, his knee crooked up on the mattress. He should be in his room, or at least farther back into the recesses of the house, because the first rays of dawn would stream in through that open window.

"Do you ever stop trying to take care of everyone and everything, Irish flower?"

"No more than you do," she said with a scratchy-sounding voice.

He looked surprised at that; then his lips twitched. There were other, worrisome things to consider, to ask, but at this second she wasn't up to it. She would give herself one minute to study the sculpted bones of his native warrior's face, the serious set of his mouth, the firm line of his jaw. His hair was getting longer, suggesting he hadn't time to cut it, and he had it back in a short braid. She'd thought about doing that, slipping off the bench one night during those casual meals with the staff to brush and braid it for him. She'd weave in ribbons and feathers so he'd look like a warrior in truth. She'd thought of it when she found a few feathers on one of her outings, probably from a caracal's kill, and put them in a cup on her dresser.

He cocked his head. "Perhaps I should let you do that. It's an aggravation to me to do it for myself, but I might like the touch of your hands." He covered one now, surrounding it with warmth and strength, and that was all it took. The tears overflowed, and the shaking swept through her very bones. She wanted to be held, but she hurt so much that her sobs made her rib cage feel like it was going to shatter and explode.

Bracketing one arm on the outside of her body, he cupped her face. He didn't try to move her, but he came all the way down until his forehead was pressed to hers, like at the enclosure. She gripped him, held on for dear life as the terror and memory of what had nearly happened, and what *had* happened, took hold. His hands closed over her rib cage again, and he kissed her tearstained cheeks, her nose, her forehead, then trailed down to brush her mouth, her chin. His kisses fell on her throat, her collarbone, the upper rise of her breasts, the lower curve, just above where his thumbs pressed into the crease. It was a peculiar feeling, her grief wrapped in those featherlike touches of his mouth that seemed to draw away some of the pain.

He stopped at her abdomen, nuzzling her, then laid his head down on her there, the braid sliding down to where her hand rested on the sheets. She freed the thong holding it, and then unraveled it, spreading it out so she could stroke it the same way she'd wanted to stroke the lion's mane. But he'd told her it was dangerous to treat a wild animal like a trusted pet. Ever.

"Jeremiah and the rest saved my life."

"Yes, they did." He lifted his head.

"And you wouldn't let me give Miah blood."

"No, I wouldn't. For one thing, you were too weak. For another . . ." He moved to her throat, only this time the purpose wasn't comfort, but something altogether different. "I won't take the risk of them third-marking you, linking your life to theirs. A third marking is a truly . . . intimate . . . exchange." She drew in her breath at the feel of his fangs grazing her throat. His breath was hot there, stroking her. *Not something you would share with a fledgling. Or a child.*

For all that Mrs. Rupert asserted that males were simple and straightforward as fence posts, and usually thought with the part of their anatomy they optimistically imagined was most like one, Elisa thought they were a little more complex than that. The sheer possessiveness that entered his tone now, intertwined with his gratifying concern for her, was entirely unexpected. There was a missing piece of the puzzle here, but fortunately Mal was willing to enlighten her.

"Do you know when Jeremiah second-marked you?"

She drew back, pressing her head deeper into the pillow. "He hasn't."

"He told you he was sorry about killing Leonidas, right before you passed out. You remember that?"

"Of course. He said it to me."

"Elisa, he was all the way across the compound, and I heard nothing."

"But I've never given him blood directly." At his look, her temper spiked. "I've no reason to lie to you. You can plumb my bloody mind, right? Look there for the truth if you're not going to believe me."

She tried to struggle up on her elbows, feeling at a sudden disadvantage like this. The sharp pain that shot through her was enough to steal her breath, but she didn't want to be in this position anymore.

"Hold on, then. Stubborn girl." He surprised her by helping her sit up, easing her into an upright position and rearranging her pillows behind her so she could manage it. She imagined she must look frightful. Seeing a glimpse of herself in the dresser mirror, she was surprised to find her face was washed, her hair reasonably combed. The place where Leonidas had hit her was still bruised, but not as much as she expected, telling her how long she'd been out.

"Chumani came in and saw that you were cleaned up. I thought you'd prefer a woman to do that, though Kohana was all set to do it. He's turned into a mother hen when it comes to you."

"So why aren't *you* off working and letting one of them watch over me?"

He gave her a look, but touched her chin, stroked his knuckles over her cheek. "Don't avoid the question. Think. How could he have second-marked you, if you don't remember it?"

He had to be mistaken. Jeremiah had never had access to her, except . . .

She closed her eyes. "After Victor. He took off and they had to go hunt him down. So when they found me, they didn't know how long it was after the attack. I was on the barn floor, next to Jeremiah's cage. Dev said Jeremiah was holding my hand, just inside the cage. I was a mess, a lot of wounds." *A lot of bites . . .*

"He marked you through the wrist. And you didn't know."

"No. I . . ." She stopped, though, thinking about it. When things had been at their worst, she'd curled up into the tightest possible ball in her bed, her fist in her mouth. She'd hoped Danny wasn't listening in to her tears, and that Mrs. Pritchett wasn't feeling the trembling that shook her so hard the bed rattled in its frame. She'd shied from sleep until exhaustion made it impossible for her to do otherwise, and when she went under, she'd expected nightmares in that darkness.

Sometimes she did get those, but before they could break her, they would shift, and sleep became the one place she was soothed. It was gray fog and warmth, a soft touch on her brow, a stroking. A child's voice would be singing to her, easy lullabies from her childhood as well as songs she didn't know but would find herself humming when she worked around the station, keeping herself on an even keel.

She'd thought maybe she'd overheard the cook singing them, but then Mrs. Rupert had asked her what the song was, liking the tune.

It had been Jeremiah. Staying so quiet in her mind so she'd never know he was there. He'd been helping her stay together. It made so much sense now, why she'd felt so bonded to him, had never truly feared him the way she had the others. Was it a second mark, or . . .

"No, it's a second mark. I'd have detected a third mark on you, and so would Danny. Because you were already second-marked by Danny, and Jeremiah is so much younger, his mark was far weaker and concealed by hers, so to speak."

His expression was dispassionate, a closed book. Alarm trickled through her. "He didn't do it to hurt me. He's never spoken to me directly, not until what he said after Leonidas's attack. Is he okay? Have you checked on him since you brought me here?"

Mal rose. "I'll send Chumani in to look after you. I need to attend to some things."

"Wait." He was beyond the reach of her outstretched hand now. "You haven't told me how they are. Is Miah okay? And Matthew and Nerida? Are the children all—"

"Goddamn it, girl." Mal stopped in the doorway and turned to face her, right before she feared he'd been about to leave without another word. She wouldn't have put it past him. One moment he was positively nurturing; then the next he was the bloody Wall of China. Of course, she thought she might prefer either of those confusing states to this, his anger suddenly pouring out on her like a hot western wind. "How many times do these fledglings have to nearly kill you for you to realize they're *not* children? They're not your personal pets or your mission in life. Should I just throw you in with them, let them mangle and violate you over and over, until it penetrates that thick, common servant's head of yours?"

Elisa sucked in a breath, pain knifing under her rib cage. But he wasn't done. He'd pivoted fully, stepped back into the room, his mouth hard and tight. Almost ugly.

"Why do you worry about them every moment of the day? Any other young woman would be pining for the mainland, for dances and boys and a record player in her room. You're *not* their mother. You were given a job, to clean up after them and feed them their meals, to be their *maid*. The same job you've performed all your life. No more and no less. It shouldn't mean more than that."

A record player? His contempt and fury took the breath from her. In one vicious stroke he erased every kind or provocative thing he'd done toward her, painted everything in her life with the same brush, so none of it meant anything to anyone.

No, that was wrong. She managed to steel her trembling jaw, closing her hands into fists on the bedsheets again. "It means something to me."

She barely got it out, but it didn't matter. He was already gone.

～

The words that had come out of his mouth were vile poison. She hadn't deserved it; he already knew that. It was like everything he'd felt at the fledglings' compound—rage, fear and unreasoning jealousy—had suddenly overflowed. His gut churning, he took himself out of the house. While he pointedly ignored Chumani and Kohana's condemning glances when he passed them in the kitchen, he curtly told them to watch over her.

His skin crawled with the impending dawn, beads of sweat breaking out as he drove through the night. He went to the shore, leaving the Jeep high above the tide line. Standing in that graying darkness, he defied the sunrise to reach out and touch him, suffering the discomfort of its near arrival as his penance.

It was the past, damn it. Well over a century ago now. But he remembered.

Remembered the beatings, everything that went into forcing him to be something he wasn't. He'd resisted, but he'd been six, like Nerida. If a body and soul was starved long enough, they grabbed onto what was necessary to survive. When at last he was broken and turned into a "tame Indian," dutifully willing to perform manual labor inside a world not his own, he'd lost his language, unsure of the syllables anymore. He didn't remember his name. His fucking name. The faces of his mother and father, their friends and neighbors, had blurred.

He'd had more in common with those fledglings than Elisa knew, and that pale mirror had stuck in his craw from the beginning, hadn't it?

He'd always told his staff they could not pity an abused cat. Just like when Nerida had dropped at his feet, expecting him to hit her, it was important not to react, not to reinforce or instill the idea that they were irreparably damaged. He'd claimed to be calm, impartial, but, blinded by his own emotions, he'd made that mistake with the fledglings, in a different way.

So caught up in the unnaturalness of their early turnings and their brutal circumstances, the dangers they posed to others, he hadn't considered the curative powers of *expecting* them to act normal, and seeing if that helped them move toward normalcy, no matter what their physical handicaps were. Such as giving Nerida a simple command to take blankets across a compound.

Hadn't Elisa suggested something along those lines from the beginning? Had he let his personal baggage, unloaded from that plane with the fledglings, make him that obtuse?

He thought again about Jeremiah meeting his gaze, telling him with undeniable dignity that they didn't need anything. How long had it been since the boy had been treated as something more than a dangerous, unpredictable monster? Mal didn't have to look far for the answer to that. Elisa had been treating them that way all along. She'd even tried to give that gift to Leonidas, as much as she could.

Damn it, he didn't know what to do with the feelings roiling through him. He kept coming back to those seconds racing across the island, cursing every thick patch of undergrowth or upward rise that slowed him down. Seeing her lying there. It didn't matter that he'd known she was alive, that she'd survive. It hadn't blunted the edge of her pain or terror, or lessened his reaction to it, seeing it all play out in his head and knowing he wasn't there to protect her.

He should have paid closer attention to Danny's warnings about Elisa. *She'll look like a baby to you, but she's strong, Mal. Terrifyingly so, because I think her fragile soul and body weren't made to survive a will that strong.*

Elisa had ignored him, hadn't waited, because she hadn't trusted him. She'd known his heart wasn't in this from the beginning, so she couldn't believe anyone would really try to save those girls other than herself. And that was his fault, damn it.

Totally unexpected . . . Again Danny's description. *She was this crazy little maid I'd just met, and she cracked a teapot over the head of a five-hundred-year-old vampire. He could have torn her to pieces, and she knew it, but she did it to distract him. To help me.*

He wondered if Willis had been overwhelmed by her, like a diamond dropped unexpectedly in his dusty lap. Mal wasn't sure he didn't feel the same way. Elisa had set something off in him almost from the first day, and that wasn't his usual behavior.

Short and curvy as a ripe peach, she made him want to take a bite, taste those juices, the flavor of her. Hell, he even got aroused when she wore her apron now. He imagined her in only that, her breasts swelling out the open sides, taunting him like freshly risen bread. From there, his active mind would see her turning to cut tomatoes at the counter, revealing that soft round bottom, her white thighs. He'd press up behind her, bury himself in the wetness of her cunt, slide his fingers beneath the apron and tease her nipples into aching hardness. Her dark brown hair, nearly the same color as the silken curls between her legs, would brush against his jaw as he drove into her, hard enough to make her drop the knife. Locking both her wrists over her head, he'd push her up against the counter, making it vibrate with the force of his thrusts into her.

He was avoiding why he was really out here. She'd been right. She *was* right. Nerida letting them out of their cells to come to Elisa's defense had been a planned, intentional act. Then there was Jeremiah's marking of her. Cleverly concealing that he could be in her mind, but sending her those soothing lullabies when she'd been afraid and alone in her bed at night, back in Australia. Though Mal hadn't known her then, tonight suggested he really hadn't let himself know her at all.

He'd lost much of his humanity, as most made vampires did, but the irony was that the painful memory of his own humanity, not vampire indifference to human frailty, had goaded his cruel words to Elisa, his near-fatal mistake with the fledglings.

They were fighting bloodlust, yes, and any of them might succumb to what had befallen Victor and Leonidas, but they'd proven themselves. They weren't rabid animals, sick and senseless, beyond help. They deserved more than he'd been giving them, and it was time to set aside his own past and its influence on his actions, and focus on what kind of future was truly possible for them.

It had been easier to give that chance to his feline brethren, because he didn't see his own human face, the betrayal and pain reflected on it. But now that he acknowledged it, he knew he had to make it right. And he'd begin by making it right with the woman who'd given them so much of herself. Who'd given far too much, because she thought she was all alone in doing so.

When he'd founded the preserve, he'd done the same, thinking he had to do it all, that only *he* cared enough, mired in the pain of the creatures he was trying to help. It nearly drove him mad before he started letting others in, recognizing their passion could be as great as his own. It couldn't be one person's mission. Not only because it took more than one set of hands, but because defeats and setbacks had to be weathered, and only the support of others could help with the pain and grieving over that.

He needed to help Elisa understand that, and a good place to start was proving she wasn't alone. A shadow crossed his mind, recalling the words he'd spat at her. He'd make that up to her, too, and not with more words. She'd be in bed at least a week. That would give him time to bring her an apology she could believe. He wouldn't require anything of her until then, letting Kohana and Chumani take care of her while he observed a self-imposed exile, no matter how much his body and other more complicated parts of him protested.

As the sky turned to rose, his skin was practically steaming and his breath was tight in his chest, warning him it was well past time to be underground. Heading for the Jeep, he sent a message to Kohana, telling him the variety of things he wanted.

There was no time to waste.

24

Despite his resolve, it took an extreme act of will to leave her care to Kohana and Chumani for the next week, as well as to stay out of her head. It wasn't until Chumani reported she'd healed enough to get back into a restricted routine, punctuated by a lot of bed rest, that he was ready to meet with her. Though it was hard not to go to her immediately, he okayed Elisa taking on a *very* limited routine and told Chumani to have the Irish maid come to his office at midnight. They had matters to discuss, now that she was back on her feet.

That would give him time for two more phone calls. He'd anticipated one of them not going well, a call to a meat supplier who was sending substandard fare, but it still left him in a foul temper when Kohana appeared at the study door at nine o'clock. Of course, as if they were mirroring each other, the Indian had a look on his face as if he'd swallowed sour milk. He stood there, saying nothing, just glaring at Mal.

"For fuck's sake, what is it?" Mal said at last. He kept his attention on the legal pad in front of him, the details he was scribbling out. Travel arrangements, logistics . . . gods, logistics. Clothes to order . . .

Kohana grunted, unaffected by the threatening tone. "Isn't it obvious to everyone she's like those young vampires' mama?"

Mal looked up, eyed him. "What are you going on about?"

"A spirit sometimes is what it is, from the time it's born. That girl was born to be a mother. She takes care of everyone. You ever watch her when the staff eats dinner? Do I need a napkin? Would Chumani like to eat her pudding with a fork instead of a spoon? Jumping up to get everyone a second helping. Clearing the dishes before any of us can lift a finger."

"She's been a servant since she could walk."

Kohana gave him a disparaging look. "I've met plenty of folk born into serving class who are lazy and resentful of it. She likes taking care of people. And I've learned enough about your kind that I suspect there's a deeper element to it, one that's snagged you pretty good, too."

It was rare—perhaps never—that Kohana had ever referred to him as belonging more to the vampire species than his native race. It meant he was truly pissed. Mal's eyes narrowed. "Yes, she's got a submissive personality. She was chosen and groomed for that by Danny's mother. What *is* your point?"

Kohana took a determined hop forward. He'd left his crutch in the hall, his powerful thigh muscles fully capable of balancing him. "You've been threatening to kill what she considers her children since she came. You think any mother wouldn't fight tooth and nail to stay with them? Protect them as best she's able? You put her on that plane, take her away from her children, you'll destroy her. You know any mother who'd survive losing all six of her children in one go?"

If possible, Mal was even more confused by the direction of the conversation. "Why are you telling me what I already know, and why the hell do you think I'm putting her on a plane?"

"Because she said so. That you hadn't come to see her since you yelled after her, right after it happened—"

"I had you take flowers to her room from me, damn it."

"—but that you were going to have some big discussion with her later tonight. She was sure it was because you're sending her home."

"I'm so glad you all believe her version of things before you even talk to me."

Kohana scowled. "I'm here now. The way she talked, it was as if you'd already talked to her. You're in her mind; I assumed you'd told her as much."

"No. I haven't been in her mind at all this week. I've found out how she's doing through you two." Which had been damnably hard, but from Kohana's expression, Mal doubted he'd be getting a pat on his back for his forbearance.

He sighed. "Where is she?"

"With the fledglings. She's manacled herself to Jeremiah's cell with a padlock. Swallowed the key. Right in front of me, too, before I could stop her."

Mal blinked, rose from his chair. Something in his face may have even given Kohana pause, because the Indian looked like he might hop backward in reflex, though in the end he held his ground. Mal spoke slowly, enunciating each word with deliberate and deceptive calm. "You're telling me you've been standing here yakking, when she's barely recovered and yet she's gone off property? Chained herself to the cell of a fledgling given to erratic spurts of bloodlust, where he could reach right through the bars and rip her head off?"

Kohana gave him a disgusted look. "I left three men there, all with crossbows trained on him in case that happens."

"Oh, well, good, then. It will work out fine if they kill him, the one she loves the most." Mal came around the desk swiftly, headed for the French doors. "Remind me to have you buried up to your neck in the leopards' favorite hunting ground. They can use your head for their personal ball of string."

"I'll mark it down for your evening schedule. Sir."

Mal snarled something unintelligible and was gone. Kohana cursed himself. Truth, he'd overlooked her reaction if Jeremiah was harmed, but since he'd known what Mal was working on, he'd been knocked off balance, hearing Elisa's absolute certainty that she was being sent away. He'd thought Mal had changed course, and it had ticked him off something fierce.

"Men are total idiots." Chumani snorted, steam practically coming out of her nostrils as he came back into the kitchen. With Elisa out of commission, she'd rearranged her shifts and was helping Kohana prepare dinner, chopping carrots so ferociously Kohana was thinking he should get the knife from her. She stopped, waved it at him. "Mal thinks Elisa will respond better to a grand gesture, days after he was so mean to her, rather than giving her a simple apology right away. And we can't say anything. Why is it men think actions are better than words?"

A lock of hair had come loose and curled at her brow, drawing more attention to the line of her slim neck, the pout of her full lips and those long, long lashes. She was wearing a V-neck T-shirt, one that showed the hint of cleavage, the cotton molded to firm breasts. He hadn't intended to let his gaze wander that way, but Chumani in a high dudgeon was hard for any man to resist. And a much younger man wouldn't, right?

The hell with that. She noted the direction of his gaze a bare second before Kohana reached out, clasped her arm in one large hand and pulled her into him, hard enough she collided against his chest, the knife still gripped in her hand. He didn't care about that. Cupping her face, he held her close with the other, sliding his arm around her waist to hold her fast as he kissed her, hard and long . . . deep. Her body stiffened, then eased, then fully melded into his, so close and hot that his need ran away from him and he dropped a hand to her waist and then farther, molding the hip and the taut, round buttock, pressing her against an erection large and aching enough to compete with a youth half his age, damn it all.

The knife dropped to the floor and her hands slid up under his arms, fingers digging into his shirt. When he finally stopped, they were both breathing hard, and he knew she was just as aroused as he was, a pure shot of adrenaline. His voice was thick when he spoke.

"Maybe because we're better at action."

She stared up at him. Her eyes were a little wild and astonishingly vulnerable. It made him gentle his hold on her neck, pass his thumb over her nape. "I didn't just do that for the hell of it, you know."

She swallowed. "I sure hope not. Because if you did, I will kick your ass, old man." Then she rose on her toes and kissed him back, fitting every curve of her body to his, as if they were two saplings seeded together, trunks and roots inextricably and irrevocably intertwined.

For so long, he'd felt like an unopened can of soda around her, all shook up with nowhere for all that violent pressure to go. It wasn't as good as he'd imagined—it was leaps and bounds better, because it was raw and unleashed, and quiet and constant as a river at once. He didn't need a shaman's blood to know this was as meant to be as anything in nature.

He was still worried about Elisa, but somehow, he knew it would be all right. Because Mal was like that unopened soda as well, and the little miss had just given it a good kick. Her vampire had blood in his eye, and the top was likely to explode right off. As he pulled Chumani closer, showing her just how steady a one-legged man could be, he thought that might not be a bad thing at all.

~

Women. Yes, maybe he had screwed up, not communicating with her, but she knew better than this. As Kohana had pointed out, she'd been a servant all her life. She knew there were lines you didn't cross.

Unless she didn't think she had anything left to lose. *If you put her on that plane, you might as well kill her.* Still, he wasn't in a mood to coddle. He'd been dealing with all manner of bullshit this week, in order to give her . . . Yeah, she didn't know about it, but damn it, she needed to learn to trust him. He embraced the irrational thought, responding to the kick of his heated blood that said it was time to set her straight.

When he pulled up in the Jeep and switched it off, he saw things were as Kohana described them, and that didn't help settle him. It was too soon after a much worse scenario. Though they'd rinsed down the area thoroughly, he still smelled traces of the blood that had been shed here.

That, as well as this situation, wouldn't be a calming environment for any of the fledglings, particularly the one to whom she'd positioned herself far too closely. Having three crossbows on him wouldn't help.

She was trying to explain the same thing to the staff. He'd heard her through her mind on the way here. "He's not going to hurt me, but you're scaring him. Please stop; just put them down. You don't even have to let them go, but you can lower them."

You'd be a lot more effective at giving orders if you were better at taking them.

He sent her that thought just as his Jeep crested the hill. Everything in her tensed up. She hadn't known what else to do. She'd thought he wouldn't listen otherwise.

It pissed him off further. As he got out of the Jeep and strode toward the enclosure, Chayton was outside of it. When he stepped forward, his face set in that same disapproving mask Kohana had shown him, Mal peeled back his lips and snarled. He used enough fang to send Chayton skittering back in shock and self-preservation. Sometimes his employees needed to remember that he was no more a tame pet than the other kind they handled on the island.

As he moved into the communal enclosure, crossed the space between them, he spoke. "Would you like to tell me what the hell you're thinking?"

Elisa blinked, rising to her feet, the manacle clanking against Jeremiah's cell door. She was still tired enough from her ordeal that she hadn't been able to remain standing as she'd hoped, proud and defiant throughout. Jeremiah squatted on the other side of the bars, catty-corner. While he didn't meet Mal's gaze, he tracked his movements through sidelong glances.

"You know what I'm thinking." She wasn't being impudent, but her voice held an edge.

"Yes. Which is why I asked, because this required no thinking at all."

"I'm doing the only thing I could to keep you from sending me home."

"If that's your goal, defying me is the last thing you should be doing. And are you thinking about what's best for them, or for you?"

That made her stiffen. "I help—"

"How does it help them to see you destroyed bit by bit by their loss of control, Elisa? How does it help them learn to be independent in a world of vampires by teaching them to be dependent on a *human*? If I tell you you're getting on that plane, you're going. That's the way it works. No argument or discussion."

"No." Her chin lifted. A chin that had a slight quiver to it, her large blue eyes so full of appeal and pain. He remembered a week ago, when they'd been wide with arousal, her mouth bruised by his kisses, versus now, when it was a hard, thin, resolute line in the sand.

"You don't have the right to 'no,' Elisa, and you damn well know it." He looked toward Bidzil, who was properly expressionless. "Get the bolt cutters."

She surged forward then, forgetting about the manacles so that they caught her up and rattled hard against the bars. He saw her wince from the still-tender ribs, but something else cracked in her expression then.

"Then what, in the name of God, do I have to do to have the right? I've done nothing but what I've been told my whole life. I had a man between my legs before I had hair there. I know what it's like to get driven off from a garbage can like an unwanted stray dog, foraging for scraps. I've had my body ripped open, the man I love torn apart within feet of me, so my dress was soaked with his blood as I was raped. It was my favorite dress . . . one I wore for him."

Her voice had become strident, hard and hoarse, a tone he'd never heard from her. He wasn't sure she'd ever uttered it herself. This was from the well of the soul, where the darkest secrets and deepest angers were kept, and she was dredging them up brutally, as if she were using a steel gouge on her soul.

"I protect them. I watch over them. I'm the only one who truly listens to them, who sees the children they once were. Regardless of how old he truly is, Jeremiah needs that stuffed bear on his bed, because it means something to him. Miah and Nerida sing to each other when they go to bed in the morning. William wants to learn to play Chayton's flute, which of course means that Matthew does, too. They are my purpose, my meaning. I have to protect them."

He kept his voice low and even. "You've *made* them your purpose and meaning, Elisa. They keep you from facing the rest. You've invested a cost in them so dear, that if you turn away now, Willis's death, your violation, you think it'll have all been meaningless. Well, things like that *are* meaningless. That's the point; that's why they're so awful."

"I can't leave them." Elisa spoke in that same awful voice, only now it was quiet, an open raw wound. "They're mine to protect. My charges."

Mal's frustration broke the reins then. With an oath, he stepped forward, backing her into the bars. Laying his hand on the chain connecting the manacle, he yanked. The link burst, with enough force that it jerked her to him.

"I'm done with this," he snapped. He wrapped the loose chain around his other hand, tethering her to him. He'd drag her back to the house bodily if needed, but a strangled noise from her, an animal scream of rage and pain, stopped him. That, and the fact he was solidly punched in the face by a small, intensely concentrated fist.

He wouldn't have given her credit for such strength, though of course she had a second mark's enhanced ability. It was the coordination and accuracy of it that told him that, somewhere during her short life span, she'd been taught to fight. A pair of thin arms shot out from the cell, wrapped across her waist and chest, and drew her back against the bars hard enough that her body collided against them with a metallic thud, the chain pulled from his hand.

The three men had their crossbows up, but in that instant they lost their opportunity, for now they couldn't shoot without hitting her. She wasn't a third-mark. She wouldn't survive an arrow going through her heart, and she and Jeremiah were of like height, their chests aligned for an optimal double kill shot.

Jeremiah's furious and frightened gaze was locked on his, a challenge and a plea at once. He'd spread his fingers out as far as they could go over her face, pressing her cheek to the cell bars. His other arm was slanted up toward her chest, fingers also spread. He was trying to protect her with as much of his body as he could, thinking Mal was going to retaliate, hit her in those vulnerable face and solar plexus areas. The way he'd been beaten for such acts of defiance.

Jeremiah knew he couldn't stand against Mal. He should have been cowering back, protecting himself. Instead he was risking everything, protecting her.

"Jeremiah." When Elisa spoke, her voice was shaking, because she was still riding her fury and pain, tears on her face. In her mind, though, Mal saw she was making a valiant effort to calm herself. Her hand rested on the boy's wrist. "It's all right. He's not going to hurt me."

She was sure of it, too. It unexpectedly moved Mal, that even in the heat of their argument she knew she was completely safe with him, at least physically. But if push came to shove, she'd take a beating as harsh as he could dish out, if that was what would allow her to stay here.

Christ.

He held the boy's gaze. He could call him that, at least in his mind, because the difference in their ages, whatever Jeremiah's true age was, was significant enough to justify it. "She's right. I'm not going to injure her, Jeremiah. But I need you to let her go, because you know as well as I do that a situation like this could result in a bloodlust surge. It would happen in an instant, and you'd snap her neck. All right? You know that."

The young man pressed his lips against those long fangs that were so perilously close to Elisa's neck. Malachi saw the tinges of red in his eye, the grip of his fingers starting to tighten.

Elisa drew in a gasp, because Mal was now flush up against her, his hands locked on Jeremiah's wrists. Slowly, his gaze remaining on the fledgling's, he guided Jeremiah's arms off her body and upward. Mal wasn't brutal about it, but he was inexorable, slowly pushing the boy back to arm's length, holding him there.

Elisa, slide out from beneath me and move away from his cell. Right now.

He was pressed pretty tightly against her, so she had to wriggle and inch downward, where the cant of his body widened the space between them. Ignoring the creak of her fragile ribs, she took hold of his shirt at the waist to give her leverage to swing below him and come out of that heated space. Chayton was there, taking her arm and guiding her back a few steps before she could turn and see.

Jeremiah was fighting it, shuddering in Mal's arms, and Elisa blanched as she realized how close a thing it had been. The boy was already thrashing and growling, the stress of the past few moments overcoming him. Whipping his head to the right, he sank his fangs into Malachi's arm. Though Elisa gasped, the older vampire didn't flinch, just waited until the boy convulsed, his jaw relaxing enough for Mal to switch his grip.

Elisa expected him to let Jeremiah go, to thrust him away and let the bloodlust fit take its horrible, pitiful course. It would throw him to the ground, or Jeremiah would rush the bars until he'd knocked himself almost senseless. Then he'd lie on the ground, jerking and crying out in that way that made her heart choke her.

Instead, Mal turned the boy so his back was against the bars, and Jeremiah was suddenly in much the same position Elisa had been, only Mal's arms held him there, high across the narrow chest and around the waist, the vampire murmuring to him as the boy fought the demonic possession of his body. Mal's arm was bleeding, staining Jeremiah's shirt.

Chayton had run to the Jeep and was back, pressing a packet of blood into Elisa's hand. "Go give this to him, but stay well clear."

Elisa nodded, and approached the bars again. "Toss it through," Malachi said, his voice remarkably tranquil, unruffled. "Gently, so it doesn't split."

When she complied, Jeremiah's head snapped around, tracking it. As soon as it landed, Malachi let him go. Jeremiah leaped upon it, and Elisa looked away, somehow unable to watch him transform into this beast, gulping the blood so fast it streamed down his chin, dripping to the ground.

We're all beasts, Elisa. We just learn control. Somewhat. Don't look away. You hurt him by reacting the way you do.

It surprised her, coming from Mal, but she immediately brought her gaze back to Jeremiah. She managed to make a soothing and encouraging noise, as if he was sitting down to the dinner table with napkin properly tucked in, knife and fork in hand. With a sinking feeling, she realized that if he'd second-marked her, he could read her reaction, no matter what face she put on it. She concentrated on soothing her emotions inside, so they would reflect what she was trying to give him on the outside.

Whether or not it helped, or if it was just the blood, he was calming. He was rocking back and forth on his heels now, sucking at the blood bag. Mal turned then, taking her arm in a firm grip. "All right. Let's go."

～

He parked on her favored knoll. They stared out over a star-strewn landscape, the whitecaps of the ocean coming through like milk with the help of the moonlight's touch. In the far distance, across the fault line into Africa, she saw a family of leopards. It was a mother with cub in tow, working her way across an open plain. A gazelle herd was at the other end. The mother would search out the young and injured, Nature's way of culling out the weak.

It made her so tired. She should ask him what he was going to do with the children after she was gone, but she didn't have the courage. She couldn't think about that plane as anything but a coffin, containing the rest of her life, passed in sterile numbness.

"Marshall Grant is the overlord of the Florida territory. He's worked with me on protection of the Florida panther population, letting me enter the Everglades in his territory as needed. I've spent some time at his home. There's a relatively dense concentration of vampires in Florida, because it has a significantly transient human population. Makes it easier to blend. Lady Lyssa has oversight on Florida, as she's the Southern Region Master."

Elisa blinked and looked toward him, her brow creasing. "I'm sorry, sir. What?"

A grim look crossed his face. "*Sir* is a title of respect, Elisa. You don't have any for me, so it seems a little hypocritical, doesn't it?"

He saw her indignant response to that. She followed all of his rules, even those she considered completely ludicrous, rules she thought had more to do with his need to order about the whole world than with anything sensible. The only time she broke them was when it was absolutely necessary, something dire required, and she was sorry she'd thumped him like that, but . . .

He kept his gaze fastened on her until the thoughts stuttered to a halt, the girl realizing he was following them like a typewriter's keys clattering across a page. "Done yet?" he asked.

She pressed her lips together, gave a nod.

"Good. I'd put a cap on that busy mind of yours, because you have one hell of a punishment coming. You don't want to make it worse. If we can get William and Matthew to a certain point in behavior and self-control, I believe Lord Marshall will be willing to take them into his household, permanently. On a probationary basis, of course. He could provide them protection and service, give them a safe place to see how they get on with the vampire world."

When the words sank in, she made a visible effort not to go slack-jawed in shock. He nodded with grim satisfaction. "That's what I've been working on this past week. There's a similar possibility for Miah and Nerida, down in South America, but I'm still working that one out. Since Lord Marshall confirmed today that he wants me to visit and discuss it, I was going to share that with you. Tonight, in my study."

"So you weren't going to send me away."

"No."

"Oh." She said it in a small voice. "I guess all that was totally unnecessary, then."

"Yeah. You could say that."

She swallowed. "Are you going to send me away now?"

"Yes." He felt the trip of her heart, and held on to silence for an extra five beats, testing himself as much as her. He chose five, because he wasn't going to make it to ten. "But only if you give me the wrong answer to this next question. What happens to children when their parents are always disagreeing in front of them about how they should be raised?"

"They tend to know they can misbehave with one parent more than the other."

"That, but even more important, it creates instability. The more stability these fledglings have, the better. You're key to that, but so am I. We have to work together. Now, if you can agree to that, I will make you a promise, here and now."

His gaze held hers as she gave him a wary nod. The subsequent pause was long enough to get Elisa past her shock that a vampire was making a promise to a human, and then she was hanging on his every word.

"I'm going to do everything I can to give them the chance to make something of their lives," he said. "Unless, like Leonidas, they cross a line over which they can't come back. I will do that whether you are here or not. You have my word."

Elisa recalled the way he'd held Jeremiah with his strong long-fingered hands, the ones he had on the gearshift and window frame now, his body half-turned toward her. He'd restrained the boy with a strength that could be ruthless and savage, but hadn't been.

"So, if I convinced you they are in good hands, would you get on that plane, go back to your Australia, and let yourself heal as you deserve? Move forward with the life you thought you might have? There will be other stock hands with good hearts. You're young. You won't be alone long."

There was an edge to his words as he said them, and he glanced away from her, out into the night. "I'd stay in close contact with Danny, so you'd know all that's happening here. You've done more than enough, more than anyone ever should have asked you to do. I know you wanted to do it, but you have to learn there are others that can help carry this load. It may even help your cubs, seeing that you have the confidence to trust them to other capable hands."

She looked down at her lap, then back up at him. "Do you want me to go?"

Those dark, piercing eyes shifted, and that edge she'd heard in his voice was there in his gaze. "No," he said quietly. "I don't. But if I ever see in your heart and mind that's what you truly want, what you need, I will put you on that plane."

"And what do you see there now?"

He shook his head, his lips curving without humor. "It's a mess, more than I'll wade through. A man can get bogged down in the female mind when it's like that and never find his way out again."

She swallowed. "What if I want to stay?"

He leaned in so those intense eyes were much closer. His hand drifted across her lap, up her arm, and then settled on her throat, a collar of flesh and bone that made every nerve ending aware of his touch. When he saw her reaction to it, crimson flame flickered in those dark depths.

"If you stay, you will not disobey me again. I mean this, Elisa." Those fingers tightened infinitesimally, making her lift her chin in response, her heart beat faster. "What you did was incredibly rash, and served no purpose. If Jeremiah had harmed you, how do you think he would have felt? And what did you plan to do once you chained yourself there?"

Her cheeks pinkened. "I hadn't really gotten that far."

"Exactly." He stopped, let out a sigh and settled back. She felt the loss of that touch, oddly wanting it back, but then he was speaking again. "You've done well with them, Elisa. You also managed to take two very practical vampires, myself and Danny, down this insane path and show us it's not entirely insane."

Her look of surprise showed, for he inclined his head. "Despite your belief that I'm a tyrant merely for the joy of it, I do notice things. And I can change my mind. Hence the calls to Lord Marshall. But this is not a full reversal of the boat, Elisa. There's a long way to go, and I know you're smart enough to see the signs that it might still go badly in the end. So I need you to give me another truthful answer. Can you obey me from here forward, no question, no detours, no arguments? Trust me absolutely, before you've really learned to believe in that trust? I know it's not an easy thing to ask, but I need to see in your heart you can do it. It's important, if we're going to succeed in this."

She wanted to. Oh, how she did. She wanted to believe the whole world wouldn't come crashing down if she let someone else hold these particular reins, but she was afraid she was running away from what had been such a heavy load for so long. And she was afraid of how she'd fill her empty hands, what thoughts would take her over, if she let those reins go.

"I've never met someone with such foolish determination and courage." He snorted, eyeing her. "You're not running from anything. Sooner or later, Elisa, we all have to face our pain. You're . . . among friends. We'll help you, the same way we'll help the fledglings. You're not back at the station, where you have to pretend all's well because you don't want to add to Danny's guilt. You can be what you need to be here. Kohana, Chumani, the others . . . They'll all help."

Tears threatened, but she managed to hold them back, give a quick nod. "I don't want to go." The idea of getting on that plane made her belly ache, and it wasn't all because she'd be leaving the children.

Those red sparks in his eyes had a matching flicker through every aware part of her body, like tiny fireflies. "All right, then. Offer me your throat."

Her heart immediately rabbited up into that very area. She put her hand on the center console and stretched over it, coming to him. He slid his arm around her waist, his hand cupping her arse as it came off the seat, and the gearshift pressed into her stomach before the impression was lost in the more distracting pressure of his fangs, piercing into her skin. She drew in a breath, her nipples tightening in that open triangle of space between them where she was painfully conscious of the proximity of his body.

The pain of the bite and ache of her still-tender ribs should have helped ground her, but instead she wanted him to pull her across, make her straddle his lap. His hard, heated length would impale her, fill this restless emptiness inside of her.

He tightened his grip, his half growl making her shiver. Her life was in the hands holding hers. Maybe in more ways than one.

"Yes," she whispered. "I'll trust you, sir. And I'll try really, really hard not to disobey ever again."

She felt a smile against her throat, and the warmth of it dissipated some of her worries. At least until she heard his next thought.

It's time to take you home and give you an incentive to do just that. It's time for your punishment.

25

Elisa tried to stay calm as Mal steered her into his office. In the Jeep, he hadn't seemed angry anymore. While she knew some of his anger was justified, given that he hadn't been about to do what she thought, she didn't know how much more she could take tonight. The week had been full of rioting emotions, as she dealt with Mal's silence and what it meant, the fact Jeremiah had second-marked her, what had happened with Leonidas, and then of course the foolishness that had driven her little drama tonight.

Not sure of what lay ahead, she wished she could escape to her bed, even if it meant having to suffer alone with that ball of sexual heat Mal had planted in her stomach with his provocative touch, his demanding words.

Mal didn't take a seat behind his desk. He gestured her to the chair in front of it, then sat on the edge of the pirate chest, his legs braced out on either side of her body. Her feet in the canvas sneakers looked small, aligned neatly together in that V-shaped space. His restless energy caged her there as much as his body.

"When you arrived here—what now seems like centuries ago—Thomas brought a letter with him, from your lady. She described you as obedient, docile to a fault. Obviously, you cleverly managed to conceal your split personality from her."

Whatever else she'd been expecting, it hadn't been this sudden switch to a sardonic tone, one that seemed deliberately intended to goad her. He cocked a brow. "Why don't you tell me what you would do in my place?"

"I'm sure I couldn't say, sir."

"Oh, now you have nothing to say. Childishly contrite and almost meek, with your eyes down and your chin on your chest. The spitfire who dared to get in my face with her asinine demands mere minutes ago would have plenty to say. It wouldn't be a pathetic and simpering 'I'm sure I couldn't say, sir.'"

She didn't know what *asinine* or *simpering* were, but they didn't sound complimentary. Her fingers closed into balls on her lap. "With all due respect, sir, you could have told me anytime this week what you were doing. Instead, you left me thinking—"

"What gave you the impression you have the rights of an equal, Elisa? Because Danny unwisely let you forget what a servant's role is?"

No, because of the way you touch me, make me feel. She didn't want to say it that way, hadn't meant to think it, but now she had. She shook her head, weary with it, stared at his knees. "You said we were in this . . . together. I'm not sophisticated, Mr. Malachi. I'm not Chumani, who can understand that what's in a woman's heart and what a man wants aren't the same thing, and be so casual about it."

He studied her a long moment, giving nothing away. The direction of her lowered gaze took her over the terrain of his spread thighs, the denim stretched over the muscle and length of them, the curve of the groin area, something she shouldn't be thinking about, but it was right there after all. Might as well enjoy something before he started chewing on her again. Then she saw the puncture in his arm, still healing from Jeremiah's bite.

He'd saved her, and it wasn't the first time. She would have been angry with anyone she cared about if they risked themselves in a way she perceived as pointless or foolish. So if he was angry maybe it was because . . . he cared.

That thought alone halted her mind in its tracks. The simple truth of it was too normal, too obvious, but she was almost certain she was right. She wouldn't ask, wouldn't question it, and if she was delusional, so be it.

Not thinking too much about why she was doing it, she slid out of the chair, knelt before him. Looking at his arm, she saw it was indeed healing, but that didn't make it hurt less. "Thank you for saving my life," she said quietly.

You're welcome.

To hear his voice now in her head, gruff and yet with a certain note of kindness, disarmed her in a way that his scolding hadn't.

"Elisa, I'm not going to let this one slide. I'm going to punish you, because you need to remember how important the boundaries are." *And because, if I don't punish you for scaring away half my life span, I might choke you.*

Had he meant for her to hear that? She assumed he did, but it made that warmth spread, despite the implicit threat. He bent then, clasping her elbows to bring her back to her feet. Her fingers whispered along his thighs and came to rest on his shirt front, close to his waist. "Elisa, look at me now."

She shook her head. The way she was feeling, she'd look at him with moony calf eyes and he'd laugh at her. Of course, by not obeying, she was just proving his point, wasn't she?

His broad chest rose and fell in a sigh. He didn't let her go. Instead, he tilted his head down, sliding his jaw against the side of hers. Though vampires didn't have facial hair, his jaw wasn't like a woman's skin. The hard firmness to it was unmistakably male. He slid his nose along her cheek, his mouth so close. Her head jerked up then, her eyes meeting his.

"Obey me," he murmured. "Just obey me, Elisa. This is a reminder of that."

He said *obey*, but she wondered if he meant *trust*. In his mind, of course, the two were interchangeable. She'd obeyed a lot of people in her life—her employers, because she needed her job; Lady Constance, because she educated Elisa for the purpose of serving her daughter; and then Danny. Danny had been the first to win Elisa's trust such that her obedience was based in love and loyalty. Hearing Malachi speak the word *obey* in such a manner made her think of that, and wonder if it was possible for him to want such a thing from her. Or, even more disturbing, whether this yearning feeling in her chest was an absurd desire to feel it for him.

"I want you to turn around and put your knees on the edge of the chair. Grip the top of it and balance yourself that way."

"It will topple."

"It's heavy oak. Your weight is unlikely to disturb it." His eyes were still so close, his mouth feathering heated breath across her lips as he spoke. His hands, gripping her upper arms, burned the flesh beneath. "Before you get on the chair, I want you to reach under your skirt, slide off your panties and hand them to me."

"I . . . What?"

His gaze gleamed, as feral as a wild cat's, sending a shard of flame rippling through her lower belly. "I found it annoying at first, but I've gotten rather fond of your fixation with calling me *sir*. So, *Yes, sir* would be the proper response." He cocked his head, and his lips brushed her cheekbone, making her shiver.

"Yes, sir," she whispered. While her own confused reaction was occupying most of her attention, she didn't miss the fact her breasts were brushing his chest, her upper thighs pressed against the heat of his splayed ones. There had to be only a matter of inches between the shallow valley between her thighs and the heat of his aroused groin.

"Good girl." He turned her then, helping her get started. Folding her fingers in the fabric of her skirt, she tried to gather it up to find the undergarment beneath. He'd taken her to bed before, made her feel amazing things, so why her hands should begin to shake now, and her mind be assaulted by disturbing images, she didn't know. Willis's kisses, gentle and then more urgent, morphing into Victor's fangs, tearing at her mouth and tongue, then Leonidas, snarling and hitting her in the face . . . Mal, angry with her, such that she thought he was going to send her away. All the emotions that came with those thoughts and images flooded her.

She whimpered, her brow creasing as her eyes shut tight. "I can't. I just can't. I want to, but I don't, and I don't know why I'm feeling this now. I think I'm going to faint."

"Shhh . . ." His arm slid over her chest, his large hand gripping the opposite shoulder and dwarfing it as he held her back into the heat of his body. "You wouldn't faint, fierce little flower, even if Satan himself blew fire and brimstone in your face. What I'm about to do will help with all of it, everything going through your head now. I promise."

"How? How can it help?"

"Let your mind go and do as I say. Keep going; reach beneath your skirt."

He loosened his hold enough that she could do as he said, but he was still there, his body lending her the strength behind the demand. When she reached bare flesh, creeping up to find the elastic waist of her panties, he was stroking the side of her throat, tilting her head into his shoulder, letting her close her eyes as she hooked the band and began to ease them off. Her hands were trembling so that when they reached the tapering part of her leg, just above her knee, they slid free and fell, landing around her ankles and onto her canvas sneakers.

Pressing a hand to her back to help her bend, he let that touch drift to her hip to steady her as she freed the panties from her ankles. When she gathered them up into a discreet ball in her hand, she had to quell the sudden compulsion to fold them neatly as she might do with the laundry. However, if she was having trouble merely handing them to him, the logistics of folding were far outside her abilities right now.

His hand came out from under her right arm, the other sliding about her waist, holding her close. When she put the ball of soft, worn fabric in his palm, his fingers closed over it and her slim ones briefly, holding her there before he took the panties and his touch away.

"Up on the chair with you now." His hand was on her elbow again, urging her forward. She managed it clumsily, needing to adjust her skirt so it wasn't caught under her knees. Drawing in a breath, she closed her hands on the top of the chair for balance. He adjusted her stance so her knees were on the edge of the wood, digging into her flesh with the reminder of the open space beneath them. She'd kept her knees closer together, but he widened them, to the point the outside of each was pressed against either chair arm. It made her balance feel precarious, vulnerable, such that she tightened her hands on the chair top.

"Stay like this, Elisa."

"This frightens me."

"Trust me." Reaching over the desk, he pulled out a drawer. "Eyes front, Elisa. Toward the opposite wall."

She knew the types of games and sexual . . . tests, for lack of a better word, that vampires played with their servants. And *play* was definitely the wrong word for it, for there was nothing whimsical or childlike about it. She'd witnessed quite a few of Lady Danny's dinner parties, but even as a second-mark, she was only dinner help, not part of the floor show the way Dev always was, as Danny's full servant. She was often sent out of the room before the real post-dinner games began, those limited to the vampires and their full servants. However, on the few occasions she'd had to come back in to retrieve a dish or bring more wine, she'd seen things that had fascinated and mortified her at once, sending her scurrying away quickly, blushing, even though she'd had an equal wish to stay and look longer. That conflict in desires was similar to what she was feeling now. What *was* he doing?

He'd taken out a handful of short ropes and now he'd cinched each of her knees to the chair arm it paralleled, which would hold her knees out wide. Leaning over her, what was straining against the denim pressing through the skirt, he looped another tether over her hands and bound them to the top slat of the chair.

"Sir . . . Mr. Malachi . . ."

"Hush," he said quietly. "This is your punishment, Elisa. Obey me as your Master."

She was still trembling, but at his words, it transformed into something different. When he tied her fast, his touch was gentle, fingers testing the bonds, making sure they weren't too tight, that they weren't uncomfortable. Then she heard the metal of his belt clink and her belly flip-flopped again.

"It'll be fifteen strikes," he said. "I'm going to do it on your bare ass. You'll call each one out to me as I do it, and as you count it off, you will say, 'I will never disobey you again, sir.' Do you understand?"

The last time she'd been thrashed had been when she was fifteen, for shirking her duties to slip away to a fair in Perth. She'd met a young, lanky lad there who'd given her a flower and tried to steal a kiss, which she'd laughingly escaped, though she'd wondered what that kiss would have felt like. Though the thrashing hurt, she wouldn't have traded that day for it. She had a feeling Mal's arm was a trifle stronger than the house mistress at the Collins' house. It made her stomach quake, but she nodded. "Yes, sir."

But first he touched that rounded area, his palm fitting to one of the cheeks to knead it through her skirt, his fingertips whispering over her sensitive flesh, so close to other, even more sensitive flesh. When he folded the fabric up, secured it in the slim belted waistline, cool air drifted over her naked, moistening flesh. He had a full, unimpeded view of her there, her legs bound and spread that way. "Count it, Elisa."

"One."

She was right. He had a much stronger arm than Mrs. Florence. She almost yelped at the sting, but managed to bite it back. "I will never disobey you again," she said, her voice breaking. "Two."

Snap. A quick strike, a reminder, and she bit it out fast. "Sir."

While it had hurt like the devil, the aftermath . . . didn't. The tingling as his hand passed over her arse almost made her want another. She didn't have long to wait.

He didn't pause much between the next three except for her to get out the words he was requiring her to say. Those hurt more, because he was hitting over the same abused flesh. Her thighs quivered, hands gripping the top of the chair. Bound as she was, she couldn't do anything to stop him, no twist or jerk out of the way, and yet something more was happening. When he stopped after the third, his knuckles teased their way along the crease between her buttocks, a shocking sensation that made her want to writhe. Before she could do more than draw in a quick breath, he'd passed that area, dropped his fingers and inserted them between the lips of her sex. He slid in so easily, the arousal made an audible sucking sound.

She would have blushed hard at that, but his pleased, feral growl sent another kind of flush across her skin. A harder strike this time, one that shoved that yelp past her teeth. "I'm sorry, sir."

"I want to hear your cries, Elisa." There was a wealth of meaning to that. Was his cock harder, straining even more against his jeans from looking at her naked and bound like this? And why did that make her even more aroused, as if they were feeding that part of each other?

Four more this time, and in addition to the pain and arousal, something else surged inside of her as well. An ache in her throat that became tears, though she couldn't really say what was making her want to cry. She was just sorry for so many things, and it felt like she needed to purge a backlog of feeling. She wanted him to keep going, beyond fifteen strokes, though of course such a thought was crazy. Her arse was already on fire, enough that strikes nine and ten caused genuine cries of pain.

"Say it, Elisa."

"I will never disobey you again. Sir."

He leaned forward, nuzzled her backside with his face, rubbing his jaw against the left cheek. His heated breath whispered over her sex and she contracted without thought, just imagining his tongue sliding in there, the way he'd done it before. God, the coil in her stomach was so tight, she was shaking all over, from something even more powerful than pain.

"More," she whispered. "Please, sir."

He paused; then she felt the brief prick of fangs before he pulled back. "All together. I want to hear you scream."

She wasn't entirely sure what he meant until the belt landed. He didn't pause to let her speak, though she tried to get the syllables out. They got lost when she did in fact cry out, not once but on each of the final five strikes. The sixteenth he threw in unexpectedly singed her nerve endings and sent her body jerking hard against her bonds. Tears had wet her face, but she said it now, six times in succession, breathlessly, an oath that suddenly meant far more.

"I will never disobey you, sir. I will never disobey you, sir . . ."

The tongue of the belt teased over her throbbing flesh, then down, playing with her soaking cunt. It had been a crude word at first, one he used, but now she embraced the primal sound of it, at least in her mind. It made her hotter, needier. Leaning in, he pressed against the back of her thigh. He was in fact hard as an iron bar for her.

"Of course you'll disobey me again. Because of who you are, and how that mind of yours works. And because you'll realize if you're very bad, I'll do this to you again. Lift your ass to me, Elisa. Lift it as high as you can, and hold it there until I tell you that you can move."

It was an awkward position, but she managed it, perhaps because she was so overwhelmed with emotional reaction she thought she could touch her arse to the back of her head if he commanded it. She didn't think about his words, about how shameless the truth made her. Instead, she waited, soft whimpers coming from her, whimpers that became a different kind of cry as his mouth closed fully over her wet cunt, sucking on those juices, licking them away and creating more as his tongue dipped into her, swirled and came back out, only to thrust in again.

It doesn't make you shameless, Elisa. It means you want to serve your Master, give him pleasure, make him crazy with lust for you until he'll fuck you a hundred different ways, wear you out and then want to take you all over again, to remind you that you're his.

She wanted him to take her while she was tied in this chair, helpless to him, his cock buried deep inside of her. She wanted him to thrust and take her over, reach under her arms and grip her breasts through the thin dress, rip the fabric away and leave it in tatters. She wanted him to do what he wanted, take her soaring to that incredible place that at times had left her perplexed and wanting, but there was no confusion now. Her fully woken body had a singular purpose, to serve his pleasure.

"As part of your punishment, I had no intention of being inside you tonight, even if you begged," he observed, that growl in his voice. "Though you're making it damnably difficult to remember why the hell I decided that."

"It wouldn't bother me . . . if you changed your mind."

"No, I'm sure it wouldn't." Stepping to the side of the chair, he lifted her chin, keeping her arched in all ways to him. With the other hand, he slipped back over the globe of her backside and found her wet pussy again, began to stroke that dense area of nerve endings with devilish skill. "You'll look at me as you climax, Elisa. Give me everything. Don't take your eyes off me, or I'll give you fifteen more stripes, and I promise they will hurt like the very devil over top of those."

She didn't need the reminder. Now that he was done, there was a throbbing heat over her buttocks that told her she was going to have trouble sitting down for the next day or so, unless the second-mark healing ability jumped in and helped her somewhat. But to look at him while this was happening was so difficult. Those dark, fathomless eyes following the widening of her gaze, the stretching of her mouth as air became too precious and small, the quiver of her body, the rock of it against her bonds as she began to jerk against his hand. When two of his fingers slid inside of her, emulating the act of his cock while his thumb stroked and massaged her clit, she could hardly bear to hold his gaze, though it was such a pleasure to look on his face, get lost in it instead of what she must look like.

"You look like the most fuckable thing in the history of the world," he said, his gaze ablaze with heat. "Obey me now, Elisa. You come for me. Spurt your honey over my fingers; clamp down on them."

She couldn't stop herself. The climax swept over like a tidal wave and though she kept her eyes on his face as he commanded, it was a struggle, because her cries became a scream. The arched position of her body made her completely helpless to him as he kept teasing, pumping, massaging, stroking, holding her chin up so he could see how it all affected her, every tear and quiver, the terror and pleasure of it at once rocketing through her.

She wanted to eat him alive. If she were free, she'd leap upon him, lick and bite until he rolled her under him, pinning her down and taking charge once again, overwhelming her with his strength and will.

It took forever to come down, and when she did, she wondered if anyone else was in the house.

Mal put his mouth to the corner of hers. "I hope the whole damn staff was in here, so they could hear how well you served me. How you belong to me."

Served him? But he'd given *her* all the pleasure, hadn't he? And taken none for himself.

Elisa, there are many things that give a vampire pleasure. Nothing pleases us so much as surrender. He was freeing her bonds, but her legs were shaking so badly, she was afraid she might topple over. She needn't have worried. He released her hands but then rebound her wrists together and lifted her in his arms.

Carrying her out of the study, he took her through the house and down the steps, down that long hallway with the cat mural. Into his bedroom and then onto his bed. When he laid her there, he began to undress her. One item at a time until she was completely naked and he was still fully clothed. He unbound her wrists to get everything off, but then retied them to the headboard. He used longer ties for her legs and bound her ankles to the gnarled wooden branches at the base, her legs parted wide so that the remains of her climax were trickling out, teasing the lips of her cunt. When he stretched out next to her on one elbow, he made it clear he would take all the time he desired to look his fill. Remarkably, it made her body start to feel restless again, as if it could reach a climax again in no time. She should be exhausted.

"What . . . what are you doing?"

"I'm turning in early tonight. For the next few hours, you'll do nothing but lie next to me. Until dawn, I will touch you, arouse you, make you greedy for another climax, but you're not going to have another. Not for a while. This is the second part of your punishment. The next time I tell you to say, 'I will never disobey you, sir,' you will mean it to the depths of your soul."

His look gave her those butterflies in the stomach. "I don't think I could do that again for a while anyhow. The climax part."

"Hmm. You may be right. But I'll please myself." Leaning forward, he began to drop kisses along the curve of her right breast, then the left, working his way around the nipples without touching them. Elisa watched the peaks drawing into intense, tight points, felt her lower belly begin to coil again. Yet when her body began to involuntarily move toward him, trying to beg for his mouth where she wanted it, he gave her a light slap in a most unexpected place, that tender place between her legs. She jumped and he gave her a reproving look. "You don't move unless I tell you to do it, *atsilusgi*."

She obeyed, and obeyed, and obeyed, until she was crying again, her body quivering with the most painful need she'd ever experienced. When he finally put his mouth on her nipples, the surge of vicious reaction took her so close to climax, but he would allow nothing but air to touch that part of her body. If it started clenching on its own, trying to create the feeling of touch or friction, he eased off, took the feeling out of reach until she'd calmed. Then he started again. He drank from her as well. Tiny sips from her throat, the inside of her thigh, his hair brushing her sex, his nose briefly nuzzling into that wet, dark place. He told her she smelled like hot need, the most irresistible smell to a man.

He suckled her breasts again. Once, he laid his body full upon hers, stroking along her flanks with his capable hands, the hard evidence of his desire pushed up between her legs, her bare, wet cunt dampening the denim. She'd never imagined anything like this, a man teasing a woman to such a mindless frenzy. He was right. She'd say anything he wanted, just to get him inside of her. But nothing would sway him, because he was teaching her a lesson, making a point. The word he'd said earlier kept sticking in her head. *Master.* He was teaching her how to properly serve a Master. How to serve him.

But to be her Master, he would have to mark her once more. Make her his fully marked servant, bound to him for all eternity. She'd be his forever, the way Dev was to Danny, serving whatever needs she had, public or private, with other vampires or without. It was a life far beyond her simple desires and dreams, and yet he was making her body override her heart, making them both believe they could want anything he desired, a dark magic she couldn't resist.

He rose up above her now, stroking her breasts, feeding her his fingers, so she could taste herself from where he'd had them inside of her. *Tell me now, Elisa. What's the lesson you've learned?*

I will never disobey you, Master. Please . . .

"Please what, Elisa?"

"Please . . . come inside of me."

"What if I take my own pleasure and don't allow you to release? Make you continue to suffer?"

"I don't care. I want to give you pleasure. That's all I want. Make me suffer, but let me be the one to please you." She couldn't bear the idea of that hard cock inside of Chumani's body. Or anyone else.

"The moment I'm inside that needy pussy of yours, you'll come."

"Then let me take you in my mouth." It was a daring, wanton thing to say, but she'd done it before, for Mr. Collins—

Quicker than she could follow, he'd seized her mouth with his own, his tongue coming in to tangle with hers, overpowering her mind. She whimpered.

You will not think of him or anyone else when you are with me, Elisa. Not ever. Do you want my cock in your mouth? Do you want to swallow my come into your body?

Yes, Master. Please.

"Say it aloud." He gazed down at her with implacable eyes. "I want to see your sweet lips form those words."

"I want your . . . cock in my mouth. I want you to come there, so I can swallow it. Have it inside of me."

"Every drop."

"Yes. Please."

He rose on his knees then, opened the jeans. He didn't give her the pleasure of seeing him fully naked, hadn't even removed his shirt, but she knew that was part of this, too. The searing pleasure of denial. But when that long, hard cock stretched out just above her face, the tip already glistening slick with his arousal, her lips parted, throat arching as she reached for him, forgetting his rule about not moving. But this time he didn't seem to mind as much. He guided the head into her mouth, watched with intent eyes and firm mouth as she took him in, and kept taking him, until he reached the back of her throat. She'd learned to relax those muscles, and she did now, giving him greater reach. She wished she could take all of him, all the way to the base, but he was a longer, thicker man than . . . He was long and thick.

His eyes gleamed at her hasty correction. When he began to withdraw, she sucked on him, tasting him with her tongue, savoring his unique flavor. Her body shuddered, saturated with want, craving release, and yet there was such a sweet anticipation to it, she didn't mind being on this cusp for him.

Thrust and withdraw. He was slow about it at first, making her hypercognizant of the way she must look, her mouth stretched around his girth, the way her eyes pleaded as they looked up at him, wanting more, and more, and more. His face got tighter, the cords of his neck hardening. His thigh muscles rippled in the loosened jeans, and she so wished her hands were free so she could fill her hands with his buttocks, feel them flex and ease in that pumping rhythm. She'd run her hands along the columns of his thighs as she knelt at his feet. His hands would be in her hair, forcing her to do his bidding, whatever he wanted from her. She'd never been so focused on one thing, and so mindless at once.

His cock convulsed in her mouth, and she was ready for him. He became far more rough and powerful then, almost bruising in his hold on her head and throat, but she reveled in it, as well as the jet of heat, the flood of seed he gave to her. A hoarse cry broke from his lips, his body pressed down on her, holding her to his desires.

When he was done, her lashes were wet with the strain of taking him, but she licked and cleaned him thoroughly. He pulled free an inch at a time, waiting for her to do her job properly, until she took a final taste of his salt and musk from the tiny slit at the end. Dropping to an elbow next to her, he let his gaze wander over her flushed, trembling body. If he touched her at all, she knew she'd explode. He cocked his head, gazing down between her legs.

"You're so wet, your curls there are gleaming with dew, like grass after a rainstorm. I want you to come for me, Elisa, without me touching you. Contract the muscles inside of you, the way your body has been doing on its own. Contract and then release, as if my cock is stretching you, working you hard. Do it while I watch."

At first it was difficult, to do something consciously that the body did in an involuntary way. But the first time she managed it, a shudder went through her. He showed his fangs, an approval. "Keep doing it. Maybe I'll take you to the edge, then make you stop."

She kept doing it, until she was doing it quite frantically, her breath rasping in her throat, hips bucking as if he were thrusting into her in truth. She kept her gaze on his face, goaded by the raw lust in his eyes, as if he'd devour her whole any moment now. Abruptly, he leaned forward as she continued to undulate. His lips parted and the tip of his tongue traced a slow, slow circle around her nipple. Then he gave her a little nip.

She contracted hard, a guttural cry ripping from her throat. He withdrew several inches, watching every expression as her body took over, performing at his demand with nothing more than his eyes stroking her. The climax swept over her so intensely she was shocked to feel a wetness gush onto her thighs like a man's seed. He bent then, brought his mouth to that offering as she was still going. A full-throated, raw shriek tore from her at the first contact of his mouth.

Inside me, inside me, please fuck me, fuck me . . . She used his word, because she'd become the feral animal now, no patience for modesty.

He shifted, and she snarled her pleasure as he buried his still-erect cock deep inside of her, seating himself to the hilt. She rocked violently against him, milking everything she could from that moment, her lips drawn back, eyes glazed as he watched her, completely in control of her, of whatever he wanted from her.

But she wasn't so far gone that she couldn't see that she'd spun a trance of her own. The hard set of his mouth, the glitter of his eyes, were also pure male animal, lost in everything she was giving him.

Give it all to me.

And she did, until exhaustion claimed her and she wound down, shuddering, trembling, her body suddenly so heavy and drained she could barely do more than murmur as he released her arms and legs and shifted her into a curl inside his arms, the curve of his body.

She fell asleep like that, not thinking a thing about laundry or chores or anything else but Malachi. Something about that gave her a twinge of sadness, but she didn't chase it. He didn't let her. He kissed her softly, again and again, an oral lullaby that took her into dreams. For the first time in a long time, she was replete, inside and out.

~

As she slept so deeply she might have been knocked unconscious, Mal waited, his mind inside of hers. When he felt that tentative touch he expected, he spoke, knowing Elisa was far beyond them both, in dreams.

You've been a comfort to her, but I'm here now. Stay out of her head, boy. This is my territory now, and vampires don't share. I'll take care of her.

It was a direct, male-to-male warning, and Jeremiah understood it, loud and clear. He withdrew, allowing Mal to settle in with the girl, his mind as well as his body surrounding her. In a couple hours, he'd wake and take her again. Throughout the daylight hours, he'd re-impress the claim and the lesson. Of course, he realized he'd just staked a very obvious claim, one even more significant than the one he'd made the day she arrived. He knew what it meant. Or rather, what it could mean, and what it couldn't.

One of the things it meant was he had one more question for Elisa, but he had to talk to Danny first. He'd need to be ready to have a strip taken out of his hide for even proposing it, but thinking about Elisa's earlier thoughts, he figured some things were just worth an ass-kicking.

Wryly he realized he had a touch of nervousness, like a beau going to a formidable matriarch to ask permission to court her daughter. But it wasn't like that. This was practical, necessary for what was ahead. A big part of him didn't even want to bring Elisa into it, but he knew it was important. She'd proven to him tonight that she could handle it. There was a room in her heart open that wasn't in his, and his intuition told him that room would be critical to securing a future for some of her fledglings.

But that was the beginning and end of it. He knew what was in her heart, so close to the surface he could see it, even with a mere second mark. As a vampire, he couldn't give her that, but he'd never met someone who deserved it more. He wouldn't take it from her, no matter what. What he wanted to do would be permanent . . . but temporary.

He grimaced. Yeah, he was sure Danny would see it that way.

26

"I NEED to third-mark Elisa."

There was a significant pause on the other end of the line, long enough that Mal thought it might be static interference, but then Danny spoke. "You're wanting to keep her? How does she feel about that?"

"It's not like that. She can still come home when this is all done. The Council doesn't have a problem with a third-mark servant being away from her Master, as long as she's serving in another vampire's household, and you've already second-marked her."

"Mal, you're confusing me, probably because you're not getting to the point, which both annoys me and makes me suspicious. Why would you want to third-mark her, if you're only going to give her up?"

He sighed. "I think it's possible four of the fledglings can learn enough control to get along passably well in the right vampire's household. The host vampire would have to take them on purely as wards, have the right temperament to work with them, safely test how independent they can be over time. He or she would also need the compassion to handle things properly if the fledglings never get past the transition bloodlust or it intensifies as they get older. But while we work with them here, getting them ready for such households, I need to travel and meet with the prospects. I want Elisa's eyes, her feel for their . . . hearts."

There, he'd said it, as foolish as it sounded, but dealing with the cats had always been intuitive to him. It meant sometimes he'd seen things even the animal behaviorists who'd visited hadn't. There were some things that existed outside of science. His chronic practicality, as Elisa called it, and her maternal bond with the fledglings, would be the proper combination of intuition. He was certain enough of it to be having this most awkward phone call, though he couldn't quite put his finger on why he felt it was awkward. Which was okay, because Danny managed to do that all on her own.

"So you've become attached to her."

"It has nothing to do with that."

"But you're not denying it."

"Afterward, I'll send her back to you," he repeated stubbornly.

"Is that what she wants? Or, the more critical question, is that what you want?"

"Danny, she can't stay here forever."

"Why not? If she's agreeable to that, she'd be a help to you there, I'm sure. And if one or more of the fledglings end up being there an extended time, she would want to stay there with them. She'd accept that. I know you'd be gentle with her, Mal. You're remote and don't deal with other vampires too often, so she'd be all right. As she gets more seasoned and experienced—"

"I'd be able to whore her out when other vampires visited. Or be forced to do so when I had to take her to the Regional vampire gathering, where the third-marked servants are required to be present for pointless games and power plays."

Danny paused. "Wasn't exactly my way of putting it, but you know our ways. It's not all like that. With the right servant, it's a mutual pleasure. And Elisa has the nature for it."

"The nature, but not the heart." Mal tightened his jaw. It was true, but he wasn't going to put it all on Elisa like that. "And while my cock might respond to it like any trained dog will if handed the right treat . . . it's not what I am either, not heart deep."

"Really?" He could almost see that slim brow arching, Danny's intrigued look. "Are you going to elaborate on that?"

"You know my history. It's not a surprise to you. I'm not like born vampires, or even most made vampires. Before I was turned, I wanted something different, even if I pissed it away." He hitched over it, because it was probably the first time in his life he'd said it. "That hasn't changed, not really."

"What was it you wanted?" Danny's voice was neutral, quiet.

What the hell? He'd opened the can of worms now, right? "A family. A home. Children. I wanted to hunt as the old ones of our tribe used to do before we were overrun with settlers, bring home game to my wife and have her prepare it. Sit with her around a fire at night, watch our children play and think about how I'd make love to her that night. I'm a vampire, Danny. I can't have that memory. I can't have the fantasy."

"Maybe not exactly like that, no. But our way of life doesn't completely exclude such a thing, Mal. And as much as you like that picture, there are things in you that are different from that, too. Things you need as a vampire that you can't deny."

"That's the problem. They're all tangled together. I'm with her, and I want . . . I want to own her. Make her mine in all ways. Take her to her knees and teach her pleasure there. And I also want to see her . . ."

"Cook your food, sit by your fire at night?"

"Yes. You're going to ridicule me, I'm sure."

"No," Danny responded. "I'm not. I love my station, Mal. I love to watch the seasons cycle, help the new lambs be born. I love sitting on the porch with Dev at night, listening to the radio and watching him whittle. I also love taking him to bed and wringing him dry, making him serve me over and over again, in a hundred ways."

"Well, the man is hung like a stallion in full rut mode, from what I hear."

"There is that." Danny's feline smile was palpable over the phone. "But it's not really that. Don't deflect. When we have to do vampire business, which is more often than he or I like, we've learned to take a great deal of pleasure from those games, because he's serving me, and every time it pushes his limits, he knows he's serving me even more. That's the magic of the third-mark bond, Mal, when it's true. It's something so strong between you that anything which gives you pleasure will give her pleasure. If you loosen up those tight laces on your vampire nature a bit, you'll give her even more. The two desires *can* go together for us."

He didn't say anything as Danny added, "You know she has it in her. My mother knew it when she groomed her to become a member of my household. But if what you were just saying is your true desire, you couldn't have found someone more appropriate. Elisa *is* unique. She's not flashy or worldly in the least. She just has an abiding desire to serve, to please. To love." The last was added in a murmur. "Mal, if she's offering that gift to you, and you want it, don't be a fool. Don't turn away from it. You may not be able to have what you wanted, but you can have something maybe as special for one of our kind. And she very well may be in the same boat at this point."

Not able to have what she wanted, but something different, if he offered it to her. But what kind of offer was it? Did it really give her anything? "If she doesn't want the third mark, I won't do it. And even if she does, if she wants to come home after, I'll send her back to you. Which is what I think will happen."

"Hmm. Regardless, you have my blessing." Now there was amusement in her voice. "Have her call me after she gives you her answer on the third mark, so I can discuss it with her, confirm it's what she wants. I assume you'll advise me where you're going, and assure me that you can protect her. Recent events . . . may interfere with her submissive nature."

"I know. That's the other thing, why I want to make sure that she's willing and able. But you have my word. Nothing's getting past me to cause her any fear or harm her. These will be one-on-one meetings with the vampire in question. Should be manageable."

"All right. Now, about Leonidas." Danny sighed. "How likely do you think it is the others will have this problem as they age, but don't change physically?"

"Your guess is as good as mine, unfortunately. We might be able to get more information out of them on their ages, but my guess is that Victor and Leonidas were of similar ages." Mal pushed his chair back. "I think the vampire next closest to them in age is Jeremiah, for all that he looks younger. There's a maturity to him far different from the other four. But unfortunately, his bloodlust episodes have the same quality as Leonidas's, though he's worked harder to fight them off."

"So we might have more time on the younger ones." Danny's tone was thoughtful.

"What are you thinking?"

"Well, this may sound a bit off, but there's a vampire, a very young one, barely more than a fledgling himself, who's earning degrees in scientific study in London. He's a born vampire, his father a well-regarded overlord in line for Region Master there. Anyhow, Lord Brian recently wrote a paper for the Vampire Council proposing the establishment of a facility to study problems uniquely applicable to vampires. Our weakness to sunlight, unexpected transition effects, the Ennui. It's not anything more than a concept at this point, but I'll send you the article. It was given to all the Region Masters. Since he's young and eager to prove his skills and worth, you might consider inviting him down to meet the fledglings, see what he thinks of the progression of terminal bloodlust, because it's a unique situation, as far as we know. If he is what he says he is, he might be able to help."

"All right." Mal made a note of it. "Send me the document. If he could figure out how to handle their fangs, that alone would be a blessing. It would give them a visual normalcy that would help them get along better in both human and vampire society."

"I thought about just extracting them when they were here, but it felt wrong. I didn't know how it would impact the marking serums."

"If there's such a thing as an expert on our kind, I'd feel better doing it after getting his recommendation." His lip curled. "Of course, it's been my experience that science wasn't even a field until a group of people made a career of acting on the dangerous thought, 'What would happen if we . . .' et cetera, and decided to call it scientific inquiry."

"Sounds like Lord Brian will enjoy your company." Danny chuckled. "Like two peas in a pod. He may never want to leave your island."

~

When he passed through the kitchen, Kohana grunted at him. "Mail and meat delivery came in."

"Yeah, I heard the plane. You get anything from your sister on the res?"

Kohana nodded. "The money I've been sending her has been helping. She's got running water in the house now."

"Good. We'll keep sending what we can." Mal cocked his head at the Indian's expression. "Something else?"

"Elisa got your gift."

"Don't know what you're talking about, old man."

"Not as old as you."

"But I'm prettier."

Kohana snorted. "So you say. Go see the girl. She's a picture."

"You getting sweet on her?" Mal inquired, even as he moved toward the opposite exit from the kitchen.

"If I was?" Kohana arched a brow. "You'd have something to say about it, I'm willing to bet. Or do you not know anything about that, either?"

Mal chose to ignore the comment and the additional snort that followed him out of the kitchen as he headed to the upper-level bedrooms. That was another reason why he preferred his island to anywhere else. Several of his staff knew him well enough they wouldn't be surprised by what he'd said to Danny about the things he held on to, old dreams. They didn't find it odd because they were things humans could want, did want. Why would it all disappear just because he'd become a vampire? Even for the born vampires, he often wondered why it was so strange and taboo for a vampire to want family, connection.

The strong cravings he felt for blood and sex might be a little over-the-top when compared to humans, and he might be leery of calling his staff his friends outright, but it didn't mean he didn't value such connections. Gods, it gave him a headache. He scowled. No wonder he preferred staying on the island.

He could hear the music well before he reached the upper level. His contact on the mainland had said he could get his hands on a wealth of 1940s popular music, but he'd apparently found a few fifties records as well, because Mal was hearing the lyrics to "Tell Me Why" by Eddie Fisher. Despite the seriousness of his conversation with Danny, it made him smile, the whimsical sound of it. That smile only deepened as he reached her open door.

Since the night she'd agreed to stay, Elisa had offered to move to the bunkhouse a couple times, wanting that validation that she was here as staff, but Mal hadn't agreed to that. So in that way she had, she'd gotten what she wanted via a different route. She'd transformed her room from a generic, comfortable guest room into a reflection of the woman now inhabiting it. There were flowers in jars, seashell arrangements with colorful soda bottles. She'd used spare cloth to sew herself brightly colored pillows.

It wasn't the validation Mal was avoiding. He wanted her in the house, far more convenient to him. His bed. When he was in his office at night, he liked hearing her putter around the kitchen with Kohana. After she was done with her chores, she'd gotten brave enough to read in the study while he worked. She'd take one of his books down and read about the cats, learn more about their behavior and the island, sometimes falling asleep on the sofa in the corner. At times he looked over and saw both of his tomcats curled up on her, one under her arm, the other behind her legs. They kept her suitably pinned and slightly uncomfortable in that position, but not enough to disturb them, that unique and diabolical method all domestic felines seemed to inflict on those willing to appreciate and indulge them.

Sometimes, when she was helping Kohana, a favorite song came on the radio and she sang along with it, as she was doing now. Her voice was a mix of cultured Brit with a spicing of Aussie colloquialism, probably because her parents hadn't been a big part of her life and Lady Constance's education had been top-notch. But every once in a while, he thought he caught the sound of her Irish blood in the pleasing notes.

Reaching her doorway, he found it a pleasure to focus on the pretty tableau before him. Several of the books she'd borrowed from his library were stacked next to the bed. A mending basket sat in a chair, a torn skirt spread over it. On the bed were some papers, and he saw she'd been scribbling, drawing some rough sketches of his cats, making notes about them, details she wanted to remember about their care and personalities when she helped out at the habitat area. In another corner she had a sewing project going, new clothes for the fledglings, using fabric Kohana had given her from their stores.

Right now, though, she wasn't mending, studying, reading or sketching. The new record player he'd gotten for her was placed on the dresser. The Eddie Fisher selection swelled in volume, filling the room. She was dancing to it, twirling now and again, swaying back and forth as she studied another record cover. She was wearing one of her maid outfits, the calf-length skirt and delectable apron, a clean and pressed blouse. As usual, the button over her ample bosom was straining a bit, giving his fingers the wicked desire to slip it. It would reveal a deeper view of that tempting valley of cleavage, one that even the severely proper brassiere couldn't quell.

He'd done that recently, in fact, surprising her when she was cleaning the back porch. He'd backed her up against the wall, slid that button free and nuzzled that valley, making her breath shorten and her hand catch in his hair. He'd been on his way out for the evening, and had been strongly tempted to say the hell with it and take her up against the wall, but managed to curtail his baser urges. She was like a drug, his little maid whose eyes went opaque with desire as she clutched him with real, honest need in her body.

Knowing his Irish flower, when the record player came in and Kohana told her it was hers, she'd probably said she'd run it up to the room and then come right back down to continue her wide array of self-imposed chores. However, she'd obviously been unable to resist playing just one record. He wondered if she knew the song or if it had been random, the top of the stack.

When she made another twirl, she saw him and gave a start. "Oh. I usually know when you're around. I guess"—she hurried toward the player—"I was too busy listening."

"Leave it on; that's fine. Or put on that next one you're holding."

"It's a wonderful gift." She paused as the current song faded. The gaze she gave him was slightly apprehensive. "Were you picking on me?"

"What?" He stepped into the room. "What do you mean?"

"I mean . . . what you said the other night, about any other young girl would be pining for the mainland, and record players, and such. I just . . . Oh, never mind. I really like this. It shouldn't be just for me, though. I'm going to take it down to the bunkhouse so they can enjoy it, but I thought it would be all right for me to have it to myself for just one night. I'll bring it back up to the kitchen for Kohana and me to listen, during the early part of the day when we're cleaning. It's so nice and easy to carry around."

When he took another step toward her, she turned away, busying herself with replacing the record, her head bent so her hair exposed her nape, the line of her shoulder. He paused behind her, knowing she was hyperaware of his closeness.

"No. And yes. No, I wasn't picking on you, not in a mean way. I was suggesting you can be both. The girl who'd like to wear a pretty dress and go dancing on the mainland, as well as the woman who's dedicated her soul to helping those nobody else wanted to help."

She remained in the same position, but he sensed her mind turning it over, trying to figure out what he was doing here, what he wanted. She was imagining a variety of things, some of which were making it hard not to get derailed and indulge in tugging her blouse off her shoulders, releasing her from the bra and filling his hands with those generous curves.

"I was talking to Danny." He cleared his throat. "You'll go with me to Lord Marshall's. I think it would be best if you did that with a third mark. Mine."

That word had a wealth of meaning, for certain, but he left it at that, waiting to see what she would do and say. As the silence drew out, he added, "While the mark is of course a permanent binding, it doesn't bind you here forever. Once we get things sorted out with the fledglings, you'd be able to go back to Danny's station whenever you wished. It's not a prison sentence."

"I would never think of it that way."

Suddenly he wanted to see her face. She was drawing her hand away from setting the needle, and he closed his hand on that wrist, turning her around to face him. Her eyes were serious, mouth soft, worried.

"Vampires require many things of their human servants, regardless of the number of marks, Elisa," he said, keeping a grip on her hand. "But accepting a third mark is always a choice. You know why."

"Because ever after, the human is fully bonded to the vampire. You own my heart, mind and soul. I serve you forever."

"It can be that way. But as I said, I'll concede your service to Danny, if that's the way you eventually want it. This has to be your choice."

Her hand in his hadn't moved. The variety of thoughts whirling in her mind were too chaotic for him to pick up one linear thread. He caught one entirely random thought—she wished she'd put away the mending before he came in.

"Elisa." He drew her gaze back up to him with a faintly impatient tone. "I know you'll do anything for the fledglings. Any number of foolish, hazardous things. But you don't have to do this for them. It will certainly help them, and me, but we can accomplish something similar if it's not something you want."

"But the chances of success won't be as great." Her shrewd eyes studied his face. "You need my help, mind to mind, the way Danny and Dev are."

"Damn it, I don't want you to do this just for them."

"Who do you want me to do it for?" Those blue eyes were intent. "For you, Master?"

His jaw tightened. That quiet word, the curl of her hand on his arm. He could be in her mind, but for some reason at this moment she was mysterious, unfathomable. "I want you to do it for you," he insisted.

The music started playing, a lovely, strong female voice, and her eyes softened. "I guess she's saying it all, isn't she? A sign, maybe?"

The woman was singing about traveling to exotic places. However, with every sight, every marvel, every dream, she exhorted the listener to remember one key thing. Elisa mouthed it, her breath whispering over the syllables.

"You belong to me." Then the corner of her mouth quirked. "Or is that your line? Do you like to dance, Mr. Malachi?" Her slim fingers twined with his.

Mal wondered if the floor had dropped two feet beneath him, because his ground had definitely been shaken. "It's been a long time. I was taught . . . waltzes, things like that."

"Is it painful to remember?" Her expression said Chumani had told her some of his past. Still, he answered the question.

"No. Because it was the first time I got to touch girls."

That quirk became a tiny smile. "Boys do tend to remember that fondly."

"What do girls remember?"

"The first kiss. The first time a boy holds her hand. The first time a man says, 'I love you,' and really means it, not just as a way to get . . . you know." She pressed her lips together, hesitating, then removed both her hands from his, but only to lay them on his chest, gaze up into his face. "I know I'm being a bit forward, but . . . will you dance with me?"

It was more than being forward. In this moment she was acting as if they were simply man and woman, circling each other, accepting bond and attraction, no worries or reservations. He should be disabusing her of such a notion, knowing its dangers, but she looked directly into his eyes, and there were no fledglings, no cats, no one watching, just the two of them standing in her bedroom, enjoying a song.

Sliding his arm around her waist, he closed his hand around one of hers, but left it on his chest, warming it between those two parts of him as he moved her into an easy three-step rhythm, mindful of the dimensions of her room. It had been a while since he'd done it, but it was easy with her moving with him, her body close from the cinch of his arm.

"Do you know the waltz was thought scandalous when it was invented, because it allowed men and women to stand close to one another, and required the man to put a hand on the woman's waist?" Elisa tilted her head, an innocently coquettish gesture. "When I was younger, I remember riding the train from Perth. There was this young boy and young girl, teenagers, on the train. I don't think their parents knew they were sweethearts, but I could tell. They were sitting in the seats behind their parents and I was across the aisle. I remember he put his hand on the dividing armrest and she put hers next to it, and for so many miles, as the train clacked along, they kept their hands like that, no more than a half inch between them. You could feel the heat between them, and not touching made it even more powerful. There was all that yearning in the air, and it just got heavier and heavier. At last, when I think they could bear no more, he moved his hand, so slightly. For just the barest second, he put his smallest finger over hers. The look on her face . . . it was as if he'd kissed her soundly and . . ."

Her cheeks flushed then, but he saw it in her mind and finished it. "And made love to her, with that one gesture."

She nodded. "Sometimes, when I'm with you, it feels that way. You give me one look, or you touch my back when you head out for your evening's work, and the heat lingers inside of me, unfolds there."

"Elisa—"

"I'm being foolish." She gave a quick smile, her hand flexing on his shoulder. "It's that song, so romantic and . . . full. Don't pay any attention to me. So when do you want to do the third mark? Right now?"

27

H E stopped, dropping her hand so he could put both at her waist, his fingers flexing. During the dancing, she'd become as appealing and romantic as a pink rose. Now, though, she was practical, flatly reasonable.

"Would that work for you?" he asked curtly. "Get it off the to-do list, and then you can go beat rugs with Kohana, or cook eggs?"

She blinked. "Since you came to tell me, I assumed you wanted to go ahead and get it done."

He did, damn it. Then he caught a stray thought from her mind, and it helped, made him understand. Lowering his brow to hers, he gave her unexpected tenderness. As a result, her blue eyes flitted up to his, uncertainty replacing that veneer of efficiency. "I do. But I want you to feel, Elisa. I want you to feel all of it. Even if you choose to go home afterwards, I've bound you to me the way no other vampire ever will. In the eyes of the vampire world, you will be mine. It's significant."

"I know." Petulance gave her tone a snap. She closed her eyes. "I want you to just do it. I don't want to feel, because it's not real, you know. I belong to you, but you'll never belong to me."

It made something tighten in his gut, even though she wasn't saying anything he hadn't already known about her, about what she truly

wanted. "But someone will. I told you, there will be other men at your
station with gentle hands—"

"I don't *want* another Willis. There was only one of him, and he's
here, in my heart. I don't need another man like that. I don't need—"
She drew a breath, tried to back away, but he held on to her arms. Began
to back her into a wall. He could feel her struggle, see it, but he saw
what was beneath it as well. When he saw her answer, his vampire
senses sharpened like a blade, his bloodlust stirring to take, claim. The
protests on her lips froze, then dissolved altogether as she became all
wide blue eyes and parted mouth, her heart pounding up into her
throat. When her back hit the wall, he lifted her up against it, sliding an
arm around her waist and cupping her buttock so her legs naturally
curled high on his thighs to hold on.

"Elisa, do you want to be my third-marked servant, bound to me
forever, subject to my will for you, whatever that may be? If you answer
no, it will change nothing about what I will or won't do for you and
your fledglings. This is your choice. Is it what you want, or not?"

"I need . . . time."

"No, you don't. It's just a matter of whether you accept it or not."

"Is it what you want?" She stared at him. "You've never had a third-
mark servant. Why do you want me?"

He should have known she'd have the courage to think about that
side of it, make it about more than her decision. She never forgot others
in her calculations. In fact, the decision to keep the record player to
herself, even for a mere night, was the first time he'd ever seen her take
something for her own.

"I take things for myself all the time," she whispered. "When I wake
up early to see the sunrise. When I pick wildflowers. When I read in
your study, just so I can smell you, see the way you look against the
lamplight, watch your hands as you stroke your cats and wish it was
me . . ."

He'd let her into his mind unintentionally. He was preparing her for
a connection that would link them that way, so perhaps that was why
he'd dropped his guard. Maybe in this moment he wanted her more
deeply in his mind than he'd ever wanted anyone there. Maybe she'd
find wildflowers and sunshine he'd missed or, more likely, she'd bring
those things with her.

She gave an unexpected giggle, a nervous sound. "Now I'm picturing wildflowers sprouting out your ears, and sunshine bursting from your arse."

"This is a serious moment," he informed her, though his lips quivered against a smile. "You're supposed to be awed at the possibilities and yet compliant to my wishes."

She arranged her face in a semblance of sobriety, though the laughter did fade out of her eyes. "I am. That's what terrifies me. Both for myself and for you. I don't know if I would be any good as a third-marked servant, at the types of things you might need from me, even if it's just for a little while. And what if I want to keep being one, but you want to send me home? I'd feel like I failed you."

"If that happens, it will be because I'm such an ogre you'll be glad to go home."

She frowned, a tiny pucker between her brows. "I don't think I have that in me. To admit I can't be what you need me to be."

He knew that. It made her so irresistible to his vampire blood, he had to bite back a need to rush this moment. There was a painful, dangerous reality to this. The third mark could damage her soul in the long run. It could even destroy it. That mattered to him, even as instinct pushed him forward, an irresistible tide. Nature was cruel, but inexorable. It would override good sense and caution and, though the result might be tragedy or loss, it knew things the rational mind couldn't. He believed in it, but he'd also seen his cats obey instinct to fight things that would be for their own benefit. The question was, which situation was this?

She moistened her lips. "I think we have to take the chance, don't we? It's just the way it has to be, like a baby taking his first steps. He may be walking toward a life of hardship, but God intends him to walk, so he walks."

He'd closed his mind to her after the wildflower observation. Not because he didn't appreciate her humor, but because he sincerely didn't want to influence her. The fact she'd picked up on his thought process regardless and given it her own unique stamp was unsettling. But it also sealed her fate.

With her body so close, her soul quivering in his grasp, as near as the pulse pounding in her throat, he wasn't going to argue with his own nature any longer. He'd embraced it long ago, after all, letting go of what he'd been before, a shipwreck that he'd lost in the current of his life too quickly to mourn its loss. That had come far later.

Maybe this drive now was all vampire, or maybe being a vampire simply tapped into the dark places that always existed in the male mind. A need to give and receive pleasure through conquering. Not all women responded to it, but almost all of them recognized it in some way.

He turned her from the wall, effortlessly hitching her up his body. She fell forward against him, curling her arms around his shoulders, dropping her head against his so he carried her almost as a man might carry his child, her body going loose and fluid against him, trusting, compliant.

He laid her down on her bed, and, following his own desires, he slid off the skirt. She wore the sneakers he'd decorated for her, and he put those to the side, taking off the short white socks. Then came the practical panties. Before they visited the mainland, he'd be buying her some very different ones, including bras that would lovingly cradle that eye-catching bosom of hers rather than strangling it. She'd wear them under her neat, practical outfits, distracting him with the knowledge she was wearing them to please him.

Her lower body was completely bare now. He opened her shirt, holding that one straining button for last, then flicked it open. Sliding an arm beneath her, he freed the bra, then scooped her forward, let her lean against him, his one knee planted between her thighs to keep them spread as he pulled the shirt down her arms to the elbows. He let the bra follow, taking the cups over her head and behind her, so the straps and the sleeves of her shirt kept her partially restrained in movement.

When he laid her back down, he kept his arm under her so her breasts tilted up invitingly toward him, those large pink nipples already tightening before his gaze, wanting his mouth. She loved it when he suckled her. Sometimes, when she went to sleep here, when he couldn't be with her, she passed her fingertips over them before she fell into dreams, thinking of his mouth there, and other places. She was fascinated with the cleverness of his mouth.

Hearing the drift of such thoughts in her mind was not helping him show restraint, but he wanted her wet and begging, beyond thoughts of fledglings or floor scrubbings, all his in every way, knowing she was entirely focused on him when he did this. He might be superstitious, but he wanted it that way, so there was nothing to taint it. He might not be the first who'd ever had her body or even her heart, but he would be the first who'd taken her like this. He'd also been the first to take her how she wanted to be taken, and that was a key difference.

"Why . . . ?" Her voice was breathy. "Why do you like me tied like this? I won't try to get away."

"You know why, Elisa. It's in your mind, and it's why it makes you wet. Tell me why. I want to hear it from those distracting lips of yours."

They parted as she moistened them. "You want me . . . helpless. Owned. Yours. You want me . . . overcome with these feelings, beyond thought."

He nodded. "Now hush. And feel."

He'd left the bedroom door open. Kohana could come down the hall, or anyone who came into the house. She could be seen like this, stretched on the bed, legs spread for his pleasure, breasts bare. He'd seen her gaze drift to that open door, and knew it was a worry in her mind, but it was something else, too. She didn't want to acknowledge it, modest thing that she was, but it excited her, in a deep, dark place. It was a statement on what she was becoming. It didn't mean he was cheaply using her and not caring who saw her naked and vulnerable. Instead, it was a way of underscoring her value that most wouldn't understand, but she did.

Danny and Dev had plowed that ground for her. A vampire female had exceptional hearing, so he knew the times Elisa had stumbled on the two of them, she'd been allowed to see what she saw. While others might look if Danny desired them to do so, no one was allowed to touch Dev unless she said it was all right. Elisa understood it enough to remember that now, and revel in the idea she could be that . . . essential.

Essential was the perfect word for it, because if the whole island started to sink into the sea right now, he wouldn't have stopped. The only thing that could have accomplished that was if he saw a true rejection of this in her mind. But instead, while the waters were fraught with hazards and the possibility of regrets, she was riding the crest of the wave far above that, accepting what fate would give them in the future, and taking the now.

He stood above her, the one knee planted between her legs as he studied her, from thighs to throat. Up to the flushed face and desire-bright eyes, the long, thick lashes and pretty wings of hair around her face. Her one foot was braced against his calf, toes curled against denim. The other foot dangled, shin brushing the side of his leg. The longer he looked, the more she trembled, and the thicker the scent of her arousal became, such that he saw the tempting cream gather on those nether lips beneath the tiny brown curls. A drop began to slide down toward the crease of her buttocks, making his fangs lengthen and saliva gather in his mouth.

Please . . . Please, Master.

It was unconscious, the plea in her mind, since she was trying not to speak, picking up on his demand that she be still and quiet, surrendering to whatever it was he wanted from her right now. That subliminal plea swept fire through him, particularly as her lashes lowered, emphasizing that surrender and yet lingering over his chest and abdomen, past his belt and then down to the arousal clearly pressing against his jeans. All for her.

Kneeling on the floor between her dangling legs, he cupped her buttocks to slide her forward to his mouth. When only his breath touched her cunt, she cried out, an involuntary whimper, and he saw the tiny muscles flex, the clit ripple. A pure, perfect new drop of honey formed as a result. He licked it away, dipping inside briefly, and she shuddered, giving another delectable whimper.

I'll give you the third mark here, Irish flower, so that you'll remember it each time your thighs brush together.

Her response was incoherent acquiescence, a sweet, wordless song to him. He kept up that slow lick, teasing her lips, the clit, the weeping gateway that would be stretching to accommodate his cock before this was done. He could hear the rush of blood in the femoral, so close, but he wanted the taste and scent of her orgasm on his mouth when he finally turned his mouth to that. She was quivering so hard in his grasp, trying so hard not to move, because she knew that was what he liked . . . usually.

You may move, Elisa. Buck against my hold, work those hips against my mouth, show me how you become under my touch, the way you are with no one else.

The way I alone want to make you feel. He didn't share that unexpected thought. But he didn't have to dwell on it, because she obeyed like a wild bird freed from a cage, her body surging up against his mouth, her restricted arms tensing, fingers digging into the bed as she undulated up, her breasts wobbling back toward her throat as her body became a crescent of need, all reaching for him. As she fought his irresistible hold, showing that delicious female conflict that always existed in the grip of pleasure—the need to pull away and yet be as close as possible—he teased her clit with more insistent lashes of his tongue. Her climax surged upward, and she was trying to resist it, but he wouldn't allow that, either.

He watched with eternal fascination as her breath became short puffs, almost like a woman in labor, and then she was making short cries, one right on top of another, staccato notes that rushed up a hill she couldn't escape.

Go over now, Elisa. Obey me.

Muscles and nerves stretched to their limit and her cunt contracted hard against his mouth, a small spurt of sweet liquid gushing onto his tongue. A scream tore from her throat, building in volume he wouldn't allow to diminish as he kept working her with his mouth. Plunging his tongue in hard and fast now, he sucked that tight bud, moving his lips over her in a random motion that kept the nerves straining to keep up, feeling the sensation everywhere so it wouldn't ebb.

He brought his fingers into play, taking over for his mouth as he turned it to her thigh, sinking his fangs into that pounding artery. Her cry escalated, her arms beating against the mattress, hands clawing the covers such that she had handfuls of the fabric crushed in it. Her lush backside was off the mattress, working her pussy up against his fingers. As her blood filled his mouth, he released that final serum, felt it swirl away into her, rushing for her heart and that deep place science said didn't physically exist in the human body. Vampires had always known it did.

The soul was the true image of divinity, because it was everywhere and nowhere, what gave life and spark, but was never fully defined or understood in its plan or desires, its needs and demands. Every living thing had it. To deny it was to deny whatever God was and reject miracles like this, simple and unfathomably complicated at once.

Her pleasure overcame her such that the other leg wrapped over his back, holding him tight to her, her soul reaching for him. He took the precious extra moment to seal the wound, then came up her body, sliding her thigh back to his side, fingers leaving a firm imprint.

Her eyes were so feverish and needy. If there was such a thing as Heaven, it would be her, always like this, completely connected to him, her naked body still shuddering in the aftermath of the ecstasy he'd given her, her eyes fastened on him in total concentration.

He opened his jeans, freeing his cock from the painful confinement. Her hungry gaze only made it jerk in further need, almost making him wince. He needed to release into her, relieve this intense pressure, that pussy clasping him with blissful friction. But first . . .

He could have her bite him, but he knew his gentle maid. Even in her most ferocious moment he doubted she would be able to bring herself to pierce his flesh. So he drew the blade he carried at his now-undone belt. He paused, considering, and then took it to his throat, a short, practiced slice. He could have chosen the wrist, but he knew what he wanted, and from the flicker in her gaze, he knew she wanted it, too.

He came down on her, staying clothed to underscore his dominance over her, but later he would stretch out on her, flesh against flesh, not denying either of them that mutual pleasure.

She'd forced her body to quivering stillness, his intuitive almost-servant, awaiting his desires. He adjusted himself, took hold of the base of his organ, so close to explosion it jerked even from the clasp of his hand, but then he fitted it to her opening, giving a muted, heartfelt groan. She was so soaking wet he sank like a heavy stone to the bottom of a warm pond.

Curling his arm around her shoulders, he cupped her head with his palm, bringing her to his throat. "Drink, sweet girl," he murmured. "Become my full servant."

He'd heard about it from others, but he'd also heard, time and again, that no words could fully describe it, like most things that mattered more than anything else. Her lips touched the spot, then closed over it, the tip of her tongue taking a delicate sip. Then her instincts kicked in, already goaded and directed by that third mark, such that she began suckling, drinking deep, taking in the amount needed to finish it.

It was like a shower of starlight, rushing through his veins. They elongated into barbed streams of light that wound through her, binding her to him. For the second mark, her mind had been open to him, but now he realized how superficial interpreting her mind had been. In a plane, one could explore the sky above the earth. But this was a rocket, giving him the ability to see the whole galaxy, plunging him into an infinite variety of unexplored areas, following that barbed chain of stars wherever they might lead.

It frightened her a little. Even as he was amazed by it, he sensed her hesitation at the unexpected invasion. Suddenly, in her deepest places, even those she had trouble facing herself, another being could share that space, be there whenever he chose. He murmured to her, even as he sent her the thought.

I will not harm you, Elisa. I'll protect you, keep you safe. I'm holding you within and without, always.

It was instinct, no plan, nothing weighed against reality or whatever their future might be, but it was truth for him in this second, so fiercely felt he wasn't sure if it wasn't actual forever fact. Beyond his understanding, but no less true for all that. She felt it, accepted it, resumed her teasing at his throat. He withdrew partially from her, then slid back in, let her feel another form of claiming now, one that had her hands seeking a purchase at his hips, trying to hold on to the denim as much as her clothing's gentle restraints would allow. Her legs locked hard and high on him, her heels brushing his back.

He was so close to explosion, but he was also immersed in the new sensations. So closely linked to her, every thought, feeling and desire swirled like new stars in truth in that galaxy. Bright points of light exploding and streaking against the sky of her soul. He could reach out and touch them, feel their burning heat in his grasp. Her muscles contracted on him as he withdrew, surged in again, and that fire consumed him, such that he let go of control and gave himself to that binding as much as she had.

He began to pump hard, driving into her, moving them on the bed. She made tiny, maddening sounds each time he sheathed himself to the hilt, taking himself as deep as he could go, cock and mind together. Maybe even his soul. He pulled back from her mouth, knowing she'd had as much as she should have, but compensated for the loss by arching her up to him and sealing his lips over her left nipple, drawing it in deep as he worked his cock inside of her and prepared to explode. Her muscles quivered, on the verge of a second orgasm.

He was able to hold out, barely, until they went together, her cries music to his ears as he released into her, a hot flush of life that made her his in all ways, blood and seed.

He wanted her to say it, and must have told her so, because she was repeating it, over and over, branding that on the new shared universe between them.

Servant. Your servant.
Mine.

~

It took a while to get oriented to the new feeling, and though he adapted more quickly to it than her, he gave her time, curled in his arms. As he'd promised, he'd stripped them both at last, so he lay naked with her cuddled against his side. Her hand was on his abdomen, shyly stroking down his pubic area and occasionally whispering over his currently replete organ, which nevertheless was receptive to the stroke of her curious fingers. For his part, he caressed her hair, occasionally dropped a kiss on the curve of a breast, teased the damp line of her thigh with his fingers, watching how her thighs automatically loosened and parted at his touch.

It was when he rolled her to her stomach to brace himself over her body, rub his cock against the seam of her soft bottom as he kissed his way up her nape, that he found the visible proof of the third marking. Never having made a third-mark servant before, he'd forgotten that aspect of it. Every third-mark bore an impression on the flesh of their full surrender to their Master or Mistress. It was not something the vampire controlled, a mysterious reflection of their unique bond.

He'd nudged his way beneath the fall of her silky hair, where the changed texture of her skin above her delicate nape warned him something was different. He lifted his head, using his fingers to slide the strands aside.

"What is it?" she asked, in a voice softened by lazily unfurling desire and exhaustion.

Though the puncture marks had healed, he was acutely aware of the first place he'd ever bitten her, when he'd made it clear to the fledglings she was his. That sweet line of throat, just behind the ear. He could still remember the placement of his fangs, probably because he was looking at two short slash marks that emulated both the shape of his fangs and marked the entry point. Between them was the impression of a flower bloom, five fragile petals drawn up like a half-opened bud, flanked by those two marks. The stem slid in a slim crescent down beneath them. *Atsilusgi.*

He leaned back down, pressed his lips over it again, feeling an oddly volatile reaction. He wanted to take her again, taste her again. He wanted to hold his lips against that mark forever, feel the fierce pleasure of knowing it was on her skin, a permanent part of him.

Your mark, Elisa. Your full servant's mark is on your neck. He showed it to her, stayed in her mind to see her slowly digest it. As a result, he was tempted almost beyond recall to follow through on his urgent desires when he saw a delicious mix of confusion, yearning and shivering pleasure roll through her at the knowledge she bore a visible impression of his ownership.

The night's duties were calling, though. At length, he reluctantly donned his jeans and shirt. He bade her to stay naked and then scooped her up in his arms, putting her on his lap. As he nuzzled her throat, he approved of the way she turned her face into his shoulder to give him access to that mortal artery, but then he tightened his arm over her back.

"In a few more minutes, I want you to get dressed, Irish flower. You were determined to get my mark and then go back to your daily duties. That's what I want you to do now."

When she gave him a somewhat dazed, disbelieving look, he nodded. "You'll do whatever chores Kohana has for you, and whatever ones you set for yourself, and you'll work hard. In fact, my office floor needs a good scrubbing from muddy boots tracking things in."

She blinked, and he was amused to see some of that haze dissipate, enough that the maid with the outwardly dutiful tongue and the internally impertinent one reasserted itself, even if she was wobbling on her feet a bit. He suppressed a smile.

"Yes, I'm aware of whose boots are primarily responsible for that. You and Kohana remind me often enough. These"—he pushed her discarded panties with a toe—"do not go back on. You'll be bare under your skirt. You'll do your scrubbing in my office once I'm in there later this evening, working on the books. You'll do the work on your hands and knees, with the hem of your skirt tucked up in your belt so I can see your pretty bare ass and sweet flushed cunt. You'll keep your knees shoulder width apart for me, and if you forget, I'll just have to give you a couple slaps of the belt, make a few welts on the insides of your thighs to remind you, won't I?"

She stared at him, and he held her gaze, waiting, seeing if she could handle this. It was a lot to ask, but his intuition told him not to hold back. At length, she gave him a short nod. "Yes, sir."

"Good. You'll go back to what we were doing before as well. Just before dawn every day, you'll go to my bed. You'll strip naked, lay upon the covers and await me there, to surrender your body however I want to savor it. It's your new responsibility, and one of your most important ones. There may be times I want you to stay there with me, sleep until your normal rising hour. Be prepared for that. For the next week, this will be the way it is. In ten days, we'll go to the mainland and meet with Lord Marshall. The things I'll require of you over these ten days will help you prepare for that."

Though all that was true, as he spoke, they became his demands, his desires, beyond simple training and preparation. He wanted her mind focused this way, to teach her how to respond and obey him without question. It crossed his mind that he wasn't sure how the others were going to react to seeing a vampire's nature unleashed like this. He'd deal with that. Chumani would probably just give him her arch look that said it was nothing new to them . . . just a different form of it.

Will doing all this . . . prepare me to be the servant you wish me to be as well? Elisa's eyes were deep, and intelligent, and something else. Something he couldn't deny or resist. Just as he had to make sure her choice wasn't all about the fledglings, maybe she was trying to decide now if his decision to mark her wasn't merely functional. He liked knowing that it mattered to her, even as it unsettled him, her inadvertent ability to shoot a bull's-eye through his thoughts.

"Yes." But he forced himself to add the rest. "It will also tell you if you think you can be a vampire's full servant. Remember, Elisa, the choice to be my full servant is yours, until things are resolved for your fledglings. Once that's done, I'll ask you again if being my servant is what you wish. If your answer is still yes"—his eyes locked with hers—"then after that, all choices will be mine. Do you understand?"

It sent a pleasurable shiver through his new full servant, but she nodded. She thought he was far more likely to decide she was not suitable servant material than the reverse. Unfortunately, he knew she was wrong. She was everything a vampire could want in a servant. In a bare few weeks, he'd claimed her, no matter his supposed practical reasons. He'd heard the truth of it in Danny's smugness, damn her.

One of these days, he'd get Dev off by himself and strong-arm the man into telling him whether Danny had had two agendas all along. She'd been servantless for two hundred years herself, but now she seemed to be playing matchmaker, thinking everyone had to have a servant to be complete.

Unfortunately, feeling this sense of balance in himself he hadn't felt in a long time—so long he didn't want to think back to when he'd last had it—he knew she might be right. And that was just plain annoying.

28

OVER the next ten days, Elisa realized the most remarkable thing was not the change in her relationship with Mal, which was extraordinarily exciting and frightening by itself, but the changes in herself. And *change* was entirely the wrong word. It was more like some dormant powerful force within her had been roused to life, taking over her entire perspective on things. It was a part of her that seemed familiar and yet wildly strange as well, like a dress that looked dark and modest on one side, but when you turned it right side out, had brilliant colors and an exotic cut. It was still the same dress, the same person, but a different way of wearing who you were.

Some of the things he asked of her were a bit frightening, and intimidating, but she followed his lead, trusting him, and discovered a well inside of her that wanted more, more, more. He hadn't striped her with the belt when she was scrubbing his floor—he'd spanked her with his open hand, which made her nearly incoherent with inexplicable desire. Then he'd knelt and taken her there, from behind, making her continue to scrub as best she could while he was doing it, until the climax swept over her.

He made it clear to Kohana that she was now solely responsible for attending his needs, whatever they might be. This included everything from keeping his rooms clean to providing him blood, fresh. While that necessarily meant she couldn't give as often or as much to the fledglings, he told her firmly the staff would fill the gap. He preferred to take the blood directly from her, something she was glad he initially did in the privacy of his office or room, because of the feelings it stirred inside of her. Plus he tended to like to let his hands wander over her, opening her blouse to tease her breasts as he held her in his lap, nourishing himself at her throat. At his command, she wore only skirts in the house, no trousers, so he could slide his hand beneath her skirt and stroke her to a shuddering climax right there, crooning at her helpless cries.

He didn't do everything privately. Several days into her new role, they were having one of their outside dinners with the staff when he gestured her over to him. Thinking he needed something, she came to his side. "Yes, sir?"

"Kneel next to me," he ordered.

There were a few glances from the table, but the staff kept on as if nothing was amiss when she settled on her knees beside him. He continued to listen to their chatter, contributing to the conversation here and there, but his hand slid over her cheek, fingers caressing her throat, tracing the vee of her blouse, playing in the cleavage, though he didn't take it further than that. That was the extent of what he wanted, for her to be on her knees next to him, silent and awaiting whatever he bid. It was fairly circumspect, except for the fact that it aroused her so strongly she knew all those second-marked staff members could smell the scent of her desire.

But she'd found that was a blade with two sides, because Mal's treatment of her clearly caused a reaction among the staff as well. That night she'd clearly scented female musk, and had seen Chumani's nipples grow erect, pressing against her thin bra. Elisa might have felt uncomfortable about it, wondering if Mal had ever done such things for the Indian woman, but her gaze had been stealing toward Kohana, not Mal. From the look the large Indian gave her, she figured if Chumani hadn't challenged him to that intimate hand-to-hand match, it likely was going to happen that night. So none of them was immune to the sexually charged atmosphere Mal was creating in his "training." She was fairly sure the fact Mal had shortened the schedule to allow staff members more opportunities to go to the mainland for R & R trips was his acknowledgment of that.

Of course, when he was off working with the cats, neither Chumani nor Kohana, nor any of the others, remarked upon it to her. She suspected he'd already briefed them on what he was doing and why. Based on that, she supposed she could have considered it playacting, preparing for a stage play of sorts. But a part of her embraced such treatment so fervently it scared her, as if her domestic training all her life had been a foundation for this. True, willing servitude.

Perhaps it was good that Chumani and Kohana didn't ask her to explain, because if she had to articulate all the strange sensations and emotions such behavior was causing her to experience, it would open a floodgate.

She could tell herself it was that third mark, that it had changed something in her, but again, she knew the cut of that dress. It was part of her, sure as anything else. She missed Dev more than she ever had, because she might have been able to talk to him about it, work through some of it.

The strength and stamina she now had were awe-inspiring, however. She could lift things far beyond her former capabilities, could run all day and not get tired. One day, experimenting on it, she cleaned the house, top to bottom, at a rapid pace. Dusted light fixtures, molding, ran all the laundry through and put it on the line. Even swept the porches and washed the windows. The more she did, the more energy she seemed to have, and though she knew she was almost manically pushing herself, she kept doing so, enthralled with it.

Nothing slowed her down that day until she ran full tilt into Mal on the stairs, flying down with an armload of laundry piled so high in the basket it was over her head. She wasn't worried, though, because her footing had become as nimble as one of the cats.

"Oof." She used the reach of her much shorter arms to see what she'd hit, though of course she already knew. She could sense him like a lock of her own hair along her face. An arm interjected itself over and under the bundle and took it from her, giving her back her vision when he indifferently dumped it over the railing so it landed with a thump on the living area floor.

"What are you doing?"

"Cleaning. I've never had so much energy in my life. Mrs. Pritchett could work me twenty-four hours a day and sit on the porch all day drinking lemonade. Fair dinkum. I don't even know where to start."

She was two steps up, almost eye level with him. Putting an arm around her waist, he drew her to him, taking her feet off the wood to capture her busy mouth in a time-spiraling-down-much-slower kiss. He kept at it for some minutes, until her body was straining against him, wanting more contact, but all he gave her was his mouth, his body pressed against her and that hard arm around her waist.

"We'll go to my room for a bit," he said at last, drawing back, his eyes dark and piercing. "I'll show you what the limits of your endurance are. And I have things from the mainland for you. Things you'll wear when we go to see Lord Marshall."

Gifts? He'd bought her a gift? Clothing?

"I can sew, sir. You didn't need to buy me things. With the right fabric, I can make a very pretty dress . . ." Her voice trailed off as she remembered what some of those vampire servants wore on their visits to the station. Oh, they wore normal daks and boots going through the Outback, but inside, they wore all manner of titillating costumes, things that had the station hands drawing straws to see who would get to bring in more wood for the stove, any excuse to get on the porch where a curious stockman might see something through the windows. Sometimes the female servants were so immodest, they walked out into the courtyard in diaphanous, flowing clothes that revealed the shadow of nipples or buttocks. The male servants might be in leathers fit tighter than anything she'd ever seen in her life.

"Nothing quite that shameless for our first trip," he promised her. He hefted her over his shoulder, her elbows propped on that broad platform, his hand spread over her backside as he went down the stairs and strode through the house. Reaching up, she touched the dangling light fixture in the main room, pleased to see the sparkle of the glass and not a bit of dust. She heard his huff of laughter and smiled herself.

"How did things go with the fledglings tonight?"

"Better. Having Leonidas gone, regrettable as it is, has helped the others considerably. And your visits continue to help settle them. Tomorrow night the girls will come here, join me for dinner. Then I'll let them sit for a while in the living area, see how they do in a more civilized environment. If they do well, we'll try the two boys the next night, then Jeremiah on his own."

"Really? Oh, Mal, that would be marvelous."

"We'll see. Nerida will probably try to eat Kohana and he'll behead her with his cleaver like one of the chickens." He sighed. "But we need to get a feel of how they'll do so I can give prospects a clear picture of their progress."

"I can be there, too, right?"

He squeezed her arse. "Nope. Going to lock you in your room with moldy bread and stale water."

She had a retort for that, but held it as he let her down in his room and gestured to several boxes on the bed that had been opened, pink tissue paper pulled back. "I want to see you in those from here forward. No more of the other."

She wasn't sure what he meant until she cautiously approached the bed. There were several dresses, as well as slacks and silky blouse combinations. Beautiful, store-bought things she'd expect to see screen starlets wear, in those casual black-and-white scenes where they were having after dinner drinks and cigarettes. However, what he'd gestured at were two boxes overflowing with undergarments. Lacy, filmy bits of cloth that no maid she'd ever known would wear, scanty and scandalous. The bras were barely full cups, just a crescent of cloth and wiring to hold the breast and lift it up. The tops would become a pair of plumped-up pillows, the way whores showed them off, only these were nice and fine things.

The fragrance coming from the box was like a garden in summer, rich and heady. It seduced the nose, made a person want to keep drawing in deep draughts, as if the box could pull a person into the heart of summer itself, all its passion and life.

"You're not a whore, Elisa. You're never to think that again."

"Oh no. I didn't mean it quite like that. Though I guess, in a way . . ." Those strange feelings swirled in her mind again, making her think maybe Dev wouldn't be much help on them after all, because he was a man and likely had never seen the world that way. "The things you've been having me learn to do for you, with you, serving you however, whenever, you want me . . . There are times I think you could strip me naked on the picnic table outside while all the hands are eating, and root me there, and I wouldn't do anything but ask how far you want me to spread my legs for you."

She closed her eyes then. It seemed harsh when spoken aloud like that. Particularly when she compared it to what she'd always believed was proper, what she'd been and what she was now. "I'm willing to do all that and more to find the fledglings a place in the world, so I guess it's all for the good."

"You're lying to yourself if you think that's the only reason you submit to me." His voice held a warning note she recognized.

"You know it's not. That's not what I meant." She reached out, her fingers grazing the stiff cup of a satiny peach-colored bra. Her work earlier in the day made her rough flesh catch on the fine fabric. A third mark didn't cure dishpan hands. At least not right away. Nor did it change the scars of what had happened before the third mark.

So she'd live for three hundred years with work-roughened hands. She supposed she could wear gloves.

"Elisa." His arms came around her, and she realized she was crying.

"I'm sorry." She tried to brush them away. "These are beautiful. Just don't pay any attention to me."

Instead, he took her to the large side chair he used for reading and sat down upon it, drawing her into his lap and bringing her close, tucking her head under his jaw. He didn't say anything, just let her cry, that overwhelming mania of energy resolving itself into this, this difficulty reconciling all the changes and what they meant, and the fact it didn't change what had brought her here, or who she truly was, deep inside. All of it coalesced into this volcano of feeling, hard to decipher with anything except a shower of tears.

She realized he was rocking her, chanting in that singsong manner. He still didn't speak his language around anyone else, but sometimes he gave her snippets, in private like this. A part of his heritage, who he'd been but could be no more. She thought the singing soothed him as much as her, a reminder carried forward that it wasn't all gone. That it would always be a part of him, no matter what. Like Willis's smile was for her.

This, as well as everything before it, would be part of her as well. She didn't have to figure it all out now. She just had to do one thing at a time, and when it was all said and done, she'd face whatever she had to face.

"There's my girl," he said softly, but he kept holding her, letting her subside into the occasional hiccup of a sob, his fingers taking away the tears as he stroked the side of her face and kept holding her cheek to his chest. "I'm sorry, Elisa. I'm sorry to give you so little time to learn how to be a third mark, making you handle this all at once. I know it makes you feel alone, because no one here can relate to what you're facing. I can call Thomas, if you'd like him to come back to the island. Dev may even be able to come for a while."

She shook her head. "No, I wouldn't possibly ask any of them to drop what they're doing just because I'm a bit wobbly over this. She'll be apples; you'll see."

Her occasional lapse into Aussie-isms always gave his dark eyes a softer light, and she took strength from that when he tipped up her chin. She dwelled on that stern mouth, the beautiful strength of his face. "I'm not sorry I marked you," he said softly. "I like the fact you belong to me. I'm discovering I have far more vampire in me than I ever expected; the things I want from you are limitless. You sense it, and you respond to it, and the more you respond, the more I want."

She trembled at it, feeling it. "Would you like me to try these things on for you, Master?"

His answer to that was a resounding yes, but she only got to the first peach set. When he saw what the bra did to her generous breasts, and the way the lace of the panties outlined the upper curves of her buttocks but left the lower curves on full display, he had her bent over a pile of pillows on the bed, her arse in the air. He sank his fangs into one of those cheeks, licked the blood away; then his tongue teased the satin crotch, a delicious friction that had her crying out until he made that pinprick mark again. He was considerate, though, careful not to snag the delicate fabrics with his fangs or create bloodstains on them. But then he set aside consideration and made good on his threat to teach her what the endurance limits of a third-mark truly were.

When he left her, she was boneless and limp on his bed, incapable of further thoughts, good or bad, though she knew that dark, swirling storm would uneasily rise again. Third mark or not, there was a part of her hiding in a room in her mind, a part that didn't fit with all of this. That part was afraid it would stay forever locked in that room, because what it wanted could never be part of her life again, no matter how much of her heart it had once held.

She told herself that was okay, that she would take this driving pleasure to serve him, in both passionate and simple ways, as a close second. The craving need for him never went away. He aroused her just by existing. For his part, he seemed to have summoned up a libido he'd been keeping under wraps on the island. But even when it wasn't about the physical, she listened for his step, his voice, his scent. She was as fully besotted with him as she'd ever been with Willis, only it brought her a pain she couldn't describe or explain, because of how different it was.

She'd met plenty of women who'd set aside one dream in favor of a more practical one, and lived long and happy lives for it. For this immediate moment, she resolved to go about her duties . . . once she had feeling in her extremities again. Chores were chores. She could take care of others, enjoy each day God gave her, and let the rest be what it was. She couldn't change it.

~

The girls did very well on their trip into the house. In fact, Nerida and Miah ended up at Kohana's elbows, watching him make cookies with wide-eyed fascination, and Mal had to intervene to explain their constitution could handle only one cookie, not twenty. Thereafter, they sat perched on stools, noses lifted like the lion cubs, inhaling the scent in a state of absorbed bliss. They touched everything. Books, furniture, carpet, walls, window treatments, pictures, dishes . . .

It was obvious how long it had been since they'd been allowed inside any type of civilized human habitation. Elisa tried not to let that twist her heart in pity, at least not in any detectable way, mindful of Mal's reminder to act as if all of this was quite normal. For the most part, he sat quietly in his chair, reading the papers from the mainland, though Elisa knew his attention was fully on the girls at all times. They were calmer than she'd ever seen them, however, such that when she sat down near him to sew, they eventually approached and settled with her. She was able to show each how to do the stitches, and gave them swatches of fabric on which to practice, their heads bent attentively.

It was likely the first time since their kidnapping they'd been given something to do that any human girl might learn to do, to help keep the family's clothes in good order.

Elisa watched Miah's head, the sure fingers. Remembering the way she'd tried to wheelbarrow away from Leonidas, she couldn't bear to think of how many times she must have been subjected to the foul appetites of Ruskin's adult male vampires. When the girl's head rose, apparently feeling her regard, Elisa met her gaze. "I'd like to brush your hair. It's so pretty, we could put ribbons in it. See, I have these blue satin ones." She pulled them out of her "magic basket," as well as her wooden brush, and immediately the little girls' fingers were all over them. Miah stole a glance at Mal, then turned her attention back to Elisa.

"All you have to do is nod if you'd like me to do that. If not, it's completely okay. You won't hurt my feelings."

A choice. Did anyone really understand the value of it, until they faced the loss of it? These children had woken up from a brutal turning to find they'd never again see sunlight, never again stuff themselves on chocolate chip cookies. Even in her narrow life of being a domestic, there'd been choices. Only in that brief moment with Leonidas and then Victor had she known what it was to be relegated to complete insignificance, to know that her desires and wants didn't matter in the least, that whatever they'd wanted to do to her, they would. It was a feeling that couldn't be described, a hellish experience, and these girls had lived it for God knew how long.

She could feel Mal's attention on her, and she stilled the faint tremor in her hands such thoughts raised. She didn't want to agitate the girls. Miah was studying her face too closely already. However, a moment later the older girl turned her upper body enough to look toward Mal again. She didn't meet his gaze, but instead fastened her eyes briefly on his chest, a message of sorts. Which Elisa figured out when the girl turned back to her and slowly, slowly reached toward Elisa's hand, the one holding the brush.

Elisa watched the slim brown fingers close over hers. Then Miah made the same gesture toward Elisa's head that she'd made toward the girls. "Brush . . . yours."

29

Elisa looked toward Mal, and he gave her a slight nod. She smiled toward Miah, trying not to show how emotional such a request, such perception of her state of mind, made her. Instead, she shifted to make it easier for Miah to get behind her. She hadn't had her hair cut since she'd been here, so she usually kept the unruly longer curls pinned up with creative use of bobby pins. Now Miah plucked them free deftly, handing them to Nerida with soft murmurs of noise that passed for language. When they were all out, she started to brush Elisa's hair.

Elisa had shifted her body such that she was facing Mal. As she raised her attention to him, she saw he was watching Miah with that peculiar stillness vampires had. It meant he had all his considerable senses focused on her, ready for anything unexpected. She had no doubt if Miah twitched in an improper manner, he'd have her whisked across the room from Elisa in a heartbeat. But she was more resilient now. She was a third-mark servant, could feel that additional strength pumping through her, even though she knew it didn't make her invincible. She was quietly ecstatic that Mal was letting this happen, and that Miah had felt secure enough in his presence to try it. She took it as a good omen for their upcoming trip, what they would tell Lord Marshall about the fledglings. Hopefully the boys would do as well.

Nerida was fishing in her basket, and had come up with several different-colored ribbons in addition to the blue. The child held them up for Elisa's inspection and she nodded. "Those would be lovely. I'll be so fancy Kohana will think I'm going to a station social instead of planning to peel potatoes. Course, I bet you'd make short work of those mountains of potatoes, wouldn't you, you clever thing?"

Nerida studied her, head cocked, and then the small mouth bowed. Elisa stilled at the hint of a smile; then the girl ducked her head and fished in the basket again. Now she pulled out something else, several strips of tanned leather that had some sparkles on them, beadwork.

"Oh, that's—" Elisa grimaced, catching herself before she made the abrupt snatching movement that could startle the girls. Too late, Nerida caught her mild dismay.

In a flash, she'd dropped it. Not only had she jerked away from the basket, but she'd curled in her habitual ball on the floor, her head ducked down from Mal's retribution. Miah froze, but unlike her sister, she held her position, tense, right behind Elisa. Mal's attention locked on her like the site of a rifle. All of this in less than a second.

"Here, now, none of that," Elisa said quietly, before anyone could decide to do anything. She lifted the beaded strip from the basket, catching Nerida's attention between the arms folded over her head. "I wasn't at all angry, Nerida. This is something I was making Mr. Malachi for Christmas, and I just didn't want to give away the surprise. Which is really kind of foolish, considering he can read my mind and certainly probably knows I've been working on it during off-hours. Chumani and Kohana have been helping me learn the beadwork, which is fairly straightforward if you already know quite a bit of needlework, but I'm sure mine is not so fine as someone who's been doing it for a while."

She rose then, went to a squat next to the girl. This time, her mind was fully attuned to Mal's. They didn't have to have a conscious conversation. She felt his acceptance of her course of action, because he was reading it as she moved forward, just as she read his reassurance that he was ready if something went amiss.

Going to a crouch next to Nerida, she held out the beaded strip. The beads were a blue background, with brown and yellow cat's eyes worked along it in a pattern, and the tanned leather had been cut into a fringe strip at the end. She'd originally imagined him wearing such a thing in his hair with feathers, but of course, she'd made it so he could affix it to the knife holster he wore at his belt if he preferred, or even tie it on as a bracelet, weaving together the fringe so it didn't become a deadly distraction for the cats. Kohana had pointed out that hazard, noting if one of the leopards took a playful swipe at it, they could lay open his arm like a fish's gullet.

"I know Lord Ruskin and his vampires did awful things to you," Elisa said, watching the attention in that solemn brown eye. "They played games, tricked you by being nice and then, when you came close, they hurt you. Which was even more unkind, because they could hurt you whenever they wished, right? They didn't have to fool you to do it. The only reason they did that was because they were horrible, soulless monsters who should be roasting in hell now, if there is a hell for such vileness. But sometimes rather than hell, I think it's better to just imagine them as dust, nothingness, no soul to roast. They just don't exist anymore." She spread out her fingers, as if shaking dust away from them, and the girl's eyes followed the motion.

Miah had intended to follow her to Nerida's side, but Mal had kept her in place with a look and a gesture, so Elisa glanced her way now, with a kind nod.

"The very fact you and Miah wanted to dress my hair says you're learning. Learning to hope, learning that this place is different. We're different. I've never tricked you, have I? I've never told you something that wasn't true. You're vampires and you can pick up my emotions as well as Mr. Malachi or any of his wild creatures. So now I want you to think, because you are a clever, clever girl. Mr. Malachi has not harmed any of you, or threatened to harm you, except when he thought you were going to harm me or someone on his staff, right? He's protecting them; that's all.

"So come sit up," she said in a firm, no-nonsense Mrs. Rupert voice. "Let's do your hair and Miah's, now that she's brushed mine so pretty. We'd do Mr. Malachi's for him, but men don't like that kind of fussing."

She tossed a smile in Mal's direction. His eyes glinted at her in that way that made her knees feel a little weak. "We'll talk Kohana into it, because he has really long hair. I can try out my gift in his hair and then make Mr. Malachi another he doesn't know about. After all, Kohana needs a Christmas gift, too."

She'd placed a hand on Nerida's arm as she spoke, curling her hand around the thin limb. It was the first time she'd ever tried touching the girl, and she did it calmly, rewarded when Nerida didn't recoil. She did feel a frisson of warning from Mal, but it was simply a caution, not a prohibition, so she exerted gentle force, rubbing her until the girl sat up, glancing under those long lashes toward Mal and then toward that beaded strip. Reaching out with tiny fingers, she took it from Elisa's fingers with precise caution.

"Just wait until we get closer to Christmas." Elisa kept the exultance from her voice with effort. "We'll make popcorn strings for the cats in the habitats. We'll use very thin strips of leather or even intestines for that"—she made a face—"because of course we can't use actual string, but I think it will still be fun . . ."

Elisa found Miah at her elbow now, reaching forward to touch the decoration. A clanking of pots from the kitchen area drew her gaze to Kohana in the open pass-through. He'd arrived from the chicken coop with his eggs and was preparing to cook. Nerida met Miah's gaze. Elisa drew in a surprised breath as the two scampered gracefully toward the kitchen, the beaded strips and brush in tow.

Elisa's gaze darted to Mal, relieved to see he'd remained seated, calm. He shook his head, a slight smile on his firm mouth. "I've told Kohana not to be alarmed and, aside from the fact two vampire fledglings now want to dress his hair up, he's not unduly concerned."

Elisa saw Kohana indeed was not perturbed, though he sent her a pained look as Nerida clambered onto the counter and combed through his hair with her fingers, while Miah pushed over a chair to get him to sit, since neither girl could come close to reaching his great height. Miah fingered the eggs, lifting one to her nose to smell, and Kohana chided her in his gruff way to put those down, because those were for the hands, and maybe he'd show her all the ways they cooked them up.

Long fingers circled Elisa's wrist. She looked away from the scene to have Mal tug her into a tumble on his lap, a sudden movement that briefly caught the girls' attention; then they went back to Kohana. "It was a nice Christmas gift," Mal told her. "Thank you."

"I'll make you another. Unless you'd prefer Kohana have it because it's a girlish fancy you don't think you can wear in front of the others. But he told me Lakota warriors sometimes wore such things."

"Warriors?"

She nodded. "You're a warrior. You fight for the cats, even these fledglings. You fight to be who you are."

"And what's that?"

"I don't know," she said honestly, dropping her head back to meet his gaze, then sliding her attention to his throat, because sometimes she was overwhelmed by the intensity in his eyes. She wondered if it was that problem as much as vampire etiquette that often kept servants from meeting a vampire's gaze. "But I think you're figuring it out yourself."

After nearly seven days of unrelenting lust, she was surprised she didn't feel his normal reaction when she was firmly seated on his groin. It discomfited her somewhat until those sensual lips curved again. "Hussy," he murmured. "Think I'm tired of you already?"

Flustered, she tried to push herself off his lap, but found herself held fast as he made an incoherent noise, a command to be still. *Remember, we keep sexual vibes low around the fledglings. They've had too many bad memories associated with that, for one thing. For another, they have an abundance of those hormones. Because of their abnormal ages and physical makeup, it manifests itself in violent and destructive ways when roused.*

Of course. She should have figured that out herself, and was a little embarrassed that he had to tell her.

I don't expect you to know everything, Elisa. That's my job. While her snort was automatic, it made his eyes spark with affection at her impertinence. *I'll be sure and prove that to you later; never fear.*

Fortunately, the radio crackled then, pulling his attention away, since Elisa was concerned she might start emanating some of those inappropriate vibes in response to that heavy-lidded look he gave her.

While no message came through on the radio, Mal's attention turned inward in that way he did when he was listening to a message from one of the staff. He helped her to her feet. "I need to take the girls back to the enclosure."

"Is there a problem?"

"Nothing to worry about." The girls had attended him instantly upon rising, and he gestured to them. "C'mon, you two. I have to go back to work. I'll bring you back another day; never fear. You did very well."

It was short, dry praise, but coming from him, it was significant.

Nerida and Miah immediately obeyed him and, while Elisa saw wariness, she didn't see blatant fear as the two girls clasped hands and walked to the doorway. Mal pointed them toward the Jeep.

"Why don't I go with you? I can stay at the enclosure with them while you go take care of whatever the problem is."

"Not this time." He nodded toward Kohana, an unspoken message. Following him out as far as the porch, she noted he didn't have the girls get in the cage in which they'd been brought. He instead gestured them into the Jeep seats. The amazement and then delight on their faces was a wonder to see, something that distracted her until the Jeep pulled out. Nerida looked back at her, raised a small hand, and Elisa waved back, feeling her heart strings tie in the usual knots of hope and worry. For once, though, hope for the girls' future outweighed the worry.

∼

After the Jeep was out of sight, she turned on her heel and moved to the kitchen. They'd worked the beaded strip around a braided strand of Kohana's hair, and it actually looked quite handsome there, though the man gave her a much abused look about it.

"I think Chumani will really like that," she observed. "Kohana, what's going on?"

He'd had a retort for the first comment, but instead he pressed his lips together.

"It's about the fledglings, isn't it?" She slid around the counter. "If he didn't tell you not to tell me, then you're not defying any rules."

"With Mal, there's no difference between an implied command and an actual one, and you know that." However, he sighed, gave her a shrewd look. "He's pretty agitated tonight. Chayton thought Mal might want to come down and check on him."

Jeremiah had been withdrawn and temperamental since Leonidas. The worry came back, but she tamped down the overwhelming urge to follow Mal. She had to trust him. "All right. I'll talk to him about it when he returns. Do you need help gathering more eggs?"

"No, but I could use some meat from the smokehouse. Bring me a few of those sides of ham." Giving her a speculative look, he added, "It's handy, having you all strong and mighty these days."

"Lets you be more lazy, more like." Though of course just the opposite was true. The staff had a variety of unspoken strategies to ensure the man sat down on occasion without sacrificing his pride. If he overdid things, his stump could get to hurting, as well as his back and other leg. A second-mark's healing ability couldn't solve everything. Chumani had made it clear things had changed between them yesterday with her newest strategy—sitting down on his lap before he could get up to start clearing the table. She'd hooked an arm around his neck while continuing to chat with Tokala, as if it were the most natural thing in the world. And of course, seeing them together, it was. There'd been a lot of grins exchanged, and Kohana's face had gotten red for a moment, but then it was as if it had always been that way.

Elisa moved to the back door, stepped out into the night and paused, taking a steady breath. It would be okay. She refused to believe Jeremiah might be getting worse, headed down the same path as Victor and Leonidas. He was just having a hard time dealing with what had happened with Leonidas. Mal could have told her where he was going. She needed to talk to him about that. She wanted him to trust her. Her emotions wouldn't go haywire in this type of crisis.

She took three steps toward the smokehouse, and pain drove her to her knees. It erupted in her mind, an agony that stole her breath, knocked her to her side in the dirt. So overwhelming, it took several seconds to realize it wasn't her pain. A cry of need and desperation, an explosion of fear, like a drowning swimmer being swept out far beyond the shoreline, losing everything he knew, nothing to hold on to. She reached out on instinct, and gasped at the sense that her wrist had been grabbed in a bruising grip. Red finger marks appeared on her outstretched forearm, an imprint of need so strong it translated to a physical mark.

Kohana stumbled down the stairs in his haste, but he recovered and was at her side in a blink. She caught hold of his shirt, fighting the pain. "Tell Mal we have to come to them. We have to come now."

30

W<small>HEN</small> they pulled up in the Jeep, she managed to get past the chaos in her head to see Jeremiah. He was writhing on the ground in the communal enclosure. His elongated fangs had torn open his bottom lip, but he'd also gnawed at his arms, for there were bloody punctures up and down them.

"I need to get closer to him," she said, the moment Mal joined them at the vehicle. "He needs to know I'm here."

To see Mal's face she had to squint through the blinding ache in her head. The vampire was in her mind, knew what was happening. Not for the first time, she appreciated how much time that bond saved, though when his gaze fell to her clawed arms, Kohana had to step in.

"She didn't do that," the Indian said shortly. "I didn't see it happen to the first arm, but the marks appeared on the second as I was bringing her here. He's doing it somehow."

"He didn't do it on purpose. Mal." Elisa bent down over her stomach, which was churning in agony. "Please."

Mal lifted her out of the Jeep. As he hefted her up against his chest, she spoke into that muscled wall. "He's in my head," she whispered. "He's afraid. He's so afraid, Mal. I know you can't let me in there, but you need to get me close as you can. And please . . . go to him."

He took her inside the first gate, Kohana bringing a stool so she could sit in that secured space. If her head wasn't so full of Jeremiah, she would have flashed back unpleasantly to the last crisis that had trapped her in this small area. But she wasn't trapped this time. This was different, entirely, and her focus was all on Jeremiah.

Mal, please go to him.

He was still holding her, bent next to the stool, but now he nodded. She got a hazy glimpse of his serious face as he gestured Bidzil to open up that inner gate. Jeremiah rolled over, tearing up the ground, and a sob caught in her throat. She hadn't seen Victor's or Leonidas's impulse control and rationality defeated by full-blown, incessant bloodlust—the battle had already been lost when she came into their lives. She hadn't witnessed this; a mind with a conscience and moral structure deteriorating, a soul who'd been through so many nightmares already that it should have been lost long ago. And would have been, except for the will of the boy who refused to let go, hanging on with bare fingernails.

He was fighting it, fighting so hard . . .

Kohana leaned over her, closed his hands on her arms where she'd started to dig into her own flesh. When she looked up, Mal was moving with purposeful strides toward the boy.

She was disoriented and suddenly terrified that he would deal with it as Danny had dealt with Victor that long ago night, that same determined look in his eye as she'd had. But that wasn't her fear. It was Jeremiah's, a trapped and wounded animal.

No, Jeremiah. No, don't, love.

But he was on his feet, making agonized grunts of pain, running away. He charged the opposite end of the enclosure. As she cried out, he hit the fence hard enough to knock him backward. He rose again, rushed at another side, with the same result.

Jeremiah, he's not going to hurt you. Come to me. Come to me.

Suddenly he was there, thrusting his arm through the small metal opening of the gate, scraping his knuckles. Mal was right behind him, but Jeremiah was fully in her head, so she saw what he was about to do right before he got there. She met him, closing both hands over Jeremiah's bloody one. In a blink, he'd reversed the hold and yanked her off the stool, so she was on her knees on the opposite fence side.

It's okay. It's all right. I'm here, Jeremiah . . .

Mal's hands closed on the boy's shoulders, but not to yank him away. He was in her mind with Jeremiah. He could see the boy's intention was not to hurt her. In fact, Jeremiah would have been holding her hand against his chest if the fence wasn't in the way, his forehead pressed so hard into the metal it was cutting into the skin. She threaded her other hand through, cupped it over the back of his head.

"It's all right," she whispered. "It's all right, dear boy. We're here. We're all here. No one's abandoned you. It's okay."

Jeremiah was panting like a dog. Now a shudder racked him, and his hands flexed, sending shards of pain through her gripped fingers. She didn't try to draw away a bit as Mal knelt behind him, put his hands over their locked ones, eased that grip. "Walk it out, boy," he said quietly. "You're a vampire; you can't drown. You just hit bottom and walk back to shore. Walk out of those waves."

Just like with Nerida and Miah, the two of them were perfectly in sync, holding the fledgling between them. In this moment, she could imagine a lifetime of doing this type of thing. With fledglings, with wildcats, learning each one's unique needs. She could truly help him, so he wouldn't have to be alone in it.

That was an odd thought, for sure, because he had a close relationship with his staff. But it was different, even closer with a third-mark, wasn't it? Mal's gaze flickered up to her, a brief thing where she couldn't tell what he was thinking, but then her attention was back on Jeremiah. She flooded reassurance into him, showing him the two of them were in lockstep around him, holding him so it didn't take him under.

She tightened her grip on his skull, digging her fingers into his hair, which reached his shoulders now, a silky blond mane. When it was his turn to come to the house, she hoped to cut it for him, hoped she could give him some of the same experience Nerida and Miah had had tonight. If she could offer him one night of normalcy, a chance to see what was possible, it could lend him hope, strength against this.

I know you can fight this, Jeremiah. This isn't who you are.

A strangled cry wrenched from his throat, his body shuddering anew, but the episode was lessening, his thrashing now becoming more of a rocking between them. She saw blood in the center of the enclosure and knew he'd thrown up, yet she sensed no hunger to him as the seizure ebbed. Just . . . weariness. A weariness so deep and profound she wasn't sure if there was much difference between it and death.

No. I won't let you give up. "Things are getting better, love," she whispered, stroking his hair. "They really are. You should have seen Miah and Nerida tonight. They helped Kohana with his eggs. Brushed my hair. Things can be different. I promise. It's your turn tomorrow. I'll teach you to play checkers, if you don't remember or know how. You can see all of Mal's wonderful books."

Jeremiah made another quiet noise. At length, he pulled out of her grasp, and backed away from Mal. As he came to his feet, he stood there, swaying. His eyes were fully crimson, his shirt bloodstained and torn. More blood dripped from his fangs to his chin. He looked monstrous, and when Elisa flinched at the thought, she realized it wasn't her thought. It was his, looking at himself through her eyes.

That's not what I see, she thought fiercely. *I see a young boy that needs my help, as I always have.*

The expression that crossed his face was so piercing she felt it in her own chest. She'd said something wrong. So wrong that she had a terrible feeling she could never take it back.

"Jeremiah . . ." She hooked her fingers on the gate, but he just backed away farther.

I won't be able to come to the house. I'll never be able to come to the house.

Turning away, he shuffled off toward his cell. Elisa saw the other fledglings watch him with eyes that were so old. They'd seen this before. And they all knew how it ended.

～

The ride back was quiet. Kohana took an ATV, and Mal drove Elisa. She sat in the passenger seat, hands clutched in her lap, not wanting him to talk, not welcoming even her own thoughts. He stopped at one of the overlooks, though. Turning toward her, he brushed his fingers along her cheek.

"Please don't say it," she said, staring out the windshield. "I can't bear to hear you say anything in your terribly practical tone. Just because it's happened that way for Victor and Leonidas doesn't mean it will happen for him. He's different. He's stronger than they were. You know he is."

"We don't know how Leonidas and Victor were before they lost themselves to the bloodlust. You didn't see that transformation."

"Didn't I just say not to do that?" She blinked back tears. Looking out at the panorama of stars and ocean, she saw a whole beautiful world that should be Jeremiah's to explore, to experience. If she could give it to him, if she had to give up her life to give it to him, she would, without hesitation, a blink. Her life had not always been easy, but compared to Jeremiah, she'd led a princess's life, every small joy and happiness magnified to a miracle.

"Whatever is happening to Jeremiah, whatever happened to Victor and Leonidas, I don't think it's going to affect the others."

That got her attention back. Her brow furrowed. "What do you mean?"

Mal took her hand, held it on his thigh. "Danny's been busy. At my request, she called Janus to her station for further questioning."

Janus was the only survivor of the four adult males Ruskin had illegally turned to serve as his "sons,"—murdering, raping thugs. He was under the supervision of one of Danny's territory overlords now. Elisa swallowed, remembering when Danny had called all four of them out in the courtyard at Ruskin's Darwin fortress. Dev hadn't known until too late that Elisa was standing at an upper window. With a deadly calm, Danny had tossed each a weapon, told them to defend themselves. Then, with a speed and skill that had been bloodcurdling, she'd decapitated three of them before Elisa could even turn her head away.

When Janus dropped his blade, his fingers trembling too hard to hold it, she'd ordered him to his knees. Then she'd told him his life was spared, because she had one wavering molecule of belief that the four of them had been a different kind of victim of Ruskin's cruelty. She'd then told him if he ever gave her a shadow of a doubt that she'd made a wrong decision, he should stake himself. Because otherwise she'd make sure his death was slow and painful.

Since that day, realizing what the four had done to the children, no matter that it was done under Ruskin's twisted supervision, Elisa had sometimes wished her Mistress had killed all of them. But at least he wasn't at their station.

"What did she find out from him?"

"That the four of them turned Victor, Leonidas and Jeremiah. Having a fledgling turn other fledglings is always a risky, unstable proposition. William, Matthew, Nerida and Miah were turned by Ruskin, who was a five-hundred-year-old mature vampire. We've all noticed there's a marked difference in the severity and types of attacks they experience versus Jeremiah or Leonidas. As I told you earlier, a normal transition is most volatile during the first three months, and then the bloodlust ebbs over time. The age of their turning, the trauma they've endured, have exacerbated that, but it's possible as we give them a semblance of normalcy, and time passes, it will eventually pass, the same way it does for an adult vampire. They'd still have the dangerous vulnerability of being weaker than adult vampires, but if I'm right, that makes their future somewhat more optimistic."

When it came to the fledglings, he never gave her empty reassurances, so he must feel quite certain. It was something. But she couldn't bring herself to say anything just yet. He shifted, bracing his wrist on the wheel. "We'll head to the mainland as planned at the end of the week. Nothing has changed for those four. Lord Marshall's household is still an excellent potential haven for two of them, and the other prospect I'm researching looks good."

Nothing has changed for those four. "But not for Jeremiah."

"Not until we see what's going to happen with him," Mal said quietly. "I'm sorry, Elisa."

Getting out of the Jeep, she walked to the front and looked out at the view. "I won't survive losing him."

There, she'd said it to the night sky, to the darkness, and to the vampire who was deep inside of her mind and soul now, in ways that went beyond the marking. She'd told herself it was okay he could never feel the same. Like a priest, he could accept the full weight of what she felt, even if he didn't feel it himself. A priest could consign it all to God's will and wisdom.

Only for some reason, that star-filled sky and moonlight seemed strangely empty of godliness to her at the moment. "It was the first time he took that bear I brought him, the way he looks at me. The way he came to me tonight . . . I'm the only one he trusts to give him comfort, to help him. And I can't bloody help him. I—"

She was crying *again*. Would the tears ever stop? When he got out, came to her, she folded into him, clutching his T-shirt. It wasn't a cathartic cry this time, those open, clean tears and sobs. This was like crying broken glass, all of it ground up inside her chest and choked out, because this wasn't going to be made better by the tears.

I know what he means to you, and you to him. We'll get through this, one way or another. Whatever you need to survive, you will, because you have me.

The sobs broke loose, because she needed to believe him. The human heart grabbed at comfort, because it was the only thing that kept one from being swept out on that tide, the one Jeremiah had feared enough to imagine he was drowning.

Every creature feared such a feeling. Particularly a fledgling vampire child, one who knew exactly what it was to be lost and forgotten, thrown to the jaws of merciless Fate.

31

FLORIDA. Elisa stood on the back balcony of Lord Marshall Grant's intracoastal waterway home in the late afternoon, watching boats passing by with thrumming motors. They'd arrived at the airport so close to dawn that when they reached the house, the host had turned in for the day, but a very efficient staff had shown Mal to his accommodations. After he'd done a thorough check of the surroundings, ensuring Marshall was the only vampire on the premises, he'd given Elisa leave to wander the grounds. She was to use her propensity for making friends with household staff to learn the many details that might be useful to their purpose here.

Lord Marshall Grant, overlord for the Florida territory, had a human servant, Nadia, who'd conceived not once, but three times. She'd lost all of them at different points of the pregnancy, the latest one practically a month before the anticipated birth. According to Mal, while it was exceedingly rare for vampire children to be conceived at all, when they were—barring any external forces, such as an enemy vampire attack or other injury—the mother carried them to term without incident.

As a result, Lord Marshall had had to endure ridiculous rumors that Nadia had done something to sabotage the pregnancy. Even vampires weren't immune from claptrap scuttlebutt based on nothing more than people's meanest imaginings. Less than a few hours into their visit, Elisa had already confirmed the rumor was complete hogwash.

While she appreciated the fine things she saw while exploring the grounds, other things had been of keener interest to her. Wide yard space, a billiards and bowling room. Through chats with the staff, she found Lord Marshall was well learned, with a good library and an interest in travel that increased his knowledge of the world, something he could share with the boys.

Near lunchtime, she'd been traveling down a hall, learning the estate so she could easily go fetch things for Mal if needed. She'd traveled with Danny several times, and from watching Dev, she knew this was the more mundane side of what was expected of a third-mark when travel occurred. One got to know the kitchen staff, the lay of the household, the surrounding environment, so the vampire's needs could be anticipated and met. That was still the primary responsibility of the third-mark, even in a household of domestics.

She stopped at an open doorway, seeing a maid with a feather duster busy at work. Elisa wouldn't have done more than pause for a hello, but she noted the room was a nursery, complete with cradle, crib, toys and all the things parents with substantial financial means would provide their child. Stepping in, she saw there was even a small tricycle. On impulse, the expectant parents had planned for the child's growth beyond the first few years. It twisted in her heart, such that she couldn't help the automatic murmur of "Bless them" as she crossed herself.

Katrine, the maid, looked her way. The trace of irritation at being interrupted softened at Elisa's gesture. "That's the truth, ma'am. Breaks my heart every time I clean in here. Can I help you with something?"

"Just learning the house for my Master. You can call me Elisa. Can you tell me how long ago they lost the last one?" It wasn't difficult to load her voice with a woman's sympathy.

"A year." Katrine shook her head. "I've heard tell how cold vampires can be toward humans, but Lord Marshall, he just hasn't got the heart to have it all taken away. Miss Nadia, she comes in here and sits sometimes. I think she was able to get past the first one she lost, though it was hard. But the second took its toll, and this last one just fairly broke her."

"As it would any woman," Elisa observed. "I'm sure it's hard on Lord Marshall as well. They were his children, too."

"No doubt, but I'm not sure if she can get past it." Katrine hesitated, but Elisa picked up a second duster and began working on the light fixtures, earning a grateful look. "I don't think I'm saying anything you won't see for yourself tonight. He's the one who bought the tricycle, had it all shined up with ribbons when he gave it to her as a gift, the second time."

The maid shrugged, lowered her voice. "He's devoted to her as much as any husband I've ever seen. But you didn't hear me say it." Katrine eyed her critically. "I'm sure none of you full-servant types think you'll have the house with the picket fence, you know? The life with kids and the husband who comes home from work with his briefcase and all that. But the idea of having a child to raise had taken hold of both of them. It's a hard thing."

"It surely is." The ghost of what she'd dreamed about with Willis couldn't help but rear its head, despite her attempt to push it away before it clouded her expression. Sure, Mal said she was free to go after this was all over, but in truth, in the deepest part of her heart, it was getting more difficult to envision it, too much of her heart now tied up in him.

Yeah, that was a mistake, but there was no help for it. She wasn't sure if she'd change it if she could, which was more unsettling than anything else. It said she wasn't the same person anymore. Of course, for tonight's purposes, that was probably going to be a good thing.

She'd found it interesting that Mal seemed fairly uptight about her presence at the dinner as well, but then, she was also his first full servant, so this was likely a new experience for him. It would be all right. At least that was what her practical mind told her, trying to tiptoe around melodramatic fantasies and worries and leave them undisturbed. They were here for the fledglings. Everything else would work out.

Tiptoe or not, the butterflies were back, particularly when she left Katrine with a few more kind and companionable words, and saw the sun hitting the horizon, heralding the oncoming night. Throughout the day, to calm her nerves about anything that might happen over the next few hours, she'd returned in her mind to their trip from the airport. That illuminating car ride had reassured her, at least temporarily. So, knowing he'd soon be waking, she decided to give herself a few moments on the balcony overlooking that sunset and water view and revisit their conversation, hoping the combination of visual and memory would calm her anew . . .

~

It was odd to see him away from the island and his cats. Instead of his faded jeans and T-shirts, he wore a pair of slacks, a white dress shirt and a slender copper tie with a pewter tie tack. His coat lay over the seat opposite him in the limo. He'd rolled up his sleeves, and he had a knee propped against the door. Sleek and brushed, his hair was pulled into a tail at his nape, so it emphasized the strong bones of his face. He looked like a lean, powerful animal pressing against the bars of his cell, ready to leap out as soon as the door was opened.

He was very handsome in the suit, but she liked imagining the shirt pulled open to reveal the bronzed chest, the tails fluttering with the wind, the tie gone. Or perhaps the tie wrapped around her wrists and tethered to the hook above the car window, so he could pull her shirt open and nuzzle and feast upon her breasts, sitting up high in the lacy bra he'd insisted she wear.

She slanted her gaze upward. "That wasn't my thought. That was yours."

"You don't seem to be objecting." Reaching over, he captured a curl around his finger, let it go to spring back against her temple. "I'm beginning to regret getting you that bra, and that scrap of panties that go with it."

"Why? You don't like them?" She was crestfallen, because he'd seemed to like them so much when she put them on.

"I think you remember exactly how much I like them. It's a wonder they survived my approval." He sighed. "I'd prefer Lord Marshall not to notice you, but I want you to be as beautiful as you are. I don't want other servants teasing you or being unkind."

Elisa gave a snort. "Every household has a few of those, Mr. Malachi. People who think because they've been a servant for a certain length of time or because they handle the master or mistress's arse-wiping, they can put on airs. They just do it because they know they really aren't any better than anyone else, and won't likely ever be. I don't pay any attention to that. And I know vampire servants aren't domestics, but I expect it works in a similar way."

"Hmm." He cocked his head. "Mr. Malachi?"

"I figure I better practice. I expect I'm not supposed to call you Mal in front of them, and with more than one of you in the room, *sir* might not be specific enough."

"*Master* might be." His eyes gleamed in the dark. It sent a swivel of sensation through her lower belly, helping to dispel the nervousness. Some of it.

"It might." But when she laced her fingers together to foolishly try to hide her growing anxiety, his mouth tightened, mood changing.

"Tonight, we'll likely both have to be what we're not, Elisa. I can't tell you how much I hate saying those words, for either of us."

Maybe it was because it was still dark, the streets so empty at the early morning hour. There was something about the cloistered solitude of a car that made it feel more intimate, less formal. The driver, separated from them by privacy glass, only made it feel more like that. So as that familiar sadness stole into his gaze, she leaned over, laid her head on his chest. Giving comfort as well as taking it when he put his arms around her.

"We're not pretending. You're as much a scary vampire as you are a person who likes quiet islands and the company of cats more than people. You make me feel beautiful and wanton and exotic when you touch me, but I'm still just Elisa, a housemaid. We know what we are. That's all that matters. If I have to go someplace I don't want to be tonight, I'll just send myself to a room in my head and shut the door. A puppet part of myself will do what it needs to do. Then, when that's all done, it'll come knocking and the real me will come out again."

"Your hands are cold." His gentle rebuke was spoken against her ear as he folded them inside his warm one. His other hand stroked her hair.

She heard that neutral tone in his voice, but now she knew enough about him to know it covered much stronger emotions. Laying her hand on his thigh, the smooth slacks, she spoke in a near whisper. "You won't let anyone truly hurt me. It's just buggering and being naked." That thigh muscle tensed, but she pressed on, following instinct. "I've done that with men who don't care anything for me except what my mouth and other parts of me can do for them, and it's not so bad, as long as you have that room in your mind."

"I don't like it, Elisa. I truly don't. And yet . . ."

Lifting her head, she looked into his face. "I understand. I've seen the way of it, with Danny and Dev. It's scary, and he'd probably not like admitting it, but Dev enjoys it because of that unexpected part of himself. The part that likes pleasing her. I have that, too, don't I? You've said so."

"Yes."

"And you'll be there with me, every minute."

"Count on it. Inside and out." He gave her a direct look now. "Have I ever given you cause to do that? Go into that room and close the door?"

She smiled. "You'd just follow me in there, wouldn't you? So what would be the point?" At his look, she laid her hand on his jaw. "This will be apples; don't worry. Will *you* be okay?"

"You really do ask the most inappropriate questions for a servant. I'm a vampire. I'm invincible, like Superman."

"Oh no." She made a dismayed face. "I forgot to pack your cape and tights."

"Well, I'll have to beat you for that."

Suppressing a smile, she settled back on his chest. But as they continued to drive through the night, she wondered if he'd ever had a room like she'd described, a place to hide when he was little. Somehow, she thought he hadn't. However, while she thought he had lost some of himself because he couldn't hide that boy safely away, she also thought he'd rediscovered some of it when he created what he was now. A whole new person, formed out of the good, the bad, the remembered and the forgotten.

Realizing from his stillness he was reading her mind like a picture show, she flushed, pressing her hot cheek against his crisp shirtfront. Her fingers curled against his strong thigh as he spoke, a velvet rumble under her cheek.

"You are a remarkable human, Elisa. So deferential, and yet you're an ocean tide. You're unstoppable, even though you're just a recurring lap of water on the toes, nothing threatening or aggressive. It's extraordinary."

"And frustrating. I heard that thought, even if you didn't share it." She tilted her head up, seeing the gleam in his eyes, confirming it. "Would you tell me how you became a vampire? If it doesn't upset you too much."

He shook his head. But he looked out the window a few extra minutes, gathering his thoughts, before he spoke again. "I worked for a family in Boston, as you knew. So much noise and too many people. There were others there, like me. Black, Indian, Asian. We were bonded by our bitterness. One night, hanging out behind a bar with brown-bag bottles, I was drunk enough to say I hated being an Indian. Hated it with every fiber of my being, every drop of my hated blood. I demanded from them, from the sky, from anyone who would listen to an obnoxious drunk, what I'd done to deserve being born a member of such a miserable, fragmented group of people. I'd forgotten my mother, the way she sang to me, the meals she cooked for me. How I'd lain with her in our cabin at night, the two of us anticipating my father's return from his trap lines. I was young, furious and stupid."

Elisa stayed silent, watching his expressions as he faced his past, his regrets. "A woman walked out of the darkness that night, a beautiful woman with cream skin and red hair, blue eyes. Drunk or sober, all of us knew about the type of women fascinated by men of different colors, who liked the thrill of taking them to their beds, of 'wallowing' below their station." His lip curled. "It didn't matter. We were men, and life was hard. We'd take pleasure where we could get it. She told me she could make me something different, something powerful and eternal. All I had to do was agree to it, and to stay with her until she tired of me."

"She was a vampire."

He nodded. "Just as she promised, I became something entirely different from what I'd been. I was with her twenty-five years, and I wasn't the only one. She liked collecting. She had an African prince, a Buddhist monk . . . even a circus performer who fascinated her because he was wholly covered in tattoos. She wasn't unkind, not as vampires go. She just thought of us as pets. She could be cruel if we got out of line, and she was powerful. But eventually she moved on to new oddities, releasing me from her service. She told me I was welcome to stay as part of her household until I decided what else I wanted to do. I stayed, too used to being her toy to want anything else, nursing my self-ish angers under the façade of the bored urbanite."

Elisa regarded him with frank astonishment. "I can't even imagine you that way. It's like a whole other person."

"I was." He paused, shifting. "Then one day I attended a Wild West show that advertised 'real' Indians, including a bona fide chief. Part of the show was a mock battle between cowboys and Indians. Of course the cowboys won, and then the chief was paraded out to surrender and become their prisoner. People responded as they were supposed to do, with boos and catcalls. He was silent, dispassionate, in a magnificent headdress of feathers."

Elisa could imagine it, because she saw it reflected in his eyes, the impact it made on him. "After the show, I went to his tent to see him and learn his story. He shared a cigarette with me, told me his people were confined to a reservation. He'd been told if he joined the show, the manager would give his starving people money, blankets, things to help them through their harsh, hungry winters. Even if the owner was a damned liar, the chief saw two options. He could stay in the cesspool and prison the reservation was, impotent to protect his people, stripped of all his power, or he could do the show, where at least he could send some of the money *he* was earning back home, and keep after the owner to make good on his promise.

"There was such a quiet dignity to him. Perhaps I was feeling less angry than I thought at that point, more adrift, and that's what moti-vated me to seek him out. But after thirty seconds of sizing me up, he said this: 'They may have taken your people away from you, but it is you who turned away from them, in your anger and pain. You are no longer one of them, and that was your choice, not the white man's.' Then he turned away, dismissing me the way he did any other white person who came to gawk at him, parents who would pay him a nickel if he shook his tomahawk for their wide-eyed children."

Elisa wanted to put her arms back around him, but it was obvious he was contained in a man's pain, and a woman's comfort wouldn't be welcome. So she kept listening, because she could offer him that.

"When I was six, I was branded with the name Malachi. My identity was beaten and starved away, and I became what they wanted me to be.

But as he said, after a while I gave up trying to get it back, and by the time I learned better, it was too late."

A muscle jumped in his jaw. "The worst day was when I realized I could no longer remember the name my mother called me. Every once in a while, I think I hear it on the edges of a dream, but when I wake, it's gone. I keep thinking one day I'll see my mother in those dreams and she'll give it back to me, but I never dream of her, either. She carried me on her back when her feet were bleeding worse than mine, when she was sick, near frozen and starving. But I can't remember her face, or the name she gave me."

His gaze went to the window, his face hard, eyes even harder. "Because I gave up who I was, gave it away, I know I don't deserve to remember that name. When I came out of his tent, I saw a tiger they had in a tiny cage. People were throwing bits of food and trash at him to get him to growl. Him, I could help. He deserved to be helped. I bought him, and that was the beginning, though it was decades before the island came to be. So here I am."

"I'm sorry. I know you'll say you don't deserve to hear that," she added quickly, "but that's not the way I meant it. I mean that it's a terrible world sometimes. But I do think whatever you may have been, you're doing good things now. And that's all any of us can do to make up for past mistakes, right?"

He looked at her, gave her a faint smile. "Of all the things about you, Irish flower, your ability to simplify matters is one I cherish the most."

She shrugged. "I've been told I'm simple, plenty of times."

He opened his mouth, but then he saw her eyes dancing, and his own lightened in response. More shyly, she reached out and touched his knee.

"Thank you for telling me that."

He lifted a shoulder. "I'd heard having a third-marked servant allows a vampire a way to unburden his soul, because he can trust his servant more than any other, having her mind bound to his so irrevocably." His gaze touched hers, the becoming flush in her cheeks his words evoked. "I thought it was romanticized nonsense. But I've never told anyone that story, *atsilusgi*. I think I've been needing to tell it. As well as to apologize, deeply, for the things I said right after Leonidas's attack."

Her eyes widened in surprise, but when her lips parted to speak, he shook his head. "The problem was I had more in common with your fledglings than I wanted to admit. Just like that chief, you made me face that harsh reality, made me see that I'd once again taken the wrong path. I don't feel that way anymore."

Glancing out the window as they pulled into the driveway of a sprawling, stucco waterway mansion, he made a quiet grunt, a comment on the house's opulence or something else, she didn't know, but then he turned his head, met her gaze squarely.

"I can't remember my name, but I took the name they gave me, Malachi, and made it my own, not theirs. If we can manage it, we'll give William, Matthew, Nerida and Miah the same chance."

32

Rᴇᴛᴜʀɴɪɴɢ to the present and that waterway view, she recalled she'd been moved by what he'd shared with her, enough to let it pass that he hadn't mentioned Jeremiah. They'd stayed away from that subject for the several days before they left, even as she'd visited the boy at the enclosure as much as travel preparations permitted. Though he'd come to the fence for her, listened to her talk, he'd had little to say. Each time she went back to her Jeep, he moved back to his cell, disappeared into his shelter and belowground as if he'd simply come up for her comfort, not his. He wouldn't speak in her mind.

Something would break loose, though. She would have faith, and pray. If God had any mercy at all, surely Jeremiah was deserving of it.

She saw lots of palm trees scattered over the short lawn behind the property and framing the view of the waterway. The swaying fronds made her think of the picture shows where Cleopatra and Egyptian pharaohs were fanned on silk couches. She could well imagine those pharaohs as vampires, so powerful and remote, yet tempting touch with their strange and exotic appearance.

The things Mal had had her do to prepare for this certainly qualified as strange and exotic, far beyond her normal experience. However, with those new experiences had come a new level of intimacy. Bedtime conversations they'd shared, things he'd told her about himself, like in the car. It was disturbingly like she'd imagined it would be between her and Willis once they gave themselves to each other, heart and soul, knowing each other like no one else ever would.

For her part, when she saw him, it was like her heart was pinned on her chest, beating so hard. One night right after dinner, a group of the staff, including Chumani and Kohana, had been gathered in the front room, listening to a radio show. Elisa had a pile of mending with her, but when she got to Mal's shirt, one he'd ripped in one of his tussles with leopard cubs, her hands had lingered on it, smoothing the fabric. She'd looked up to see him watching her with an entirely unexpected expression. For a blink, she thought he was as absorbed in what she was doing as she'd been in his shirt, the rest of those in the room disappearing. Under his stare, she'd flushed, and quickly bent to her task.

She wasn't entirely stupid. She knew how silly lust could make the mind, how it could dazzle with thoughts of love and emotion that didn't exist. But just like that conversation in the car, those quiet moments in his bed, curled in his arms, hadn't been all about sex. Not while listening to his voice rumble through his chest as he answered the questions she had, then asked his own, their conversations meandering like an easy river. She felt things from him during them, things she was hard put to explain.

The staff did act differently toward her now. They'd been affectionate and kind from the beginning, but the ones who'd been so casual about giving her a hand into the Jeep, or nudging her out of the way in the kitchen, were a little more circumspect. Even Kohana's occasional hugs had that flavor. It had taken her a few days to put her finger on it, but she'd realized it was the way men treated a woman who'd clearly been claimed by another.

On top of all that, there was that third mark, the way it made her feel, so completely connected to him. He hadn't said he wanted her to stay on the island forever, but he hadn't said he wanted her to go back to the station when all this was over, either. He was leaving it up to her. She could stay, and every day that passed where she served as his third-mark servant was one day further from the life she'd once expected to have. She wasn't sure how to feel about that. Sad or simply . . . accepting?

She thought about what Mal had said, about his past, present and future. Lord Marshall and Nadia, losing their babies. Danny and Dev, their fierce bond, how and what they'd fought, side by side. She and Willis, looking toward a simple, lovely future and having it all taken away in one terrible moment. Yes, they were all different, but they were the same, too, weren't they? All of them wanting and needing, capable of being hurt and grieving. Capable of love.

Imagining William and Matthew here, as part of this household, she knew why Mal had reached out. He'd taken the risk of committing a severe offense with his presumption, because certainly two vampires who would never grow any older in appearance were far different from three born vampire babies who would have. But he had exceptional intuition. He thought this would be a good home for them and that, approached correctly, Lord Marshall and Nadia would consider the idea.

So when all was said and done, to make that happen, he needed her to set aside her trepidation about whatever might happen tonight. She wouldn't let him down. Taking a deep breath, she took one last look at that view, the disappearing sun, and decided to head down to his room and give him a proper waking. Then she'd change into those tiny scraps of underwear and clothes designed to show her off as something she was not, but that she could be, if the reason was important enough. And it was.

～

She wasn't surprised to find him still in the bed, since they'd arrived so close to dawn and he was young enough that such near-sun exposure could sap his strength. Even when he needed sleep, though, he slept restlessly. It was as if the human he'd once been ached to be out under the stars, rather than in a dark room like this, the curtains securely closed over special heavy blinds such that not a trace of light came through. Because they lived by the water, there were no subterranean rooms, but Lord Marshall had outfitted the rooms well for even his younger vampire guests. Another good sign for William and Matthew.

She'd noted Mal's penchant at home for keeping all the French doors open at night. Sometimes he even took his paperwork out on the porch, listening to the cats calling across the island during their nocturnal wanderings. She thought of his childhood, how he'd run away, but they'd caught him, time and again, and locked him up.

The covers were half-off of him, his upper body twisted so his back was to her. The sheet was low enough she could see his hip, the rise of a buttock, for he slept naked, God bless every fine inch of him. She leaned in the doorway. It wasn't often she got the chance to ogle without interruption, though she knew he was awake—merely not awake enough to acknowledge her.

Given everything she'd learned about predators, if not for their aversion to light, vampires would be nigh invulnerable, at the top of the food chain. No wonder they preferred to keep their existence a secret from humankind generally. Whole legions of vampire-hunter teams would form to try to root them out during daylight, when ones like Mal were weakest.

She didn't like that thought. But then something amazing occurred to her, something she hadn't considered before. That was one of the reasons a vampire had a full servant, her senses enhanced so that she could hear the movement of household staff on the upper and lower floors, could scent the lingering traces of anyone who'd passed by this room in recent hours. She'd never thought of herself as anyone's protector, certainly not a formidable vampire, but she'd been equipped to be just that. Well, *protector* was a little strong. More like a small, yappy guard dog, one who would make absolutely sure Mal knew someone was coming, if ever his senses were thrown off.

"Yappy guard dog? Like one of those fuzzy mop dogs we saw when we pulled in last night?"

"Those fuzzy mop dogs are Horace and Helmsley, who apparently belong to Nadia's mother, Latriska. She stays here and does bookkeeping for Lord Marshall, because she's a very accomplished bookkeeper and secretary. She's not marked, but Lord Marshall chose to bring her here anyway after Nadia lost her third baby."

Mal rolled over then, raising a brow. "You could have been an intelligence operative during the War."

"Who says I wasn't?" She struck an exotic pose at the door. "Don't I look like Mata Hari? Her maid, at least. Or her maid's maid."

The skin around his eyes creased with a smile. "You look like a foolish, delightful girl who needs a spanking. And you would have been barely out of short skirts during the War. Come here."

She considered his near nakedness, too well hidden by the blanket now that he'd turned over. He'd been so serious in the car, so many demons plaguing him. She was glad to see those gone, but she thought she could drive them further off.

"I think I'll get far more out of it if I say no."

"And how do you figure that?" His brow arched, his eyes taking on that wicked glint her body recognized, already warming.

"Well, you'll insist on chasing after me, which means you'll have to jump out of bed, and I'll see you all bare-arsed. A girl has to get her thrills where she can. That's what Danny always says. Or at least she said it when she caught me taking a peek at Dev. He was washing up behind the house, because he'd spent a day in the bush and was coated in mud and grime. Danny said he couldn't come in until he was two coats of dirt lighter, so he grumbled, went to the pump out back and stripped down, all of it. Mrs. Pritchett was at the kitchen window and her eyes fair popped out of her head. I decided we needed to have more wood for the cookstove, because the window cut off too much. Plus, Mrs. Rupert was crowded in next to her, and they're stout women. I couldn't squeeze in to see."

He was regarding her with fascination, but when she wound down, he crossed his arms over his bare chest. "Your idea won't work."

"Why not? I—"

She gave a short shriek, for he'd moved faster than she could follow, such that all she sensed was a brief jerk, her feet leaving the floor, and then she was in the bed, turned beneath him. The sheet floated down over the two of them like a disturbed cloud. His hands were sure and firm, one palm spread behind her shoulder blades, the other gripping her hip, his body between her legs, pressing against the thin fabric of her skirt. Like many males upon waking—something she'd quite recently learned, never having woken in a man's bed before Mal—he was a more than impressive size. So impressive she couldn't help the involuntary arch against him, the drawing of her lower lip between her teeth.

"Are you wearing any panties?" His tone shifted to that husky murmur she recognized meant he was no longer willing to play, the hunter taking over.

"No. You told me not to do that, ever, except when you instruct me to it."

"And why did I do that?"

"Because you wanted me to be accessible to you whenever you wanted to . . ."

"Say it, Elisa." He bent, caught her ear in a brief nip, then worked his way down the side of her throat, teasing that flower mark with sensual intent before piercing her over it without preamble. She gave a tiny moan, her fingers flexing on his biceps as he took his first blood of the evening.

"When you want to be inside my c-cunt. With your tongue, cock or whatever object pleases you."

Even after ten days of intense training, she could still stumble on such a bald declaration. But he was relentless, and she'd realized quickly that it was more than his desire to have her properly prepared. She was his first fully marked servant, and he was exploring this side of his vampire nature, stirred from dormancy to sudden, full, raging life. He'd explored it with great creativity, until she'd assured herself anything that happened in Florida would pall in comparison.

It was a reassuring lie, of course, because it would be far different to have him do these things to her in front of strangers, or worse, be touched by others when she was under his command. However, she was going to handle it fine. She'd accept no other outcome.

She was already wet. She worried she would drip on the floor tonight, not wearing any undergarments. Particularly if he kept teasing her like this throughout the evening.

Vampires like that, Irish flower. We like smelling your arousal, knowing it's so strong that your honey is trickling down your lovely thigh, over your calf. Even in a room full of servants, I'll be able to tell the arousal is yours.

When he pressed harder against her, she lifted her hips to him, stroking her damp center against his full length, despite the irritating boundary of cloth. But she'd learned. She kept her hands on his upper arms, knowing it was up to him what he wanted her to do. He might command her to lift her skirt, or do it himself, as he did now. Using one hand to bunch the fabric, he pulled it up to her abdomen, curving his body off of her with a ripple of muscle to accommodate it.

I'm going to fuck you now, Elisa. Leisurely, deep, and take my time with it. I'm going to eventually come, but you will not. If you think at any point you can't hold back any longer, you tell me, because I do not want you to come. I want you so close to it you're about to lose your mind, but that is all.

Oh, if that was all. It was a desperate, wry thought. She was already hot through and through, because that had been part of the training as well, such that she could become wet and ready for him with barely more than a command to do so. At the same time, she could hold back. Based on his training, she could straddle the line of near dying from the desire to come, and an incurable hunger to please his every desire. His pleasure at her obedience was as much nourishment for her soul as her blood was to his body.

Finding out that such a carnal ability to serve was directly connected to her concentrated desire to serve in more mundane ways had been a revelation for her. In their quiet discussions after such intense lovemaking, he'd pointed out things in her nature that had been there all along. He believed that Lady Constance had seen them as well, explaining why she'd taken Elisa in, knowing she'd be a treasure in a vampire's household. Knowing that didn't offend her; if anything, it somehow made her feel even more connected to the one place she'd considered home. And she guessed her lack of offense just reinforced what they'd all known about her.

He pushed into her now, that wetness easing his way, though she gave a tiny little groan, because he was extremely thick this evening. He wasn't rough, but he was rough enough, insisting and making her work her hips up and back to accommodate him until she was gasping at that friction. He pulled open her blouse so he could see the thrust of her breasts toward him, the way the aroused nipples pushed against the thin fabric of the decorative bra.

When he was settled to the hilt, his hips pressing her thighs wide, she let her gaze course up his chest, to the finely molded shoulders and corded neck, the dark hair falling over his forehead, emphasizing those severe cheekbones and stern lips, the dark eyes that made her think of arcane starless skies.

I want to touch you, Master. May I?

Whatever you wish to drive your arousal higher.

She wanted to torture herself, and so she did, sliding her hands from his arms, lingering on the slope of his back, down to the firm buttocks, digging her fingers in there, kneading to pleasure herself with the feel of him driving deeper, withdrawing, then flexing to drive in again. Her kneading began to match his rhythm, her heels overlapping her wrists to let him drive in deeper. He wrenched another cry from her throat as he bent and suckled her right nipple through the satin cloth. Letting her feel the press of fangs through it, he went still, not puncturing or tearing it. The moist heat of his breath, the slow circle of his tongue over her jutting nipple, enhanced the sensation.

No, no . . . It wasn't a protest; it was proof of how helpless he was making her, such that she had to admonish herself to hold on. She didn't want to stop anything he was doing, but she knew he was going to test her to her limit. Already, her body was coiled so tight, a ravenous creature whose hunger was being denied.

Obey me, sweet Elisa. You serve my pleasure, not your own. Let me see you tremble and flush, so close to climax, your pussy already gripping me as if it will never let go.

He was as good as his word, being slow and leisurely about it all, giving the other nipple the same attention as her nails dug into his arse, moving up to claw his lower back as he became more insistent, as he drew his strokes down to slow glides. He murmured to her, growled at her, worked up to harder thrusts, now pumping into her faster, and she gripped him even more, giving him a tight, slick fist he couldn't resist, knowing she was cheating somewhat, but she didn't want to fail him, and she wanted to see his pleasure.

Of course he slowed down again, commanded her not to grip him with those devilish internal muscles, and built her up again until she was crying out on every stroke, a wail of tormented need that gave his eyes those flickers of crimson and had his fangs bared when at last he released into her.

Oh God . . . She couldn't resist that. As those streams jetted into her, bathing all those sensitive tissues, she couldn't stop herself. She let out a strangled cry of warning, straining with all she was to stop her reaction, the climax hitting her wall of control like a battering ram.

He used that speed again, unexpectedly. In a blink, her mouth, open on a cry, was being nudged wider. He thrust his cock in there, his knees straddling her shoulders, holding her down. She strangled on a stutter-ing scream when, with his other hand, he thrust several cubes of ice directly inside of her. The ice had been left in a bucket by the bed, and now he held another piece against her clit as well, that one diabolical hand sealing in the overwhelming sensation. He kept ramming into her mouth, still coming. He'd left a small patter of drops across her belly; she felt them, even as she took those further expulsions of hot seed on her tongue. He tasted of salt and metallic blood, the unique semen of a vampire.

Pulling out, he gripped the base of his cock and milked out the last flood before her eyes, a white viscous fluid over the generous rise of her breasts. He spread it with the tip of his cock, rubbing himself over her as his body shuddered one last time. She could smell him there, right under her nose, and she already knew he wouldn't allow her to bathe. He'd want her to have that scent on her all night, that primal male mark-ing. Lord Marshall would detect it immediately.

She had no room for shame. She was fair writhing with the excru-ciating feel of the ice melting inside of her and the piece he still held against her clit. Having her climax aborted so abruptly left her with a peculiar feeling of volatility. She'd do anything he wanted her to, just to gain release. It didn't matter whom they'd be with tonight; she'd bend herself over his dinner plate and let him rut on her. She'd even take Lord Marshall's cock in her mouth at the same time, if it was the proper, guestlike thing to do.

As she lifted her lashes to gaze up at him with greedy eyes, his eyes gleamed with a mixture of reactions, but she received the most impor-tant message from it. That was exactly the state of mind he'd intended her to be in. He didn't want her to be afraid or anxious.

You serve me, Elisa. That's all you need to worry about.

She managed a nod, still gasping, and let out another short scream as he teased the ice inside of her with one probing finger. He had his cock back in her mouth, his other hand sliding along her jaw, caressing the stretch of her lips around him. Though replete, his cock had not yet softened, because he often didn't, as long as her breath and moist heat could hold him like this.

"We'll let that melt," he said softly. "Then you'll help me get dressed, and we'll take care of that spanking. Servants stand at dinner, so I won't have the pleasure of seeing you squirm on a sore backside. But I'm sure we'll more than make up for it."

Then, despite all that, his eyes darkened. Pulling out and sliding down so he lay on her body, he caught her mouth in a hot, deep kiss. His fingers curled under her neck, spearing into her disheveled hair. *Follow my lead, Elisa, and trust me. I'll take care of you.*

33

THERE was quite a difference in a dinner out in the middle of Western Australia and one here, in easy reach of everything needed to make it fancy. Even at the Pearlmuttons, she'd never seen anything like this. Lord Marshall had amassed more wealth than Elisa thought was possible. As she and Mal passed the dining room, she glimpsed a small army of servants at work and a long table set with gleaming gold leaf china. The Persian rug stretched completely over the dining room floor. A large chandelier made up of crystal teardrops and blown glass shaped like tulips hung low over the table. She expected the servant who changed out the bulbs inside those fragile things had to have a delicate touch.

A classical music piece drifted down the hallway from the open door of the solarium. It made her miss the crackle of Kohana's radio and his penchant for accompanying Negro spirituals in his rough baritone. Of course, that longing might be because her nerves were knocked awry. One of the efficient household staff had just informed Mal their dinner party had expanded.

Two additional vampire guests had arrived at dusk, members of Lord Marshall's territory. Though the housemaid made it clear it was a last-minute decision by Lord Marshall, Elisa still felt remiss in her duties, particularly when Mal tensed at the news. However, as he escorted her to the main level of the house, his hand slid across her lower back, a brief touch of reassurance, and she knew he wasn't angry at her.

She told herself it was just as well. If they'd known ahead of time, she would have worried pointlessly over it. Despite that bit of practicality, a flood of apprehension filled her as they drew closer to the solarium and she heard the voices of the other guests as they enjoyed pre-dinner cocktails. Mal stopped her in the hallway then, brought her back against his full body, lowering his head to nuzzle her throat, a one-touch reminder of all he'd done to her over the past hour. It brought all her unreleased passion surging forward, a tidal wave to obliterate that flood. Her nipples hardened, her body softened against his, and he made a quiet noise of approval.

You can do this, Irish flower. You serve me. Keep remembering that.

That, and the fact they were here for the fledglings. She firmed her chin, and her resolve.

As they continued down the hallway, a house servant slipped out of Lord Marshall's private study, several doors before the solarium entry. The servant left the door cracked, giving Mal and Elisa a direct view of the room's occupants.

The woman who must be Nadia sat in a man's deep reading chair, perhaps where Lord Marshall liked to read the paper at night. She had her legs drawn up, arms folded over her body. Despite the coiled position, her mother, Latriska, was brushing her hair, but Nadia might have been a doll. Her gaze was on the fire in the fireplace, seemingly unnecessary because of the Florida heat, but she was painfully thin and shivering, with a wrap over her shoulders.

A tall, handsome man—Lord Marshall, for Elisa couldn't imagine it would be anyone else—briefly bent to lay a kiss on the top of her head. Her eyes closed. When he bent farther, moving to her lips, she visibly flinched, turning her face away.

Elisa drew in a breath, for Lord Marshall straightened and noticed them there. Nadia's refusal was an act no vampire could let pass, not and save face in front of others of his kind. She wished they'd gone another way to the dining area. But Elisa's regard for Mal increased tenfold then. Before Lord Marshall could decide how to react, her Master stepped closer to the door, drawing Elisa with him and putting his hand on the door latch to widen it slightly, yet maintain their privacy with the block of his body in front of the opening.

"My lord, it's a terrible thing to lose a child," he murmured. "Perhaps later, Elisa could sit with Nadia. She has a gift for bringing light into the most soul-sick heart."

He hadn't tried to pretend he hadn't seen it, or awkwardly changed the topic. He'd met it head-on, with quiet compassion. And Lord Marshall, his hand still resting on Nadia's shoulder, showed how deeply he appreciated it when the vampire's typical dispassionate mien dropped briefly. Elisa saw a haggard male, uncertain how to comfort a female who obviously meant a great deal to him.

Mal courteously pulled the door closed and they continued down the hallway toward the solarium. It was a dilemma Elisa couldn't imagine. Even after such a brief time as his full servant, she knew if Mal was in such a deep depression, she'd be in that same mire with him, because the bond was that strong. For a servant to turn so emphatically away from the touch of her Master, when the physical passion was so constant and undeniable, was a strong indicator of how trapped Nadia was in the tragedy of losing three unborn babies. But the whole vampire-servant link required her to accept her Master's will, physically and emotionally.

What will he do if she doesn't come out of it? Vampire hearing was so acute that anything vital or sensitive now needed to be spoken mind to mind.

In our world, he has only two choices. Put her somewhere under his care but out of his household, and take another servant. Or kill her.

Recalling that brief glimpse of Lord Marshall's face, she shook her head. *He won't do it. He won't put her aside.* Instead, his household would slowly be swallowed by their shared despair. *He loves her too much.*

She'd simply spoken what had been obvious to her, but the second she had the thought she tensed up. *I mean . . . I know vampires aren't supposed to feel that way about their servant. You know, they can "love" them, but not be "in love" with them. I do understand that. I—*

She had her hand in the crook of his elbow. His settled over it as he gave her one of his unfathomable looks. *Breathe, Elisa. We're about to go in now.* His mouth tightened. *And I believe you will be the only female servant present at dinner.*

"Oh, crikeys," she muttered, forgetting to say it in her head only. Mal gave her the hint of a smile, though there was a fierceness to his gaze, that possessiveness. Both gave her courage, helped her settle the bad kind of collywobbles. *Oh, crikeys.*

~

Lord Marshall's two visitors, Cynthia Maher and Jonathan Kreager, were here to discuss business issues with him and to offer their annual tithe. Since Lady Danny was currently a Region Master, Elisa knew the tithe was a requirement of all vampires in a territory, in return for the overlord's protection and investment of the monies to the benefit of them all.

When Lord Marshall joined them, Elisa was able to get a better look at their host. A made vampire who'd been turned at an older age, he looked in his forties and had handsome silver threaded through his dark hair. Along with eyes of a remarkable emerald green, he had a stature that made it clear he was a male who commanded respect.

Cynthia was a stained-glass artisan who ran a shop in Miami. Her servant, Christophe, was a Frenchman of exceptional beauty. He kept his silken brown hair out of his eyes with the occasional graceful head toss. It managed not to look too effeminate because of the sensual mouth and straight, sharp nose, though Elisa thought Dev still would have teased him about being too much of a sheila. He was handsome and well proportioned, however, dressed in slacks and a dress shirt open at the throat, revealing a glimpse of muscular chest.

Jonathan Kreager's tastes apparently also ran to men. Elisa knew such things existed, of course, but none of the vampires in Danny's territory buttered their bread that way. With his thick red hair, long-lashed blue eyes and pale skin, Jonathan actually *was* girlishly pretty, a slim Fae prince without the wings. His servant was just the opposite. If Jonathan was a fairy prince, Gustav would have been one of the mountainous Vikings who stood at the head of a longboat, bellowing orders and eyeing convents on the coast of England, ripe for pillaging. He had chocolate brown eyes, a trimmed beard that caught the candlelight with a copper sheen, and hair queued on his shoulders, more of a thick, unruly mane than a head of hair.

In deference to his bulk, he wore clothes that had obviously been tailored to his size, and the linen shirt tucked into camel-colored trousers worked well on him, along with calf-length dress boots. Interestingly, she noticed he wore a collar, a thick band of leather. A chain tether disappeared down the shirt, and from the faint imprint of it, it also appeared to go into his pants.

It's attached to what's known as a cock harness, Elisa. In addition to the collar on his neck, he has one around his cock and balls, to remind him to mind his Master. Some vampires like using such devices on their servants.

She couldn't even imagine where one would obtain such a thing. But the world was much more vast than she realized.

The two servants were giving her the once-over, not in a crude way, but as she'd told Mal. Servants sized one another up. Though of course this was a bit different, because the three of them weren't going to be polishing china or scrubbing floors together. Fortunately, their regard didn't feel sleazy or inappropriate. As they all moved toward the dining room, the Frenchman gave her a conspiratorial wink. Gustav cocked his head, then held his forefinger and thumb close together in a subtle gesture at his side, indicating his amusement with her diminutive size. It reminded her of Kohana, the teasing more playful than insulting.

It made her feel somewhat better. She did notice that when Christophe winked at her, Mal gave him a narrow look. He instantly became the perfect servant again, his expression revealing nothing, eyes focused on the back of his Mistress's chair after he seated her at the long table.

Cynthia was willowy and elegant, her hands how Elisa would expect an artist's to look, slender and interesting, the nails trimmed short, though painted a glossy pink. She wore a soft flowing dress in a matching pink that looked like an Impressionistic painting, a melting of different shades that shimmered like a sky when she moved. It molded to her curves and yet enhanced the fragile bone structure of her neck, her hair pulled up on her nape. If she hadn't known otherwise, Elisa would have guessed Christophe was the vampire and Cynthia the servant, but when Cynthia tilted her head back to see what mischief had caused Mal's look, that sharpening of her gray eyes, as well as the flash of fang, corrected the impression.

"Forgive him, Malachi. He can be such a terrible flirt. Later, you're welcome to try to beat it out of him, but you'll only achieve personal satisfaction, no real results. I've tried all sorts of torments, and it only grows worse."

Jonathan lifted a brow at Mal's noncommittal response. His speculative smile clearly showed his appreciation of Mal's looks, something that startled Elisa, though Mal seemed to take it in stride. It reminded her that, though he preferred not to attend vampire socials, it was not his first one. "You're an Indian. When were you made?"

"Nineteenth century."

"That's remarkable. I wouldn't have expected our kind to have penetrated the pioneer country at that time. Too much nature and sun for our tastes."

"It was in the East. I ran into Lady Diana there. She made me."

"I've heard of her. She's somewhat of an oddity, isn't she? I've heard she's getting to have a touch of the Ennui and stays pretty much on her estate. She still has her harem of made vampires, though, as diverse as a box of colored candy. The Council limited her to making one every decade recently."

The conversation then turned to equally inane chatter, but Elisa's attention remained on Mal. He'd tightened his hands on the arms of the chair, a slight motion but one she noted. She wondered if it was the subject that made him uncomfortable, or the environment itself. The room had no windows, perhaps for long dinners that went close to the dawn hours.

Kreager sat back, murmured to Gustav. As the servant left the room, the vampire cocked his head toward their quiet host. "Lord Marshall, I know you typically prefer such things to begin during dessert and coffee, but I have a new toy, a prototype from an inventor friend with an interest in the sensual arts. Seeing as we have a lovely new female servant here tonight, one almost delightfully virginal in her exposure to our entertainments, I thought we might use her as a test subject for it."

Gustav had returned quickly. When Jonathan gestured, the servant went to Mal, handing the item to him with a courteous half-bow. Elisa got a better look at it as it was handed over, and wasn't at all sure how to react. It was like a man's cock, only shorter and curved. There appeared to be a notched piece near the base.

"I'm sure you've all seen a vibrator, though they're harder to find among polite company these days than they were earlier in the century. The phallus part is self-explanatory," Kreager noted, "but the piece at the bottom is the new offering from my friend. It fits against the clitoris. He said the dual stimulation can bring a woman to orgasm, over and over."

He looked toward Cynthia, eyes flashing with devilish mischief. "You may want to purchase one, sweetheart. You can taunt Christophe by using it on yourself. Perhaps being replaced by a mere toy might make him behave better."

With the far less congenial glance he sent toward the suddenly far more tense-jawed Christophe, Elisa saw Jonathan's pretty face was a deceptive mask for that relentless control vampires all seemed to wield so aptly. She thought of the chain running into Gustav's trousers. Whatever kind of master Jonathan was, that look held more than a hint of it.

The vampire angled a considering eye to Lord Marshall, his tone becoming casual, and kinder than she would have expected. "It's also useful for a woman who is feeling somewhat . . . separated from her sexual self. For whatever reason."

The idea of forcing a traumatized woman to perform sexually made Elisa blink. But then she thought of how a third-mark could lose herself in that relentless sexual drive and wondered if her disapproval might be misplaced. Further, Lord Marshall showed his first reaction since the appetizers had been served. Interest flickered across his face at Kreager's words. After a considering pause, he nodded to Mal.

"I agree with Jonathan's idea for entertainment. Your servant will demonstrate the device throughout the sampling of our next two courses."

"Excellent, my lord." Jonathan inclined his head. "By then, if it does as it should, Gustav and Christophe will be fair about to come out of their trousers. Dessert will be very lively. We can orchestrate a good performance to honor your hospitality."

Elisa only half-heard the comment, her attention frozen on that object in Mal's hand and the plans for it. There were certainly . . . objects that had been used at the dinners Danny had hosted, whispers about them. Her mother had referenced such things with casual crudity when Elisa was a small girl and they were beyond her comprehension, but this was her first direct exposure. It appeared it was about to be her first direct experience with it as well.

Elisa, come stand beside my chair.

She'd worn a black demi bra that pushed her breasts up impossibly high. The dress she wore was a slinky black thing with sparkles and a silver sash, silver heels. She'd dressed her hair with several costume-jewelry diamond pins and been amazed at how glamorous she looked, a tiny, curvy pixie. Despite his earlier remarks, he'd had her wear a black slip of a thong, an amazing piece of work that covered nothing, designed merely to be titillating to the male species. At the thought of taking off the dress, wearing only such things, she grew cold and a little timid, but Mal took care of things.

When she came to stand before him, he untied the sash of the wrap-around dress with little fanfare, letting it slide open, revealing her provocative underwear. Her tiny tremulous breath made her bosom quiver. She was aware of Christophe's more discreet but no less avid regard.

I will poke his eyes out with my butter knife, and then you won't have to worry about him.

Let him look, Master. He'll see the traces of your seed over my breasts.

His gaze flickered up to her, hot approval there at the reminder and the address. It helped steady her, and so she kept her focus on him. He slid his hands along her waist, his thumbs following the line of the thong in front, indulging himself in the caress, but soothing her with it as well. Then he slid lower, over the crotch of the panties. She'd been wet when she'd put them on, so the panel was already damp and she shuddered at the contact, earning sharpened attention all down the table. It was like wolves scenting blood, only in this case their killer senses were tuned to sexual arousal.

Even Cynthia seemed quite interested, but that didn't surprise Elisa, because of Danny. For whatever reason, Elisa found two women taking their fill of each other less shocking than two men. Maybe because she was a woman and knew how easily females could embrace intimacy.

You'll have to tell me some stories about Danny and other women. In vivid detail.

Mal teased the panel to the side, slid a finger inside of her, proving she was already wet and slick, ready for the device. She colored all manner of rosy for him to do such a thing, but the vampires seemed to take excessive pleasure in her blushing innocence.

Mal fitted the device to the opening and slid it in, following the contours of her body with the ease of intimate knowledge. She gasped, swaying at the invasion, particularly when he positioned the notched piece over her clit, such that it felt like a finger pad sitting on that bud. There were adjustable straps to go with it. Using the hold of her underwear, as well as those straps, he had her secured in it very quickly. But Cynthia wasn't entirely satisfied.

"Have her leave the dress, Mal, and walk across the room. I want to know if it can be worn comfortably while moving."

Mal gave her a nod, and Elisa shrugged out of the dress, though she had to suppress the strong urge to hold on to it.

Walk for me, Irish flower. Show me that pretty ass, the way it swings in those high heels.

Walk for *him*. Not them. She held on to that. But before she could move away, Jonathan spoke again.

"Turn it on, so we can see how she walks with it that way."

She was beginning to really *not* like him. Still, Mal nodded, and made an adjustment. A sudden, astounding wave of vibration spiraled up into her sex. On top of that, the notch started stroking across her clit, altogether too distracting and intense, particularly since she'd started this evening fully aroused.

Walk, Irish flower. Obey me.

He wanted to see her walk, too. Ironically, it helped, to know his lust was being stimulated, showing her off this way. She'd obey anything he told her to do, which just made his reaction intensify. There was no telling how far that would take them tonight—or how far it would incite this group to go.

She moved away tentatively, breath coming fast. There was no way she could walk normally, not with that friction rocketing back and forth across sensitive tissues, but she tried, and got dizzy. She'd made it just past Jonathan's chair when she swayed. Gustav's hand closed over her arm and elbow, steadying her, but then Jonathan turned and his servant's hold became something different. His large hands shifted to her upper arms, holding her back against his massive chest as Jonathan leaned forward with interest and wiggled the base of the thing, simulating a short thrust, which pushed the clitoral stimulator harder against her.

She cried out, arching against Gustav's hold, and she couldn't help it. "Mal."

Easy, girl. I'm here with you. Close your eyes; imagine it's me.

When Mal had been able to arouse her in a way no other man had, she'd thought it simply skill. He was a male who'd looked beyond his own release to develop the ability to pleasure a woman. But such talent could be applied indifferently, and received indifferently. Any man with such skill would have been able to arouse her. So she'd thought.

While another man could touch this device and ratchet up her sexual response through his knowledge of a female body, other key parts of her were repelled. She didn't want Kreager touching her. Gustav had steadied her out of helpfulness, but now he was holding her for the benefit of another vampire, and she found his grip constricting, stealing her breath, no matter that he smelled like cinnamon spice, something she usually found reassuring. As the room seemed to bend inward, she realized she was being overwhelmed by panic. She shut her eyes, fighting for calm.

"Oh no, you don't." Jonathan's voice was amused, though not unpleasantly so. It didn't seem to matter to her nerves, however. *Trapped, trapped, trapped.* "Don't go hiding on me." He withdrew the vibrator enough to slide it back in, and those tissues reacted with preclimactic violence. She gasped and he chuckled, but with command in his tone. "Open your eyes."

"She has them closed on my command," Mal interjected, though there was an edge to his voice that Elisa caught, even if no one else did. "She is new to this, Kreager, and I don't want to overwhelm her."

"But overwhelming a servant is the best way to break them in." This from Cynthia. "And watching their ultimate acceptance as they face utter surrender . . ." Wistful memory was in her tone. From the shift in the direction of her voice, she was looking at Christophe. The idea that the confident Frenchman could ever have been feeling what Elisa was feeling now was astonishing but also somewhat reassuring, but it was a fleeting feeling, lost in the perilous sense of being in a shrinking box, the air going away.

Lord Marshall spoke. "She's right, Malachi. I'm overruling you. Host and overlord's prerogative. Open your eyes, girl."

You don't need to do so, Elisa.

But she did, didn't she? And not just for the fledglings. She wasn't going to look too hard at that, but she felt it in her bones. She was his. He just had to command her. *He* had to do it. *Please, Master . . .*

A brief pause, a flash of something like seething frustration, but it wasn't directed at her. Then he spoke in her mind, calm, firm, just like he did for his cats. *Open your eyes, Elisa.*

She managed it then, shifting her gaze to the flat expanse of linen tablecloth, focusing on dinnerware, because all her internal focus was on the build of her body toward climax, toward . . .

"No . . ." She panted it out, but it was already too late. Kreager kept moving the vibrator, his fingers brushing her wet sex with unconcerned intimacy as she stiffened in Gustav's hold, unable to control the orgasm that rolled over her relentlessly, heedless of her shame at being so easily coaxed to it with an inanimate object, in front of strange, staring eyes. She flung her head back on Gustav's massive chest and cried out, aware that her nipples were stiff and prominent, pushing against the barely there bra. As the climax took her over, Jonathan let go of the device to cup and squeeze her breasts, furthering the reaction of her body under his practiced hands.

It wasn't enough to keep her coming for long, though. Not like the never-ending, drawn-out moments she experienced with Mal, savoring his pleasure as he did things to make each orgasm a more mind-altering, prolonged experience than the last. Still, she was making soft bleats of spent passion, pressing her cheek to Gustav's shirt and the solid chest beneath. Jonathan nodded his satisfaction and tossed another question out. "Has she ever taken three men?"

"No." Mal's expression had become granite. Lord Marshall apparently picked up on what might be boiling behind the dispassionate mien.

"Is there a problem, Malachi? You came here as a guest in my home, a supplicant for a favor. Have you been on your island so long you've forgotten how to be a vampire?"

Mal shifted his gaze to the overlord. Elisa saw the flash, the hot fury, so brief it could have been a trick of candlelight, because now his expression became courteous, mild. "No, my lord. I've not forgotten anything about being a vampire."

Mal let his attention rove over her displayed body. The fluid from her climax was running down her thigh, the vibrator still going inside of her, working the oversensitized tissues so she twitched and mewled, unable to stop herself, but no one seemed to mind. She was the center of a great deal of aroused attention. Cynthia's avid gaze caressed her abdomen, the way her legs trembled and the vibrator filled the flesh in between.

Elisa clung to how Mal's eyes warmed on her, putting the fury away. He let her see that her desire pleased him, stoked his own. In the passion-filled privacy of his bedroom, she'd felt the power of that, time and again. It steadied her, and as it did, she gave herself back to him, mind, body and heart. *I'm fine, Master. I can do anything you demand.*

That dark gaze dwelled on her face for a long moment, then shifted to Lord Marshall. When Mal spoke, his voice was still all polite courtesy. "What is your pleasure, Lord Marshall? My servant is lovely, young and eager to please. However traumatic she might find this situation, whatever she has known before this moment, her personal circumstances, it should certainly not interfere with her presence and performance for your guests."

Had he lost his mind? His championing of her bolstered her beyond description, but trepidation shot through her as well. It wouldn't take much to upset the apple cart for William and Matthew.

If one grazing shot at his hypocrisy is all it takes, then it's not the right place for them.

The even thought startled her, but at the same moment Marshall Grant's jaw eased. He inclined his head, a faint acknowledgment. "Touché, sir. I expect we can all be a little protective of our servants, when they do so much for us. But I think you'll agree that it's possible for her to handle more."

He'd adjusted the mantle of his authority with little difficulty, and now she found herself pinned by his steady, implacable gaze. "What about it, child? Can you serve your Master's needs, no matter what they are, in this company or any other? Can you be his full servant in truth? You see, no matter her 'personal circumstances,' if I told Nadia to join us, get on her knees and serve every vampire in here, she would do it.

It is because she has proved that capacity to me over and over, that I give her consideration now, *not* asking that of her. So are you ready to begin earning that high regard from your Master?"

It was odd to be having this kind of serious conversation, pinned against a mountain of a man, her body naked and spread and impaled upon a vibrating phallus, making it devilishly hard to think. But on top of that, Lord Marshall Grant was a lying wanker.

Elisa was dead certain he wouldn't have asked that of Nadia even if she'd never whored herself out for him in her entire life. He cared for her too much, in a way he wasn't allowed to show here. The same way Mal cared for Elisa, and didn't want to be here, wanted to be back on his island where the world was about so much more than this. And it was likely why Danny preferred her station, where she and Dev could be as close as they wished. It made Elisa think that the vampire world might be in for an eventual surprise, as it changed its attitude about servants, one pairing at a time. Unfortunately that wasn't going to happen today.

"I am ready . . . to be . . . whatever my Master demands," she rasped. Lord in Heaven, the vibrator was starting to arouse her again, moving past painful overstimulation.

"Prettily said. Then I'll ask your Master for the 'right of demand,' so that I might make the next request."

As the silence drew out, an obvious cord of tension stretching from one end of the table to the other, her apprehension was mirrored in the increased stillness from the other two vampires, watching the byplay.

Elisa knew that unyielding look on Mal's face. Knew it was tied into a hundred different things, memories of humiliation, of being forced to do something alien to one's nature, against one's heart. He didn't want her to suffer that, no matter that he had every right in his world to demand it of her. And that alone made it possible for her to accept whatever Lord Marshall offered.

You're my Master. You'll protect my heart, hold it in that room I mentioned, right? I'll pretend you're holding me in your lap, telling me stories of lions mating and leopards chasing one another around trees. About how harsh Nature can be one moment, and yet loving in the next. I want to serve you, Master. Let me do it.

His lips tightened. "What may my servant do to bring you pleasure, my lord?"

"Not an unequivocal assent." Lord Marshall sat back, studying him, and yet in some sense Elisa felt that Mal had not displeased him. "Jonathan's idea intrigues me. We have two handsome male servants here and one lovely female. I need a third male. Will you take whatever position I decree, Malachi?"

Please say yes. If he was involved, it increased her chances of getting through it. His hand upon her, his touch.

Mal inclined his head. "It's always a pleasure to enjoy my servant."

"Very well. Then you will provide the occupation for her mouth. Gustav will take her from behind and Christophe will have the pleasure of her pussy." Lord Marshall raised his glass. "I want her arms bound behind her back so she's at the mercy of the three of you for movement. My conservancy would be a much better location to enjoy the spectacle. The staff can bring the rest of our meal out there, and it's a shame to waste tonight's breeze off the water. May I suggest we head in that direction?"

34

Just like that. As if he'd decided there'd be cards and charades after dinner. Instead, it was, "Oh fine, gents, let's have a bit of three-way buggering while we enjoy our port and cigars and Cynthia enjoys her sherry." Though it appeared Cynthia preferred whiskey mixed with blood.

Gustav had lifted her off her feet, holding her waist, and brought her to Mal, who was still sitting in his chair. When he drew the wet vibrator from her, she tried not to grab hold of him, but it was a near thing, her lower belly clutching over the sensation, her release flowing down her leg. As the others rose to go to the other room, he picked up his cloth napkin, pressed it to her inner thigh, soft strokes that kept her stance wide. Then he leaned forward and gave the curve of her breast a quick nip.

I can do this, sir. I can.

I know you can. He lifted his face to her, and she'd never wanted to lean down and kiss him more, but she stepped back at his gesture and he rose. Lord Marshall was at his elbow, engaging him in conversation. He and Mal moved toward the door with the other two vampires, the servants left to follow on their own. She knew it was part of the way things were tonight, so she squelched the tiny spurt of lost feeling that came from being so casually dismissed.

Christophe's hand landed on her elbow, holding her back with a pointed look. Now it was just her, Christophe and Gustav. And she in scanty underwear. She tried not to think about it, but it was an act of supreme will not to try to cover herself. Christophe gave Gustav a nod, and he brought the flagon of whiskey from the sidebar, pouring a full glass and extending it to her.

"Drink it all down, *ma cherie*," Christophe murmured. "One fast gulp, hard, like a man. It may seem like a lot, but it takes more to affect a third-mark. It goes away quicker as well, but this should be enough to get you started. We'll take you the rest of the way."

She nodded, not questioning their solicitude. She'd learned to recognize the good servants, the ones who understood they were all in it together and the best way to get along was to help one another out.

"They'll want you stripped and bound here," the Frenchman continued, producing a silk black cord. "Gustav will do the stripping honors, so you allow him that, eh?"

"I can undress myself," she said, and winced at the quaver.

"Use our strength, *ma cherie*. You'll need it." Christophe's eyes twinkled. "Though it is fortunate that Gustav is the one who will take you from behind, because despite his mountainous size, it is my cock that is the more formidable of the two."

"So he says," Gustav rumbled. "But only because he plays with it so much it's lengthened like an overstretched spaghetti noodle."

She blinked, tears from the whiskey's burn blinding her, but she couldn't help but feel the spurt of humor. Whether from the alcohol rush or not, she didn't know, but it was enough to give her a tiny smile. "Thank you."

"*Pfft.*" Christophe waved a hand. "Think we haven't been where you are? The first dinner I attended, it was like being thrown naked into a vat of horny, violent rugby players. I thought it was what Hell must be like, all those twisting, writhing bodies. But then something happened. Even now, there are times I remember it . . . fondly."

As he spoke, Gustav unhooked the bra quite deftly. She stiffened as his large hands settled on her hips to slide off her panties, but she used Christophe's shoulders for balance as she stepped out of them. He left her garters, stockings and heels. "This is a very nice look. They will like this."

She was shaking again, standing there all naked in front of the two of them as if it meant nothing. Christophe guided her wrists behind her and Gustav knotted the rope around them, drawing her shoulders back so her breasts were further lifted for Christophe's avidly appreciative gaze. "Ah, a nice touch."

Taking a swig of the whiskey straight from the bottle, he cupped her head, moving in to seize her mouth. She let out a surprised noise but then she was focusing on swallowing as he gave her more of the searing liquid. Gustav braced her behind so she felt the heat and pressure of both of them, a prelude of things to come. Christophe bent and fastened his whiskey-scented mouth on one nipple, suckling it quickly, and then the other. She bucked and gasped, overwhelmed at the sensual attack.

"There you are. All pointed and hard they are now, your pussy glistening again. You're ready and they'll love you. So will we, pretty sweet morsel. Come now, and don't worry."

She wasn't quite sure how or what to think. It was the most remarkable thing she'd ever experienced, the way they now both stripped as well, setting their clothes aside with a matter-of-fact air. It helped, that feeling of camaraderie, though they weren't the ones about to become a shish kebab. Gustav was in fact wearing what Mal had called a harness, and his stiff cock was enormous from the restraint, the straps tightly binding his testicles and the base of the shaft.

Taking the bottle from Christophe's hands, she upended it just as he'd done. As she choked, Gustav helpfully pounded her on the back and Christophe rescued the bottle before she dropped it. Through bleary eyes, she noted Christophe was as well-endowed as he'd said, but she held on to the fortitude of the alcohol, the arousal of her own body. She would use that and let her mind drift without anchor, not hold on to anything but the fact it would eventually be over. She would be pleasured beyond bearing, right? But treated as chattel, as an amusement, not a treasure. She closed her eyes, but before she could balk or bolt, she was nudged into motion.

They led her into the conservancy, a glassed-in room that faced the waterway. It wouldn't be too difficult for a passing boat to discern what they were doing, even with the distance of the backyard and the dock for Marshall's yacht. She was fully on display. The vampires were scattered about on the casual furniture in the outdoor living area. She met

Mal's gaze first, saw him look with hot approval at her appearance, though his attention lingered on her breasts as if he knew another male's mouth had been there, and he possibly didn't approve. But her arms had been tied, and she wasn't sure anymore what she was supposed to allow or not allow.

His jaw relaxed a fraction. *You don't have to make those choices, Elisa. That's my job. You've done nothing wrong. They know what they are doing. Just follow their lead.*

Christophe stretched out on the sturdy and long tile table set up in the center of the room, and Elisa didn't know whether to praise or curse the efficiency of Marshall's staff in providing it. The Frenchman's cock had only gained in size since they left the dining room. It was rising high and hard, ready for her. Gustav lifted her up like a tiny doll and guided her to spread her legs, straddling his fellow servant's body. Elisa caught a panicked whimper in her throat. It was diabolical to tie someone's arms like this. She was afraid, and these were strangers.

No, she was fine. This wasn't Victor. She didn't want Mal reacting to her spurt of panic, trying to call this off. Lord Marshall wouldn't be tolerant forever. *I'm fine. I'm fine.* And she was. Christophe and Gustav were considerate and experienced, conscious of what brought a woman pleasure. That was the whole point of this. Her pleasure as entertainment. It would not be painful . . . not physically.

She didn't have to worry about pregnancy. Lady Constance had told her a long time ago that, while third-marks could be fertile with a human or vampire, something in the makeup of third-marks kept them from impregnating each other, another reason they were preferred for dinner games with their masters and mistresses. She wondered if that was another reason Mal had wanted her third-marked before this trip.

She couldn't keep her mind distracted any longer. Gustav had one arm around her waist, the other hand curled around her throat. As Christophe's cock pushed into her cunt, the broad head sliding intimately against slick petals, she tried to relax, tried not to think. Maybe it had been merely a few weeks, but she'd gotten used to accepting only one male there. No matter how Mal had overwhelmed her, she'd been able to choose. Choice was a fleeting thing. She closed her eyes, their desires be damned, and tried not to let the tears show, but they liked that, liked seeing them seep down her cheeks. She heard it in Cynthia's murmur.

"The first-timers are delectable. Their sweet tears, even as they get hotter and hotter. It's a delicious struggle for them. The way they experience pleasure and emotion together as they learn what surrender to their Master truly means."

She let out a groan as Christophe worked his hips and made his way in until she was seated to the hilt. He took over for Gustav, curving an arm around her back, bringing her down so he could suckle a nipple anew. She started at the unusual sensation of oil drizzling across her buttocks, and then Gustav's fingers were massaging that tight opening between her cheeks. There was no way she could have anything else inside of her. With Christophe, she was full to bursting already.

When Mal rose and approached the table, her eyes opened, heart pounding, a plea there. Gustav curled one oiled hand in her hair, arching her throat to draw her face upward. As Mal opened his slacks, she fastened her gaze on his cock. He was astonishingly hard, demonstrating that some part of him was aroused by this, as she'd anticipated. She couldn't cast any stones, could she, given that she was fast becoming a warm, gushing fountain again?

"Take me deep, Elisa," he ordered with quiet firmness.

That made it click for her again. She was his servant, serving his pleasure and will. What they did to her served that, and so her pleasure would be his pleasure. Damn it all to hell.

She opened her mouth. At the first press of the broad head, the way he stretched her mouth to take him all the way in, her mind started to settle; something soothed in her belly, even as the rest of her body stayed agitated, restless. He pushed in deep, then pulled out slow, his intent focus on every change in her face, the way her lips slid over his length, moistening him with her mouth. Christophe remained still inside her for now, his mouth a slow, provocative pull on her nipple. As Mal's fingers dug deep into her scalp, his other hand caressing her throat, that agitation became a spiral of reaction. Almost before she realized it, she was being pulled from trepidation down into a more mindless state—a state of mindless eagerness. She suckled Mal hard, drawing in her cheeks. As she did, she lifted her arse, instinctively offering to Gustav.

"There it is. They lose themselves after a while and then they become proper little sluts, willing to do anything for you." That came from

Jonathan. But his tone was amused, almost affectionate, the slur oddly not derogatory.

Either way, she'd found her center again. Having Mal in her mouth, him taking control, that was what had made her settle. This was now being commanded and arbitrated by him. She was the servant, created to serve a Master. This Master.

She let out a cry as Gustav started easing his cock into her arse. It burned, holy Mary, it burned. She shuddered, sucking Mal harder. She was going to split in two.

"She's tightening up," Gustav murmured. "I don't want to push. She's a virgin here."

Mal's fingers stroked her hair. "Christophe, suckle her nipples harder. Knead her breasts as you do it, almost bruising her. It makes her hotter and wetter. Her nipples are very sensitive."

She cried out again as Christophe responded enthusiastically. While sensation spiraled faster through her, Gustav replaced the head of his cock with his fingers, one, then two, stretching her, his thumb teasing her rim, creating a rocket of sensations that had her surging forward on Mal, pushing her breasts deep in Christophe's mouth, and relying entirely on Gustav's hold on her waist to keep her upright.

Then Gustav's cock was back. As her hips lifted and fell, and Christophe surged in deeper, Mal pumped into her throat harder. *Take more of me, Irish flower. Make me come with that clever mouth of yours.* Somewhere during that thought, Gustav pushed through the tight rings of muscle and drove deep. Christophe, in perfect sync, did the same.

She screamed against Mal's cock, the burning pain and sense of fullness overwhelming, but Christophe was still teasing her breasts with his lashing tongue. He alternately kneaded them with his hands and then let their weight fall, creating an excruciating tingle in her nipples.

Keep working me, Elisa. Don't forget your first duty is to your Master.

She was sobbing between pain and pleasure as she attacked him anew, sucking, licking frantically, accepting his punishing thrusts into her mouth, making those harsh moans at the back of her throat. She was losing control over her body in truth, just as Jonathan had said. She was a mindless, sexual creature, meant for fucking, buggering, every part of her given to their mouths, cocks, hands in a way she'd never experienced before. It was heinous, carnal, euphoric and utterly mind-shattering. Having her hands tied behind her back where she couldn't cup Mal's testicle sac, or dig her fingers into his thighs, was an intimacy she longed to earn. Maybe he'd give her that after she served him properly. Maybe he'd let her clean him with her tongue after she brought him gushing forth.

Her body was rushing toward a hard, shattering orgasm the likes of which she knew she'd never experienced as well. It was a rough-and-tumble fall down a steep hill, headed straight for a cliff, and no clawing or struggles were going to stop it. Christophe and Gustav were going at it now, smacking into her and grunting like the intent male animals they were. But she felt Mal's eyes on her, and knew where her responsibility lay.

I'm going to come, Master.

Not yet. Not until I've come.

She was afraid he'd say that, but she renewed her effort, in a race with her own body as Christophe and Gustav inexorably dragged her that way. Mal's hands were tightening in her hair, ruthlessly pulling at her scalp in a way that added to the sensation. She added her own plea to the demands he was sending her.

Please come for me, Master. I want to swallow you, feel you flood my mouth.

He let out a quiet snarl, and then he was coming, pushing into her throat so she had to work hard not to gag, her eyes tearing as the first stream shot down it, so profuse it hit the back of her throat and bathed his cockhead, filling her mouth. She had to close her lips tight on him, spreading the hot semen over him even as she frantically swallowed, wanting every drop. Apparently Gustav was given permission to loosen the collar on his cock, for he released then, right behind Mal. Christophe joined him a mere moment later. Three men filling her with their seed and heat, their passion and strength. She couldn't hold off another second, her body spasming.

Come for your Master, Elisa.

She let out that raw, guttural cry, the one that said she was beyond feminine screams or shrieks. This was pure animal, the orgasm rocketing through her arse and cunt, the sensitive tips of her breasts, one still being teased and nipped by Christophe's clever tongue. Mal's hands had taken over for Gustav's, holding her head up, hand fisted in her hair, working her on his length so that she had to milk the very last drop of sensation from him.

She didn't close her eyes, she was sure of it, but it was clear she blacked out, because for a while, everything was gray and hazy. She vaguely stirred when Gustav eased from her. Christophe did as well, leaving behind very sore, well-used tissues. Mal's handkerchief was on her face, at her eyes, wiping the tears, and then his mouth was there, kissing them away. When he straightened, she tried to find his cock again, wanting to clean him with her mouth. He let her do that, let her suck and lick the stickiness away from his semierect shaft, teasing the ridged head with the tip of her tongue. As she did, she was aware of Gustav and Christophe cleaning her at his direction. She was also cognizant of a quiet sense of approval from their waiting audience. She'd done well. She hadn't let her Master down.

At length, she was helped to a sitting position. A cup of wine was placed at her lips. Mal was holding it, his other hand stroking her face. He wouldn't let them care further for her, and as her world oriented, she was aware the other vampires were talking among themselves, the floor show over and therefore no longer the center of their attention. They'd moved on to an animated discussion of politics. Gustav and Christophe were already cleaned up and taking their places behind their respective Master and Mistress. She knew Mal should be joining the other vampires, not tending to her like this.

"Hush," he murmured. "I'll do as I please, and my servant won't be giving me orders. You did well, *atsilusgi*. So very well."

She nodded, but at length she closed her hand over his wrist, lifted her lashes up to him. "I'm fine, sir. Truly. Please go back to the others. I'm just going to go to the bathroom and clean up."

He gave her a steady look, then nodded, helping her down off the table. But he gestured to Gustav. "Please see she gets to the bathroom."

She thought it was interesting he'd bypassed Christophe, but then, Christophe had been more flirtatious with her, hadn't he? Whatever that said about her Master, she didn't know, but she knew it somehow warmed her. And she needed that warmth, because as the reality of what she'd just done started to hit her, wine or whiskey couldn't seem to dispel the cold that was spreading through her lower abdomen.

Gustav was a quiet presence at her shoulder. She made it out of the room, halfway down the hall, before the shaking started in earnest and she had to stop, lean against the wall, her arms closing around herself. She fiercely willed her mind to be blank, to be as nothing but the air or the potted plants or the very clean floor runner with vibrant jewel tones.

Gustav waited on her, saying nothing, and she was more grateful for that than she knew how to say. When she continued on, he was just a step behind. He didn't touch her, apparently realizing it would make her more aware she was hobbling down a hallway completely naked, as if it was the most normal thing in the world. But she sensed he was ready if she stumbled.

When she reached the bathroom door, she put her hand on the knob, eyes brushing his before darting away. "Thank you, Gustav. I'll take a few minutes to clean up, get dressed, then be back."

He cleared his throat. "They prefer you didn't. Get dressed, that is. We attend them for the rest of the evening in the altogether. It lets them play with us as they like, when they like, with no impediments. There won't likely be anything that intense the rest of the night, though. Just more petting and such."

She nodded, one slow movement with a head that felt weighted down with granite. "They don't give you any time to protect yourself, do they?"

"No. That's the point, and they know it. They know our souls, that there's something in us that will surrender to it." Reaching down, he cupped her face with that tremendous hand. It was pure comfort, nothing else. "It's hard at first, but those who are meant for it will embrace it after a time. It's how you please your Master. That means everything."

She'd figured that part out, even though now that it was over, she didn't want to understand. She didn't even want to think. Since he was going to stand there until she went into the bathroom, she did, closing the door. As soon as she heard his heavy tread back down the hallway, her knees gave out and she crumpled onto the tile floor. Pushing her fist hard against her mouth, she contained the sobs that welled up into her throat, her other arm wrapped around her body so the pressure didn't break her ribs with their force.

She knew she shouldn't be acting this way. If Mal decided to take a look inside her mind, it wouldn't be good. He might not love her, but he did obviously care about her, the same way he cared about the well-being of his cats, the people at his station. She knuckled at her eyes, baring her teeth at herself. The only frustration he should feel was with her lack of sophistication. Lady Danny never cried, never broke down like this. In fact, if something flustered Lady Danny, she'd go rip that something's head off its shoulders and then ask for a nice spot of tea afterward. With a biscuit.

When things were crumbling, she tried to make herself smile, but this time it didn't work. Willis had been killed months ago, but all of a sudden it was as if she was grieving anew, not for him this time, but for *her* loss. The sobs were coming harder, and she could *not* come unglued like this, but she was.

It was a large bathroom, so she figured that was why she didn't hear him come in, but suddenly Mal was kneeling behind her where she was crumpled beside the tub. His arms slid around her, his thighs spread in a squat so he was able to pull her into the vee they made. She turned in his arms, burying her face in his chest, curling her hands hard into the fine shirt she'd spent so much time ironing for him so he'd look properly respectable in front of Lord Marshall. Now she was going to wrinkle it and blotch it up with tears. And the tile was cold under her bare bottom.

"Here, now." He gathered her up and lifted her, and was sitting on a small couch—a couch in a bathroom, imagine it—holding her so close in his arms she was sure he'd hold all the pieces together. "Easy, sweet girl. Easy."

He did that soft singsong he did, the one with no real words. It was what he sang as he moved among the cats at night. Their ears would prick, following him with those mysterious cat's eyes as he sang to them in his mother's tongue that no one else got to hear. Except her.

"I miss him so. I miss being loved as me. As everything I am, nothing more, nothing less."

He rubbed her back as her sobs became those tiny sentences, confessed to the safety of his damp, nonjudging shirtfront. "Sometimes I'm afraid, wherever he is, he's angry at me, because his love for me is what got him killed. That maybe he wishes he had fallen for some other girl. And that thought's unbearable. Early on, I had this awful dream, that I had died, and I came to the gates. It wasn't like the Pearly Gates, not the way they say, but like the entrance to a wonderful sprawling station, with children running about, and laughing, busy people, and lots of sunshine. He was standing against those gates, and he told me I had to go, because I couldn't be there. That he didn't want me there. And his face was angry."

"That was your worry, projecting itself in a dream. He doesn't feel that way."

"How do you know?" She lifted her face to him then, though she was sure her face was as blotchy and wet as his shirt.

"Because whatever waits for us after, once we get there we understand all the things we didn't while we were alive." He curled a lock of her hair around her ear. He didn't look the least bit hurried or concerned, though she well knew he shouldn't be in here. He gave her an admonishing look and continued. "There's only acceptance and love, and when we come back together, we know it's all as it was meant to be."

"Do you really believe that?"

"For you, yes. Because you deserve such a place." Tracing her brow, he moved along her temple to the curve of her cheek, gathering a new tear there. "My mother made me feel the way you described. She loved me as I was. I don't remember it too much, because I had to let go of so many things to survive. But I remembered it better when you came along."

"Why is that?"

He gave her that exasperated look now. "Because *you* make me feel that way. Though I can never return the gift, because I can never be all that for you, can I? Tonight proves that. But I thank you for reminding me of the feeling."

"A gift isn't something you have to return," she said softly, though her heart hurt as she said it.

"It should be. I'm sorry, Elisa. I tried to stop regretting the things I couldn't be, but there are times I deeply regret not being able to give you the gift Willis gave you. And that I have to demand more of you, because of what I am."

Then that bleakness was gone from his voice and he was focused entirely on her again. "There's more to this than your grief for what you've lost, though. I'm seeing shame in your mind, and fear. I won't tolerate that. Tell me why you feel that way."

It took Elisa a while, but at length she managed it, letting it unfold in her mind so he could see the full, embarrassing scope of it. "Before Lady Danny came, there was a girl, a maid in her mother's house. Mary. Lord Ian took a liking to her, maybe even more than he liked Lady Constance, because he always preferred someone who would submit to him. And after Lady Constance died, he had no boundaries. He made Mary . . . He taught her to . . . become excited when she was humiliated and degraded. The worse he treated her, the more . . . excited she became.

"She didn't start out that way. She just wanted to please him. He was this fine gentleman with his fine clothes who made her feel so different . . . But in the end, when Lady Danny came, she sent her away, with such a look of disgust. Like she was simply trash, good for nothing but to be spit upon and thrown away. Because Mary had no self-respect. She'd thrown it all away for the way he made her feel, a sick need she had to fill, like it was opium."

Mal was silent for a bit; then he spoke in a quiet, conversational tone. "I'm rethinking William and Matthew. I think they'd be far better off with Kreager and Gustav."

"What?" She wasn't sure if she'd heard him right, and pushed up to look at him. "Mr. Kreager isn't the way you are with me. He's cold, and a little cruel. I can see it in Gustav's eyes. How could you think such a thing? Where is your mind?"

It was the slight twitch to Mal's mouth, the way he tightened his hands on her arms so she couldn't pull back, that brought her to a halt. She firmed her lips. "You're teasing me."

"No." Now his gaze sobered. "I'm proving something to you, Elisa. What you described being done to Mary, it's quite possible to do that to a submissive. It requires seduction of the baser parts of our personalities, those deep needs that we can't deny in ourselves. Follow that with emotional manipulation, eventually reinforced with outright physical abuse, and at length, in her mind she deserves every bad thing done to her. She becomes a kicked dog, who only cringes and stays in place, waiting to be kicked some more. That's not you, Elisa. You have passion and courage. Enough courage to face what's really happening here."

He curled a finger around a lock of her hair. "What bothered you so much about what just happened? That your body took pleasure in it? Elisa, the body has no morality. It enjoys sex, food, sleep, a warm sunny day or rain pattering against the skin. The body is purest innocence in its impulses."

"No." She shook her head. "I understand all that, and maybe there's some of that, but it was more. I mean, you can read it from my mind, can't you?"

He cocked his head, his touch gliding down from her chin to her neck, thumb sliding along the carotid in a meditative motion, stroking that mark of his in a way that had the pulse jumping beneath his touch. "I'd like to hear it from your lips."

"Because how I choose to say it tells you things my mind can't."

His eyes crinkled with that faint smile. "Smart girl."

She sighed. She wanted to look away, but of course he wouldn't let her do that, made her hold his gaze. "Before, I could do it, because it was just one more thing. Let Mr. Collins lift my skirts, clean the china, dust the banister, make the beds. You know? It really didn't mean any more or less than any of the rest of it. But you made it mean something different. Well, you and Willis. You made it matter to me, who was doing it. How it made *me* feel. And that seems so selfish, so different from what I've been taught, but all I could think when all that was going on just now was how . . . alone I felt, all in my head. I've never felt that way when you've . . . done things to me. It seemed like my body was betraying me, saying awful things about who I really am, when I only want to feel that way with you."

She shivered. Shifting her, he shrugged off his jacket and wrapped it around her so she was snug inside it and it draped down to her knees. Bringing her close, he kissed her, something that started out warm and slow, then became heated so quickly she was gripping him hard with both hands when his head rose at last. "I like knowing you feel that way, Elisa. I like it very, very much."

She saw it, in that possessive male look he gave her, flashes of what he'd sent Lord Marshall and Christophe. It made her tremble, and when he recognized it, he stroked her abused muscles. "But you need to understand something else, Elisa. When you follow my commands and submit to such things, it fires my blood, because you are serving me without question, with trust. There's no greater gift a servant can give a vampire than that. You have awed me tonight.

"You could have acted like you were forcing yourself to swallow a medicine you knew you had to take for your own good. Instead, you gave yourself to the moment, took pleasure in it, let yourself get swept away by it. That's what a true submissive will do, if she believes it's her Master's will. And though I'm far beyond the gentle, beautiful feelings you and Willis had just started to share, watching you tonight, I was overwhelmed to have you in my life, bound to me as a third-mark. I have never wanted a woman at my side more than I want you to be there. You are brave, beautiful and mine. And the vampires in that room are quite aware that not a one of us could have done what you did tonight. That is the gift you give us. That you gave me."

He stopped, obviously feeling he'd gone over the line of usual vampire etiquette for expressing feelings, but Elisa was now the overwhelmed one. She'd be replaying those words in her head when she finally took herself off to bed.

When I finally take you off to bed, he amended.

The ripple of pleasure was real, a reinforcement. With a determined set of her chin, she rose then. Standing between his splayed thighs, she took the jacket off, but he surprised her. Sliding an arm around her waist, he pressed his cheek against her midriff, beneath the weight of her breasts. As he stayed that way for several moments, it gripped her heart. Resting her fingers on the shining ebony wings of his queued back hair, his coat held in her other hand, draped down his back, she bent over him, holding him to her.

"You may be a vampire," she said. "And some of this . . . it's what you feel. But it isn't how you feel it, or show it. You're different. I do know that. And that helps, too."

"It helps me that you know it." He rose then, her Master back, but she knew for certain they were in this together. It was a bolstering reminder that he was doing this for her.

"No. I'm doing this because of you, Elisa. What you showed all of us. We're doing it for them. For the fledglings."

As he put the coat back on, she helped him straighten it, smooth and brush off the shoulders. He tucked his shirttails deeper into his trousers, adjusted his belt. It was such a tempting male movement it made her hands itch to follow the same track. Lord in Heaven, as if she needed more of such activity. But then, she never seemed to get enough of him.

Determinedly, she gave herself a quick look in the mirror, taking the time to brush out her hair with the brush on the counter while he watched with quiet interest. Taking the brush from her when she got self-conscious, he finished it, making the curls shine like silk on her shoulders. "Leave it down. I like it this way."

It was silly, how it made her stomach flop, but it did. She couldn't smile, but the promise of it was in her heart. "I expect we should get back to the party, sir. God knows what they'll want to do next."

"I believe it's going to be charades." He tugged a lock of her hair. "Vampires enjoy their party games just like humans. And considering they use their servants . . . their very naked servants"—his gaze roved over her—"to handle the physical part of the game, it's very entertaining."

"You all have turned the corner," she informed him.

"Kangaroos loose in the top paddock?"

"A whole herd."

35

Gustav was right, though. Despite the fact the charades did result in Jonathan deciding he wanted his large servant to kneel in front of him and suck his cock there in front of everyone during after-dinner drinks, things were a little less intense. During Gustav's task, which he handled with remarkable grace for his size, his large hand gripping his Master's sizeable cock to take him deep in his throat, Elisa returned to Mal. Folding her legs beneath her, she sat at his knee on the floor while he, Lord Marshall and Cynthia discussed various issues. Their business interests, tidbits about the cat sanctuary. Jonathan threw in a comment here or there until his voice got strained and he moved to a corner. When they got there, instead of resuming, Gustav turned away from the vampire, bracing himself on hands and knees, putting his face to the floor so his Master could slam into him, fucking him to a fast completion.

While the three vampires talked, Elisa couldn't help but keep a fascinated eye on them under lowered lashes. Gustav's cock was enormous, leaking seed, the cock harness biting hard into his flesh. In the Viking's face, she saw the grip of mindless passion she was sure that had been on hers earlier, and knew he wasn't even aware of them anymore, only of his Master's desires. When Jonathan finished, Gustav straightened, pivoted on his knees once more and cleaned the vampire with the bowl of water, damp towel and soap brought by a quietly efficient servant. Afterward, Jonathan tucked himself back into his trousers and returned to the group, calling for another drink. Gustav, still hard and erect, returned to stand at the wall with Christophe, eyes down. Her pussy was aching and wet again.

Remarkable. She was going to have many things to discuss with Dev, next time she saw him. Or maybe not. For all that he was approachable, Dev was station manager after all, next in charge after Danny herself.

Be sure and ask if he's ever had to pantomime The Wizard of Oz *as a charade choice.*

You are an evil man. You just wanted to see me skip arm in arm with Christophe and see all sorts of . . . things . . . move.

At least on you. Of course, I think that's when Kreager started getting worked up again.

It didn't seem to work you up.

Mal took a sip of the iced tea he'd been brought. As he did, he closed his other hand over hers and casually brought her palm to his lap, resting it on the sizeable erection his seated position, the shadowed lighting and his tailored trousers were hiding. She drew in a breath, but he tightened his hand over hers, moved her palm in a slow glide down the full length, until she could feel the firm nest of testicles at the base. *If I wanted to take you on all fours right here, just like Gustav, you would do it without hesitation, wouldn't you?*

Yes. Her gaze lifted to his, then swept down, but not before she saw the fierce satisfaction in his face, felt an answering response to it in her own body.

Good. But next time I take you, I want to have you all to myself. When we are alone, near dawn, I plan to possess you quite fiercely. You might be a little sore from earlier, but I'll relish that, easing into you, hearing you whimper but seeing the desire in your eyes to take all of me, feel me come where Christophe did, burning that memory away . . .

Will you do it that way because I'm yours, your property?

His gaze stilled upon her. She wasn't sure what her expression was, since she hardly knew what she was feeling, but she held her breath until he responded.

And if my answer is yes?

She stared back at him. Then her eyes lowered once more, her other hand curling on her thigh. As incomprehensible as it might be, she knew her answer, down to the level of her soul.

Good.

She could feel the slipperiness of her pussy against her calf, folded beneath her. Cynthia turned an amused eye to Mal, her nostrils flaring. "Whatever conversation you're having seems to be affecting your servant. Would that we could all listen in." Her gaze lingered on Elisa's hand, still curled over Mal's cock, defining it in the pants. Despite having just climaxed, Kreager had a similar avidity to his gaze.

Mal put Elisa's hand aside with a reassuring squeeze and gave a faint, disarming smile, but it was Lord Marshall who came to the rescue. "You've been doing your own teasing, Cynthia. Christophe's cock hasn't taken a rest from its high position most of the night. Same goes for your servant, Jonathan."

"I find the cock harness keeps his mind focused there." Jonathan shrugged, but glanced fondly back at Gustav. However, Elisa noted a bit of challenge in the look that suggested Gustav's mind was not as docile as his actions suggested. "He's a bear to manage when he's not reined in, but when I take it off at dawn, he fair explodes."

Cynthia gave him a feral smile. "Now you're just teasing me. Perhaps we will swap servants at dawn, Jonathan. I'd like to try handling your bear. And I know you can scarcely contain your interest in my pretty servant."

"A negotiation we can save for the drive back home." Jonathan flashed fang at her. "We don't want to make others of our group feel excluded."

Lord Marshall gave a dry chuckle, though Elisa noted the humor sounded a bit forced. "I've no problem leaving such activity to the two of you. Malachi and I have some business to conduct before the dawn hour, and given his earlier protectiveness, I expect he cannot wait to have his servant safely away from you both."

During the exchange, household staff freshened their drinks. Katrine met Elisa's gaze, gave her a nod. It had been strange and unsettling at first, domestic servants coming and going while she knelt naked at Mal's feet, but Elisa found she was almost getting used to it. In fact, with him stroking her hair, occasionally teasing the line of her shoulder, she almost felt . . . Well, *comfortable* wasn't the best word, but she wasn't as unsettled as she'd been before. Gustav, Mal, even Cynthia and Jonathan, maybe had been right. Something in her, with him as her Master, worked with this. It was probably best not to think too much further on it. At least tonight.

The night was drawing to a blissful close. The staff had brought in coffee. When Mal chose a dark Colombian, he lifted Elisa's wrist to his mouth, nuzzled her there, a sensual warning before he pricked her gently, drained some of her blood into the cup, flavoring the brew. She saw that Cynthia had done the same, bringing Christophe forward so he pressed against the back of her chair, his arm over her shoulder, forearm resting with casual intimacy on it. She dipped her head to rub against his skin after she made the puncture.

For all that she'd just experienced, and even what she'd experienced up to now with Mal, this was still the most intimate thing about being his servant, because it was the one thing that was never shared. Since third-marking her, Mal would only use her blood for nourishment, only allow her to provide for his needs in this way. To be able to bring pleasure to his life, protection, sustenance . . . Elisa shivered as if his breath had moved over her skin. It really would be better if she thought about this at some other time, when she wasn't in some half-dream state, in the middle of a decadent, macabre fairy tale in the altogether.

As if to underscore it, she'd apparently lost the last thirty minutes, half dozing under Mal's fondling touch, a languid state of arousal. Cynthia and Jonathan were rising, making their farewells to the other two vampires. Christophe and Gustav were given leave to retrieve their clothes. As they left the room, Elisa was surprised both paused to give her a friendly glance, a nod of good-bye. She gave the same back, finding it easy to put warmth in her expression. It had been very strange, all of it, but they'd done their level best to help her get through it, and she couldn't help but think well of them for it.

Mal rose to join Marshall in escorting them all to the front drive, but the pressure of his hand on her shoulder told her he wanted her to stay where she was. *Marshall and I will likely talk in his office a few minutes before we come back in here. Relax, and enjoy the view. If you're hungry or thirsty, the staff will come in and ask if you need anything after the vampires are gone.*

I'm fine, Master. She was still floating, still in this curious world where she almost wanted to be naked, kneeling at his chair, waiting for his next command, so she could do whatever he desired. It was really all so odd . . .

She laid her head on the side of his chair where his hand had been braced, feeling the warmth. When she woke tomorrow, she'd be horrified with herself, wondering what had happened to the Elisa of a day ago, and how they'd managed to unlock this room inside herself she didn't want to close. Right now, though, she didn't want to think at all.

With his uncanny intuition, had Mal suspected who might come into that room once it was devoid of vampires? Someone who also perhaps wanted to absorb the warmth of the Master she loved, where she could safely do so? In truth, when Nadia slipped into the conservancy, Elisa wasn't surprised at all to see her.

From her shadowed corner, she watched the woman go to the windows, stare out, but she trailed her fingers over the headrest of the chair that Marshall had occupied, then pressed her palm there, even as she continued to look out at the waterway, the wavering lights.

Modesty and self-consciousness returned in full force. Nadia wore a dark blue dress, nothing provocative about it. It only emphasized her thin paleness. However, it was obvious that in full health, the woman was stunning, the type of beauty like Lady Danny that would turn a man's head all the way around like an owl.

"He missed having you with him tonight." The impulsive words were the first that came to Elisa's tongue.

Nadia fair jumped out of her skin, her head whipping around, eyes wide. Elisa cursed herself. With Nadia being a third-mark, Elisa had assumed the woman would detect her immediately. Another sign Marshall's servant was not at all well.

Nadia cleared her throat then, but made a visible effort to appear composed and courteous to one of her Master's guests. "I didn't see you there." As she took in Elisa's state of undress, her face tightened. "It appears my lord and his visitors were well entertained."

"He didn't . . ." Elisa bit her lip, knowing it wasn't supposed to be the same with vampires and their servants as with monogamous couples, but then decided to hang it. She'd proceed with what *she* would want to know, if it was about Mal. "He didn't participate. He just watched."

Nadia studied her a long moment. However, instead of easing the set of her shoulders, she suddenly clenched her hands into fists, folded them across her body and stared back out the windows. "It would have been better if he'd fucked all of you. Then he won't come to my bed . . . needing."

Elisa swallowed. This woman was third-marked, so her vampire master obviously knew her thoughts. During that avoided kiss earlier, Elisa had registered only the physical act. She hadn't thought about Lord Marshall receiving the double blow of knowing what went through his servant's mind as she recoiled from him. However, even with just instinct going for her, Elisa wasn't picking up revulsion. Instead, it was fear.

It was so obvious, she knew that Lord Marshall must know it as well. And there was no way, short of taking the woman by force, to get around such a fear. For all his ruthless desire at dinner, she hadn't sensed that kind of cruelty in him.

Nadia was terrified she'd lose a part of her heart again. Or that she'd already lost it for good.

"Did he tell you why we came?"

Nadia sighed. Running a tremulous hand over her face, she gave her limp hair a harsh tug. Turning away from the window, she sat on the arm of the chair where Lord Marshall had been, as if that was her normal place. Her palm molded over the place his hand would have rested, as if absorbing the touch she wanted but couldn't accept. "Yes. That you and . . . I'm sorry; there's a robe in the closet there. Would you mind putting it on?"

Gladly, Elisa thought, practically scampering over there. It was a woman's robe, perhaps one Nadia kept here as an extra. She could well imagine her stretched out with Lord Marshall, having long, erotic encounters in front of that glass wall that looked out over the water, in the darkness where the boats couldn't see. The robe would be for when they walked to the end of that dock hand in hand . . . Or were such romantic ideas about vampires and their servants foolish?

"I'm sorry," Nadia said. "You're quite lovely. I mean no insult. I just . . . It's all so unbearable sometimes. I shouldn't be talking to you like this."

"I'd much rather you talk to me like this than treat me like a guest,"

Elisa said honestly. "I'm worried about my two boys, and I'd rather us speak plain about them. It's one thing if Lord Marshall wants them, but I'm more concerned if *you* want them."

Before Nadia could reply, they heard footsteps coming down the hall, along with Lord Marshall's voice.

"No apology needed, Malachi. For one thing, I know you'd damn sure do it again, and with more force if needed." There was wry humor in the tone. "You need something from me, but you were only prepared to go so far to get it. If she'd truly been near breaking, you would have cut your losses and figured out another option. You have principles, which explains why you stay on your island. There's not a lot of room for such nonsense in our world. Jonathan and Cynthia can become somewhat tiresome at times, particularly Jonathan, but they're young. Not much older than you, but you have more self-possession, which tells me you've learned a few things they haven't yet. But you don't get on my nerves by acting like you know every damn thing, either."

"No, my lord," Mal said in a neutral voice. *And I heard that, Elisa. What? I was just saying he doesn't know you that well yet.*

As they entered the room, Mal gave her a look that promised retribution, but then he nodded, drawing the overlord's attention to Nadia. Apparently, Lord Marshall had been as lost in his head as Nadia, for he looked as startled to see her there as Nadia had been to see Elisa.

When Nadia's Master looked toward her, it was like seeing a person who'd had half of himself amputated stare hungrily at that other half, far beyond his reach, while he slowly bled out on the floor. Nadia's yearning was no less painful, for all that her eyes remained downcast, her fingers dug into the chair arm.

It wasn't that difficult to understand, Elisa realized. She'd met parents in the bush who'd lost children. It was so hard for them to come back together over it, because the grief was so sharp and deep they could barely handle it themselves, let alone comfort each other. This couple had lost three. Were she and Mal going to make it worse, or better? Was this a mistake?

No. She trusted Mal's intuition. When he took a seat in a chair near Lord Marshall's, she came to him. As he ran a finger over the robe's lapel, she registered his amusement at how it dragged the ground at her ankles. Before she could make a face at him, discreetly of course, he pulled her down on the chair arm.

After a moment's pause, Lord Marshall had taken his own chair. Nadia didn't move from the perch that mirrored Elisa's, but her body quivered as if undecided whether to stay or go. Glancing at his servant, Marshall laid his arm on the rest, settling his hand just above her knee. He didn't push back the fabric of the skirt, so Nadia didn't get the full impact of the heat of his palm, the press of his fingers into her flesh, the way Elisa did when Mal automatically slid the robe out of his way to clasp her thigh.

But Nadia at least accepted the hint of intimate contact. A promising sign, to Elisa's way of thinking.

36

"So tell us more about these fledglings and why you think I can provide them a safe haven," Marshall said, making a visible effort to focus on Mal.

With a courteous nod, Mal began. He reviewed the fledglings' circumstances, how they'd come to be at the sanctuary. He'd sent Lord Marshall that information and discussed it with him briefly over the phone, but now he gave him more detail, answered questions. While Elisa understood why he had to explain the violent catalyst that had sent the fledglings to his sanctuary as a last resort, Lord Marshall's brief look toward her, as well as Nadia's, was a little difficult. Particularly when Mal mentioned how she was violated and Willis was killed. But then he was past that part and she could relax again. Somewhat.

"After spending time with them, I believe the devolving bloodlust shown by the three boys has to do with how they were turned. The others have periodic bouts, but they are little different from what you see in vampires when they are first turned. Their age may keep the transition from ever fully completing, but I think it will be no worse than managing a human's problem with epilepsy, particularly in a controlled environment. However, my gut feeling is that the transition will eventually conclude for those four; it will just take longer."

As Mal discussed the progress the children had made since they'd first arrived, Nadia rose, moved back to the windows, staring out at the night. When she sank into her lady's chair there, curling her feet under her, Lord Marshall glanced her way, his mouth tightening, but he gestured to Mal to continue.

Elisa listened for a few moments, but her eyes were on the woman, her attention flickering between that and the changes in Lord Marshall's attitude. He'd gone from somewhat interested to politely allowing Mal to say his piece. It was clear that the key to his acceptance of William and Matthew was the woman who was now tuning them out.

Making a murmured apology, as if she needed a bathroom break, Elisa slipped out of the room. She hurried to her guest room, a smaller room adjacent to Mal's. Retrieving the item she wanted, she trotted back to the study, holding up the robe so she didn't trip over it.

"It's a fucked situation, all the way around, Mal," Lord Marshall said as she came back in. "It sounds like you've got a good handle on it. I'm not sure why you don't keep them down there, rather than throwing them out to the wolves like this."

"For the same reason I rehabilitate as many of my cats as possible to be released into their intended habitats. It's the way it's supposed to be, allowing them to maximize their full potential."

"What about your cats that came to you from people's homes as pets, or circuses, where they've performed for years? How many of those can be rehabilitated into the wild?"

"Very few," Mal acknowledged. "Because what they were intended to be was so twisted it is very difficult to find their way back to Nature."

"And vampires whose growth is forever stunted so they'll never look older than children? Wouldn't they be the same?"

It was always the same argument. Elisa bit down on her tongue, knowing she had no place to interrupt the two vampires, and would only make things worse if the perception was that Mal had no control over his own servant. But it was so difficult. More difficult now than even before, because after spending these past weeks seeing things through Mal's learned eyes, she knew they were terribly valid points.

But she'd seen things he hadn't—he'd as much as said so, and that was why he was here. He believed this was the right course to pursue.

So instead of getting frustrated by the topic, she slid around the two males, over to where Nadia was, and took a seat on the carpet next to her chair, opening the drawing pad on her lap.

"I've taken to sketching the cats to help me keep track of things about them," she said, low, glancing up at the woman's face. "You and Lord Marshall should come visit there. It's truly an amazing place. There are over a hundred wild cats." She held up the pad. "These are cheetah cubs. You've probably seen them, but I'd never seen one outside a book. To me, they look very different from most cats. Almost more like fuzzy baboons, without the red backsides."

Giving a tired, vague smile, Nadia leaned forward and picked up the sketchbook to politely peruse the pictures. Elisa rose behind her, bracing her hands on the chair back so her knuckles grazed Nadia's thin shoulders. The woman shivered, and Elisa automatically began to draw back, but her hands were seized, the album almost toppling from Nadia's lap. "No, don't move them," she whispered.

The poor girl was literally starved for touch. Elisa recalled then how much Mal had touched her since he marked her. He never left the kitchen in the morning without grazing her body with his own, or kissing her, sliding a palm over her backside, a hip, the line of her throat. Tonight, no more than a few minutes at a time went by without him stroking or caressing her, and she didn't feel it was all for her own reassurance. During dinner, Cynthia and Jonathan had touched their servants frequently. And the yearning between Marshall and Nadia for it was palpable.

Mal had shown her that lions liked tactile communication, almost more than any other cat species. They rubbed faces and bodies together frequently. For all that they were solitary, vampires apparently had that in common, even if only with their servants. And their servants quickly became dependent on it, or perhaps were already naturally inclined to crave it. Without prompting, she began to rub her palms in slow circles along the tops of Nadia's bony shoulders. "See the next one? Turn the page there."

When Nadia did, the woman glanced back up at Elisa. "That's not a cat."

"Actually, it is. It looks like something between a sloth and a bear, doesn't it? It's called a binturong, and when it passes gas, it smells like fresh popcorn. I told Mal it must have done something that the Creator liked, since he gets a nicer smell than most of us get."

A tiny chuckle hitched the woman's shoulders, and Elisa moved from there to her neck. The shiver had a different component, one she well understood herself. She unbound Nadia's hair from the ribbon that held it, unfurled it over her shoulders and began to comb through it with her fingers, taking time over the scalp, with a slow massage of the fragile line of skull. She loved it when Mal stroked her head, and Nadia seemed to respond the same way, tilting into the touch while she turned the next couple pages. As she did, Elisa explained various more tidbits about the cats. She even shared Mal's leopard story in an even lower tone, making Nadia chuckle again. Since she knew Mal could hear everything if he chose, and Lord Marshall, too, the low tone was mainly courtesy to the males' conversation.

She tightened her fingers on Nadia's scalp, a brief pause, as the woman's fingers pinched up the next page. "The next sketches are of the fledglings. If you don't want to look, you don't have to, but I didn't want you to feel like I was trying to trick you."

Nadia paused, her head inclining briefly. As she stared at the last page of cats, considering her next move, Elisa continued to stroke through the long blond strands. While not as thick and lustrous right now, it made her think of Danny's hair. She'd sometimes brushed her lady's hair before she went to bed, particularly if Dev had to be out on the station early mornings to go deal with the herd or check things with the hands. But she'd seen him sit on the top porch step at night, Danny leaning back between his knees while he did this, a firm scalp stroke that trailed off into the loose tresses. Sometimes he'd curl them around his callused fingers and tug.

Elisa paused, realizing the relationship she kept using as a guide of how a relationship should be involved a vampire and her servant, rather than a husband and wife. It was a startling yet undeniable fact. Before she could figure out how to react to that, Nadia drew her attention again.

"Why would you be so honest?" the woman asked, not lifting her head.

"Because I care about them." The answer was simple and straightforward. "Mal's taken in cats that were pushed off onto someone who felt reluctantly obligated to try and help, and the cats often end up in equally bad circumstances again. This isn't a pair of dresses I'm asking someone to take off my hands because I don't have the heart to throw them away myself. They're chil—young vampires, with feelings and thoughts, who've had such a crook time of it they don't trust anything good in their lives. Even if the best they can ever do is me and Mal's island, as long as he'll let us stay there, they'll know they're cared for and wanted. But they deserve better if we can get it for them."

Nadia turned the page. "Oh. He's beautiful, isn't he?"

"Yes. That's Jeremiah." Elisa swallowed over the sudden thickness in her throat. "As you heard Mal say, he's not doing so well right now, but he's really the closest thing they have to a leader. He's so serious and thoughtful. His eyes can get red at times, but when they're not, they're like that perfect gray-green a field has in midsummer. His hair is the color of fresh straw, but so thick and silky. He'd have been a very handsome man, one of those with a smile that makes a girl think of doing foolish things. And he is so brave, Nadia. The incident Mal spoke of . . . where we lost Leonidas. It was Jeremiah who took his life, though you could tell it tore up something so deep inside him to do it."

"Well, of course." Nadia traced the boy's face on the page. "If they've been through all this together, and they were turned close to the same time, then he got to see Leonidas when he wasn't . . . beyond help. He not only had to watch Leonidas lose his grip on any semblance of control; he had to be the one who ended it for him. As truly awful as that was for Leonidas, can you imagine how Jeremiah felt, watching it unfold?"

"To know you can do nothing to fix the suffering of someone you care about?" Elisa leaned down, putting her temple against Nadia's. She slid her arms around the woman, laid her hands over her cold fingers on Jeremiah's face. "Yes," she whispered. "Because I see it in your lord's face, each time he looks at you."

Though becoming a servant might incite greater pleasure in those casual caresses, Elisa had always loved the familiarity of touch. Strokes, hugs, lying side by side with another warm body at night. If Dev had to be out at the dawn hours, Danny sometimes impulsively pulled Elisa into the bed with her. Curling around her maid, she held her softness close. It was mildly arousing, for Danny's hands tended to drift over a throat, trace a curve of breast, or rest on the rounded part of a hip, but it mainly confirmed connection, a sense of belonging that Elisa had welcomed.

One or two remarkable times, when Dev had come to his Mistress in the morning hours, usually after working long hours, Danny had bid her stay. He'd stripped down to his shorts and then coiled around them both. When he held them close, dropping into exhausted slumber to Danny's tender amusement, Elisa had felt nearly content. Had they been teaching her even then?

She thought about Gustav and Christophe, who hadn't known her at all, but put her more at ease with their calm contact and provocative embraces before they led her into such intense play with their vampires. And now Nadia, not finding it at all odd to allow Elisa to touch her this way. She even tilted her head, inviting Elisa to press her lips to her throat, to brush along the pumping artery. Elisa saw a faint imprint, knew that was where Lord Marshall must feed most often. When she touched the tip of her tongue there, Nadia quivered in the loose grip of her arms.

Then Nadia turned a page and there were William and Matthew. Since the incident with Leonidas, Mal had let the two share communal enclosure time. In this sketch, they'd been playing keep-away. They'd wrestled over the ball until William got it away and sat on the younger boy, a smug look on his face. Matthew had snarled and then subsided, giving him an annoyed but accepting expression. Elisa had drawn the pose, though it had to be from memory. In less than two seconds, when William's guard dropped, Matthew had bucked him off and they'd been at it again.

She described the scene to Nadia, continuing to nuzzle at her throat, partly because Nadia seemed to like it so much, and because Elisa herself was unexpectedly enjoying it. At this moment, it was as if she had become Gustav or Christophe, taking the lead, Nadia submitting to her caresses willingly. It had a lovely, intriguing quality to it, primarily because she imagined how Mal would enjoy watching her do this with another woman at his behest, two female bodies twined together. Had she really just had that thought? There probably weren't enough Hail Marys and Our Fathers to cover that sinful idea.

"Their fangs won't pull back?" Nadia asked, her breath a little short.

"It's such a shame, because they're so lovely otherwise. It must make them terribly self-conscious."

"It does at times. Nerida chipped one of hers on a rock one day by accident and the chip didn't fill in as it would with normal vampire healing powers. It made Mal think that we could try filing them back, which wouldn't interfere with the marking glands. There's a vampire scientist he's inviting to the island, and if he comes, he'll see if he has any ideas about that. If the boys came here before then," Elisa spoke carefully, casually, "I'm sure Mal could arrange for Lord Brian to include you on his visit."

As she straightened, she slid her hands at Nadia's waist up so her knuckles were pressed underneath the woman's bosom. Before she could change to a more appropriate position, Nadia caught hold of one of the hands, turned it slowly, discreetly, so it was molded around her right breast, her thumb pressing against the nipple that was so tight and needy Elisa felt an answering response in her own breasts.

The men continued their conversation without interruption, but Mal told her what she already suspected. *Marshall is following his servant's response like a starving lion, Elisa. Don't stop. It's helping them both. Sweet, clever girl.*

It wasn't so much cleverness as intuition, a desire to help, but the compliment made her glow, so she wouldn't argue it. She teased the nipple gently, squeezed the curve in a way that made the woman tremble and gave Elisa a spike in arousal again. She'd been pleasantly flustered by Danny's more sexual caresses, but hadn't ever instigated them herself. It didn't do for her what touching Mal did. However, Nadia's silent urgency, her barely disguised need, was intoxicating. And heartbreaking.

Nadia lifted her attention from the sketch pad back to the window. A boat outlined in its own running lights was drifting by, like a small constellation against the dark water. "Do you know I carried this last one long enough to produce milk? I mean, it's odd, because vampire infants don't drink milk. If the mother is vampire, she feeds them from a puncture wound on her breast, so the baby can still bond through the breast-feeding. If the mother is human, like me, you mix one part of your human milk with two parts of the father's blood. There are those who say that the milk isn't really necessary, it's just there to make the servant feel like a part of it, but I think they're wrong."

She shifted the book closed, though Elisa noted her hand stayed as a marker on the page with William and Matthew. "Marshall had a midwife come and pump out my milk, because those first few days I just lay there like I was dead. It had to be done often. Milk just trickled out and soured on the linens. One night, he came to me like a ghost in the night, when all I thought I wanted was my tears, and he put his mouth there and suckled me." Nadia swallowed hard, telling Elisa the woman was silently weeping. "I felt his tears as well, dropping on my breasts in the darkness. He was gone once it was light. But not because of the sunlight. He stays away because I've made him stay away, and yet I want him so close as well. How do you explain a woman's heart to a male at a time like this, when even we don't understand it? How can I love him more than breath and yet hate him and the whole world at the same time?"

Her voice was a bare whisper. Elisa wondered if she knew her Master was listening to every syllable. She thought she heard a falter in Marshall's conversation with Mal, absorbing the blow of those words.

Elisa slid around to her side, pulling up a straight chair. Pressing her leg against Nadia's, she put her arm around the taller woman's shoulders and took her other hand. "Sometimes life is so horribly cruel that none of us can make sense of any of it. You need to give yourselves time. When something awful happens, sometimes we're like children. We want it to be fixed and all better right away. We want it to make sense. But things like this . . . Oh lovey, there is no why to it. It was a truly horrible thing. I don't think anything will ever make up for what you've lost. But we all have to go on."

Nadia opened the book again, looked down at the album. "I don't want them to be a substitute. That wouldn't work, and it's not fair."

"I don't think that would happen. They're not babies, and as much as I fall into calling them children, which aggravates Mal, I know they're not. They're young vampires that need home, family. Protectors."

"Do you think they would need me?"

"Without question." Elisa was sure of that one. She squeezed Nadia's hands, met her gaze head-on. "The way they bonded to me, they remember their mothers, if only as a ghost in their minds. I think they'll need that, as well as Lord Marshall's firm hand and kindness, to feel like they can make it in the world . . . and maybe they'll help you, too." She drew a breath. "I lost someone so dear to me, in a most horrible way. If I hadn't had the care of these childr—fledglings, I wouldn't have seen the point of anything.

"As many hideous things as I've seen happen to people, even if I can't explain most times why they happen—though sometimes I can, when they're worthless bludgers"—she gave her a quick, teasing nudge—"one thing I've seen happen, over and over. A person figures out how to deal with it, and down the road, they appreciate the good things again. It's not some big, miraculous moment, and it always takes far longer than we expect. Just all of a sudden, one day, they realize they enjoyed sitting out in a spot of sunshine, or something made them laugh that hadn't made them laugh in a while. Or they reach out and touch someone they haven't, just because they want to do so and it feels good."

Nadia glanced over her shoulder, to the profile of her Master. "He can't wait that long. He'll have to put me aside." In her voice, Elisa could hear how that would be the final coffin nail. Nadia wouldn't survive that. She'd beg for death instead.

Elisa put her other hand over Nadia's, squeezed hard enough that the woman's eyes came back to her. "He won't. I've been in your house less than a day, and I can tell how that man feels about you. You may be his servant, but you're his heart. And it's broken. All he wants is the chance to fix it, to bandage it, and make it better for you. Let him in, and don't be afraid. I'd lay money he'll stick by you, no matter how long it takes."

"How good a gambler are you?"

"I usually win money at the station house races." Elisa gave her a wink. "I know what horse has the most heart, the one that will bust his arse to win."

Nadia let out a strangled hiccup of a chuckle, but then her gaze lifted, went back to her vampire. Elisa saw that heavy yearning come back into her eyes, the one she'd had when she sat on his chair arm alone, rubbing the place where his hand had been before. Need was overflowing in the woman's face, like the tears that were still making slow tracks down her face.

Marshall stopped in midsentence, looked toward her. "Everything all right?" he asked quietly.

She shook her head. "But things don't feel awful right now."

He seemed to mull that over, glancing at Elisa. "I'm glad to hear that," he said carefully.

"My lord . . ." Nadia pushed out of the chair, almost stumbling, but Elisa steadied her with a hand, catching the book as it fell from her lap. Marshall rose immediately, but Nadia drew herself up, pale and fragile there, outlined by the windows. Her body was starting to shake, the woman like a dam near breaking.

"I need you to take me to your bed. I need you to hold me while I cry out a thousand tears. Maybe a million. And I need you to be inside of me, holding me so close, so that I don't break into pieces and blow away like glass shards. I'm so frightened, but I need you not to take no for an answer. I am dying inside of my head, and I need you to be the Master you've always been to me. You've been gentle, but I need your ruthlessness too."

As her voice faltered, her eyes lowering, Elisa had the rare treat of seeing a vampire look poleaxed. "I hope you can make sense of all that in my mind, because I can't explain it better than that. I'll probably need to go through that over and over again for a while, because I'm not sure if tomorrow will be better, or the next day. But I want to find those better days, and I can only do that with you. Please . . ." Her voice broke. "Please don't give up on me. Don't set me aside. Elisa says you won't, but—"

In a blink too fast for Elisa to follow, Marshall was there, pulling Nadia against his chest and wrapping his arms around her. "I will never allow you to be anywhere I'm not. Not ever. Even if you begged for death, I would go into the sun before I let you be without me. I cannot bear your pain."

Inches away from them both, Elisa was caught up in that fierce declaration, her body transfixed by the harsh truth of it. There was only one word that covered it, but she wasn't brave or strong enough to say it in her mind. It was too close to her own painful yearnings.

When Mal's fingertips grazed her shoulder, she let him draw her away. Though her mind was still reeling with it, she had the presence of mind to leave the sketchbook on the sofa, exchanging a significant look with him.

As they gave the couple their privacy, Elisa knew the impression they'd made on her mind would linger for quite a while—the puzzle of vampires and servants, love and submission. Was three hundred years, the normal life span of a full servant, long enough to figure it all out? And was that what she wanted?

37

"I THINK I could have simply sent you as an emissary and stayed home where I didn't have to wear a damn suit." Mal stretched like a lazy cat, comfortable again in his jeans and T-shirt.

To Elisa's combined joy and anxiety, Lord Marshall had asked them to stay an extra couple days, and started talking about the logistics and timing for him and Nadia to visit William and Matthew at the island. If all went well there, they'd bring them to Florida for a trial period. Fortunately, those two days had not involved any other vampire visitors, and Lord Marshall had been content to keep their evening social engagements to simple, easy things. The four of them played cards, walked along the private waterway boardwalk, and viewed slide shows of Marshall and Nadia's travels to Egypt and Greece. In an entirely vampirelike way, Elisa nevertheless felt like they'd discovered their first friends as a couple.

During one of their evenings together, Marshall had mentioned a pavilion on the beach that had carnival rides and other attractions. Picking up on Elisa's excitement about it, Mal had decided he'd take her there for their last night in Florida. Marshall had an early evening engagement off premises and Nadia had surprised them all, asking if she could accompany him. For her part, Elisa was relieved that Mal had graciously declined when Marshall gave them the choice of coming along.

So here her Master was, driving her to the carnival. As he parked the car Marshall had loaned them, Mal enchanted her by opening her door for her and taking her hand, like any other young couple. Mal looked young, after all.

"I'm young for a vampire."

"Well, to the rest of us, being over a hundred years old is a little long in the tooth." Elisa slanted him a glance. "Truly."

He grinned at her, giving a quick flash of those long fangs before he tucked them away. "So, Ferris wheel first?"

She looked up at the brightly colored lights, and wanted to go that way eventually, but knowing she was here at his indulgence, first she wanted to see the one thing that interested her the most. "How about the carousel? Willis was starting to teach me to ride a horse, so I can show you a few things."

"The things I'd like you to show me would likely scandalize our audience," he noted, watching the children running past, parents in tow.

"Well, the adults maybe. The children are too young. They'd just think adults are silly and disgusting and go about their business." She gave him a smile as he paid for their tickets. Her skin tingled under his regard. She and Nadia had shopped yesterday and Nadia had insisted on buying her a pretty yellow sundress with a low bodice and slim straps on her otherwise bare shoulders. From the moment she put it on it was clear her vampire master liked it. She'd worn the canvas sneakers he'd decorated for her, those protective cougar eyes blinking at her. Other than that, she'd worn no other adornments. She had no jewelry, and in truth preferred to keep her neck bare, because even when he wasn't hungry he had a delicious habit of sometimes brushing his lips over her nape, a provocative tease.

"Elisa, you can take your time here," he told her, pocketing the tickets. "I'm not going to drag you back to the house the second I get bored. I like a carnival, too."

She flushed a little. "This was just a really nice thing to do. It's . . ."

"No one's ever taken you somewhere just because *you* wanted to go." He slid his knuckles along her cheek, his dark eyes searching her face. "Though I'm not pleased to hear that, I'm glad to be the first to do that for you. You can thank me by not worrying about the time, or whether we need to be doing something else. I am commanding you to have fun. That's the only thing you're allowed to do. In fact . . ."

He gestured to the left, at a tent hung with souvenirs and pretty trinkets, including a variety of shell bracelets and necklaces. "Before we go to the carousel, we need to get you some jewelry."

"If you get me one, Kohana will want one, too. You know he gets terribly jealous about such things."

Mal gave her a sidelong look, but picked one out, paid the vendor. She noted the man gave them a narrow appraisal before taking Mal's money, but Mal met his gaze. Something in his expression was apparently unsettling enough that the vendor cleared his throat and became occupied with getting them change.

She realized that, between her time with Danny and on the island, it had completely slipped her mind how people would react to seeing an Indian man and a white woman together as a couple. Of course, vampires were very fair-minded, in a sense. They didn't discriminate between black, white, yellow, red—they considered all humans inferior. Among their own kind, prejudice existed between made and born vampires, but power and strength were the main determinants of the respect a vampire was owed from his or her own kind. Of course, that wasn't just the case with vampires. The vendor's intimidated response proved that.

It will be fine, Elisa. Unfortunately, most Indians that these humans know look poor and disheveled. And they're usually drunk. I'm confusing enough that they'll think I'm some exotic race from overseas, and you're a pretty servant girl temporarily taken with my foreign ways.

She knew that would help. It might be far different if he were a colored man out with a white woman of wealth or breeding.

The world is full of nonsense. Don't worry about it. It will not interfere with your enjoyment of the fair, atsilusgi. *I promise you that.* At the dangerous glint of his gaze, a hint of fang, she believed him.

"Turn around," he said.

Obeying, she held her hair off her neck. He'd wanted her to wear it down, so she'd only tied a wide yellow ribbon around it to keep it out of her face. He brought the string of pale white shells down in front of her eyes. It had a pendant of blue glass, worn to smoothness by the ocean waves. *A blue that matches your eyes.* When he brought it to her throat, she realized it was a choker. As he hooked the fastener, it pulled snugly against her throat.

Everything in her went still and expectant, her body, mind and other, deeper parts of herself recognizing the significance of him choosing that type of adornment, even if just a trinket. An additional hold upon her, overlaying that flower and fang mark on the side of her neck. Her mind immediately went to Gustav, that collar on his throat, the way it ran down to his . . .

I don't think my servant needs quite as much restraint as all that. But I do like the way this looks on her. When he turned her around, his tone stayed light, but the look in his gaze told her, thrillingly, that she wasn't mistaken. "Now, while you wear this, you are only allowed to think about what you want to do here, whatever will make you happy."

Being with him. Every minute.

She didn't let herself look away, giving the thought free rein to be out there between them, because she couldn't hide it anyway. She wouldn't even try. He held her gaze an extra moment, his fingers strong and sure on hers. "Let's go to that carousel," he said at last.

She knew exactly which horse she wanted, the minute they got close enough to see them. After Mal handed over their tickets, she went right to a galloping black charger who looked like hellfire could come out of his nostrils. He was far taller than herself. The one next to it was a white pony with pink ribbons and blue flowers. Considering it sourly, Mal sighed and lifted her onto the charger. He caressed the line of her panties through the skirt, a discreet stroke through the silky garment he'd decided to let her to wear today. Then he threw his leg over the pommel of the white pony, seating himself and wiggling his arse in a prissy, princess kind of way. It made the children nearby laugh. It made her laugh, too.

It was a different side of him, for sure, but one she liked immensely. She'd seen him playful with his cats, but there was a seriousness to that, for of course cub play was also learning hunting skills. She wondered sometimes if humans were the only ones who could afford to play for the sheer, foolish joy of it, no skills involved. But apparently, her vampire remembered some of the way of it.

"If only vampires could be photographed. I'll have to draw a picture for Kohana and the rest."

"It will be hard to do that with your hands bound around your back from now until forever," he threatened, but with a heated glance that reminded her just what he liked to do to her when her hands were bound behind her back.

Then the carousel started. As her horse started to go way, way up, she gave a happy little shriek, much like the other children. Mal's went up only a foot or so, such that his long legs stayed well-grounded through the heels of his boots. Watching him with laughter in her heart, Elisa realized something else. She'd remembered Willis teaching her to ride the horse without thinking about what had happened to him, the first time she'd ever done that.

Perhaps it wasn't only Nadia taking steps back toward what life could be, new possibilities, rather than what she'd dreamed she'd always wanted.

～

Mal watched her cling to the charger's reins, giving herself to the same joy as the children. Despite how hard life often could be for cats in the wild, when a good meal was taken, or an optimal spot of shade found, all was well with them. There was time to play with cubs, groom, doze in that boneless cat way. They embraced those good moments because in Nature, to dwell on the bad was to waste them.

He'd never seen a human pull it off. Human or vampire, they all seemed to get caught in the psychology of their memories, those terrible events that had happened to them. Some would say animals lacked sufficient depth of intelligence to appreciate how terrible the world could be. Some would say the same of Elisa, seeing only a domestic's limited vision, her apparent obliviousness to what her world could have been if all these terrible things hadn't happened to her, or if she hadn't been born in the circumstances she had.

He didn't see that. He saw a woman who refused to let any of it knock her down, and was so resolved in it she managed to spread it to those around her. Their second night here, Nadia had joined them for their early dinner. There'd been faint color in her cheeks, and a cautious warmth and intimacy had been obvious between her and Marshall. He thought of the fledglings, how they looked to Elisa for meaning in their lives. How Danny had been willing to go to extraordinary lengths for the girl. And he had to turn that mirror on himself as well. He'd third-marked her as if it was the most logical thing in the world, when he hadn't been able to summon up a reason strong enough to do it to a human for over twelve decades.

She hadn't pursued any of it intentionally or overtly. She merely followed her own unique code of decency and integrity. She would even deny she had much of a hand in the choices others had made, probably claiming they all had the strength of character to make those decisions themselves.

She was a gem. A gentle, beautiful girl who would always be underestimated because of that pretty, submissive soul she had, not an ounce of true rebellion in her. She wanted to please, to love, to serve . . . and the only thing that made her veer away from what someone wanted from her was that stubborn core that refused to allow her to do what she thought wasn't right. When that happened, to her mind it wasn't rebellion or defiance—she had to do what was right, because that was best for everyone, even when they didn't believe it.

And a servant, above all else, looked out for those she served.

~

When the carousel stopped, he slid off the horse and helped her down the same way he'd helped her on, only this time he held on to her, pressing her against the horse's side as he kissed her, threading his fingers through her hair, following the lines of her throat with his thumbs, a slow stroke up and back, taking his time with it. Often, he'd let demand surge up, take over, but this time he just enjoyed feeling it. The way her body slowly melted into that fit with his, her arms around his waist, palms skimming up his back and holding on.

"Oy, now, got to make room for the next mob," the operator called out from the center of the carousel. "Take your pretty sheila off to the strongman contest and impress her with a stuffed bear, mate."

When Mal turned his head to give the man a wry look, Elisa blinked and waved, a huge smile splitting her face. "How ya going, mate? What are you doing halfway round the world?"

The meaty, bald specimen of a man responded in kind, his wide grin creasing his face all over, showing a couple missing teeth. "Well, blimey charlie, what'd ya know? A pretty sheila on my carousel, in truth. I hail from Sydney. Don't know what the hell I'm doing all the way over here among the Yanks. Gone wobbly, I expect. That your husband?" Then he snorted before she could answer. "Course not. No woman I know kisses her husband like that. Get on with you now and enjoy the fun, but come back round in a bit on my break. I'll shout you a lemonade if you'll tell an old bastard all about home."

He'd squinted hard in their direction, showing that while his hearing was impeccable, his eyesight wasn't as good. He'd been able to make out the embrace, but the difference in their races apparently hadn't registered, not enough to bring him up short or stifle his teasing. Of course, in Elisa's optimistic mind, Mal saw an entirely different logic. Like maybe he was one of the good sorts to whom it didn't matter. She'd met men in the bush who liked Aboriginal women, and while they mostly had an entirely different opinion of a white woman being with a black-fella, he might be one of the rare ones who didn't hold it against a sheila who stepped across those lines. He was working at a carnival after all, a world usually populated by those on the fringes of society at best.

So, choosing to believe that instead of impaired eyesight, she gave him another affectionate expression and a wave. Then she took Mal's hand and let him lead her off the carousel so they could load a new group.

As she glanced over her shoulder at the man, Mal caught the wistful look. "You miss home a lot, don't you?"

"Yes. And no." She looked up at him. "Dealing with so many strange and new things, it's exciting and exhilarating and all that, but some-times I get lonely for what's familiar. The comfort of people who've known me awhile, the things I've always known. But I've already started feeling at ease at your place, with Kohana and the rest. It's just hard. Changing, that is. Isn't it?"

He decided to keep his answer to a nod, knowing exactly how she felt. But then he couldn't help himself for asking. "Am I one of the new and strange things?"

"Definitely. Particularly the strange part." Then, remarkably, she pushed him off balance and took off in the crowd, laughing over her shoulder at him, daring him to give chase.

He caught up, of course, grabbed hold of her, but before he could decide on his retaliation, she seized his other hand and pointed. "Look. Bicycles."

There were an array of colorful bicycles that could be rented for people to ride them on the beach and boardwalks. "See the red, shiny one? Isn't that fine? There were boys who used them in Perth for deliveries and such, and I always thought they'd be so lovely to run errands, but I never learned how to ride one. No boy to take me out on a ride." She gave him a telling smile. "Do you know how to ride one?"

"I do." It amazed him that she didn't, but she wouldn't have had much opportunity for that kind of play, or even learning something so utilitarian, not when her days had been filled with cleaning, laundry and helping the housekeepers of her respective employers. "Would you like to learn now?"

"Wasn't I being rather obvious about it?" At her impish look, he gave her a pinch on her bottom that had her gasping and pushing away from him with an amused but disapproving look. "You're not supposed to do that in public."

"You're not supposed to sass your Master. Before the night's over, you might need another of those spankings you claim not to like."

Her lashes lowered in a suitably demure look that was pointless when he saw the eagerness in her mind, hot visions that made him want to do exactly that, right now. But he curbed the impulse, because he really did want to give her this. There were two sides to her euphoria tonight. Part of her was celebrating their success at Marshall's, but the other was staving off the knowledge she would soon have to let two of her fledglings go, trusting their lives to another. For her—for any parent—he expected it was an altogether terrifying thought.

He paid for a two-hour rental, boosted her on the handlebars and took them off to a quieter part of the causeway, a concrete canal area that gave them enough room to do what he intended. She enjoyed the ride, holding on to his hands on the bars, stretching out her legs and leaning back into the crook of his shoulder, the sea breeze caressing her face. She was laughing, trying to keep her skirt properly tucked in so the wind wouldn't ruck it up, and when she turned her face into his jaw, her lips touched his throat, a provocative tease, more so because of its innocence. She was really, truly irresistible. He wondered if even Danny had ever seen this side of her. It was the first time he'd seen her wholly free of all her responsibilities, the young girl she actually was shining through in full, springlike force, infecting everyone they passed with smiles.

When they reached the canal area, he stopped the bike, letting her slide off the bars, and then patted the seat. "Your turn. If you do well, you can ferry *me* around on the handlebars."

"Thank goodness I have a third-mark's strength." She grinned and straddled the seat, tucking her skirt beneath her. Her sundress was close-fitting and came modestly above the knee when she sat, so there'd be no danger of it rippling into the spokes. "All right, so I just put my feet on these pedals and push, right?"

"Right. But balance is the trick to riding a bike. It's like when you balance on a fence and have to keep your weight centered. I'm going to hold on to the back as you get it. Keep the handlebars straight. I won't let you fall, so don't worry about that. That's usually what makes it hard at first, a fear of falling."

"Oh, I've fallen plenty of times. That doesn't bother me. You just get up, dust yourself off and keep going." Catching her bottom lip in her teeth, she put her feet on the pedals. It took a few tries, but then she was going, and he was moving with her, keeping the bike steady as the handlebars wobbled back and forth and she got the way of it. A couple of times the front wheel turned abruptly, but he was able to reach forward and steady it, trotting along beside her, letting go when she seemed to have it in hand again.

"I think I've got it," she said at length, after they'd made several long passes up and down the area. Pausing, she put one foot on the ground to brace the bike. The canal had taken them into a tunnel, illuminated dimly by the streetlights outside of it, but with their enhanced sight, neither really needed them. She studied the graffiti painted along the inside walls. There were the expected curse words, but also protestations of love, a religious emblem or two, and artwork, done in broad colors and strokes.

"Look." Elisa pointed. A lion, in bright yellow with a bristling orange mane, had his mouth open wide, fangs showing. Swirled around him in red letters was the motto, "I am Lion. Hear me roar." His tail was threaded through the *O* in roar.

"Can you imagine one of your lions roaring in here? The echoes would knock us down."

"Do you miss my island?"

When she lifted her long lashes to him, her eyes thoughtful, he wasn't sure why the answer was so important, such that he didn't look for it in her mind, or question what it was about her expression that held him so still.

"Yes. Very much. More than I expected. I like being there, as I said. I mean, as long as you want me there." She amended that with a nervous little smile, and this time he did look for the thought. Her life had always been transient. She was telling herself that she knew better than to consider any place a permanent home. He still wouldn't let her quarter with the staff, after all.

"Elisa—"

"I want to do it now on my own," she said. "I'll be okay."

He nodded, but watched carefully as she hopped forward, then put the other foot back on the pedal. He held on long enough for her to get some forward momentum, and then he let go.

Elisa laughed, a delighted, nervous sound. "Oh, this is wonderful. You can go as fast as you can pedal." When she increased her speed, he knew he wouldn't be able to keep pace with her and pass as human in front of the others biking or crossing the concrete to reach the beach. He stayed at a jog, slowing to a walk as she got farther ahead. As he watched, she made long, wide laps around him, becoming more and more confident. She rocked her body back and forth, taking advantage of her third-mark balance to let the bike make a serpentine track.

When a man passed her on his bike with his arms straight out, she had to try that as well. Of course her bike hit a loose patch of concrete, and she went tumbling. Heedless of whether or not he appeared to be more than human, he was there in an instant, but his worry immediately dissipated at her wry laughter.

"Got too cocky, didn't I? Guess there's a reason they call it that, because it seems it's mostly men who try that kind of foolishness before they're ready."

Mal squatted, lifting the bike off of her, and saw she'd scraped her knee. She beamed up at him. "It will be gone in a moment, but isn't it marvelous? Mr. Collins's son fell off his bike one day and had one just like that. He told me it was going to be an even bigger scab than the one that Tommy Saunders got. He was so proud of it." Her laughter became a soft smile. "He still wanted me to bandage it up and kiss it, though. Boys are funny that way."

"Yes, they are." Staring at her, he felt so full of . . . feeling. It took his voice, but at the same time made him want to say all manner of incredibly foolish things. He'd never been happier in his life than right now, with her, like this. It was a most astounding thought. He had a good life at his sanctuary, no question, but he'd never felt so full of another person, so in need of them. He wanted to share that with her, but didn't. He'd never opened himself up like that, as human or vampire, perhaps because he'd gotten too used to protecting himself from what might change. Like her, assuming nothing was permanent. But he did follow another, safer impulse.

"Well, seeing as it's going to be gone in a few moments, we won't need the bandage. But the kissing . . ." Bending over it, he placed his lips there, spending several discreet moments stroking his tongue along the abused area, sending a little quiver through her as he held her thigh beneath the dress hem, caressing bare flesh, feeling the heat between her legs increase. After giving the knee a thorough washing, taking away all the blood, he made her laugh by pretending to spit out bits of gravel. Then he pressed a single kiss to the center.

"You ripped your hem. I owe you a new dress."

"Seeing as you bought it, and I ruined it, I think it's just the opposite."

"Yellow isn't my color. And you look much better in that bodice."

She giggled at him, then put her hand over her mouth, an admonishment not to give herself to such youthful silliness. "Well," she said at length, "if anything is owed, I think the bicycling lessons were a fine trade."

Abruptly, her expression changed, her eyes becoming large and deep, her mouth soft. "I want to speak to the carousel operator, and then I want to go back to Lord Marshall's. I want to pack our bags and go back to the island tomorrow. I want to be in your bed with the canopy, and all the sounds of the lions, leopards, cheetahs and cougars. I want to see Jeremiah and the others, and give them the good news. Will you take me there?"

Despite her earlier words, she didn't say, "Will you take me home?"

He was a damn fool for wishing she had. She understood how things were. She always had, always would, and he was supposed to appreciate that in her, not want her to get soft and sloppy over him. He'd told her once they got the fledglings resolved, he would ask her again if she wanted to be his third-mark, if she wanted to stay with him, and after that all choices would be his. But looking at her, he didn't know if he'd ever ask the question. She fairly oozed commitment and family. Even if her answer was yes, it would be because of that generous heart and deeply submissive nature. It wasn't what she truly wanted. He couldn't take that away from her.

"Yes, I'll take you there." He helped her up. As she brushed against his body, he held back the urge to crush her against him, give her a much more heated kiss, one that would erase all those reasonable thoughts. It had to be the magical stardust of the fair, making the impossible possible, and the unlikely far too appealing.

She couldn't afford to have her heart broken again, he reminded himself. She didn't have the emotional distance necessary to be a vampire's servant. Kohana had told him that in his usual impertinent, blunt way, and Mal knew the gruff Indian had told her the same, in less direct terms. The way she'd handled herself at Grant's had proven it. Her natural submission had gotten her through it, but it had torn something up in her, her body betraying her heart.

However, he didn't interact with vampires that often. He could count on one hand the number of times over the past five years. He wasn't an overlord or Region Master with political aspirations. He didn't even really have to bring a servant for most trips. He could probably keep it restricted to Region Master or overlord demands, and seeing that that would be Lady Lyssa and Lord Marshall, both of whom had servants Elisa now knew and liked, it would be manageable.

Even if the fledglings all left, he could offer her the choice to stay until she felt comfortable returning to Australia and Danny, when enough time had passed to help heal the ghosts that lingered there for her. That was logical, reasonable, no commitment involved or promises that could be broken.

If it was such a logical choice, he could say it right here, right now, and it would be done. She'd certainly accept it, and that would be that. But he couldn't make his lips move to form the words. Whatever it was—the biology of the third mark, the way it made a vampire view his third servant, or something deeper he didn't care to analyze—nothing inside him had any interest in leaving the damn offer open-ended.

Which meant, for her own good, silence was his best option. He'd be like the damn Sphinx and let her go—let her go home—as soon as the fledglings were settled.

38

Nadia and Marshall would come to the island in a month, and the boys would be brought to them a month after that. They'd agreed to that schedule based on Mal's determination of how long it would take to ensure the boys were ready to be part of an actual household.

Elisa thought he might have to amend that timetable, however, because since they'd let the boys know they had a future, they were making progress in leaps and bounds. Over the next several weeks, it became a regular thing, having the boys visit the house one night, the girls the next. On one memorable evening, Mal deemed all four ready to be there. They'd taught them cards, and Nerida had even shyly climbed from Elisa's lap into Malachi's, holding his cards for him. She'd shown a particular trust for him ever since the Leonidas incident, and though he tried to appear immune and unaffected by it, Elisa could tell their smallest vampire's trust touched him.

The boys fell right into Mal's trap when he offered them a game of fifty-two-card pickup. They'd had so much fun racing each other to pick up all the cards, though, she wasn't sure they really understood it was a joke, not a game, or if they even cared. They were all starting to verbalize more, fangs notwithstanding. Lord Brian was scheduled to visit around the same time as Marshall and Nadia, which meant they could be part of discussions about that and other matters regarding the fledglings' state.

The news for the girls was equally good. Mal had made contact with a Lord Mason in South America. Through Lady Lyssa, Mal had found out the little-known and unusual fact that Lord Mason had created a foundation to assist human women who needed to escape dire circumstances. His initial focus had been women in the Middle East, but he'd been known to expand that reach. While of course Miah and Nerida weren't a perfect fit for his philanthropic endeavors, through the conduit of Enrique, his full servant, the vampire lord became interested in their situation, and agreed that he might give them a home at his estate. If they learned enough control, he could find them a place in one of his women's communities where they would essentially disappear from vampire eyes, and have his marked protection.

So almost everything was looking bright as sunshine. On those evenings at the house, Elisa would talk to them about the places they would be going. Nadia had sent gifts for all of them, not just the boys, but for the boys she'd also sent a photo and sketch album like Elisa had, so William and Matthew could see the house, the rooms they were creating for them, and what their new benefactors looked like.

While Lord Mason was not available to come to visit the girls, Enrique and his wife, Amara, would be coming to visit.

"Lord Mason's full servant has a wife?" Elisa's brow had lifted to her hairline at that news. The children had gone back to their enclosure for the night and she was in Mal's room. As always, he wanted her stretched out naked on his bed at the near dawn to feed, as well as to enjoy other things she had to offer him. It was a part of her day she always anticipated, perhaps too much, but he seemed to thoroughly and deeply enjoy it as well. Enough that tonight he'd decided they'd turn in a couple hours earlier than usual.

Even now, his gaze was caressing her skin. He'd had her lie on her stomach, her legs spread so he could enjoy the curve of her arse, her dampening pussy, as he stripped off his shirt. Pulling open the top button of his trousers, he toed off his shoes. Coming to sit on the edge of the bed, he molded a palm over one buttock. She laid her cheek on her folded arms, watching him, waiting for his answer.

"Yes. They're both third-marked, both Lord Mason's servants, but Enrique came to him first. Later, when Enrique married her, at her request, Mason made them both fully his. It's a unique situation, one we don't see too often."

She nodded, looking down at the pelts beneath her hands. Usually she liked to take her fill of watching him undress, a secret pleasure she could pretend was all hers. But his words gave her a brief shadow. "How would you feel about something like that?" he asked.

The question surprised and discomfited her. "Ian was Lady Constance's consort, sort of like a married couple, but he had a full servant, Chiyoko. I guess it'd be similar to that, right? Like if I'm your full servant, you could marry or keep as a consort that lady vampire Kohana said comes to visit you."

"Used to come visit. She doesn't anymore, hasn't for a long time." He pushed a curl off her cheek. "But that's not what I meant. If you go back to your station and fall in love with someone like Willis . . ." Mal paused, his jaw tightening. "Elisa, I would allow you to marry. You know that, right? It would have to be someone already inside the vampire world, second-marked of course, or willing to be brought in that way, but I know you want a family. I don't want you to be alone just because you're my third-marked servant."

"I don't feel alone now." She pleated the sheet with her fingers, neat, straight rows. He covered both her hands with his.

"Look at me."

She raised her chin, but her eyes couldn't quite focus on his, skittering away to the dresser, the wall. Putting his hand on her jaw, he made her look at him. Still, she got only as far as his not-perfectly straight nose. During one of their early-dawn conversations, one of those post-coital murmurings while he held her in his arms, he'd told her it had been broken before he was turned. On one of his escape attempts from the mission school.

"It would be so much easier if you were like the rest of them," she said desperately. "You know, Lady Danny and Lord Marshall. They're so different from me in everything . . . It's like they're royalty, and no one has ridiculous thoughts about being with royalty. You appreciate them from a distance, and even if you have some kind of Cinderella dream, you know it's a child's fairy tale. You're like Willis, but you're not. You're like Danny, but you're not. And it's so easy to get caught up in that in-between world, thinking things about you." She took a deep breath. *Stop it; stop being a stupid ninny.* "No, that's quite fair. I'm glad you said that. Yes, if I meet someone, and want to marry them, that will be a lovely, *brilliant* thing to know. Thank you, sir."

He blinked at her, but then he stilled, listening. Elisa looked up at him, but before he even said anything, she knew what it was, because it had been happening far too much of late.

"Bidzil says there's a problem."

The pleasure of the earlier evening evaporated, a heavy weight in her chest with the reminder of that *almost* in the optimistic forecast for the fledglings. "I'll go with you. He calms down when he sees me."

"It's not a seizure. He . . ." Mal's forehead creased. "Chumani says she thinks it's best if you do come."

As promising as the future looked for the other four, Jeremiah's star had been moving in an altogether different direction. In fact, while Elisa had been glad to see the four at the house tonight, a large part of her had felt she should be at the enclosure, so Jeremiah wouldn't be alone. Chumani had stayed with him, but she knew it wasn't the same.

She went every day to him now, since he couldn't leave the fledgling compound except for the nights Mal took him alone to the preserve. He'd become so erratic he couldn't be trusted out among the other four. Which meant of course Mal wouldn't let her come, either, but he would faithfully let her see what the boy was doing through his mind. The enhanced binding of the third mark gave her a far more vivid view than the brief channel he'd held open through the second mark.

Jeremiah would run across the plains at full speed as if demons were pursuing him, then would come to a halt, so abruptly his heels gouged into the ground. He'd stand in that spot, swaying. After a time, he might climb a tree and stay up there for hours, staring out into space. Whereas the other four were more and more verbal, he was monosyllabic or silent most of the time now.

When she went to see him, her reading and talking to him seemed to calm him, make the bloodlust seizures less intense when they happened. Since she was spending more time with the four outside the enclosure, they didn't mind that she devoted all her attention to him when she was there, but she didn't like their knowing looks, the sad set to their mouths, a reflection of what she often saw in Mal's face. It mirrored the ominous sense she carried, and despised herself for feeling.

Mal had sent Jeremiah's blood to the scientist. Lord Brian said Jeremiah's blood confirmed he was escalating in his violent tendencies, the transition indicators intensifying, not abating as they should be. The young scientist said he'd like to come and study him, even if he couldn't help. Like a lab rat. Elisa didn't even particularly care to think about what scientists did to those poor creatures, let alone what Lord Brian might do to her boy.

Since he was less communicative, she'd tried talking to him in her head, but he didn't respond. She'd told him they'd figure out something about the bloodlust, that he'd always have a home here, that Mal had promised nothing bad would ever happen to him. When she said such things, Jeremiah looked at her with eyes that had gone so flat . . . so empty. Every once in a while it could make her shiver, because it reminded her of Victor or Leonidas. When she thought such a terrible thing, she immediately banished it from her mind. Jeremiah was still Jeremiah. While she couldn't seem to penetrate the distance between them now, she would. They needed time; that was all.

They were on their way in a matter of a few moments, roaring out of the valley. As they rounded the sharp curve on the highest overlook, Elisa emitted a sharp warning cry. Mal cursed, hitting the brake at the same moment. At the top of that knoll, staring out at the expanse of plains, the moon hanging down and spilling silvery light across them, was Jeremiah.

"Stay in this Jeep," Mal said, his tone adamant. Elisa nodded, though her hands gripped the dashboard.

Mal had every sympathy for the boy, but he got out of the Jeep in full predator mode, eyes trained on the fledgling, his hands loose and mature body ready to handle whatever needed handling. Chumani was alive; he could feel her life essence, but she wasn't answering his call. He cursed himself for not staying linked to her. On top of that, he was far too aware of Elisa, tense and worried in the Jeep behind him, but not worried about the right things. He could keep Jeremiah from her, but things could always go wrong.

The boy didn't turn, not even when Mal was right behind him, but he did speak.

"Joomani's fine." The sibilant words were slurred even more than usual by the fangs. "I . . . held her air. Made her sleep."

Hardly reassuring, since Jeremiah sounded detached, not in touch with the reality around him. Then he turned and Elisa let out a tiny cry. The excessive slurring was because his fangs were gone, ripped out of his mouth by his own hands. He was holding one in each bloody palm. Not holding. He'd staked his hands with them, so that they were pushed through the palm, the sharp curved tip emerging on the other side.

Elisa.

She was out of the Jeep and halfway to him, but Mal's explosive command reverberated inside her mind, stopping her. All vampires had some level of compulsion on those they marked, but it was the first time he'd ever used it, more instinct than skill, his will cracking out and whipping around her like a single tail, bringing her to a halt as if he'd grabbed her around the waist. It was just enough to help her regain her senses, but she swayed in place, everything about her aching toward Jeremiah.

As the fledgling stared at her, Mal saw the gray-green gaze change. From flat deadness, to a haunted pain so raw and agonized that it drew Elisa another tiny step toward him, despite the compulsion's hold.

Recognizing a lost cause when his servant's heart was involved, Mal moved in closer. As much as he wanted her far away from this situation, he knew what was going on here was something different from what he'd observed these past few weeks in the boy's declining state. He wanted to put himself between Jeremiah and Elisa, but he kept seeing the boy holding her, trying to protect her face and chest. He'd give it a few moments, trust his gut.

"'Top dere," Jeremiah said thickly, raising one of those gruesomely punctured hands. "'Ay back, Leesa."

"You're hurt. You need help."

He shook his head. "It burns. But doesn't . . . 'urt. Nutting 'urt." He looked at his hands, then up at her. "I wanted t' talk to you . . . like dis. Out of cell . . . my will. Fer once, nutting contwolling dis moment . . . but me." He cast a fierce look Mal's way, an appeal and veiled challenge at once. Because Mal sensed the desperation in it, he gave him a slight nod, not conceding to the challenge, but granting the appeal. But he stayed very, very close.

Jeremiah looked back at her. "How old . . . I?"

"We don't know, sweetheart." Elisa's mouth was taut with pain for him, her eyes bright with it. "They didn't—"

"'Wenty-foor." He spoke the words softly, softly enough that Elisa stopped, having to replay it in her mind. *Twenty-four.* And then her eyes widened. Mal knew she was twenty-two.

"Ruskin took me when . . . nine. F-fifteen years. Wit' him . . . longest. Should be . . . dead. O'er and o'er. Victor, Leo . . . nias. Pwotected me. Dey . . . normal, like . . . all were. Leo . . . not mon'ter. He was . . . friend. Den . . . wasn't. Can't haf fwiends . . . in hell. One day . . . will be me. Looking at you de way dey did, wanting . . ." He swallowed. "Wanting to tear you into pieces. Do 'orrible dings to you, no matter how I feel."

Elisa took another step forward and Mal sent her the quiet message.

Elisa, he's right. Don't move any closer. He's holding on to control by a thread, and you must help him with your stillness.

She nodded, but her hands locked together before her. While Mal was gratified she had no fear, trusting him to protect her, he didn't want her testing the limits. The pain of those fangs in Jeremiah's palms, the agitation that boiled beneath the eerie calm, all of it could take this into a very violent place, very quickly.

Jeremiah continued, speaking slowly, so each word came out as clear as it could through the impediment of his torn-up mouth. "Mal act . . . t'ward you, way man act t'ward woman. T'ward you. Hated him for it. Doan remember anyt'ing but rage, and heat. Like when Rushkin would flog, starf us. We tore people apart . . . so angry."

She flinched, and he gave her a slow, appraising nod. "Done dat, too many times. Don't remember all . . . faces. Never gif you what he does." When he closed his eyes then, Mal heard it in Elisa's mind, the boy speaking as he wished to speak, the words unbroken even if the emotions behind them weren't.

I ache for it, die a little bit seeing it. I want to be as a man is . . . I don't know if this is what Mal feels, or something twisted, a child and a man's love. It consumes me, Elisa. I know what I do and don't want anymore.

It was the first time he'd said her name fully, rather than the childish Leesa abbreviation, and Mal could tell it struck her mind, made her throat ache. Beyond that, she was rocked on her axis, as much as he was, to hear the grown-up voice and fully formed thoughts. After months of limited and broken forms of communication, what they were hearing were the thoughts of an undeniably adult male.

I can't do it. I can't wait and see if I'll become like them. If I did, no woman will see past what I look like. Can you imagine lying with me? Letting me touch you like him? He nodded toward Mal. *Kiss you that way? Imagine it. Close your eyes, see it. Let me show it to you.*

Elisa didn't want to do it, but she did. Jeremiah, stroking her face as he'd seen Mal do, his hands going to her waist, lips pressing against hers. Childish lips, childish hands. A shudder went through her, repelled despite herself, and she opened her eyes to see tears in his.

"Jeremiah, no. It's not—"

No. He shook his head fiercely. *It's how you should feel. It's how a normal, decent human being feels. I marked you, because I didn't ever want you to be in danger and not know about it. Which was stupid, because how could I help, really, locked in a cell all the time? But then, I was able to sing to you, make you feel better, and that was something. It meant something. But it's always on the edges, you know. Not really living.*

He took a deep breath, turned his gaze to Mal and spoke the clearest he'd spoken yet, so forceful it pushed past the lisp. "I'm done. I want . . . it . . . to . . . be . . . over."

≈

"No." Elisa whispered it. When Jeremiah looked back at her, she saw a sudden calm in his gaze now, laced with a sadness so deep and so familiar. She'd seen it the day he'd killed Leonidas. She'd turned away from the truth then, but there was no turning away now.

I wanted to tell you like this, out here, without a bloodlust attack, so you know it's not because of that. I wanted to feel pain—he gestured with his hands—*to know that it doesn't matter to me anymore. Nothing is worse than the agony of what I've become, Elisa. Of what I'm becoming. You have to let me go.*

He turned back to Mal. *I want to do it today. I like the place where we watched the cheetahs. It will have a good sunrise. Give me a stake and I'll sit there. I'll do it when the sun comes up, or the sun can take me.*

"No. No. *No.*" She didn't care about compulsions or Jeremiah's control. She surged forward, and came up against the hard wall of Mal, holding her away from the young vampire. She fought to get past him, but Jeremiah took a step back. His body shuddered, his eyes sparking with crimson. Proving, as Mal had said, how very hard he was fighting to hold on to control.

"You can't do this," she cried out. She fought Mal's grip, ignored Jeremiah's rising agitation in favor of her own. Mal didn't speak in her mind, didn't admonish her out loud, as if he knew the only thing that would hold her back now was physical strength. "You can't give up. There are so many things you can live for. So many things . . ."

She trailed off as he stared at her, that terrible knowledge in his eyes. *What, Elisa? What things? I'll never leave this island, never leave that cell. I'll never be more than a freak, dependent on others. I don't want that.*

Abruptly, his fists clenched on those gruesome impalements, and he bared the bloody gaps in his mouth, his eyes going red. "I doan want dat!"

It was a howl, but it had to chase them down the hill, because Mal had already picked her up bodily and was speeding away with her. He left the Jeep behind to cut through the forest, putting distance between her and the vampire fledgling who was now screaming his rage to the night, a vibration that rivaled even the cheetah's eerie calls. It brought silence to the island, every being going stock-still as they heard and scented a predator in pain, a danger to them all.

~

"No." She kept saying it. She wouldn't give in to tears, wouldn't bear to be touched. When he dropped her on their porch, she bared her teeth at Mal just like Jeremiah had and went after him with fists and fury, until he hauled her down to their room, past Kohana's startled face. Once there, Mal closed the door, leaning against it as he let her go. She threw herself back at him. He blocked her attempts to move him, to strike out at him, tolerated her screams in stoic silence, let her go until she ran herself into complete exhaustion and collapsed at his feet, pressing her face against his thigh, letting the sobs take her. *No, no, no . . .*

When he at last bent, curled his arms around her, she latched onto one of them with a deathlike grip. As the sobs grew harder, more pain-ful, she bit into the arm, bit deep, screaming her anger and pain, tasting his blood. He held her without flinching, came down to rock her, hold her. "No . . ."

She kept on until she was depleted. She had her face in his arm and never wanted to lift it. It was just too much. She couldn't lose anymore; she just couldn't. She didn't ever want to get up again. She didn't care if he left her like this, like refuse on the floor, unnoticed and mindless.

Instead, he curled over her, stroking her back. He wasn't saying any-thing, because there was nothing to say. She could retreat into numb-ness that way, not deal with anything. But Jeremiah wasn't as merciful as Mal.

His bloodlust had apparently passed, because now his voice trem-bled in her mind, vulnerable. *Please don't, Elisa. Don't grieve for me. This is how it was meant to be. I died a long time ago, what I could have been, what I wanted to be. I need to go, and go with your blessing, even if it's the hardest thing you'll ever do.*

She sensed an edge of tension, and fear. She couldn't bear for him to be afraid.

I don't . . . It's not fair, but I don't want to go alone. I will if I have to, but you . . . you're my family. Please help me do this.

I can't let you go. I can't let you do it.

The choice isn't yours. Mal promised me. This one choice is mine. And it wasn't easy for him, because he knows it may take your heart from him. So remember that when you're angry with him over it.

She lifted her gaze to Mal. "No. Talk him out of it."

"I can't, Irish flower." Mal cupped her tear-swollen face. "Your pain is tearing me apart, but he's right. And deep in that practical soul of yours, you know it as well. You've known since Leonidas."

"No. If it's in my mind, I'm wrong. This is wrong. I'm Catholic," she said desperately, echoed it in her mind to Jeremiah. She heard what sounded like a choked chuckle, the first time Jeremiah had shown a sense of humor, grim as it was. The quiet request came again, ruthless, inexorable.

Ah, Lees. Please. Help me. Only you can help me.

39

H<small>E</small> wouldn't be talked into giving her one more day, wouldn't prolong her agony or his. That numbness returned, settling over her as she cleaned her face, changed into a different outfit. The blue dress Jeremiah had liked the most. She'd first worn it for him at the station, and he'd reached through the cage to touch the hem when she'd been sitting what Mal would have considered far too close to his cage.

Dressing up to watch someone die. Her fingers trembled and she made herself stop, take a deep breath, wait until they stilled to begin again.

When she came out on the porch, Kohana was there, and Chumani. Tokala and Bidzil. All of the other hands as well, an unexpected show of support. She managed a jerky nod. Tokala steadied her as she went down the steps and he followed her to the Jeep where Mal leaned, arms crossed, expression somber. Tears came to her eyes to see he wore dark slacks and a dress shirt.

"Tokala will go with us," he said quietly. "He'll have a crossbow to finish it, quick and painless, when Jeremiah says so. We won't make the boy do it."

"He's not a boy. He's a man. A young man."

Mal nodded. "So he is. I'll be near. There's a supply station near that spot, and I can be inside it when the sun rises."

When she'd regained consciousness from Victor's attack, she remembered how, for the first few minutes, she thought of the most absurdly normal things. How she needed to get up and help Mrs. Pritchett, despite her broken bones. How the curtains needed airing and the fan turning over her bed needed a good dusting.

"You'll be horribly uncomfortable there. It's not reinforced enough. And you'll be stuck there until dusk. I . . . You can go back to the house. Tokala will bring me."

"I'm not leaving you out there alone, Elisa."

"Please . . . I need . . ." She was fighting to keep her voice even. "I need to know after this, I can come back here, and you'll be in your bed, and you can curl around me like you always do, and we can dream. Please."

After a long moment, his jaw tight, his mind obviously deep inside of hers, seeing the truth of her words, what she needed, he inclined his head. "Let's go, then."

Tokala took the back and she sat in the passenger seat, her fingers curled around the steel bar.

Lees?

We're coming, Jeremiah. She glanced at Mal, his stern profile illuminated only by the Jeep headlights and dashboard. "Is he at the enclosure?"

"No, he's where he wants to be for this. That's where we're going."

She knew the location. Though not as elevated as the knoll in her dream, it had a profound view of a long rolling plain that passed through the blue line of the African portal, and beyond that, the sea. Three different possible worlds to visit.

Jeremiah had made sure he wasn't near the other fledglings during his end, but she was sure they knew where he'd gone. She wondered what kind of good-byes he'd said to them.

They didn't speak again. She held that lack of feeling to her like a shield until they pulled up and stopped, just twenty feet away from where Jeremiah was sitting. He had his knees drawn up and hands linked around them, rocking on the point of his buttocks as he looked up at the vast sky, the spray of stars across them.

Dear God, give me courage. I can't do this. I can't.

She looked toward Mal then, her eyes pleading. "Say something to help me do this."

"I don't want you to do it. I want to take you home right now, and protect you from this. I don't want you to feel one more moment of pain in your life."

Mal's quiet words were so fierce, the heat blasted over her chilled skin. What she'd taken for stoic acceptance was hiding a great deal more. She nodded. He knew what she needed to hear. He didn't want her to do this, but she had to do it. She knew she had to do it.

She got out of the Jeep, Tokala with her, and turned to look at Mal. "Do you need to . . ."

He shook his head. "He and I have said our good-byes. You're sure you want me to go?"

She fought an ache in her throat that threatened to become another flood of tears. "No, but I need you to go. Need you to be there."

"All right, then." He held her gaze. "I'll be in your mind, Irish flower. You can do this. He needs you, and you are better at being needed than anyone I've ever met in my life."

He slid out of the Jeep, because he'd use his vampire speed to return to the house, but as he moved a few steps away he turned, gave her a last intent look. A wave of pure feeling came from him, spreading out inside her like an amorphous blanket she could wrap around the chill. A moment later, he'd disappeared into the forest.

When she looked up at Tokala, the man nodded, passing a hand over her hair. "I'll be right close." He nodded to the tree a stone's short throw from Jeremiah. "When he's ready, you just motion to me, and I'll come closer."

Her throat too dry to respond, she started walking.

Jeremiah watched her come to him, those gray-green eyes now crimson-free. When she got there, she spread her skirt, lowered herself to the ground next to him and gave him a sidelong glance. "So here we are," she said softly. "Sure I can't interest you in a game of cricket instead? Riding a bicycle? Mal bought a bicycle for me when we were on the mainland."

"Not enough players for cricket." The blood flow from his tooth extraction had stopped, so now, for the first time since she'd met him, he was speaking almost normally, the fangs no longer an impediment. Noticing his palms had healed, she wondered what he'd done with his fangs, if they would also turn to ash at sun's first light. He'd cleaned himself up, perhaps wading in the nearby lagoon, and had gotten rid of the shirt. He was clad in just the trousers she'd made him. Reaching out, she stroked his hair away from his forehead, the first time she'd ever done it without caution or calculation. That hardly seemed to matter now, did it?

He leaned into the touch, staring at her face. "It's thirty minutes until dawn."

"I know." Her voice quavered, but she quelled it, pressing her fingers into his flesh as she dropped her hand to his shoulder. "I know you're not a little boy, Jeremiah, but can I hold you? Would you like that?"

In answer, he shifted so he was underneath her arm, crooking his legs over her lap so she could pull him close to her side. He laid his head on her shoulder, his hair brushing her neck, his lips pressed close to it, making her feel that always-present vampire awareness of her humanity, the blood pumping beneath her skin.

"I won't bite you," he murmured.

"I wasn't worried about that."

He was quiet a moment, the two of them looking out at the spectacular view. "I saw your dream that night," he continued after a moment. "The one on the knoll with the cougar. It was a good dream."

"It was, wasn't it? It's amazing . . ." When her voice quavered, she stopped, steadied it. "It's amazing how our minds can take us places we can't go. Doesn't matter if we're rich or poor; nothing can take away the ability to dream. There's a part of us inside that always goes where it wants to go, not where anyone tells us we're allowed."

"Yeah. Nobody can take it away, even when we think they have."

"Exactly like that." She tightened her arm around him. "Oh, Jeremiah. I wish . . ."

"I know. Don't." His hand landed on her forearm, squeezed a little too hard, but when she drew in an involuntary breath, he eased it. "You know, I've thought a lot about it. You remember what you said about being Catholic?"

"Yes."

"When I was little, before I was turned, my mother had my sister. She was deformed. She died after three days."

His fingers stroked her arm, drawing things on it, random circles. His body was warming, she could tell, and wondered if it was a bloodlust attack. Then she remembered how Mal's skin got hotter if he stayed outside too close to dawn, a warning. She repeated her chant in her mind. *Dear God, please help me do this.*

"I'm sorry that happened, Jeremiah."

"Before my mother died and I had to go to the orphanage, she told me my sister was so special that God wanted her back. When I think of things like that . . ." He paused, and she felt a wetness against her neck. Cupping his face, she let her fingers whisper over a single tear track. "I think . . . maybe, if I'm lucky, I'm something that God wants back. It's just taken me longer to get there."

Elisa tightened her arms around him then, holding him as close as she could. "I can't imagine God not wanting you back, Jeremiah. You remember what you said, about wanting to be a man like any other?"

He lifted a shoulder, an acknowledgment, and she pressed a kiss to the crown of his head. "You are a man, but not like any other. You're better than most. You've taken care of your siblings, for that's what the others are. You reached out to me, saved my life in more than one way. If anything, you'll be an angel, a mighty angel like Michael, watching over all of us."

He nodded. "I'd like that. Though I might like just being . . . me for a while. Do you think they play cricket in Heaven? And football?"

"Of course they do. I know they do."

His other arm slipped around her back so they were holding each other. She saw the sky lightening, felt it in her bones. *No, no, no . . .*

It's all right, Elisa. Then he lifted his face to look right at her, eye to eye. *Thank you for being this strong for me. For all of us. And thanks for that bear.*

It was such a simple, absurd thing to say. As if he knew it, a tremulous smile curved his lips, a sweet, gentle gesture, entirely at odds with the hand that closed around her arm with a man's decisiveness and a vampire's strength. *When it's time . . . you help me.*

She looked down. Drawing her arm from his waist, he closed her hand around the wooden stake he'd had hidden under his leg. Now he notched it in the right place between his ribs.

If Tokala does it, I'll have to let go of you. Don't make me do that, Elisa. Please. When the first shaft of sunlight hits us.

He laid his head back down on her shoulder, putting his arms back around her, so that stake was pressed between them. With her third-mark strength, it would take one thrust. She wrapped her other arm around his back again, stroking his head, and began to sing to him, that soft lullaby that he'd sung to her, to give her comfort in the midst of nightmares.

So much flashed through her mind. The first time Danny had introduced them to the fledglings, the day Jeremiah took the bear from outside the bars. His serious, thoughtful expression, the savagery in his face when he'd killed Leonidas, his friend, rather than let him harm Elisa. Then she imagined his mother, the one who'd given birth to a sick daughter but a beautiful, healthy son, one she'd never anticipated having to leave because she herself had died. His mother waited for him. She would be there for him, with wide-open arms, because a mother had to love a son like this. She just had to.

It gave her the courage she needed. The rose and gold of the sky increased, the split second before the sun emerged. Then the first ray lanced across the plains. Her third-mark senses were so developed now she could see it track its way across the terrain, the marshes, the dense foliage, all those habitats suitable for the different cats, the different creatures that made this their home.

What was your name, Jeremiah? Do you remember?

He nodded against her neck, his body already starting to tense from pain. Her eyes closed at his answer, tears free-falling down her cheeks onto his head.

Jeremy. You knew, Elisa. You always knew me. Please . . . It's starting to hurt.

Keeping her eyes closed, she pushed the stake home, a simple, unremarkable movement. It went through his heart at the same moment that first ray of light touched his heated flesh. Quick and painless, as Mal had said. Or at least quick. As the heart ruptured before that sharp point, she thought she'd staked her own.

I love you, Jeremy. May God bless you in death the way He couldn't in life.

~

She lowered him to the ground when he became too hot and his body began to burn from the inside, but she kept light fingertips on his forehead. She teased that lock of longish blond hair until even it was consumed and she was sitting next to a Jeremy-shaped form of ash. The looser pieces fluttered like tiny curled and dry gray autumn leaves. Tokala stood close now, staring at the stake she still held clasped in her hand. She put it aside and placed her hand on the boy's chest, applying slight pressure. As she suspected, it crumbled, the ashes spinning free as the morning breeze from the ocean picked up in strength.

She began to scatter the ashes in earnest, taking up handfuls and flinging them out over the plain, letting them go where they would, anywhere Jeremy wanted to go. Tokala bent and helped her, reading her intent, until all that was left was a dark imprint in the ground. She knew wind, rain and grass growth would eradicate that soon. Nature kept going, no matter what.

She wanted to get up, and she did, but the world was so very bright. Oddly, it felt like she was floating. She passed her knuckles over her cheeks, taking away the tears, and knew they had made their trails through an ash coating, because Tokala's face was marked with it as well. The ashes had swirled around them on a capricious wind, as if Jeremy had decided to play one last boyish trick on them.

Turning, she made it several steps to the Jeep before her knees went out from under her.

~

Despite the sunlight that could flood the front room, Mal was as close to it as he could be, standing at the top of the stairs that led to the lower bedroom level. From here he could see the porch, and it was like watching a relay. Kohana got her out of the Jeep, and Bidzil carried her up the stairs. Chumani took her then, carried her through the door, which Chayton held open. When the woman brought her to Mal, he saw his Irish flower was shivering, and coated with ash. He should have said no. He should have been the cruelest bastard in the history of the world, and told her no.

He took her immediately. She felt too light, too insubstantial, and it worried him, badly, because she should be no different from when she'd left. It was as if her spirit, the part of her that kept her weighted to the earth, real and alive, so touchable, had left her. That alarmed him even more.

"It's done," she whispered. "Oh, Mal. It's all done."

He didn't want to see how many layers of meaning she attached to that. Kohana had come in, was speaking to him, something about a bath.

"Have it brought below. I'll bathe her and put her to bed. She'll sleep with me."

He hated so many things at the moment. He hated he couldn't be there with her. He hated that Jeremiah had asked her to do this and yet even he, as much as he cared about the girl, couldn't deny the boy's last request. To die alone was a terrible thing, and Jeremiah's life had been filled with too many terrible things. But as strong as she'd proven herself, he wasn't sure she was strong enough for this.

Kohana's impotent anger simmered in his eyes, a reflection of Mal's. The other hands had worried, too, coming out to see her off like that, helpless to do anything else.

Now, seeing nothing in her mind but that hazy, numb fog, he was sure he'd made the wrong call, that he should have denied Jeremiah. But the boy would still be gone, and his mind would have called out to her at the last, tearing her to pieces.

His angry phone call to Danny, shortly after Elisa's arrival, haunted him now. *You didn't tell me the girl's life depends on theirs.*

The other four fledglings had a future. They were well on their way to not needing her any longer, and in a handful of weeks they'd be gone. In her mind, he saw she already believed herself to be completely alone, and he saw no sure way to convince her otherwise. It was the first time in a long time he'd felt the kind of fear that was overwhelming her now.

The fear of losing something that could never be replaced. A wound that could never be healed, such that whether mortal, vampire or servant, life was no longer a blessing, but an agony of memory.

40

Mɪᴀʜ and Nerida had left last night, a week after William and Matthew. Mal spent the first part of his evening overseeing the dismantling of the fledglings' enclosure. The materials wouldn't be wasted. They'd be put to use for the other cats. He wished everything had such a practical solution.

Despite the mildness of Florida and South American winters, Elisa had knitted all the fledglings sweaters, caps and mittens to remember her by. All four young vampires had worn the full ensemble when they got on the plane. She'd given each one a tight, long hug before they boarded, even blinked out a few tears. Then she'd gone back to being a ghost. A ghost maid, haunting and cleaning others' messes for eternity.

A few days after Jeremiah's death, she'd emerged in her apron and work dress, and resumed her duties with quiet efficiency, no matter how he or anybody else tried to bully her into doing otherwise. Until their departure, she'd continued her schedule with the fledglings, including their nightly visits to the house. By the time they left, they were all successfully sleeping in the subterranean guest bedrooms during the daylight hours, though Mal and the staff had temporarily added padlocks to those doors, a measure that would have to be employed by Lord Marshall and Lord Mason to protect servants until it was certain the violent transition seizures had passed, or the fledglings had learned enough control to manage the episodes themselves.

Elisa helped him and them in whatever way needed in preparations for their new lives. When Nadia and Marshall visited, as well as Lord Brian, Enrique and Amara, she conducted herself appropriately, such that only Nadia detected a difference. Once Mal pulled her aside, explained the situation, the woman was even more kind and concerned, but unfortunately she didn't have Elisa's unique ability to penetrate the thicket around a broken heart. Apparently, neither did he, damn it all.

He was her Master. He could be in her mind, but now he understood Lord Marshall's frustration. In her grief for a child, a woman could go somewhere that not even a vampire seemed to be able to reach. And Elisa's grief was more than Jeremiah's—Jeremy's—death. Throughout the events with Victor, Willis, Leonidas, the stress of being thrown into a new environment and of enduring her first vampire gathering as a third-mark, she'd held herself together. Now they were gone, that was all done, and in her mind there was nothing. She was nothing.

Right after Jeremiah's death, during the bath he'd given her, she'd been little more than a doll, responding with short answers to his questions, begging for sleep when he wanted her to say more. He hadn't had the heart to push her, and so she'd slept. And slept. It had been that way ever since. The couple times he'd tried a physical approach, she would arouse under his touch because he knew her body, enough to bring her to climax, but he wasn't touching her heart or soul. Afterward, she curled into a ball and tears trickled down her face because of that emptiness. He'd pull her close anyway, coil his strength around her, try to get her to talk, to feel. But she just retreated into automatic responses and domestic efficiency until he wanted to tear the house down, create a complete wreck of it to see if it would elicit a different, enduring response.

Elisa's vague smiles and frustratingly helpful behavior were like a branch cut from a tree. For a few weeks, if watered, it remained green and vibrant, deceiving the viewer into thinking it was still alive, still attached to the tree. But now that the fledglings had gone, he knew what was going to happen. She was going to begin to wither, rapidly.

Unless he could figure out how to reach her.

~

"Damn it." He swore hard enough the tomcats scattered off his desk. Going to the French doors, he stared into the night. She was asleep now, of course. When she wasn't doing her chores, that was what she did. She didn't want to eat with the hands or do anything else. Even the promise that they would visit both sets of fledglings in a month or two elicited little more than a distant smile out of her. He didn't know what to do with her.

"Are you going to send her home?"

Kohana stood in the hallway, in the shadows. Mal remembered the night she'd come there in her nightgown, daring him to chase her.

"So she can be Danny's problem?"

"Well, I guess from your perspective, that would be tit for tat, right? Seeing as that's how you felt when Danny sent her here."

He narrowed his gaze. "Trying to start a fight, old man?"

"You're older," Kohana said automatically, but he pinched the bridge of his nose, an uncharacteristic sign of frustration. "She dusted today, Mal. Dusted. I told her not to, not to do anything, and she looks at me with those wide eyes and says in this quiet, even voice, 'What *should* I do, then?' How the hell can you answer a question like that?"

"She'll work through it, Kohana," Mal said with an assurance he didn't feel. "We're just frustrated because we don't yet know how best to help. Sometimes all we can do is wait and be here. Be around her."

"You can do more."

Mal frowned at the entirely unsubtle accusation. "Really? Enlighten me. What can I do? Turn back time, change all of it for her? Refuse to let Jeremiah take his life, force him to suffer, just to make her feel better?" Which, in hindsight, he damn well would have done, if he thought it would. It proved his own mind wasn't in the right place right now.

"She fell in love with you, Mal. I'm not saying it's the deep kind of love that two people need to get through something this hard, but it was a start toward it. And it's all she's got. Use that. It's the thing you have that none of us do. Bring her back with that. Give her hope. Tell her you love her."

"I'm a vampire, Kohana."

Mal lifted a brow as Kohana slammed his fist into the wall hard enough to make the pictures jump. One fell to the floor with a clatter of broken glass.

"I don't give a damn about vampire rules, and I have eyes, just like every damn person on this island does. You love her. You fell in love with her the first time she wouldn't back down from you, no matter how much the odds were stacked against her. This isn't the vampire world. It's just us. Whatever we have to pretend to be to the whole damned world, fine, but we don't lie to ourselves here. Not ever. You told me that, long ago.

"As far as being a vampire, and what that means to the two of you, that can help, too. That's part of what makes her tick, right? The thing that made Danny's mother pick her, and all that." He took another hop forward. Even with the limp, when he drew himself up, Kohana showed the blood he carried from his shaman father. As well as the blood of his great-grandfather, the chief from that long-ago Wild West show. The voice that came from him now drew from them both, and every ancestor in between.

"So use the best of both, Mal. The man you could have been and the vampire you are, and help her. Just because you can't remember what your mother looked like doesn't mean you don't have her heart, the power to love another the way she did."

Mal pressed his lips together. "Get out now, Kohana. I mean it."

The man nodded. "You know where I'll be."

When he stumped back to the kitchen, Mal looked out into the night a few minutes more. Then, sighing, he returned to his desk. Picking up the phone, he braced himself to make the call he'd been avoiding. As he went through the necessary operators to connect to the number at Danny's remote location, he knew it was daylight in Australia, but he couldn't put it off any longer. After Dev received the call, Mal was glad he didn't have to do more than say, "I need to talk to Danny." Apparently, Dev heard it in his voice. He went to wake his Mistress immediately.

As expected, Danny didn't waste time on preliminaries. "Tell me."

He relayed all the facts to her. How the other four fledglings were doing, Jeremiah's decision, how he'd chosen to execute it, how Elisa had helped him. Then he found he didn't know what else to say.

"Bloody hell. I never thought to have Janus give me *when* they turned the three boys. We just knew Ruskin's four monsters were fledglings, and fledgling turnings are horribly unstable. Only in Oz would Council have ignored violations of that magnitude for that long. It's like we're not on the bloody same planet with those European bastards."

"It wouldn't have changed anything," Mal said quietly. "Don't worry about that. I didn't think about it, for the same reason. We'd already assumed he was a few years older. We just didn't know how much older."

"How is she doing?" Danny asked, her voice weighted with tension, concern.

"It's like she's fallen down a well. And she has no desire to come out of it."

The oath on the other side echoed his own sentiments. "She's been part of the serving class all her life. They don't have the luxury to entertain depression, let alone have it. If she's doing that, then she's gone far beyond where she should go."

"I know that." He set his jaw. "But she's still . . . dusting. Cleaning every damn thing. Mending clothes. I tried to stop her. Kohana tried to stop her. But we have nothing else to offer her."

"Really." The one word was heavy with speculation. "Do you want to send her home to us? Do you think that will help?"

"What do *you* think will help? That's why I'm calling." He wasn't in the mood for damn games.

"My first instinct is to bring her home, to watch over her." Danny paused. "But can I do that better than her Master?"

He sat on his desk, heedless of the paperwork that crumpled beneath him. Knees splayed, elbows planted on them, he resisted the urge to splinter the receiver. "Danny, would you please stop being a goddamn woman and speak plain?"

"I'm speaking plainly enough," she responded in that cool tone of hers. "A servant isn't about having someone to fetch for you and give you physical release when you need it, though all that comes with it. It's something deeper, something that keeps us connected to the pulse of our soul, Malachi, whatever that is."

"You held off getting a servant twice as long as I have, way longer than most vamps wait, but now you're lecturing me on what it means to have one?"

"Mal, can you stop being an emotionally constipated male and admit that if I told you to put her on the next plane, you'd tell me to bugger off in twelve different ways?"

He remembered Nadia, standing before Lord Marshall, begging him to be ruthless with her, to be the Master she needed him to be. He closed his eyes.

"As an emotionally constipated male, I'd only need one way to tell you. Fuck off. Less words, less syllables."

A wry chuckle at last. It squeezed something around his heart. He sighed. "Help me, Danny. I don't want to send her back, but I don't know how to reach her. Except, something Kohana said . . ." He hesitated. Even among close vampire relationships, there was very little as taboo as what he was thinking about saying. "He said I do have the key, but it's something vampires . . . We don't offer it to humans. Can't offer. Right?"

At the sudden, weighted silence, he realized he was right. It was ridiculous, dangerous to even bring it up. As a relatively young made vampire, he was far more likely to be accused of dangerous sentiment, the remains of his human background, which would merely heighten his inferiority in the eyes of other vampires. Even Marshall, after that emotional outburst to his servant, had made an attempt—albeit a poor one—to pass his fierce words off the next day as merely helping his servant, not a true reflection of his devotion.

Total horseshit.

Though Mal didn't give a damn about vampire opinion, he'd quickly learned, as all vampires did, that a perceived weakness could be a terrible danger for that vampire, quickly exploited by others. He had too much at stake here, too many depending on him appearing strong in all ways. A more powerful vampire with an issue against him could take it all away. Danny had had Dev for only a couple years. As Elisa so eloquently put it, the female vamp would think he'd gone wobbly. He shouldn't say anymore.

Then he thought of those empty, wounded blue eyes. *Damn it.* "You know what Elisa said to me, a while ago? She said no one, even vampires, can do without love. And she thought maybe that was why vampires had servants. Because of the way we are, humans are God's gift to us, to let us love. If you don't say something soon, I'm going to hang up and pretend we never had this conversation."

"Well, her logic makes sense, doesn't it? We'd need that from our servants, because we sure as hell aren't good at loving our fellow vampires." His gut loosened anew as he heard the warmth return to Danny's voice. "She's quite something, isn't she?"

"Yeah, in more ways than one." Mal shifted, scowling at the sound of Kohana rattling his pots. "Since she's been here, a couple things have happened that made me wonder if there's more to her than we know. I can't go into one of them"—he thought of her ability to see the fault lines that only he and Kohana were able to see—"but the other was Jeremy's second mark. She had a physically empathic connection to him, when he was in distress. Kohana has done some of his medicine-man hocus-pocus, meditating or some nonsense, but he says there may be some Celtic magic in her ancestry. Just a residual, nothing too fancy. Maybe a great-grandmother wisewoman type of thing."

"I'm sure Kohana appreciates your great reverence for his skills," Danny said dryly. "And while I wouldn't be surprised, because people are often more than they themselves know, I think she'd be every bit of what she is, even without that. My mother saw something special in Elisa, Mal. In the short time she was in my service, I saw it, over and over again. That day she hit Ruskin with a teapot . . . Hell, it was like watching a field mouse attack a lion.

"It reminded me of the night I walked into a pub and met a man who thought he had nothing to offer, but he was the biggest damn hero I've ever met. It's what makes them special to us, Mal. They can't overpower us; they aren't superior to us in any way . . . yet it's funny how all of a sudden we find we can't do without them, right? And," she added, "If you ever tell anyone we had this conversation, I'll deny it, and then rip your throat out to appease my offended sense of honor. Got it?"

He blinked, not entirely sure she was kidding. "Got it. I think."

She huffed a snort, then continued. "Mal . . . I know where you're going here. We don't have to speak of it directly, but I'll tell you this. You and I both know when a problem confronts us, we usually already know the solution, however unlikely it seems. So the only thing I'll say is this, and take it for what it's worth. Vampires and servants are what they need to be in front of other vampires. What they are behind closed doors . . . that's between the two of them. Understand? For most, it's no different from what the vampire world sees. But for some of them—maybe more than we realize, since no one will admit it—it's something different. Nothing gives a woman a reason to live like knowing someone needs and wants her, more than he wants or needs anyone or anything else." Her voice softened. "You convince her of that, Mal, and you'll get her back."

"So what gives a man reason to live? What keeps Dev going?"

"A cold beer and a soft arse. Men are much easier to recall from the dead." She laughed, then sobered. "Call me if nothing changes for the better, Mal. If you need us, we'll come. She's very special, to all of us."

41

Two nights later, when Mal told Elisa he needed her help at the cat habitats, she went along dutifully enough. As he drove the Jeep, she didn't turn her face up to the night. Instead, she simply stared into space through the windshield. Between gear shifts, he reached over and touched her leg to draw those vacant blue eyes to him.

"Elisa, do you want to go home?" he asked.

"If you no longer need me here, I can go if you want me to," she responded automatically. "They always need an extra pair of hands at the station."

"Do you *want* to go, Elisa?"

Her hands tightened in the folds of her plain work dress. Mal saw it clearly in her mind. She didn't want to be asked what she wanted. She didn't want to wade into the jungle of her feelings, wanted to be on the fringes of her consciousness only. She didn't want to think.

"Will this take long? I told Kohana I'd help him bake apple pies for the day-shift hands, for their breakfast."

"It will take as long as I require."

That got her attention. He'd been gentle these past weeks, seeing the fragile state of her mind. But his emotions had been so involved, he'd forgotten what he'd told her from the very beginning. *You don't help a traumatized cat get past the trauma by acting as if the trauma is still happening.* Life went on, so they all had to as well. She was his servant, and he was her Master.

Her gaze flickered toward him, then away, her lips pressing together, a combined sign of frustration and nervousness. Good. Both were new. As he drove up to the habitat area, Chumani raised a hand, coming out of a wire enclosure they'd put up temporarily for the new arrivals.

When Mal got out of the Jeep, Chumani nodded to them. "They're ready for the next feeding, the little monsters. Milk's in the warmer and should be the right temp. I'm headed up to the northwest corner to help the young lions hunt. The zebra herd's looking likely tonight."

"Good luck. Be careful."

The Indian woman gave him a nod, and Elisa a quick stroke down her arm, but she didn't linger over it, going about her business. Mal gestured to Elisa to precede him to the wire cage. "We received a litter of ocelot kittens found by a ranger. A poacher had their mother. Since the ranger station didn't have the resources to nurse them, they asked for our help. Unfortunately, their eyes were already open, and we don't have a nursing mother right now, so we'll deal with their human bonding later, when we get to the rehab stage. For now, we need to get them stronger. This is a job that takes a good bit of time, so you'll take over for the hands. You can drive back and forth from the house for the feedings."

She'd stopped at the wire fence, and saw the kittens in a box lined with grass and leaves. Though their eyes were open, they did in fact appear weak, uninterested in their surroundings and not moving around as they should be. The mewling noises they made were muffled.

Mal took her to the makeshift sink and directed her to wash her hands in the strong antibacterial soap. Then he removed two bottles from the warmer. "Exotic cats are very sensitive to fatal intestinal problems, which is why we're careful about giving them the wrong kind of bacteria. They can also aspirate if you don't feed them correctly. That means the milk gets into their lungs and they drown. We'll go slow this first time; don't worry."

Her eyes had gotten dark, the blue like deep ocean. "Mal, I don't want to do this."

"I don't recall making it a request. You stay here, you pull your weight. You're one of my staff, aren't you?"

"I'll go home. I just said I would."

"Fine, then. But you'll do this until I arrange a plane." Guiding her in, he put pressure on her so she was sitting on the ground, and then he sat down behind her, sliding her into the space between his thighs, bracing his back against the fencing. Her body stiffened. Since those couple of attempts to break her out of her catharsis through physical demands, he'd restrained himself to incidental contact only. That had been a mistake. He realized now it was easier to shut herself down to full-blown lust than casual intimacy like this. With both virtual feet firmly planted in her mind, he saw how one part of her mind rejected his closeness, while another part desperately wanted it. Being a vampire who'd abstained for well over a month now, he was more than willing to start forcing her to face her desire, rather than letting her hide from it.

The babies were making more noise, detecting the milk scent. He picked up one and deposited it in Elisa's lap, putting the bottle in her other hand. "Here we go. Now, the hardest part is getting it in his mouth. Wrap the hand around his head, where you're covering his eyes, and put your thumb under the jaw. It basically shuts down all other stimuli and helps him focus just on eating . . . Once in—there you go—you want the milk to drip into the mouth—"

For the next few moments, he instructed her in the proper angle to hold the bottle, how the kitten should be positioned, and at what rate to administer the milk. How much would be enough. She was trembling as she handled the baby, but he acted as if all was well, keeping his voice low, firm and calm, steadying her hand until the kitten was nursing enthusiastically.

They repeated the process with each of the three kittens, but it wasn't until she was done, holding a lap full of sleepy babies, that she touched the animals for more than the milking function. Her now-free hand touched the back of one. Normally he would have discouraged human affection, but given the circumstances, he let it go. As he watched her stroke the kit hesitantly, he saw the slight adjustment in her mind, the crack of the door, as she let herself be aware of the dependent body in her lap, the beat of his tiny heart, the way he'd taken nourishment from her. As the moment lengthened, her body eased some more, leaning back more fully into his. Putting a hand on her brow, he guided her head to lie on his shoulder as they watched the kit doze off, exhausted from his struggle to live.

"Do they . . . do they have a good chance of making it?" She pressed her lips together as if she hadn't meant to ask.

"Kittens and cubs have a fairly high mortality out in the wild. If they don't have any complications as babies, though, and you care for them the right way, they should. Maybe like Chumani, you'll be the one to teach them to hunt."

"Then one day they'll learn enough, and they'll leave. And they could die."

"Yes, they could. Or they could live the lives they were meant to lead, hunting, having babies of their own."

"It's too painful," she whispered. "It's just too difficult."

One of the kits had maneuvered to the edge of her lap, his head slowly dropping off the edge of her skirt. She steadied him, sliding him back down into the bundle with his siblings, making Mal want to smile at her instinctive mothering, even as he felt the pain of her words.

"It's only too difficult when you shut us all out, face it all alone. When you think you're all alone." He slid an arm around her waist. "I don't remember as much about the traditions of my people as I should. But I know that when a brave wanted a woman to be his, he would ask her family's permission. If they agreed, from that point on, until they were wed, he would supply her with venison. So at the wedding ceremony, a blanket and venison were presented as his part, to show he would always provide for her, give her shelter and food."

Her mind was turning over his words, trying to connect them to the ocelots, but of course there was no connection there. He was encouraged by the curiosity, lethargic though it was.

"There's this movie called *Broken Arrow*, with Jimmy Stewart. Have you seen it?" When she shook her head, he continued. "He marries an Indian woman, and the marriage ceremony, while not necessarily Cherokee, picked up on some of those old traditions. I don't recall the exact words, but they went something to the effect of: 'Now we won't feel cold, because we'll keep each other warm. We won't feel the rain, because we'll give each other shelter. And we won't know loneliness anymore, because we have each other.'"

She swallowed. "Mal, don't. Please don't."

"You can't stop me. You don't want me to stop. It hurts; I know how much it hurts. It's been tearing me apart, feeling your pain. Give it to me; let me share it with you." He put both arms around her, and she latched onto his forearms, digging in, turning her face into his shoulder, trying to pull him in and deny him at once.

I love you, Elisa.

She went very, very still, and he felt that storm rising, knew he was drawing it to the surface, but he wouldn't let it have her, would stay wrapped around her when it hit. He held her tighter, just to let her know. She might not realize it, but he needed the steadying as much as she did. He'd never told any woman he loved her, vampire or otherwise.

At length she spoke, a quiet, broken whisper against his shoulder. "Are you telling me this to make me feel better?"

"Yes and no. Yes, because I'm hoping such a pathetic offering will lift your spirits, and no, I'm not telling you *just* to make you feel better. It's not a lie. You are my servant, Elisa. Not as a temporary measure for your fledglings, not as a matter of convenience. You are my servant because that's what I wanted, and you are bound to me. You're mine, and I want you to stay that way, always."

He brushed aside the hair on her nape then, and laid his lips there, teasing the artery, scoring it with his fangs, reminding her of what was hers to give him, what he could demand. Her soul recoiled, afraid of such passion, such feeling, but his hands were already cupping her breasts. With the kittens sleeping in her lap, and not wanting to disturb them, Elisa couldn't move away, and he stroked his thumbs over her nipples. They were highly sensitive, her whole body suddenly leaping to fire as if everything she'd kept tamped down had been released by his cursed ability to arouse her no matter what.

The flood of anger and passion she felt was gratifying and also a warning, so he took the role of aggressor before her emotions could turn against her.

"No . . ." It was a broken whisper, her only plea, but in answer, his fangs sank into her throat, taking what was his, those clever, devil-blessed hands continuing to stroke, knead, and now pinch, making her surge into his touch, squirming on the ground as he woke other things up, below the waist.

Put the ocelots back in their box, Elisa.

∾

Elisa did it, one at a time, though her hands were now shaking for a different reason. As soon as the last kit was situated, Mal's hands descended farther, the heel of his palm pressing against her clit, accessible from her cross-legged position in the skirt. He moved the fabric out of his way, so that his callused palm was against her panties, a silky pair, because he'd gotten rid of her others, wanting her in only those pretty, lacy things he'd bought her.

It wasn't a marriage proposal; she understood that. She wasn't sure she knew what love meant to a vampire, but she knew it wasn't something they said to a human. Mal wasn't like a lot of vampires, and his words meant far more to her than she wanted them to mean. She wasn't ready to feel this, this need for him. She was too fragile and brittle. She'd break into a million pieces.

No, you won't. I'm here. I won't let you break. He moved his fingers upon her, and the sensations spearing her were violent, tumultuous. With a sound somewhere between snarl and sob, she twisted in his arms, surging up to find his mouth, not caring that his fang caught her lip, bringing a new taste of her blood. She wrapped her arms around his back as she scrambled around until she was straddling him, her knees planted into the ground on either side of his hips. She clawed at his T-shirt, finding bare skin and then ripping into him with her short nails. She bit his mouth in return, earning a growl and his hand on the back of her skull, holding her steady.

She fought him, now trying to get free, even as she continued to rake at his flesh. She wanted pain and punishment; she wanted to be driven completely out of her mind into that place he could take her. She wanted to do things that she'd imagined only in the darkest part of her soul, and when she was done, she wanted to be so humiliated by her own actions she'd never look at herself in a mirror, as if she'd become a vampire, turning herself into something that had no reflection, no reminder of what she once was.

She was crying when he put her on her back in the soft grass. He held her down, held her body with his body, kept her arms pinned out to either side as, instead of ravaging her, he kissed her, soft, gentle. She snapped at him, cried out her anguish and pain. Still he kissed her. Forehead, temples, eyes, down to the mouth again, over and over, until she was shuddering, trembling so far inside she thought she'd never stop. But she no longer fought him.

He made it clear that he was in control of this boat, no matter how stormy her seas. He was at the tiller and he would keep it going the way he wanted to go. As he continued to linger on her mouth, then whispering over her cheeks, the bridge of her nose, her rage became such deep emotion, she was lost in it. But not in darkness. At least not that kind.

She lifted her eyes, stared into his brown ones. The proud face, the fall of hair over his forehead. She'd seen glimpses of his mind in this volatile moment, knew he'd worried that giving her the kittens' care might enhance her grieving, but he'd followed his instinct, hadn't he? Since the day she'd stepped off the plane, he'd tried to teach her how life was supposed to be, how it followed its natural course if the mind would just get the hell out of the way. If she let herself accept the pain, the joy, everything life had to offer, she'd experience what Jeremiah never could. Clawing her way to that belief was the best way to remember him, honor him.

She understood that, could see the light of it, but it was so far down the tunnel from where she was in her mind, she didn't think she had the courage to make that walk.

You won't do it alone. Mal's voice, his thoughts.

I'm alone there. I don't know how to come to you, toward that light.

Then I'll come to you. And you'll take my hand, and I'll lead you back to it. I won't let go, no matter how much you tear up my back or bite me, little Irish flower. I'm used to cats that claw and bite.

Reaching between them, he slid her panties off, rising up to open his jeans. She trembled harder, swallowing, not sure. But then he was covering her again. Keeping her warm and sheltered . . . not lonely.

Her body knew better than her what to do, for it was wet and willing for his entry. He slid into her, inexorable, working his way through the tight tissues until he was seated all the way in, his testicles pressing against the crease of her buttocks. Her body shuddered for an entirely different reason, and he saw it, his eyes darkening further.

Since Jeremy's death, he'd touched her body only. This time he was at the gate to her heart and soul, and he wasn't going to be denied. He was there, lodged inside of her, connected. Her fingers curled into his shoulders. The gouges would heal, but she could feel the stickiness, where she'd scraped skin down to the blood that beat through him.

"I'm lost," she whispered. "And I'm afraid."

"Call me what you know I am, Elisa. Don't be afraid. I'm here."

She stared at him, understanding the significance of the request. The leap of faith, the belief that she could trust. That he, a vampire, would give her sunlight, until she found her way out of darkness again.

I'll be in the darkness with you. I won't leave you alone there.

Her breath was shortening, for he withdrew, then slowly slid back in, working those tissues that responded to him so immediately. Her body knew. All of her did.

"Master." She stammered a little, not sure, but he put his lips to her cheek, moved his body on hers, inside her, again. A slow, rhythmic movement, in, out, his buttocks flexing with precision under her heels as they slid shyly up his thighs to rest on the curve of his arse. His arm slid beneath her, holding her banded that much more closely to him. Deeper thrust, even more devastating penetration, bringing pleasure into the grief, making it painful and yet something she couldn't stop.

"Master."

Yes. He nipped her shoulder then, scraping her with a fang, flexed his body to leave a wet, hot trail along the curve of her breast, his agile tongue licking so close to an aching nipple. *Your Master, Elisa.*

"Ah . . ." The rhythmic thrusting was bringing a climax, sweeping out from her sex to her lower abdomen, speeding up her heart underneath his mouth. His fingers convulsed on her wrists, now pinned again as he underscored the point.

Let go of your thoughts, Elisa. Submit to me; surrender all of it to your Master. Your pain and pleasure . . . it's all mine.

She fought it; she had to do so. But he wouldn't be thwarted. She remembered the question she'd asked him that night at Lord Marshall's, if he would take her fiercely because she was his property. He'd said yes.

And you said, "Good." It did such things to me to hear that, Elisa. Your glorious, sweet submission. Your willingness to be mine. To let me have you, care for you. You will come for me now. With everything.

The pain and pleasure, the grief and joy both.

"No . . . I can't."

You can, and you will. You will obey me. Always. Now.

He was right, because the reaction sped up through her, overriding her fears and objections. It knocked her planted mental feet from beneath her, transforming that tunnel into a hill. She tumbled down it, toward the blinding light she couldn't face, but he would give her no other choice.

She cried out, her hands straining under his hold, body arching up for him, and when he moved over her nipple and drew it in, suckling, she detonated. One orgasm crashed over the first, even as tears ran down her face and her heart felt like it might explode, spiraling among too many emotions and needs, everything from the past few weeks coming together in a way she couldn't resist. They were all gone, they'd left her, but not him. He was still here.

He came inside of her during the worst part of the storm, and she needed it, that heated flood, the sense that he was still with her, marking her body as his. When he finally came to a stop, easing his hard thrusts that pushed her against the grass, made her feel his strength, he put his mouth over her trembling, tearstained one, and ended as he'd begun. With those gentle kisses. One after another, they captured her sobs, took the tears off her face. His hands tightened on her wrists and he drew her back up into her straddled position, staying inside of her, connected. As he wrapped his arms around her, held her flush against him, she buried her face in his neck and cried until she had nothing left, letting it all wash away.

42

She hadn't said yes. Mal was all too aware of that. She'd stay with him because he'd said it would be so, and she'd submitted to it. Her grief and pain had been too thick. It would take time before she reached the point that the acceptance was fully embraced from her side. She would need to work through it, truly believe it was the way things were meant to be. Believe in him and what he wanted to give her. So he told himself.

He was not going to dwell on the fact she hadn't told him she loved him in return. He knew she did; he could read her mind, saw all the evidence of it. She just hadn't said it, was all. Damn it, he was not thinking about it night and day like a schoolboy.

The most important thing was that she was getting better. She was feeding the kittens and joining the staff for dinner again. Though she listened more than participated, her eyes thoughtful, her mind sometimes going off into space, she was there. After she ate, she often came and knelt inside the span of his feet, leaning her head against his knee. She was coming to him for comfort. When she came to his bed at dawn, it became as much about catharsis as lust. During the night, when she was doing chores that required more physical exertion than thought, her mind was too idle. That accumulation of grief needed to be lanced in his bed.

Often she'd fight him, in a way he was sure she'd never done in her life. She made him overpower her, take her down and push her into that zone where there was only mindless surrender. Then afterward, when she was more peaceful, she was closer to the Elisa he knew, asking him questions about what had happened that day on the preserve, and telling him little tidbits about the day she and Kohana had shared on the compound.

He took her out with him every several days, but even when he wasn't with her, he talked in her mind. At some point, she started talking back, showing rare glimpses of her humor.

A slow thing, but healing was happening. He would *not* be impatient with her reserve. He couldn't take her all the way with his will alone. He could get her to the edge of the tunnel, but she had to be the one to make the final step into the sunlight. She was the human one, after all, and the sunlight was where she could walk, not him. But in those shadows, he could be whatever she needed, and he made efforts to be sure he was, the vampire world be damned.

So things were going better. He'd even told Danny that, and she'd wisely not pried at the edges of that optimism. Then around midnight one evening, he received an urgent message from Kohana. He was needed back at the compound. *Now.*

"She walked out the door without saying a word to me, crossed the yard, opened up the front gate and planted herself there." Kohana nodded toward the nearby clearing where Elisa squatted, staring up at the night sky. The Indian sat on a stump placed against the fence, his shotgun at his side as he worked on oiling a set of door latches. "I told her to come inside the fence. She told me to leave her be. It's damn disturbing to see her still like that. Usually she's everywhere at once and I can't get her to stay in one spot." He gave Mal a narrow look. "You upset her again? What does her head tell you?"

Mal gave his man a scowl. "Not a whole lot right now. It's about as still as she is on the outside." And that bothered him almost as much as her physical stillness bothered Kohana. The fact the big Indian had chosen to sit here, watching over her instead of hauling her like a sack of grain back into the compound's secure perimeter, said volumes about how the little Irish flower had wormed her way into all their hearts.

Mal realized he'd seen more than a hundred and twenty summers now. It was interesting, how he always thought of it that way. There were four seasons, but it was the summer that always marked a year. Perhaps because it was the peak of growth and change, and held the promise of fall and winter endings behind its warmth and stability. Like her. It was the sadness and happiness together, how she twisted them together so tightly inside herself, that made her such a fascinating creature of both light and shadow.

He could certainly probe her mind much more deeply to find out what she was thinking, but that curious blankness made him proceed cautiously. He'd reserve that right for when the information could not be obtained by the courtesy of simply asking.

When she'd first come to the island, Kohana had told her the truth. Mal didn't use the marks to pry that often. They were for communication. But since he'd third-marked her, the times he'd stepped into her mind, he'd found himself not wanting to leave, a desire unexpected and unprecedented. He was different from other vampires, and he'd wanted to keep it that way. He'd told himself he had no need of a servant. And he'd been lying to himself. Maybe in a lot of ways, for a long time.

He moved across the field. She seemed impossibly fragile and small to him, sitting out here. If there were any cats about, which there weren't, he thought they might be more likely to view her as a cub than a meal. Her back was straight, though, chin up, her resilience in danger of cracking her right down the middle, like a clay pot.

He stopped behind her. "You shouldn't be out here by yourself."

She nodded, one quick jerk of her head. When she spoke, her voice seemed hollow, as if she were deep in a cave. "You know, when I was a little girl, about the only thing useful my mum ever told me was that we could wish for things all we wanted, but not to ever expect them to happen. That life had its own plans for us, and we needed to accept and adjust to that, not spill our hearts away on nonsense that was never going to be. But . . . it was such a simple dream. I thought it would be okay."

As his brow creased, she swallowed noisily. "I mean, was it so much to ask, marrying a man who was like me? He liked being Dev's backup as station manager. He could have done it all his life. I saw myself as his wife, working in Lady Danny's house, maybe even taking over for Mrs. Pritchett as head housekeeper when she decided to retire to her little house in Darwin with her daughter."

Her voice became louder, yet more unsteady. "Willis and I would have a couple babies, a boy and a girl. They'd grow up on the station, and Dev would teach them things, the same as we would, and maybe they'd even get schooled and go on to be something a bit better than us. She might be a schoolteacher, or a nurse in a hospital. He could run a pub, be a businessman. I thought about that for Willis and me. We could run one of those hotel and pub things, where I handled the hotel and he handled the pub; then we'd pass it on to our son. And we'd have the money to give our daughter a beautiful wedding when she found a good man who worked hard and could take care of her. It seemed like such a small dream. Why would God care if I had that for myself or not?"

Pushing away irrational jealousy, Malachi moved around her, settled on his heels where he could put a hand on her knee and see her face. It was tear-streaked, of course. He'd heard it in her voice, trying to hold strong and yet quavering like grass helpless to the wind's desires. Her blue eyes shifted to his face. Instead of meeting his gaze, she roved over his features, and then surprised him by reaching out and laying her hand on his brow. Her slim, chapped fingers spread out over his cheekbone and the bridge of his nose, tracing them.

"You're so handsome. I don't care what the world says about white people needing to stay pure. There's not much pure about any of us, whatever our color. But I didn't really understand the men who took up with black women. They seemed like they came from such different places, you know? How could it possibly make sense, beyond just a matter of lust? But they had children, and I knew they loved one another, some of them. But you, since I've come here . . ."

She dropped her hand to his shoulder, and those fingers curled into his shirt, held on fiercely as her eyes closed and her face hardened against an emotion that was fairly eating her.

"Elisa, tell me what's the matter and we'll fix it."

A half sob burst out of her, raw and painful. She rose as if she was intending to dash away from him, but he caught her arm. When she struggled against him, he simply swung her up in his arms and took her place on the ground, settling her in his lap even as she thrashed.

"Here, now, enough of that." He shook her a bit, just to get her to mind, and felt alarm as she went limp, curling her hands into herself and her body into a ball in his embrace, as if guarding herself against his touch. "Elisa, if you don't tell me what's wrong, I'm going to get very annoyed with you. You've been feeling better lately. What's changed?"

Had she decided she didn't want to stay? His gut wrenched at the thought. Had she decided she needed to go back to Australia and nurse her memory of Willis? A specter he was beginning to have some hard feelings toward, fair or not.

"Nothing. Nothing is wrong. Which is why it's so awful, how I feel. I know you're a vampire. I'm human. We agreed I'd be your full servant to help find the children a place. And then I'd probably go home to Danny. But things changed, and what you said the other day . . . I don't know what it means, but a part of me really wanted to hear that."

That cold knot in his gut loosened slightly, but not enough. There was a very large "but" in her words, and the suspense was fraying his nerves.

"A part of me wanted to go home, so badly. I miss the station. I miss my life there, but even if I go back, that life is gone. Because I'll walk in the barn and remember . . . and Willis won't be there." She took a long pause, during which he heard the hitching shudder of her breath. "*You* won't be there," she whispered.

He closed his eyes, relief filling him. But she wasn't done.

"I keep thinking about you, the way you run with your cats, and wrestle with them. How you were when we were traveling. God help me, the things you can make me feel, the way my body is shameless when it comes to you. I didn't understand it in Dev, the way he is with Danny, even when I saw hints of it. They whispered about it on the station, a big strong man like that, so in control of so many things, but he'll do anything for her. Serve her any way she desires. The same as I'll do for you."

She straightened in his arms then, meeting his gaze, dashing away her tears with the back of her hand. "I know I'm supposed to be adult and mature, all sophisticated and not say these things straight out, but there it is. I've gone and fallen in love with a vampire, an Indian, and a man who's all wrong for me. You won't let me fuss over you and mend your shirts. You won't come in from a long, hard day and eat my food and then fall asleep in your chair, your reading glasses slipping off your nose. You won't sit there and snore while I darn your socks and think about how I need to trim your hair this week, because we'll be going to the station social and you need to look nice for that. Will you?"

She gave him such a decided, accusatory glare, Malachi was at a loss how to respond. Then she pushed off his lap and stood, putting her arms akimbo. "But none of that means anything, none of what I want, because I'm carrying your baby."

Bursting into tears again, she bolted away from him and ran.

~

Fortunately, because of his vampire speed, he was able to be slack-jawed for about thirty seconds and still catch up with her. The daft girl had run for the forest, rather than the house, and he was impressed to see he reached her almost at the same moment as Kohana. Using his crutch, the man had taken off after her as soon as he'd seen his employer sitting stock-still as if he'd been hit in the head by a large sledgehammer.

When Malachi overtook him, he veered off, slowing down to rub his abused single leg. It meant they had their privacy when Mal caught her about the waist. It overcame him then, realizing that he was holding not only her, but also their child, under the grip of his forearm. Great Spirit, he wasn't sure any vampire had ever become a father this young. It brought its own worries, glorious and terrifying at once. Easing his grasp, he turned her, putting that away for now. But he didn't put it away fast enough, because he was caught unprepared when she rammed her fist into his belly. As hard as any third-mark could do it.

While he was swearing, profusely, she looked shocked and dismayed by her own actions. However, instead of apologizing as he would have expected, she crossed her arms tightly over herself, forming a shell. "I shouldn't have said all that. Stupid, stupid girl. I'll go back to the house and pull myself together and then we can talk about it like reasonable people, when you're ready. I don't rightly know what to think of it myself yet, and maybe we need a couple days to decide how best to approach it. You will let *us* approach it, right?" Her gaze darted up to him, fear suffusing her features. She lowered her arms so they were coiled protectively over her abdomen. "I know this is your baby, but . . . I'm its mother. I'll be its mother. Her, him, whoever it is. I will get some say in that, won't I? I won't be like some nanny that . . ."

"Elisa, hush." Now that he was certain his internal organs hadn't been ruptured, he took a firm hold of her shoulders. Though his mind was still reeling over all the implications of the past few minutes, this at least was something he could address. The little he'd heard of born vampires, those coming from a vampire and human servant pairing, was sadly similar to what she'd described. While the human was given some early parenting responsibility, the child would be vampire. As he or she grew, amid the vampire attitudes toward humans, the human parent was usually viewed as more of a servant than a parent by the time the child reached adolescence.

But he wasn't those vampires, and Elisa wasn't most servants. He thought of how the fledglings had viewed her, for all their ferocity and uncertainty. He also thought of Danny's words, how a servant helped a vampire keep in touch with his own soul. He'd make sure his child knew that about a human servant, and that he or she would never think of their mother as a servant, except as the highly respected and beloved helpmeet she was to their father.

He managed to suppress a smile, because he was fairly sure she would misconstrue it when she was staring at him with such a mixture of apprehension, frustration and worry. Everything she'd described, she'd already done for him. She'd mended his clothes, fussed over the scratches from the lion attack. Made sure he fed properly, and when he wanted the blood in a glass, she garnished it with a slice of fruit or a dash of spice, "cooking" for him. She hadn't cut his hair, but she'd talked about braiding it, had made him that Christmas gift to adorn it.

She'd also stood by him at Lord Marshall's, hadn't backed down from anything he needed. Given the demands he suspected were made of a wife in the lonely and harsh Outback, he was pretty sure she was overqualified to be a vampire's servant.

She'd taken his lack of response the wrong way. She was struggling against his hold again, and he was fairly sure she was going to start kicking in a few moments. Because he wanted to do so, he simply swept her off her feet, took her to her back against the soft earth and laid himself upon her. He slid his hand beneath the skirt, found the soft petals of her sex, catching her attention immediately. Her thighs quivered and he hardened, feeling how they loosened, how instinctively she surrendered to him, no matter her agitation. Though a vampire might have a more aggressive degree of it, he expected most husbands were the same about their cherished wives. That hungry need to dominate, to possess and claim. As well as trust and depend on her love. Those things were nowhere near as inconsequential as he'd believed them to be for so long.

"Elisa." He murmured it, bracing his elbow by her shoulder, feeling her heart race beneath the press of her breasts against his chest. "You are the child's mother. You think, after all you know of me, I would take that away from you? That I would take that away from my son or daughter?"

She stared up at him, her lips parting as he kept up that teasing stroke. "I can't . . . think when you do that."

"I know. You've been thinking far too much." He eased a fingertip into her, stroked the inside and felt fire when she whimpered. "It's not good enough. I want all the way in."

He lifted off her enough to get his own clothes out of the way. Then, with barely a hesitation, he ripped the panel of the panties. She gasped at the barely leashed violence to it, but her gaze went opaque and her teeth sank into her bottom lip when he put his broad head to that tight opening and pushed in, just until he'd gotten the head past the gate.

"Beg me, Elisa. Tell me what you want."

"I want you inside. All the way. In every way."

That fire expanded in him. "I love knowing my child is inside of you, Irish flower. I want you as my full servant, and every bit of what that means. Mother of my child, the woman who belongs to me utterly, connected to my soul, serving me with every ounce of hers. You're right. It may not be what you imagined wanting, but I think it was meant to be.

"I can't offer you much," he added. "Three hundred years of life, and the occasional vampire event you and I will have to endure together. But I will love you and care for you. I will try to give you the best life possible. I can only tell you how I feel. I want you with me, in all ways."

She considered it for a long moment, and then a tiny smile bloomed on her soft mouth, her eyes cautious but hopeful, filling his heart with warmth. "Well, it's not fifty years working myself to the bone on a station through drought and flood, but I guess it will do. And I will have a baby with you. Maybe more than one. I know vampires don't usually do that, but we're not the usual thing, are we?"

"I believe in miracles, when it comes to you." He gave her a smile back, one heated with desire and need both. "I don't want you to leave. I won't allow you to leave. You're mine, now and always. Understand?"

She nodded, and he slid deeper inside of her body, into the clasp of her eyes. He would take those doubts and worries, and prove to her she'd made the right decision, that she would never regret giving her life to his. He'd take it as seriously as the oath he'd made to protect his cats and his island, all the things that really mattered.

She locked her arms over his shoulders, burying her face in his neck, but then she proved that she didn't need access to his mind to know he could use some of the same reassurance.

I'm yours, Master, now and forever. I promise. I love you, too.

~

Elisa woke in their bed alone, but that was all right. She knew he was nearby. She curled under the pelts, her naked, well-used body pressed to the sheets. Stroking the furs with idle fingers, she let the promises spoken and unspoken wash over her.

The life he offered her wouldn't involve rings and white dresses. But he'd bound himself permanently to her out of a need to claim her for his own. She remembered the night he'd third-marked her vividly, how it had overtaken everything, even his supposed reasoning that it was merely important for their travels, for the fledglings. But tonight he'd stated it baldly. He wanted to protect her, wanted her to share his life. While she was scared about some of it, she wasn't uncertain. She wanted to be with him. Everything else would come in time, wouldn't it? That was the way it was supposed to work, with or without rings and dresses.

She'd seen the girls who had the storybook wedding, seen them years down the road after babies and tears and hardships. The relationship was always evolving into different things, but if the binding was true and strong, then that part never changed. It just went from new and shiny to deep and lasting, slowly drawing them through life together, taking them through light and darkness. The question wasn't what they were, but what they wanted to be to each other, and how important that was to each of them, even if they could never be it.

A home wasn't sticks and stones anyway, but a heart that never closed its door to her, no matter what other awful things had to be faced.

The sensibleness of her thoughts settled her, so she decided to get up. Rising, she put on her clothes and went out to find him in the new twilight. He liked doing that, liked rising so close to the tail end of the sun, as if he wanted to test his strength against it, a strength that would increase as he aged. He was sitting on a piece of split-rail fencing out in the backyard, gaze tilted to the sky. Yet his gaze came down when she stepped out onto the back porch, and she knew he'd been waiting for her.

From his expression, she also knew he'd been following her thoughts, so nothing else needed to be said. He slid off the rail and opened his arms, and she went into them.

"I dreamed of Jeremy."

"Oh?"

"I've been afraid to sleep, afraid of dreaming of him." When Mal's arms tightened, she closed her eyes. "He was twenty-four, tall and earnest. It was how he really was, trapped inside his child's body. He looked at me, as if asking permission; then he leaned in, took my hands and gave me one kiss." She tilted her face up to him, gave him a smile, her blue eyes deep and vast. "It was sweet, lingering. It made me feel warm inside. When he lifted his head, he offered me the kindest smile. He said, 'I know your heart belongs to Mal, but I wanted my first kiss to be you. Hope you don't mind. Or him.' Then he gave me a rascal's smile, but I think that was meant for you."

"I don't doubt it," Mal said dryly. "The little bastard." But there was a fondness to his voice that told her he understood.

The next part was a bit harder to get through. As if he sensed it, he stroked her back, gave her the ability to continue. She couldn't quite get it out yet, so she jumped ahead. "After a time, he turned away and walked down a beach. A beach like the one we saw in Florida. He broke into a run to catch up to Leonidas . . . John. As he ran, he became younger and younger, until he was nine, really nine, before Ruskin caught him.

He was walking next to John, and John gave him a fishing pole to carry. John's hand was resting on his shoulder, but then he lifted his other one in a wave to Victor, farther down the beach. I wish I'd known his real name."

"I know. What happened before that?" His voice was quiet, easy, telling her she could say it, that even if she had to cry over it, it would be okay. So she looked up at him, at the handsome features, the gaze that could be so unexpectedly kind and understanding. "Before he took off after John . . . after the kiss, Jeremy knelt down in front of me. He laid his head on my stomach, stroked the baby. He said . . ." Her voice trembled, eyes filling as she'd feared. "The baby and you would have to take care of me, now that he's gone."

We will, no fear of that. Sitting her up on the top rail of the fence, he leaned against it himself, letting her hold on to his shoulder as they looked out at the deepening night. They sat quietly a moment; then Elisa spoke again. "You don't seem to mind the kiss."

"Did you think I would?"

"Well . . . vampires are a bit possessive." She dared a teasing smile and was encouraged by his expression, the way he cupped her face and passed his fingers over her lips.

"So are certain Irish maids. Chumani said you taught her to sew, but only with the explicit understanding that she wouldn't be mending any of *my* clothes."

Elisa sniffed and would have pulled away, but he held her there with his sure grip. His expression became more serious. "I can't imagine any boy who wouldn't want you as his first kiss."

"Oh?" She flushed at the compliment, was entranced by how his eyes heated over her response. It was there in his eyes, the way he felt for her. Here, just the two of them, he wasn't hiding it in the least. A promise in itself.

"You remember what I told you, back at Lord Marshall's, about wishing I could be what you needed?" He shifted, touching her face. "There was a time I dearly wanted to be able to tell a girl, 'I love you. Come be mine forever. Be my wife.'"

She drew in a breath at the intensity of his gaze, the way it held hers. "But when they took away who I truly was, I chose being a vampire," he said. "I chose anger over love, and became something new. Something that couldn't be what you hoped to find with Willis. I've never met a woman who made me regret that, more than I've felt it with you."

She swallowed. Framing his face with her hands, she gave him her heart in her eyes, her touch. "I may not be fancy or complicated and understand everything about vampires and servants, but I think God made pretty sure that love is something that's clear as clean glass when your heart's open. I'll be whatever you need, whatever you want to call it. Just love me back. That's all I need. I can handle anything else."

Taking a deep breath, she offered him a smile that competed with the shine of the stars above. "You might not have been my first kiss, but I promise you'll get the last one. If you can catch me."

Then she bounded off the rail and was running back toward the house, laughing. Those sneakers he'd painted tripped through the grass, her curls bouncing. Mal watched her go, indulged himself in giving her a head start, and wondered at the miracle of finding *his* heart so open whenever he was around her. She was right. Whatever vampires and servants were supposed to be, they already knew what they were, could be, for each other.

He'd been like his cats, trying to live in the now, never dwelling too much on the future. But the future was suddenly unfolding in front of him, and like the moon shining on this meadow, turning everything gleaming and silver, including her, it was full of promises meant to be kept.